DARKFIRE

A BOOK OF UNDERREALM

GARRETT
ROBINSON

DARKFIRE

Garrett Robinson

The author greatly appreciates you taking the time to read his work. Please leave a review wherever you bought the book or on Goodreads.com.

Interior Design: Legacy Books, Inc.
Publisher: Legacy Books, Inc.
Editors: Karen Conlin, Cassie Dean
Cover Artist: Sarayu Ruangvesh

1. Fantasy - Epic 2. Fantasy - Dark 3. Fantasy - New Adult

Second Edition

Published by Legacy Books

To my wife
Who gave me this idea

To my children
Who just make life better

To Johnny, Sean and Dave
Who told me to write

And to my Rebels
Don't forget why you left the woods

GET MORE

Legacy Books is home to the very best that fantasy has to offer.

Join our email alerts list, and we'll send word whenever we release a new book. You'll receive exclusive updates and see behind the scenes as we create them.

(You'll also learn the secrets that make great fantasy books, *great.*)

Interested? Visit this link:

Underrealm.net/Join

For maps of the locations in this book, visit:

Underrealm.net/maps

THE BOOKS OF UNDERREALM

THE NIGHTBLADE EPIC
NIGHTBLADE
MYSTIC
DARKFIRE
SHADEBORN
WEREMAGE
YERRIN

THE ACADEMY JOURNALS
THE ALCHEMIST'S TOUCH
THE MINDMAGE'S WRATH
THE FIREMAGE'S VENGEANCE

CHRONOLOGICAL ORDER
NIGHTBLADE
MYSTIC
DARKFIRE
SHADEBORN
THE ALCHEMIST'S TOUCH
WEREMAGE
THE MINDMAGE'S WRATH
THE FIREMAGE'S VENGEANCE
YERRIN

Darkfire

A Book of Underrealm

Garrett Robinson

ONE

THE WESTERLY ROAD SNAKED ON BEFORE LOREN FOR endless miles, winding its way until it vanished in the feet of the Greatrock Mountains that loomed far, far ahead. Summer hung full in the air at last. The heavy sun roasted her as it set, forcing her to throw back the hood of her black cloak.

"This seems as good a place as any to stop for the day," said Jordel. "Make for that copse of trees just off the road."

Loren looked up and saw it: a small cluster of oaks in a circle, trunks close together enough to provide cover from the road. The barest tug on Midnight's reins made the horse turn easily. Annis and Gem clutched Loren a bit harder. The mare's hooves fell less rapidly now that the day wound to a close; she was a powerful horse and sure-footed, but they had ridden hard that day, and Loren knew she would appreciate the night's rest.

"At last," grumbled Gem, sitting behind Annis, who sat behind Loren. "I thought my legs might fall off."

"If you think you are weary of riding, think of how Midnight must feel having to carry you all this way," said Loren. "Be grateful, at least, that we are not walking."

"Gratitude comes hard when I am weary and saddle-sore," said Gem. "Let me dismount, and my thanks shall flow like a river."

"If only that were true," murmured Annis. "I should dearly love some cool water in which to bathe and escape this heat."

Jordel made them approach the trees slowly, in case another party camped within. But the place was empty, and all gave a great sigh of relief as they slid from their saddles. Loren went to take the reins of Jordel's horse while he secured its burden.

The wizard Xain, trussed up and secured to the flanks of Jordel's horse, glowered at the Mystic as he was lifted free. Jordel took great care, lowering him gently to the ground before tying his hands to a tree.

A gag prevented Xain from speaking, but he looked at Loren with venom in his eyes as Jordel bound him. She could only match his glare for a few moments before turning away with a shudder. Every time Xain looked at her, she saw again the madness in his eyes when he had fought the Mystics upon the King's road. Her mind filled with the vision of men and horses twisting in darkfire, black flames clutching at their flesh and their clothing, consuming everything until not even the bones remained. Despite the warmth of the summer sunset, Loren felt a chill creep up her spine.

"Here, Loren," said Gem. "Help me get the bedrolls. Your blasted steed still nickers whenever I draw near."

"You thought she was fine enough when first you saw her."

"She had not tried to bite me then. I am a brave warrior, but I value my fingers."

Loren rolled her eyes. Midnight had merely tried to smell Gem, but as a city urchin he had had precious little to do with horses. She did not feel like explaining this again, so she pulled the bedrolls from Midnight's back. Annis took hers without comment, bleary-eyed; the girl looked as though she had slept as they rode.

"Get yourself to sleep," said Loren. "You are weary."

"Yet I do not wish for slumber," said Annis quietly, looking askance at Gem, who stood nearby. "When it comes, it brings dreams dark and terrible. Dreams of the wizard."

Loren looked away. She faced the same nightmares, but wakefulness was no refuge—her mind's eye turned often to Xain's madness even while awake.

She dropped the bedrolls at Gem's feet and took both horses to the other side of the grove where they could graze on the lush turf. On her return, she unfurled her bedroll upon a soft piece of ground free from rocks.

For a moment she paused, rubbing the fine green cloth between her fingertips with a smile for the kindly clothier in Wellmont who had made them. Loren hoped the woman was safe and well, free from the ravages of the Dorsean army that besieged the city.

It had been two days since Xain had cast darkfire upon the King's road. They had not found Vivien afterward, and Jordel suspected that she might have lived. That was why they had ridden so hard since, testing the mettle of their horses and putting many leagues behind them. Jordel had risked everything for Xain, and if Vivien had indeed survived, he would now be an outcast among the Mystics. His own order would be hunting for them, and so would the King's law. Their only hope was that the fighting in Wellmont would distract their pursuers long enough for them to escape.

Thoughts of the Mystics brought forth one memory in particular for Loren: the moment Xain had attacked her with his flames, only to have the fire gutter out. He had tried it thrice, and thrice been thwarted, until he forced her to drop the blade—the blade that now hung on her belt, concealed beneath her cloak.

Her bedroll was laid out, and now she was smoothing it overmuch, her hands searching for any small motion to distract her from her thoughts. She went to tether the horses before going to Jordel. The Mystic had laid his own blankets a bit apart from the rest of theirs, and now he dug into his pack for food. When Loren approached, his gaze rose to meet her.

"I thought we might step beyond the trees for a moment," said Loren. "To look at the road ahead and discuss our path for the coming days."

Jordel eyed her carefully and nodded. Loren did not need to discuss their journey. They both knew he meant to take the Westerly Road until they reached Feldemar in the north. But the Mystic had warned her carefully about speaking of the dagger in front of Gem or Annis, and so she had to get him alone.

He stood and went to inspect Xain's bonds one more time. Before they left the trees, he turned to Gem. "Keep an eye on the wizard. If he should move, shout for us. We will not go far."

"Aye," said Gem. "Though if he thinks to tangle with me, he shall find me no easy mark."

Loren smiled at that, and she saw Jordel do the same as he replied. "Still, do not fail to call for us. We shall not be gone long."

The Mystic led her out of the trees to the north, stepping beyond them into the last red rays of sun. The grassy, rolling lands before them wavered with heat, and the air had grown stuffy, with hardly a breeze to freshen it. The Mystic's keen blue eyes fixed on the Greatrocks far away for a moment before he turned to Loren.

"What troubles you?"

She looked over her shoulder to make sure neither of the children had followed them, and then she placed a hand on the dagger at her hip. "Something that happened on the King's road when Xain was overcome with madness," she said. "You saw how he was. He would not have hesitated to kill any of us if it would have led to his escape. He even turned his flames on me. Yet they died upon the air, and I do not think that was his intent. I saw the look in his eyes, Jordel, and he meant to kill me. Something stopped him."

"Indeed," said Jordel. "Something you hold even now."

"My dagger." Loren nodded. "I thought as much. But how? What is this blade, that it can turn aside a wizard's wrath?"

Jordel's brows drew together, and he turned from her to look east. When he turned back, it was not with an answer.

"Where did the dagger come from? Before your parents had it? Where did they get it from?"

Loren balked. "I do not know. I never spoke with them of it. Indeed, my parents never knew I was aware of it. I found it by accident as a child, and never saw it again until I stole it. The day I ran away from home."

Jordel nodded. "Very well, then. I will tell you something of an answer. The full story would take many days in the telling, and we do not have such luxury. But even this small piece carries a heavy burden. The more you know of this dagger, the greater the danger upon you. That is why you must never reveal anything of it to Gem or to Annis, unless you wish to bring them great harm. I do not say this lightly, or out of jealousy. Those who hoard knowledge for their own gain are a corrupt kind of men, for wisdom should be open to anyone who wishes to reach for it. Yet some knowledge tempts the heart, and in that temptation lies death. Do you understand?"

Loren snorted and looked towards the sky. "How can I? You speak in riddles. Tell me the truth plainly, and mayhap I shall see what you mean."

Jordel nodded. "I shall. But only because you have pledged yourself to my service. I pray you will remember that oath well, Loren. With it you have earned my trust, and could land my head on the chopping block. But mine would be only the first life lost in a great calamity that threatens all the nine lands. Do you hear me?"

She nodded earnestly. "I do. I promise, you will not regret accepting me."

"With what you have done already, I could never regret it. So be it. Sit with me, and let me see your dagger."

At that Loren hesitated. Rarely had another laid

hands upon her weapon, save for Auntie in Cabrus, who had stolen it. And now that she knew something of the dagger's history and value, she was even more loath to relinquish it.

Jordel did not grow angry at her reluctance, but only gave her a rueful smile. "You must trust me, Loren. And remember, you pledged yourself to my service."

Loren's heart skipped a beat. Yes, she had pledged her skill, such as it was, to Jordel. But in her heart she had thought of it as a gesture, an oath to accompany him and to fight by his side, so long as he kept his word and never asked her to take a life. Little had she thought he might demand her weapon, or considered that she was bound to deliver it. Mayhap her vow had been made in too much haste. But it was done now. She drew forth the dagger and placed it in his hand.

Together they settled themselves on the grass, Loren sitting on her black cloak. Jordel wore one of plain brown, for his Mystic's cloak of red made him stand out far too easily. He drew the dagger from its sheath, and idly his fingers traced the black designs worked into the blade before he spoke.

"This dagger is a weapon of the mage hunters from days long gone," he said. "You remember I told you that in my early days as a Mystic, I was one such?"

"I do," said Loren. "Do all mage hunters carry such a weapon, then?"

"Not for many hundreds of years. You know that

in the Fearless Decree, the High King Andriana forbade any wizard from sitting any throne, after the dark times of the Wizard Kings. What many do not know is that the Fearless Decree was not only an edict: it was a treaty. Andriana knew that if she passed such a law without the consent of at least some of the other Wizard Kings, she would throw the nine lands into war."

"You mean the Wizard Kings gave up their power of their own will?" Loren looked at him with wonder. "Why would they do that? Their rule was unquestioned until Andriana stripped them of it."

"You must remember that even among the Wizard Kings, there were many of kind heart and just mind," said Jordel. "Those who abused their strength made the Fearless Decree necessary. But some saw how power could corrupt, and they agreed to give up their thrones for the sake of their kingdoms—and for another price. In those days, all mage hunters were under the High King's command. And if the Wizard Kings were to be stripped of their thrones, they would not let the High King maintain a force that could find and kill them at will. So the mage hunters were given into the control of the Mystics and robbed of much of their power. Weapons like yours—like this dagger—were destroyed, by royal decree."

"Yet this one survived," said Loren.

Jordel nodded. "And not by accident. Few know of this, but the Mystics saved some of the weapons in secret, hidden away from both the mages and the

High King herself, and kept them as one of our most closely guarded secrets. That is what makes your blade dangerous."

Loren shook her head. "That, I still do not understand."

"The dagger is not simply a weapon of fine make. It is imbued with power—magic to help the mage hunters track and slay wizards they were ordered to destroy. You saw one such power on the King's road."

She sat a bit straighter, and her eyes widened as they beheld the dagger. "Xain could not touch me with his magic."

"Just so. It is proof against his fire, just as it would be proof against any other kind of wizard. It has other gifts as well, more than I can explain just now. In time, I will help you unlock its power. But first we must find safety, and I am afraid that is in short supply in the land of Selvan."

"You still have not made yourself clear," said Loren. "It has power, yes. Is that why the Mystics fear it so? Why would I be seen as such a danger if it were found in my possession? I did not even know of its abilities."

Jordel's mouth soured as though he had bitten into a bad fruit. "It has little to do with your knowledge, and more to do with the politicking that still holds far too much sway in the nine lands. You see, the High King gave her mage hunters over into the service of the Mystics, and then ordered them to have all such weapons destroyed. This was a royal decree, to be carried out upon pain of death. Yet the Mystics chose to keep some of the weapons intact, and became guilty of treason. What they chose to do, they did at great risk to themselves and our order. Yet I might have done the same. They worried that the Fearless Decree would not last, and the Wizard Kings would return. If that were to happen, the Mystics would need to end their threat."

"I think I take your meaning at last," said Loren. "You fear that if the High King knew the Mystics kept these weapons, you would face her wrath. But I find that hard to believe. This happened many hundreds of years ago. Can such a decree still be held so dear today?"

"It might not," said Jordel. "Except that wizards have again grown in power in the kingdoms, thrones or no. It began when they established the Academy upon the High King's Seat. In the centuries since, they have wormed themselves into positions of power in every court. Then, only twenty years ago, they found a Mystic in possession of a weapon like yours."

Loren paled. "What happened to him?"

"He was put to the question and died in the High King's dungeons," said Jordel, his voice growing heavy. "Yet he remained steadfast. He never revealed the truth: that the Mystics still keep other such blades in secret. Still the High King Enalyn, with wizards whispering in her ear, was full of wrath, and she reaffirmed the Fearless Decree. If ever another weapon were found, she would know that the Mystics had been false in their promise to destroy them."

Jordel turned the dagger over in his hands. Then he sheathed it and held it out to Loren by the hilt. She almost feared to take it. Never had she thought she held a secret so terrible that it might lay low an entire order of warriors. An order whose purpose, she realized, she still did not entirely understand. Finally she reached out her hand for the blade. Her thoughts turned to Cabrus, and to the constable Corin.

"Is that why some who have seen my dagger feared me so?" said Loren. "Did they think I was one of you? A Mystic, working for some high members of your order?"

Jordel nodded. "Just so. Scarcely any know of the existence of such weapons. Most who do are of the Mystics, and they have many agents throughout the nine lands. We are fortunate that you have never met a high member of the Academy, for they would have taken the dagger from you and used it to terrible effect."

"I understand much at last. Yet it brings me no comfort."

"As I said. Most knowledge is a gift, but not all. And if the children were to know this tale, and ever mentioned it to another in a moment of carelessness—"

"You do not need to describe it. I will say nothing to them."

"Good," said Jordel. "You have my trust. In the

short time we have known each other, you have done much to earn it."

Loren's cheeks flushed. Never in the Birchwood had anyone placed much faith in her. Other than Chet, of course—though he had never stated it so plainly. So much of their friendship had happened without words.

"Gem and Annis will think we have left them," she said.

"Indeed," said Jordel, moving to rise. "Let us sup and then rest well, for tomorrow there are many leagues to ride."

Loren followed him back through the oaks, and as she did so she pulled the edge of her cloak tighter, swathing the dagger in shadow.

TWO

The next morning, Jordel woke them early to eat a meager breakfast. At first he had let them handle their own food. But after the first day's ride, he had seen Gem stuffing his face by the campfire. Then he took all their food into his own saddlebags, rationing each meal. Loren did not mind, but the children had complained terribly—especially Gem.

The boy groaned as he tried to gnaw on a roll of hardtack. Mayhap their stock of it had gone stale, or mayhap the bread was simply rocklike in nature. Sometime since Jordel had revealed that it was the primary foodstuff he had packed in his saddlebags, Loren had given up trying to determine which was the case.

"You mean to starve me, Jordel!" said Gem loudly. "I am already nothing but skin and bones. Give me more, I beg of you, or I shall waste away and die, and the nine lands will lose a brilliant mind."

"I have eaten less than you, though my body is far greater." Jordel did not look up from his horse, his fingers busy securing Xain to the charger's back in preparation for the day's ride.

"The body requires less sustenance than the mind," said Gem. "My thoughts range far and wide, and they burn the food in my belly far faster than your brawny muscles, Mystic."

"Keep your tongue hushed, Gem," snapped Loren. "Would you have the whole of Selvan know who we are?"

Gem balked, his shoulders drooping in embarrassment. But he looked sullenly at her. "There is no one for miles in any direction. Let the birds carry the tale of our passing, for all I care."

"We must ride hard today," said Jordel. "Tomorrow I hope to reach the southern tip of the Greatrocks, where lies the joining of Selvan's Westerly Road and the road from Wellmont. If we are lucky, we shall arrive before my order and the King's law. I have held out hope that the Dorsean invasion keeps them distracted, but then again it might not. Certainly the Mystics, at least, would have sent some riders, if Vivien returned with her tale."

"What makes you so certain she survived?" said Gem, nodding at Xain. "That one's fire took care of all the rest of them."

"Yet one corpse was missing," said Loren. "We would do well to imagine the worst, and prepare for it."

"Wise words, I suppose," said Gem with a shrug. "And if she did indeed perish afterwards, let it be a pleasant surprise."

Jordel turned, and in his eyes Loren saw a baleful fire burning. Gem saw it too, and he quailed where he sat on the ground.

"Vivien is a Mystic of my order," said Jordel. "She has taken no action except in keeping with our laws, and those of the King. Her death would be a loss to all the nine lands, and you will not say otherwise again."

Gem's bravado finally fled him, and he turned his eyes to the ground, gnawing again on his hardtack. "I meant no offense. Only I do not wish to be caught by the King's law any more than you do. She was a mighty warrior, and a good woman, I am sure."

Behind Gem, Loren saw Annis' eyes flash. The girl had disliked Vivien from the start. Her opinion had not improved when the Mystic attacked their boat upon the Dragon's Tail, nor when she pursued them out of Wellmont. Loren herself held no love for the woman, who had eagerly tried to kill the mercenaries they found upon the road. Only Jordel's mercy had stopped her.

But now Loren decided to speak before Annis could stoke Jordel's ire further. "None of us wish to be found, Gem," she said. "So ready yourself to ride, and quickly. Speed is our best ally now."

Rather than quelling Annis' dark mood, Loren succeeded only in shifting the girl's attention to Xain. Immediately she regretted having spoken. The wizard had done Annis great harm, both in mind and body, and they all knew why their progress upon the road was slower than Jordel wished.

"It is hard to ride with great speed when the horses are so overburdened," said Annis quietly, and Loren heard the ire beneath the words. But then the girl turned away and blushed, as if embarrassed, moving to help Gem pack. Jordel must have heard her, but he made no comment. He only frowned, and turned a sharp gaze on her back.

They readied and mounted without another word, and Loren's world again became an endless string of road vanishing beneath Midnight's hooves. Soon enough, though, the day gave them one great difference: it began to rain. Though the hot sun had beat down on them heavily ever since they left the King's road, now it seemed the first signs of fall had come stealing through the air. Fat pellets of water struck them like hornets, and they all drew up the hoods of their cloaks.

"This is both a curse and a blessing," said Jordel, looking up. "If anyone lies in wait for us, we shall be harder to see. But it slows us down, and if we are indeed pursued, that may be disastrous."

"It depends, then, on whether they are before us or behind us," said Gem. "But our road is set, and so what use is there in worrying? There is precious little we can do either way."

"A wise way of thinking, little scholar," said Jordel, and he flashed Gem a brief smile.

Loren could almost feel the boy puff up with pride behind her. She hid a grin; Jordel no doubt meant to make Gem feel better after his outburst that morning. It seemed to have worked.

For many miles, the road had run beside a stream—a small branch of the Dragon's Tail, flying down from the Greatrock Mountains to join the river that formed Selvan's southern border. They had washed themselves in it on their first day of riding, and Loren could still imagine the touch of the cool water on her prickled skin.

But they had left the stream behind early that first day, and now the land rose and fell in steep, rocky hills, the earliest and smallest foothills of the mountains that lay ahead. The Greatrocks were hidden from view as often as not, though every time the land rose they could see that the road carried them true to their destination.

Not long after midday, they stopped to rest. Jordel turned them aside at a great cleft in one of the foothills, where a flat and rocky face shone white against the green grass. The rock curved up and over, forming a sort of half-roof that sheltered them from the rain. As soon as the horses had stopped, fetlocks brushing the mud that had formed on the ground, Annis and Gem flung themselves off with whoops of glee.

"A quick bite to eat," said Jordel. "Then we move on." He dismounted, but he left Xain slung behind the saddle.

Loren went to him, stepping close to speak quietly, though she doubted the children could have heard them over the rain. "I have thought about Annis' words this morning."

Jordel looked wearily over at where Annis and Gem sat in the shelter of the hill, eating some of the salted beef he had given them as a rare treat. "Who could blame her for her anger? Xain's actions in Wellmont were less than honorable."

"Twice he might have killed her, and you as well. Yet you still have not explained why you undergo such risk to help him."

"I do not do it only for Xain, but for all the nine lands, and the people who dwell here. They will need his help, and the help of others like him."

"You have said that before. But what sort of men are like him? Liars? Men who would harm children without a second thought?"

"Those actions were not entirely his own. You know he consumed magestones."

Loren shrugged. "Indeed. What of it?"

Jordel looked at her in surprise. "I thought you might have guessed this already. There is an excellent reason that magestones are forbidden by the King's law. They do not only grant a wizard great power, or unlock hidden parts of their gift, such as Xain's darkfire. They are like a poison in the mind, bestowing a terrible hunger. Any wizard who eats a magestone will think of little else until they get another. If a wizard resists, their mind will twist until they are no longer in control of their own actions. Their body, too, will suffer. That is why Xain harmed the Yerrin girl, and that is why he fled my care. Had I known he was under such dark influence, I might have done things differently."

A frown came to Loren's face. It seemed to make sense to her; after all, Xain had never been a friendly man, but he had become a monster once he started taking magestones.

But then she remembered Brimlad's boat on the Dragon's Tail, after they had fled the town of Redbrook. In her mind's eye, she saw the greed in Xain's face when he first beheld the black crystals. Now she turned to look at him lying across Jordel's charger. Rage twisted his features, as it so often did these days. Her stomach turned.

"He took them of his own will, knowing what would befall him," said Loren. "And he never told *me* what might happen. I might have prepared for it. I will not forgive him so easily."

"I do not ask you to. Understanding does not

require forgiveness, but it may ease a heart stung by betrayal. And your thoughts of Xain may yet change when you see how he will suffer."

Loren thought she knew something of that already; in Wellmont she had seen the wizard with his hair falling out, his teeth cracked and broken, and his skin sallow and sunken. He had told her he was poisoned by Vivien's magic, and that only magestones could break the spell. Loren now knew that had been a lie.

She had no more words for Jordel, so she took her ration and sat in the shelter of the hill to eat. As she held some hardtack under the falling rain to soften it, she studied Xain. The angry smolder never left his eyes, even when Jordel forced some food into his mouth around the cloth that gagged him, and even when they ended their rest to set forth upon the road again.

THREE

ALL THAT DAY THEY RODE, THE RAIN COMING HARDER THE farther they went. It kept them from driving the horses, and Loren saw Jordel's frustration slowly mount. Every so often she caught the Mystic glancing back at Xain, as though he thought the wizard could somehow have summoned the storm that plagued them. But that was madness; if Xain could have conjured his powers, he would have cast off his bonds and fled in an instant. And he would not have brought rain to pester them, but more likely flame to burn them all. Loren shuddered at the thought.

Mayhap she imagined it, or mayhap she was looking for it now, but each time she looked at Xain he seemed to be faring worse. An unhealthy white sheen had come over his flesh, and she did not think the rain could make his skin quite so clammy. His eyes darted everywhere, and his arms would not cease their twitching. She could imagine him wanting to scratch himself, the way he had in Wellmont after he had first started taking the magestones.

Jordel pushed them to ride after sundown, until the very last light had almost faded from the cloudy sky. Then he hastily found a site for their camp, in the lee of a tall hill where the ground had not been soaked quite so badly. Once again Loren gave quiet thanks for her fine bedroll.

Their eager pace paid off; before noon the next day they spotted the lights and smoke of a village ahead on the road. Almost at the same moment, the rain began to lighten. Soon it had reduced to little more than a drizzle, and Gem lowered his hood with a whoop of laughter.

"At last! How I have longed for a real bed and some warm food in my belly."

"And you will have both, though we have precious little time to waste," said Jordel. "Be sure to enjoy it."

Though his words were gruff, Loren could hear the relief in his voice. Whatever this place was, it seemed to be some sort of sign to Jordel: a sign that if danger had not found their party yet, the chances of it happening would lessen greatly hereafter.

"That will be the village of Strapa," said Jordel. "It sits at the joining of Selvan's Westerly Road and the smaller road that leads to Wellmont, which no king of Selvan has seen fit to name. No horseman or caravan may travel this way without passing through it, unless they wish to journey for many miles around."

"Curious that I have never heard of it," said Annis. "My family's wagons venture often upon the Westerly Road."

"They do, but they would never stop in such an insignificant place as this," said Jordel. "They would carry on to Sunvale, a few more hours' ride north."

A league before they reached the first houses of Strapa, Jordel turned them left and off the road. Mountains loomed up above them now, and the hills at their feet were coated thick with pine. Into the trees he led them, picking an unerring path through their trunks until the outside world was lost from view. Not for the first time, Loren was struck by the skill of his woodcraft, and wondered where he had learned it.

When they had reached a small clearing far from the edge of the wood, Jordel commanded them to stop. A large pile of rocks lay at the clearing's west edge, forming a small sort of cave that the rain could not reach. The Mystic dismounted, handing his reins to Loren, and went to inspect the caves with his sword drawn. Once he had been in and out of the rocks and inspected them all around, he returned with a grim smile.

"It is empty, and no tracks or droppings have been left for many a long month," he declared. "It will serve."

"Serve for what?" said Gem.

"To hold our unusual cargo, of course. Did you think to enter the village with a wizard trussed up on my horse like a fallen stag?"

Loren was surprised she had not thought of that herself. The sight of Strapa had been so welcome after their long and wet days upon the road that she had had little thought for anything other than finding the first inn she could. But of course Jordel was right. They could not haul Xain along with them as they refreshed their supplies.

Jordel lifted Xain down and deposited him within the cave, sheltered from the sky by the rocks that sat overhead. Then he produced another coil of rope from his saddlebag, and worked behind the wizard for a moment to secure his wrists to the boulders.

"That will do," he said. "Come, we can ease our horses' burdens somewhat. Gem, you will ride with me."

"You mean to leave him here alone?" said Gem, aghast.

Loren spoke up as well. "That seems unwise, Jordel. I thought you meant to leave a guard."

Jordel looked at them with a small smile, a light

dancing in his eyes. "You forget that once, I was a hunter tasked with finding men like Xain. He shall not break the bonds I placed upon him."

"But if he should?" said Annis, her voice quivering. She looked from Xain to Loren, as though seeking reassurance. Her hands shook as she clutched her reins, and Loren felt pity well up in her breast. "If he should manage to escape, will he not come looking for vengeance?"

Jordel looked at her with kindly eyes, but Gem's face grew melancholy, and he slid from the saddle to stand before the Mystic. "We cannot just leave him here, mayhap for some wandering soul to discover. I will stay and keep watch over him. Only do not forget to fetch me some food, for I may well starve before you return."

Loren tried not to laugh. Jordel put a hand on Gem's shoulder and answered him solemnly. "Your offer is a valiant one, young rogue, and I thank you for it. But I have told you that Xain will not escape, and I ask you to believe me. Even if I am proved wrong, you could not keep him here if he were unbound."

Gem lifted his chin. "I could stop him."

"I will not doubt you," said Jordel. "But I will feed you. And Annis, if by some chance he should break his ropes, I do not think he would seek us out. More likely he would flee from here as fast as his feet could carry him, and hope to avoid us for all the rest of his days. Trust me, and come."

They mounted and left. Loren looked back over her shoulder once before they left the clearing, to see Xain staring after her with a baleful glare. Just before he vanished from sight, she saw him begin to struggle against the rope that bound his wrists. It made her shiver, but she forced herself to believe in Jordel. He was a mage hunter, after all. Who knew better than he how to restrain a wizard?

Jordel must have sensed their unease, for as they picked their way through the forest he spoke to them lightly. "Strapa is not a place to leave your purse strings unguarded, and yet it is no grim village either. Any hub of trade will attract wandering villains and thieves, but those who live here are good folk, for the most part. Keep a clear eye and a strong bearing, and you shall find no trouble. We will fetch ourselves new supplies quickly, and then continue north on the Westerly Road."

"It seems that Selvan is thick with those who pursue us," said Annis. "Not only my family, but the Mystics as well. Why do we not travel through Dorsea, west of the mountains? That would put us farther from danger."

"The borders of Dorsea will not stop my order, nor your kin," said Jordel, "and indeed, I think they will guess that that is our destination. Thus, we must not go there. Furthermore, with war brewing between that kingdom and this, travelers from Selvan would be most unwelcome. You are a child of the courts, and

Gem, of the streets. You might disguise your voices. But Loren's heavy accent would do us no favors in that land."

Loren turned so quickly in surprise, she nearly fell out of her saddle. "What accent? I speak as plainly as any other."

"Indeed," said Jordel with a faint smile. "As plainly as anyone from the Birchwood, born and raised in the kingdom of Selvan. As anyone listening to you could plainly hear."

Gem laughed out loud. Annis giggled, "There is no reason to be upset, Loren. He speaks only the truth. Your voice is quite . . . regional."

"It is *not!"* cried Loren.

"No, it is quite impossible to hear you have come from the forest, raised in a small village by parents who most likely chopped wood," said Gem, speaking in an outlandish fashion, lilting the first sound of every word.

"That sounds *nothing* like me!" Loren was growing angrier by the second.

"You had best still your tongue, Gem." A light danced in Annis' eyes. "Or she might beat you with her great wood-chopping arms."

Loren hunched her shoulders and cast her hood over her face, fuming, while Gem and Annis continued their jibes. At least the children were happy again, and the air seemed to have grown less stale, somehow. Xain's presence had been a heavy weight upon them, and now his absence freed their tongues and lightened their hearts.

So they came at last to the village of Strapa, little more than a few buildings clustered in the looming shadow of the Greatrocks. Loren saw several homes, not dissimilar to the houses of her village in the Birchwood, sending a curious pang of homesickness shooting through her. Never before had she found cause to miss her village, for no fond memories had ever drawn her mind there. Any times of happiness had been with Chet, or the old storyteller Bracken, and all were dwarfed by the looming shadow of her parents.

Yet now, seeing this simple place against the backdrop of the mountains that rose above, she thought there was something noble to a life lived in such a place. True, her youth had not been easy, but many in her village had seemed happy—as did many she saw walking the streets of Strapa now. She had seen much excitement since fleeing the Birchwood, and much peril. She could hardly imagine returning to a life such as this. And yet, to her surprise, some part of her missed it, longing for the day when her greatest fear had been not chopping enough logs to please her father.

But as their horses picked a slow, careful path through the streets, Loren thought she saw some truth in the warning Jordel had given. Many curious eyes watched them as they went, and not all sat in friendly faces. A goodly number seemed to be sizing up the party, as if looking over a meal before feasting. But

Jordel's frame was impressive, and he carried a broad sword at his waist. And though Loren bore no open weapon, still she was tall for a girl. She threw back her shoulders, trying to look larger, and when she caught their glances they must have seen something in her eyes to deter them, for they quickly averted their own.

Streets spread out from the town's middle like the spokes of a wagon wheel. As they neared the center, houses gave way to inns and taverns and shops of trade. From its center, four roads led away: one to the southwest, that ran to Wellmont; one to the southeast, from which they had come; another north, where they were bound; and finally one narrow road, with buildings pressing close on either side, that went northwest.

"Where does that road lead?" said Loren, nodding.

Jordel followed her gaze. "You have a sharp eye. That road leads out of Strapa and into the Greatrocks themselves. There is a pass that leads through the mountains, along perilous heights and into deep valleys. It does not see much travel, for it is a treacherous journey."

"A secret mountain pass?" said Gem, his eyes all alight. "Why do we not take that path, Jordel? It seems to suit our purpose, to hide us from watchful eyes upon the open road."

Loren had thought the same thing, but Jordel shook his head firmly. "I considered it as we rode north," he said. "But that way lies great danger. And I fear it would add weeks to our journey, or mayhap months. Now more than ever, secrecy must give way to speed. Time pulls us ever nearer to our doom, and faster the closer we draw."

That made them fall silent, and they stayed mute as Jordel led them to an inn. There a stableboy took their horses, with many curious glances at Loren's green eyes. Jordel slipped him a copper sliver. Inside, the common room had hardly an empty seat. The rain had driven the town's inhabitants into the warmth of fire and ale. Though the place was boisterously loud and everyone seemed too interested in drink and conversation to notice four weary travelers, still Loren felt exposed as they stood upon the threshold, searching for somewhere to sit.

"There are too many eyes in this place," said Jordel quietly. "I had not counted on such a crowd. It will go ill for us if our presence here is remarked."

"Yet we stand like fools when food awaits," said Gem, licking his lips. "I think I smell a stew."

"Mayhap staying in the town is ill-advised," said Jordel. "It might be better to return to the forest."

Annis and Gem gave a loud groan. Loren, too, loathed the idea of spending another night upon the muddy ground, and already she could imagine the comfort of a straw mattress beneath her.

"Jordel, we are soaked through," she said quickly. "The children might fall ill if we press on too hard. We shall do ourselves no favors if we exceed our limits, and the road grows ever longer. If any here would remark upon us, they could have done so in the streets."

Jordel's mouth twisted. "Very well. But we eat in our room, and we leave at first light."

Gem gave a tiny whoop. They went to the back of the room, where the innkeeper was already eyeing them greedily. Jordel gave her coin, and she had a serving girl lead them to a room with a single mattress. Soon they had filled their bellies with meat and broth, and sat in lazy silence and contentment.

"I would wager you are happy we stopped here now, Mystic," said Gem.

"Gem, be *quiet!*" snapped Loren. "If I hear that word from you even once more, I shall make you regret it."

"Indeed, you should use more care," said Jordel. "I do not trust the thickness of these walls. But I will not deny that I am grateful for a hot meal. We will have few enough of them before Feldemar."

"Must you always douse my hopes?" said Gem, flopping over on his stomach in a huff.

Loren found herself still preoccupied with her strange homesickness, and said nothing. Annis looked at her with interest, picking a bit of gristle from between her teeth.

"You are curiously quiet, Loren. Whatever troubles you?"

"Nothing," said Loren, shaking her head. "This place. It brings to mind the village I came from, that is all."

"Longings for home are no strange thing for a traveler," said Jordel.

"You have heard enough of my past to know I have little reason to miss the Birchwood," said Loren, and a bitterness crept into her words.

"Reason rarely governs the heart," said Jordel softly. "I have met boys whose fathers were taken with drink or horrid memories of war, or who simply had black hearts. They were beaten every day since they could walk, the father seeking revenge on his own flesh and blood for a pain that can never be soothed. Yet when these boys told me of the day their fathers died, they wept hot and bitter tears. Few hold only hatred for home and family, no matter how justified."

"I do," said Loren fiercely. "I would die before returning. I think you speak from your own mind, and know little of ours, Jordel. The three of us have suffered much in our youth at the hands of those who should have protected us."

She looked to Gem and Annis for support. Yet Gem did not meet her eyes, but merely stared at his fingernails and picked at them with his small knife. Annis pulled her cloak around her a bit tighter, then raised her gaze.

"I have little wish to return to my mother," she said quietly. "Yet not all my memories of her are ill. She used to take me to the sea that surrounded the High King's Seat, and together we would play in the waves. She did not even bring retainers, or any guards that I could see. She stopped when I grew older—yet if she had always acted thus, I might not have wished to leave so badly."

Loren turned away from her to stare at the wall. "You had a luckier childhood than I did, then."

"Did I?" said Annis bitterly. "Things changed when I grew older. How often did your father bring you to a deep pit beneath your castle, there to show you how he killed people slowly for information? Did he ever ask you to pick up the knife and join him?"

Loren's ears burned with shame and embarrassment, but she did not turn to let Annis see it.

"We are granted little choice in the way we come to this world, nor whom we enter it with," said Jordel from his chair by the door. "Yet we hold great sway in what we do after. You all fled your homes because of something inside you, some special fire, like a torch that lit your choice clearly. Not all would take such an opportunity. Though that flame be born from hardship, you should not spurn it."

"I would rather have had parents who were not cruel, and who raised me to be a simple woodsman's daughter," said Loren. "Free from excitement I might be now, but also free from peril."

"Neither would I object to such a life," said Gem.

But Annis looked at both of them with sharp eyes. "I think you miss your guess about yourselves, the both of you. Together we have walked many miles, and I think I know something of your hearts. I could not see either of you living a simple life in the woods, or in a noble's manor. You would be as out of place there as an oliphaunt in the High King's court. None of us are the sort who are meant for that life. I think we are meant for . . . this." She gestured vaguely about them with her hands.

"And what is this, exactly?" said Gem.

"Our life," said Annis simply. "Do you not see that it suits us? I cannot see how any of us might have taken a different road than this."

"So says the merchant's daughter," said Loren, though she did not mean it to sound so scornful as it came out.

"These are somber thoughts," said Jordel quickly. "And it is ill-advised to dwell on them, for we must keep our wits about us. We need provisions for the road ahead. Loren, will you come with me?"

"What of us?" said Gem and Annis together.

"Far too many have seen us already," said Jordel. "I would rather not reinforce the tale of four travelers bearing our descriptions, all traveling together. There is safety in numbers, they say, yet fewer may avoid being seen altogether. Sleep if you can, or else wait quietly—but neither leave the room, nor answer the door if any knock but us."

They left the inn to emerge into the drizzle again, Loren still plagued by too many thoughts of home.

FOUR

THE INN STOOD NEAR THE CENTER OF TOWN, AND SO they found themselves surrounded by shops and traders' carts from beyond the village. Jordel set to work, and soon he had filled their packs with meat and bread, as well as new waterskins so they could carry more upon the road. He bought a saddle as well—Midnight had not had one when Loren stole her, and the ride north had been harder because of it. She ran to the inn and hung the saddle in Midnight's stall before joining Jordel again. Many of the vendors tried to speak with them, but the Mystic replied with lone, terse words, and they all soon fell silent. Loren had brought the children's packs as well, and slowly they too began to fill.

As they passed the door of one shop a little way from the town's center, Loren chanced to look inside. Upon the walls she saw many bows hanging on pegs, and stacked on the floor were full quivers. Above the door hung a yellow sign with a drawn bow and arrow: a bowyer's mark.

With her thoughts already turned towards home, Loren thought of Chet. Before she had fled the Birchwood, she had taken a bow and arrows from his home—one of the first things she had stolen, though certainly not the last. That bow had been broken on the streets of Cabrus as she fled constables, and it had felt like a piece of her heart broke with it. She stopped in her tracks.

"Jordel," she said quickly. "Might I have a bow?"

He looked at her curiously, and then turned his eyes to the shop. "That seems an odd request. I did not take you for an archer."

"Only a little. I used to hunt in the forest, and that is how I kept myself fed on the road to Cabrus. But my bow was lost, and . . . and I wish for a new one. Please."

Jordel frowned. "I have coin, but it is not endless. We may well need all of it before we reach our destination, and I can no longer turn to my order for more."

"But we cannot think to pay for all our food," said

Loren. "Soon enough we shall need to hunt, and meat costs far less when bought with an arrow. We shall save coin, not lose it."

His brows rose. "Are you indeed so skilled a hunter? Then very well. That seems good sense."

Loren's ears burned as they entered. In truth she was not so good as Jordel made it sound. Certainly she had nothing near Chet's skill.

It was a small shop, the walls pressing close on every side. Bows of all sizes and shapes covered the walls. Though medium-sized hunting bows were by far the most common, Loren also saw much longer bows meant for war, as well as shorter bows curved in a strange fashion she had never seen before. In one corner of the room stood a work bench, with many spars of wood stacked beside it. Also there was a large box that held sinew for stringing. Its faint smell permeated the room.

No one was inside when they entered, but their footsteps must have been louder than Loren thought. In a moment the back door opened, and the bowyer emerged. He was a man of middle age, mayhap a little younger than Loren's father. His features were rough, his chin dusted with the stubble of several days, and though his hair was fair in color it bore much dirt and grease. His clothes were well-worn and faded, but looked as though they had once been colorful—blue and white was his tunic, and his breeches a light grey.

"Well met," he said. "I hope you have come to buy a bow, for I have run quite out of underclothes."

Loren stared at him and blinked, but Jordel smiled faintly. "A shame. From your wares, I felt sure you were a clothier."

The man smiled back. "I am glad you take a joke well—not all customers do, and it may cost me more coin than I would wish. Yet what worth is a life without laughter? What do you seek on this dreary day?"

Loren swallowed and stepped forwards. "I was looking for a bow I might hunt with. I had one, but I . . . lost it."

The bowyer looked her up and down. "Lost it? I prize my wares highly, good lady. Why should I sell you a bow you might leave under a rock and forget?"

Her cheeks burned, and a flash of anger made her speak hastily. "It was a gift, and I treasured it, for it kept me well-fed upon the road . . . and for other reasons. But it was broken in a fight. And if I may not do with my own things what I wish, then mayhap our coin will be more welcome elsewhere."

Her words did not have the effect she thought they would. She had thought to make the bowyer flinch with talk of money. But he did not seem to notice the threat, and his eyes flashed when she spoke of the fight. Slowly his gaze moved from her to Jordel, and she could see him inspect the Mystic's broad frame, as well as the sword on his belt. When he spoke to Loren again, his voice bore more courtesy.

"I meant no disrespect. Another jibe, and this one ill-advised, I fear. You seek a hunting bow, you say? Let us see what we might find."

He walked to the wall, looking over the bows that rested across pegs on the wall. None were strung, but every so often he would reach up and test one by bending it in his hands. Twice he looked back at Loren, eyes roving from head to foot, judging her height.

Loren glanced at Jordel and saw something curious. His face had grown grim, and he looked back over his shoulder as though he wished to leave. She did not understand what could have made him nervous—she would have to ask him later.

"You say your bow was a gift," said the bowyer suddenly. "Who gave it to you?"

Loren shifted and looked down. "Someone important to me. A dear friend."

"I did not mean to turn your mind to thoughts of loss. I am sorry."

"He is not dead. Only we have not seen each other in a long, long time."

"More than death can take those we love," muttered the bowyer, looking at the wall again. Loren's cheeks flushed at his talk of *love,* but she said nothing. "Here we are," he went on, lifting a weapon from the wall.

He moved to his workstation in the corner and selected a string. Its ends were looped and tied already, and he wrapped one of them around one end of the bow before placing it on the ground. He pulled the other end down, looped the string through the groove carved into it, and then inspected the bottom end to ensure nothing had come loose. Satisfied, he went to Loren.

"Give that a draw, my lady," he said. "Unless I miss my guess, you shall find it a perfect match."

Loren lifted the bow, doubtful. It was a few fingers shorter than she was used to. But she placed her fingers to the string and drew it regardless.

A thrill rushed through her. The bow drew more easily than any of Chet's—yet the power was unmistakable. She could *feel* the string's desire to leap forwards, the tension that yearned to send an arrow speeding through the air. She released the draw slowly, relishing the feel of it.

"This is a masterful work of craftsmanship," she breathed. "I have never laid hands on a bow so fine."

"I am glad it is appreciated," he said, and he bent at the waist towards her. His fingers raised to his lips, then his forehead in a strange gesture. "Especially to a lady such as yourself."

Loren blushed again, looking down at her cloak. "I am no noblewoman. Only a simple villager, like yourself."

"A village girl indeed, for I can hear it in your voice. Yet not simple, I am certain. Like knows like. You are neither of you simple travelers, it is plain to see. Some folk wear adventure swathed around them like a cloak, and you are two such."

To Loren's surprise, Jordel stepped forwards and spoke brusquely. "You mistake us, friend. But I thank you for finding my daughter a suitable bow for her hunting. Tell me the price, for we must be on our way, and quickly."

Jordel reached into his cloak, two fingers sinking into his coin purse. Though he tried to keep it hidden, for a moment the purse was revealed, and Loren saw light flash in the bowyer's eyes.

"It is haste you need, eh? Well, then, I will not keep you from your travels to—forgive me, I have forgotten where you were bound."

Loren almost said *Feldemar*, but Jordel spoke first and saved her. "South to Wellmont. I have cousins within the city and wish to look after their safety."

The bowyer's eyes glittered. "Indeed. Well, that is a fine and worthy goal, good sir. A pity, though, for I thought you might be headed north—mayhap through the mountain pass."

"We are not. We have just come from the north, riding the Westerly Road."

"Indeed, indeed," said the man, nodding. Still he did not reach for the coins or ask for a price. "A pity, as I said, for I do not spend all my days here in my shop. I have been known to hire my services as a guide, you see, for I traveled the mountain pass many times in my youth. If you were heading that way—"

"We are not," Jordel said again, steel in his voice. "Now give me a price."

The man looked into Jordel's eyes, and then into Loren's. "It is rare I meet two travelers as interesting as you. And the girl and I share a bond in loss. Take the bow as my gift. And if you should meet any upon the road who seek to ride north upon the mountain pass, you tell them of me, eh? After all, with war brewing to the south, the Westerly Road will not be safe for much longer. Tell them where to find me, and that I am for hire. Albern is my name. Albern of the family Telfer."

Jordel went to Albern's work station. He drew two gold weights from his coin purse and laid them carefully upon the table. "For the bow." Then he walked out past Loren in a rush, forcing her to scramble after him. She turned one last time at the doorway. Albern stood with arms folded, watching them leave with a faint smile on his lips. He raised a single finger, like a wave good-bye. She turned and ran into the rain after Jordel.

FIVE

THEY SPENT A RESTLESS NIGHT IN THEIR ROOM. LOREN lay for a long time with her new bow beside her—Jordel had given the mattress to her and Annis, while he and Gem slept on the floor.

At long last she fell asleep, and when she woke the next morning it was to a world transformed. The faint blush of approaching sunlight shone through the high window. She could hear the morning's first birds singing, and the air itself smelled fresh and inviting.

She roused Gem and Annis—Jordel was gone, probably fetching breakfast—and they each readied for the day, Gem with many grumbles about waking so early. Loren had left her boots by the fire downstairs to dry, and she ran down in bare feet to fetch them.

There she found Jordel, fetching breakfast as she had thought. Once she pulled on her boots, she helped him with the plates, and they returned upstairs.

"The day is bright and free from rain," said Loren. "It is a portent, I think."

"Mayhap," said Jordel uneasily. "But I shy from relying too heavily on omens. And during the night my mind has dwelt much on that bowyer."

"He seemed a friendly enough sort, if a bit sharp." In truth she had quite liked the bowyer, with his disarming smile and quick wit.

"Enemies wear two guises: one of wrath and one of a smiling face. He guessed much more about us than I would have told him willingly."

"You denied it," said Loren. But her words sounded weak even in her own ears. Albern had known they meant to travel north—she had seen that much in his face. But what would he do with that knowledge? He could not have heard of them here in Strapa, so far removed from Wellmont. Could he?

Such thoughts lent her haste as she cleaned herself with a bowl of water and ate her meal. She urged Gem and Annis to hurry, and soon they left their room with bags slung on their back. As they stepped outside into the growing dawn, its warm sunlight seemed less friendly and more like a beacon of warning. Jordel ushered them quickly to the inn's stables—and there they found someone waiting for them.

A man paced before the wide wooden doors, slowly, deliberately, one hand on a sword. His head was shaved clean, but he wore a thick beard that was immaculately trimmed. Light brown eyes snapped to them the second they rounded the corner of the inn, and recognition flashed within them. With horror, Loren saw the red cloak draped about his shoulders.

Jordel froze beside her. But when the man saw the looks on their faces, he stood stock still and held his hands up.

"Wait!" he said quickly, but quietly, in almost a whisper. "Jordel, it is I. We must speak."

Jordel looked uneasily at him and did not move. "Derrick. What brings you this far west?"

The man—Derrick, Loren supposed—looked over his shoulder. "No need to bandy words with me, Jordel. I know of your deeds, and yes, some in our order are hunting you. That is why I have come. I am here to help."

Hairs rose along Loren's back, and her hand pulled at the edge of her cloak, ensuring it covered her dagger. She did not like this. Nor, it seemed, did Jordel, for he still looked uneasy.

"You may trust me, Jordel," said Derrick. "I represent many in the order who know you are faultless in this—or at least, that you do not deserve exile."

With a heavy sigh, Jordel loosened his grip on his

hilt. "Very well. But if we must speak, then let us do it with all speed. You must know my journey is urgent, and never more so than now."

"I know it well," said Derrick. "Come. I have secured a house in the village outskirts. Leave your horses—it is not far, and there is no post for them there."

Loren looked at Jordel with fear. But he nodded and bade them to follow the Mystic. Once they were out of sight of the inn, Jordel dropped back to murmur in Loren's ear. "I sense your unease, and I share it. But Derrick is a good man, and we have served together before. I think we can believe him if he says he means us no harm—but keep a wary eye."

"Always," said Loren. "And mark my words: I do not like this."

Derrick had spoken the truth—the house he led them to was only a few minutes' walk from the inn, on the eastern edge of the town. It was a small hovel, scarcely more than four walls and a roof. No other dwellings stood within many paces of it. The white smoke of a cooking fire drifted out from a hole in the roof. A small girl stood before the door; she had wide, frightened eyes and wore a dirty dress that had once been white.

"We will not be long," Derrick told her. "Keep watch for anyone approaching." He reached into a pocket and drew forth a silver penny. The girl nodded but said nothing.

Inside they found a crude wooden table and a few

chairs—not enough for all of them. On the back wall were a bookshelf and a window, while in one corner stood a small cooking pot and a fire. Black smoke stains covered the ceiling. Derrick and Jordel sat, while Annis and Gem looked at Loren.

"I will stand, thank you," she said.

"Very well," said Gem happily. "I will gladly take my place—"

Loren gave him a little shove. "You will not. Take the chair, Annis."

Annis did, but she moved it against the back wall beneath the window, as far from the table and Derrick as she could.

"Now, Jordel," said Derrick. "You can imagine that I have heard much of your exploits since you left Wellmont, but I would hear the words from you. One cannot trust what one hears when only a single side makes their case."

If the request made Jordel uneasy, he gave no sign of it. "We left Wellmont searching for the girls you see here. In my company rode five members of our order—Vivien among them. Tell me, does she live?"

Derrick nodded. "She rests in Wellmont, tended to by the finest healers we could muster. The city could ill afford to spare them, but some of our brothers and sisters joined the fighting on the wall as a form of payment."

Jordel gave a heavy sigh of relief. "That is good. I did not wish for any harm to befall her. And I know she will be pleased that the Mystics aid Wellmont in its struggle."

Loren was less joyful at the news. Well she remembered how Vivien had attacked their boat upon the Dragon's Tail. Almost she could see it in her mind's eye, the woman's short and slim form blasting them with magic while a starving Xain fought desperately to keep her at bay, only succeeding thanks to magestones. Beneath the window, Annis looked as though she shared Loren's displeasure.

Derrick leaned forwards, pressing his fingers into the table. "But what happened upon the road, Jordel? You know that is my concern, not the battle of Wellmont."

"We found a mercenary army on the King's road, marching rapidly upon the city," said Jordel. "We had already spied them on our travels, and I had guessed they were marching that way—rightly, as it happens. Fortunately we were able to warn Wellmont of their coming. It was not comforting news to bear, but it would have been far worse if they had been unprepared."

Derrick fixed him with a steely gaze. "Still you avoid my question, Jordel. What of the wizard? You know he is at the heart of this whole matter. Our order interferes little with the wars of the nine lands."

Jordel fell silent for a moment, though he did not fail to meet Derrick's gaze. "The wizard Xain was with the girls," he said. "We found them together on the road after he had fled. I had thought to recruit him, but he spurned me. When I found him again, he attacked us. He struck down all our brothers and sisters, aside from Vivien and me, before I could subdue him."

"And then?" said Derrick. "You did not give him his justice, I take it."

"I did not. For I still have need of him. I have borne him since then as a captive. He is powerless now, for his body is greatly weakened."

"Weakened from magestone cravings?"

"Just so."

Derrick sat silent for a moment, and then produced a knife from his belt. Loren tensed, but he only lifted it and began to pick at his fingernails. "You know the King's law, Jordel. Magestones are no trifles to toy with. Possession is cause enough to put him to death."

"And you know that our order has never failed to overlook such transgressions when it suits us." A note of anger colored Jordel's words, as though this were a longstanding grudge he wearied of discussing. "Always we ignore the dealings of the family Yerrin because they are a powerful ally, and many of their clan are useful to us. Yet we hunt down the poor wizards who fall victim to their wares, knowing they could never have obtained them if we put a stop to such smuggling."

Derrick put the knife on the table and spread his hands. "Ours is not to question the orders of our masters, Jordel. You know this."

"It is everyone's duty to question injustice," Jordel said quietly.

"You mention the family Yerrin," said Derrick, and his eyes fell upon Annis. "Tell me, girl. Are you the daughter of Damaris that Vivien described?"

Annis' eyes widened with fear, and she turned her face away from him. Loren saw her cheeks darken, and she pulled up her hood to hide it.

"Answer enough, I suppose," said Derrick. "You make a strange party indeed. I suppose the boy over there is brother to the Lord Prince, and this girl is the king of Dulmun." He nodded at Loren.

"Nothing so grand," said Jordel. "Merely travelers I have taken into my charge, for they are all of them good-hearted and have few other places to turn."

"The Yerrin girl could turn herself towards home and start riding," said Derrick.

"She has her reasons, and I will not question them. We both know how perilous the family Yerrin can be."

"True enough," said Derrick, leaning forwards again. "But tell me now, Jordel—where is the wizard? You claim he is no danger. Why then is he no longer in your company?"

Jordel fell silent. Loren felt the hairs on her arm prick up. She heard Gem's loud swallow.

"The lack of magestones works heavily upon his mind," said Jordel. "He will recover. I will see to it. And when he does, he may be trusted again. But he must be kept from any ability to do harm until that time."

"But where?" said Derrick, eyes wide now with urgency. "You cannot have kept him in that inn. Where are you holding him?"

Loren felt an itch growing under her skin, a feeling of great danger, and her throat was dry. She wanted to stop this conversation at once and order them all to flee. Annis and Gem looked at each other, and then to Loren.

Jordel's face grew dour, but he did not flinch. "That, I cannot tell you. You and I have seen much together, Derrick. I must ask you to trust me, and to say nothing of my presence nor my destination when you return to our order."

"What could I tell them?" said Derrick. "I know nothing of your intent, nor do I expect you to tell me. I trust you in this. Can you not trust me in return?"

"Not with Xain," said Jordel.

Derrick leaned back with a sigh. He pushed his chair back, stood, and paced behind it. "That saddens me, Jordel. I thought things might be different between us, and I wish they were. But you know my duty is to our order before all else."

Before they could react, his hand flew to his sword hilt, and he gave a sharp whistle through his teeth. Even as he drew his blade and Jordel leapt to his feet, the door of the house crashed open. Mystics in red cloaks stormed through the door.

SIX

LOREN WAS SAVED ONLY BY HER SHARP REFLEXES, heightened as they were by her growing sense of danger. When the first Mystic swung his blade, she dropped to the ground and rolled past him. From the floor she struck out at the open door with a mighty kick. It slammed shut just as a woman tried to burst through, catching her head between door and frame. She slumped senseless to the ground, her red cloak billowing on the floor around her. No more followed.

Gem and Annis scrambled for the corner while Loren was still fighting to her feet. Another sword swing nearly took her head off, but again she leapt from its path. Four Mystics had joined Derrick now—two stood beside him, pinning Jordel in the corner, while the third went for Gem and Annis. The last had set his sights on Loren, and she could almost sense his frustration as she eluded his attacks. He was a large man, greater even than Jordel, and two heads taller than Loren. His nose was flat and wide, and there was a murderer's fury in his glare.

Almost she reached for the dagger at her belt, but she stopped herself at the last second. She would not kill this man, nor anyone else in the room, and if they recognized her weapon and survived, she was doomed.

Her opponent thrust his blade forwards, but by now Loren had found her balance and sidestepped easily. He wore a heavy coat of chain, and his sight was somewhat obscured by an open-faced helmet. It was an easy matter to avoid his strokes again and again, stepping back each time. But she had no way to retaliate, and one strike from those massive arms would end the fight.

The children were faring worse. Gem had dived beneath the table and pulled Annis with him, but they had not been ignored. A Mystic grabbed Annis' leg and dragged her out. She clung to the table, screaming, while the Mystic tried to pry her fingers loose. Gem emerged and flew for the man's legs in a tackle, but his slight form did nothing. The man dropped his sword and reached for a dagger, lifting it high to plunge into Gem's back.

Loren gave a shout and ducked another swing, running past her foe to help. She leapt and seized the Mystic's knife hand before he could strike, and the weight of her jump bore them both over. They landed on the table with Loren on top, their weight smashing the flimsy wood to splinters. This man wore no helmet, and even as he winced from the fall, Loren seized his collar. Her fist drew back and she struck once, twice, three times, twice on the cheek and once in the temple. His eyes rolled back in his head, and his hands flopped to the ground.

Annis cried a warning even as Loren felt the presence of the huge Mystic behind her. She rolled to the side at the last second, and a flashing sword pierced the space where she had been—then carried on and into the body of the Mystic she had knocked unconscious. His eyes snapped open as he gave a startled cry, only to gurgle his last breath as blood bubbled from his lips.

Loren cried out in horror, but the Mystic barely looked distressed. He straightened and tugged on his sword—but it stayed put. He looked down at it, piggish eyes squinting as he tugged harder. But the sword was buried deep in bone and flesh, and had sunk into the wooden table beneath for good measure.

Her gaze snapped to a flash of movement as Gem dove to the ground behind the man. She saw his aim and leapt shoulder-first. Sharp pain shot through her as it struck his chain mail, but her weight threw him backwards. He struck Gem and tumbled, his head slamming into the bookcase on the wall. The shelves fell, sending leather tomes crashing down on him just before the bookcase itself.

"Gem!" cried Loren. She saw a tiny, scrawny leg jutting out from beneath the mess. But it wiggled with life, so she seized and tugged. Gem emerged from the pile, sputtering and cursing with a sailor's tongue.

Loren looked to Jordel. He stood against the room's far wall, backed into a corner. Three Mystics still faced him, Derrick standing between the other two. But Derrick's swings were wide and sloppy, and it kept his companions from striking. Jordel was holding his own, at least for now.

Before Loren could run to help him, the bookcase shifted. The giant Mystic threw it off and clambered to his feet. He had lost his helmet. An angry red gash crossed his forehead, and on his cheek was a welt that would surely bruise. But his eyes were angry and bright as ever, and he had recovered his sword.

"Get behind me," said Loren, seizing Gem's arm and throwing him back. The Mystic advanced. She raised her fists helplessly, backing up step by step.

He struck with the force of an ox, but just as slowly. Again she was able to dodge him—but he carried on past her, heading for Gem and Annis. Loren leapt from behind and landed on his back, where she clung as she wrapped an arm around his throat. She gripped her wrist with the opposite hand, using the strength of both arms to pull tight around his windpipe.

The Mystic staggered and fell to one knee. But though he was slow, he was uncommonly strong. One hand reached back and seized Loren by the nape of her neck. Bodily he flung her off, hurling her over his shoulder and into the wall beside Gem and Annis. She struck it hard and landed badly, all her breath knocked out. Her arms scrabbled on the floor as she tried to rise, but she could not force her legs to move.

He stood and took another step forwards. Gem put himself between the man and Annis, eyes burning with defiance. At the last second he leapt, trying once again to take the Mystic down by the legs. A meaty fist lashed out and struck him, and Gem fell heavily to the ground. The Mystic turned and went for him, slowly, with the inevitability of a rock slide. His sword flashed in the light through the window as he raised it high.

Annis gave a cry of rage and hurled herself forwards. She fell to her knees before Gem, wrapping her arms around him and defiantly staring up at the Mystic. The man paused for a moment, his sword held high.

Frantically, Loren looked around. She had fallen near the cooking fire, and the kettle still sat in the coals. Her hand wrapped around the handle as she scrambled to her feet, and she threw the pot with all her might at the Mystic. It struck him hard in the back of the head, and he fell forwards. The children barely scrambled out of the way in time. The man landed hard and did not move again. Annis drew her legs away from his prone form and clutched Gem harder. All the boy's limbs shook as he held on hard to her sleeve.

Loren wanted to ensure they were all right, but she had no time. Jordel was still backed into the corner, his blade dancing to keep Derrick and the other Mystics at bay. Loren picked up the kettle again and cracked the closest one over the head. Derrick and his companion turned in surprise—but when he saw what Loren had done, Derrick whirled on the last Mystic in an instant. He plunged his sword into the woman's chest, through her cloak and mail. The Mystic's surprise erupted in a death gasp, eyes staring wide and fearful into Derrick's, and then she fell.

All of them froze in shock—all except Derrick, who drew his blade from the corpse with a harsh tug. He turned to Jordel, who raised his weapon again—but Derrick only wiped his sword clean on the fallen woman's cloak and returned it to his scabbard.

"Forgive me," said Derrick quickly. "I had no choice. And this one was a poison within our ranks—the order will not miss her. I could not help you openly before, but now there will be no witnesses."

Jordel's face twisted in wrath, and he did not lower his weapon. "You brought violence upon a sister of the order, Derrick. It is not your place to judge who is fit to wear the red cloak."

"They would not have stopped until you lay dead,"

said Derrick. "And so you must go, quickly, for there are more of us in Strapa. I am not in command—I was only sent to earn your trust, for our masters knew of the past that you and I share."

All was silent, and for a moment Loren feared Jordel might cut Derrick down. But at last he sheathed his sword, though the grim look did not leave. "Very well. You say there are others. Where are they?"

"Away from here, outside the village, yet near enough to strike. Even now they may approach. Gain your horses and flee Strapa before they find you."

"It will go ill for you when they find you alone. What will you do?"

Derrick looked at his feet, ashamed at last. "I thought I might ask a boon of you in that regard, though I have done nothing to earn your favor. I do not wish to be exiled. I am a Mystic true, though you may doubt it. But they cannot find me unharmed when all of you have fled."

Jordel's face softened, and he nodded. "I understand." Then he drew his weapon and lifted it high.

"No!" cried Loren. But Jordel struck before she could interfere. The pommel of his sword crashed hard into Derrick's head, and the man fell.

"He is not harmed—not as sorely as some of the others, at any rate," said Jordel. "This way it will seem he was overcome trying to prevent our escape."

"You believe his tale, then?" said Gem. "It seems a fine enough thing to say after he already lost the fight.

But I do not put much faith in the words of one who slew his own companion."

"I thought something was amiss before then," said Jordel. "Derrick is a good swordsman, yet he fought poorly to keep the others from striking at me. In any case it is done, and we should hearken to his words. Out the door. Quickly!"

Loren led the way, throwing the door open—but she froze on the threshold. Before her stood another five redcloaks, all with arrows drawn. She barely had time to fling the door shut again. Five sharp *thunks* sounded against it.

"There are more outside," she said. "Armed with bows. We are trapped."

"Things are not as dire as all that," said a voice.

They looked to the window in the back of the house. There stood Albern, the bowyer, his face freshly shaven, a spark of grim humor in his eye.

"A pretty sight you all make," said Albern. "Though I imagine I might look worse after a fight such as that."

"You were watching us?" said Loren.

"I keep an eye on those who interest me. But you can provide me no amusement if you perish. Come, if you wish my help to escape. Otherwise try the front door again, and see if you can persuade your foes to show mercy."

Loren met Jordel's look, but they needed only a moment. What choice did they have? Together they lifted Gem through the window, followed by Annis, with Albern lowering them gently on the other side. Then they climbed through themselves, leaving the half-dozen Mystics behind.

SEVEN

THE WOODS WERE ONLY A FEW PACES FROM THE HOUSE, and Albern led them there in a low running crouch. Without thinking, Loren muffled her footsteps, running toes-first as she followed. It was a useless gesture, though, for Annis still crashed along as loud as ever. Once within the safety of the trees, Albern stopped to duck behind a wide trunk. Loren followed suit, and together they surveyed the house. The Mystics had only just begun to circle around, approaching it from a dozen paces away. They seemed unaware that their quarry had escaped.

"They shall notice our absence soon enough," said Albern. "Fortunately, we will be well quit of this place before then." He set off again, leading them deeper into the woods.

Soon they came to a small clearing. There, to Loren's great surprise, stood their horses—along with two more, a sprightly bay and a swaybacked plow horse.

"The bay is mine," said Albern. "The other was for supplies—though I suppose the children may ride it, if they can ride at all."

"What supplies?" said Loren.

"He means to take us into the mountains." Jordel fixed Albern with a keen glare, and not an entirely happy one. "Was this your plan, then, bowyer? To take advantage of us in a moment of peril? I do not like schemers."

Albern shrugged. "I told you yesterday—I rarely see such interesting travelers as yourselves. When I am interested in something, I look after it. And I did not have to look after you very long before I saw your pursuers close in. Once they did, I hazarded a guess that you might be more in need of a guide than you let on."

Jordel still looked displeased, but Loren spoke before he could. "Jordel, you know we cannot take the Westerly Road now. They will follow us upon it, and our two horses are overburdened. We must travel the mountain pass."

"Very well," said Jordel. "We will take your services, bowyer. Though you will receive a fair price for your guidance, and not a penny more, no matter how urgent our need."

"I would ask for nothing greater," said Albern. "I long for the diversion as much as for the coin. Though diversion does not fill the coffers, as they say. Two gold weights now, and three more when we reach Northwood at the northern end of the Greatrocks."

Jordel's brows lifted slightly. "Five gold weights is a great bargain."

"I told you I wished to ride again," said Albern with a grin.

"I shall pay you three now, and five in Northwood," said Jordel. "But if I wish to take a different path than you say, we shall take it. And you must ask no questions about our journey, or our business."

"Done and done," said Albern. "Though remind me never to let you bargain on my behalf, for I fear I might end up a pauper. Come. Let us be off."

Jordel handed him three gold weights, and then mounted while Loren helped Gem and Annis to the back of the plow horse. Midnight greeted her with a nicker as she swung atop the mare's back, black cloak billowing behind her. But when Albern made to lead the horses north, Jordel stopped him.

"We have . . . a burden," said the Mystic. "West of the town, hidden in the forests. We must retrieve it before we go."

"It must be a valuable cargo indeed, for you to fetch it while so hotly pursued," said Albern.

"You mean to go back for Xain?" said Annis, half angry, half afraid. "How do you think we can travel the mountain pass while dragging him behind us?"

Albern frowned, and he looked from the children to Jordel.

The Mystic fixed him with a grim smile. "Do you still wish so badly to guide us, bowyer? You might have taken a little more care when looking into your charges before you took them on."

Albern was silent for a moment, but then he shrugged. "Your business is your own, and I have said I will not ask questions. Neither will I answer them. Let us fetch this man, then."

"But our enemies are almost upon us," said Annis, voice thick with fear. "They may catch us even as we try to reach Xain."

"I hear your protests—and the unspoken thoughts behind them, Annis," said Jordel with a sigh. "If you hate the idea of riding with Xain so badly, I have no hold upon you. You may leave if you wish. But I will not abandon him in the woods to die."

"Nor I," said Loren softly, though it pained her to see the look in Annis' eyes. "We may as well sink a dagger into his back ourselves as leave him bound without food or water."

Annis did not answer, but turned away to hide beneath her hood. Gem put a hand on her shoulder, his other arm still wrapped around her waist as he rode behind her.

Jordel turned the horses and guided them south, picking their way quickly but carefully through the trees until they were well away from town. Then they cut west, riding at a brisk trot until they reached the woods beside the road. There they waited for a moment, looking hard in every direction to ensure no eyes were upon them, before crossing the road at a gallop to reach the other side.

"And now we are nearly home free," chirped Gem. "See, Annis? You worried for nothing."

"Hist!" said Loren. "Confidence curses luck, especially when you need it most. Say not we are safe until we are in the mountains and know that we are not being followed."

Jordel led them unerringly through the forest in the direction of Xain's hiding place. Loren wondered at that, for she could see no path for the Mystic to follow. He seemed intimately familiar with these woods. She thought there must be a tale there, but as with so many matters concerning Jordel, she had no time to ask.

Soon they reached the clearing where the great stones were stacked in a pile. The small cave was dark, and for a moment Loren could not see Xain. Fear fluttered in her heart. Then she spotted the shape of his boot, stretching almost into the daylight, and soon saw the rest of him as her eyes adjusted to the darkness within.

Xain did not look pleased to see them—nor did he

look well. His face seemed more gaunt and pale. His hair stuck out, thin and wispy, and blood had turned his eyes pink.

Jordel dismounted and brought the wizard forth, pulling him to his feet after untying his hands from the rocks. Then he tied Xain across the back of his horse as he had before.

If Albern was dismayed, he did not show it. But he surveyed Jordel's doings with a cool and reserved eye, his mouth set in a stern line. Loren could not imagine he was pleased at this development—if nothing else, it would slow their progress through the mountains.

"I ask again: have you any regrets, bowyer?" said Jordel. "Now is your last chance to return to your shop. After this moment there is no turning back, and I will not risk our lives in the mountains with a guide who wishes he were elsewhere. You may keep the gold I have given you, if you wish, for no doubt you saved us from the Mystics within the village."

"I will tell you again," said Albern. "I am not in the business of asking questions. One grows weary of staying in the same place, never leaving home or seeing new sights. I think a man such as yourself understands that."

His words were haughty, yet Loren saw Jordel relax. Still, he pressed the question. "You have seen already that we are fugitives from the Mystics—I am a member of the order myself, recently exiled. You should know also that we flee the King's justice, though I can promise you we have done no deed too ill. Our only crime is keeping this wizard from the constables, for his will is not his own."

"It is magestones, then?" said Albern. "I thought as much. He has the look. You do him a great service, though I doubt he is of the mind to thank you for it."

Xain's angry glare over the cloth that gagged him was answer enough.

Jordel hauled Xain's head up as he pulled forth a waterskin. This he jammed into the wizard's mouth, around the gag, and poured. Xain drank from it greedily, but coughed after a moment as he took too much in. Jordel closed the waterskin again, and then climbed into his saddle.

"Very well, Albern of the family Telfer," said Jordel. "We accept your service. And I thank you for your persistence in offering it, though I was at first reluctant to accept."

"And I thank you for the chance to put my feet upon the road again," said Albern. "Strapa is a fine place to live, yet one who has spent most his life wandering will weary of any place in time."

He nudged his horse north, Jordel following close behind. Loren shared a look with Annis, who still seemed afraid, and then trotted close behind.

EIGHT

THE WOODS WERE SILENT AND EMPTY, AND SOON they passed Strapa heading north. The forest grew sparser, and Loren was nervous as she imagined the Mystics hunting them through the trees. But in no time they came upon a road, not wide but well-worn, running northwest through the trees towards the Greatrocks.

"This is the beginning of the mountain pass," said Albern. "It rises steeply up into the foothills, twisting and turning as it finds its way into the mountains proper. Then after a time it descends into the wide river valley before climbing once more."

"How long is the road?" said Jordel. "We are in need of haste, and already I mourn for the speed the Westerly Road would have given us."

"Normally less than two months," said Albern offhandedly. "But there are many branches in the mountain pass, and though some are a touch safer, they take longer. If you wish for speed, we can ride hard and reach the town of Northwood in a month—but I cannot promise you better. Even that may not be possible."

Jordel ground his teeth. "A month. Far too long, yet I suppose it cannot be helped. Very well. Lead on, and if ever you must choose between the faster route and the safer one, choose the faster."

Albern had told no lie; the road began to rise almost as soon as they set hooves upon it, and soon the trees gave way to gently climbing hills. Atop the first one they paused and turned back for a moment, looking down at the lands that rolled away south and east. There, far below, they could see gentle wisps of smoke rising from Strapa's morning cooking fires. But the town was hidden by the forest, and they could see nothing of the buildings or people.

"Still no sign of our pursuers," said Jordel. "With luck they are chasing us up the Westerly Road and have not guessed we have taken this route instead."

"Even if they hazard such a guess, it will not serve

them," said Albern. "I promise you this: no one living knows this path as well as I, nor can they travel it faster."

"Yet those who chase us are quite resourceful," said Jordel. "Do not be overconfident. There are many in my order who can surprise even me, on occasion."

"You would know best," said Albern with a shrug. "Come. Let us get on with it, then."

They rode all that day in silence and haste, for the road was still wide and they could trot or gallop upon much of it. The sun burned brightly while they rode—but by the time it dipped and they stopped to make their camp, clouds had gathered again to hide it.

"Such is always the way in the mountains," said Albern. "Summer takes far longer to reach the Greatrocks than the lowlands."

Still, it was not quite cold enough that they regretted their lack of tents. They laid their bedrolls upon the ground and fetched provisions from their packs. Jordel had seen to it that they were well-stocked—yet still he rationed their meals, for now their road would be much longer than he had at first thought.

"My lady," said Albern. "I never learned your name."

Loren smiled. "I am Loren of the family Nelda," she said. "Well met, and I apologize for our earlier lack of courtesy."

"Current circumstances make it easy to forgive," said Albern. "But now we have a bit more time for pleasantries."

"And I am Jordel, of the family Adair. This is Annis of the family Yerrin, and Gem of Cabrus."

"Of the family Noctis," said Gem haughtily. "I know at least that much of my parents."

Jordel bowed his head. "As you say."

"Well met, all of you," said Albern. "And I heard from your words earlier that that one is called Xain." He nodded at the wizard, now lying on the ground near their camp, wrists and ankles bound. Xain looked back in anger, one eye almost pure red now with blood.

"He is," said Jordel. "Of the family Forredar."

"Forredar?" said Albern, his eyes widening. "That is a noble name."

Loren's ears perked with interest, but Jordel did not meet her gaze. Instead he seemed eager to change the subject. "If you know of the magestone sickness, you know we must post a guard for his sake. It is of great importance that the wizard not be allowed to flee."

"I would have suggested it in any case," said Albern. "For there are dangers in the mountains, too, besides those who may chase us. Wolves and bears, and darker things farther on."

"What cheery news," said Gem, looking into the night with discomfort.

"Fear not, little master," said Albern, jostling his shoulder. "We will keep you safe from any crawlers in the night. I will stand first watch, if you allow it."

"I would thank you," said Jordel. "For we rode

hard on the road to Strapa, and one night's rest has not yet cured our weariness."

"It is settled, then," said Albern. "A good night to you all, and hopes for a fair morning!"

He strode off from them, climbing atop a small mound that stood nearby to keep watch. His bow he laid across his knees as he pulled out some food and began to eat.

Loren studied Jordel in surprise, for he had let Albern take the watch without question. It was a great show of trust—and yet she remembered how Jordel had taken her own measure almost from the moment they had met in Cabrus. From then on he had trusted her implicitly, though it had taken her far longer to return his faith. He seemed to make up his mind about a person in mere moments. And though at first he had been wary of Albern in the workshop, he must have seen something since to convince him of the man's honesty.

"Though we did not choose this road, I am glad we are upon it," she said to him from across the fire. "The mountain pass may be uncertain, but I feel more hopeful now than I did at the prospect of riding the Westerly Road."

"I, too, feel less need to peer over my shoulder," said Jordel. "Yet still I fear what such a delay might bring. But our path is set, and there is no looking back now."

They supped, and swaddled into their bedrolls to sleep.

So began their trek through the Greatrocks. For some days the journey was uneventful, if strenuous. Albern did not wake them at all the first night to trade watches. When they asked him the next morning he said only, "I have had many years' good rest in Strapa, and my wits are sharper when not fat with sleep." But on the next night and every night thereafter, he traded watches with Loren and Jordel.

Whether riding or walking, the bowyer moved with a vigor that the rest of them found infectious. He spoke with all of them in turn and laughed often, and his cheer did much to raise their mood, which had been somber on the road from Wellmont. Sometimes he would sing as they rode, most often in the mornings; his voice rang clear on the dawn air, echoing back to them from the mountains all around.

They left the foothills on the second day and entered the mountains proper. Then the path grew steeper and narrower, though still wide enough for four horses to walk abreast. But they rode in single file, for Albern told them that the edges of the road were not to be trusted.

"This path was built for trade and travel, and not for war. The king never strengthened it so that an army might march upon it—for if soldiers needed to move from north to south they would take the Westerly Road."

"Which king built it?" said Gem.

"That I do not know," said Albern. "It has been here as long as anyone can remember, and I have found no tales of its making."

Loren looked at Jordel with interest, but he shook his head. "I never learned of it either. Indeed, few write of the Greatrocks. They are Selvan's western border against Dorsea, and are nearly impossible to cross. Few scholars believe they serve any other purpose."

"They are not just a border," said Albern. "They are a world unto themselves, with their own laws that were made by no king."

Often Jordel and Albern would speak together when the party rested. Always Jordel would ask how far they had come, and how much farther they had to go. Albern would draw crude maps for him in the dirt, show him the twists and turns of the pass, and advise him of the best route. Jordel listened more than he spoke, and always accepted the routes that Albern presented. At first Loren would sit with them and listen, but she soon abandoned the meetings, for she found them frightfully boring.

Xain became little more than a piece of luggage in Loren's mind. Upon the road to Strapa, when the horror of his attack was still fresh, she had thought of little besides him. But now there were mountains to catch her attention, and Albern's songs, and the narrow path to keep an eye on. Xain's presence grew less fearful, and she watched dispassionately whenever Jordel would move him from his horse to the ground. But she caught Annis eyeing the wizard often, and the girl's looks were still anxious.

When Xain did not haunt her, though, Annis often looked at Albern with interest. After a few days she finally ventured to begin a conversation. "Tell me, bowyer. Were you ever a soldier?"

Albern looked at her in surprise. "Why, yes. For many years in my youth I marched with the Ruby Crowns."

"A mercenary?" said Annis. Her voice dripped with hushed enthusiasm, as though he had told her a great secret that she ought not to know. "You must have traveled far."

"Far enough, and yet I saw very little," said Albern with a shrug. "I have fought in battles as far east as Idris and as far south as Hedgemond. A frigid place that is, I tell you."

"Some mercenary captains would stay in our manor on the High King's Seat from time to time," said Annis. "My sisters would always flutter about them to hear stories, but they told me I was too young."

"Most likely they were right, for I know the sort of stories mercenary captains tell," said Albern with a snort.

"What of mercenaries themselves?" Annis leaned forwards, smiling. "You must have a fair few tales."

So Albern began to tell them stories whenever they broke from riding. He would recount brief tales during the midday meal, and longer ones when they camped for the night, while Annis and Gem watched him wide eyes and, often, open mouths.

At first Loren did not pay much attention, for she was not overly fond of mercenaries. They worked for coin, which she found distasteful, and their trade was death, which she found abhorrent. But Albern dwelt little on those things. More often he told them of jokes shared with his companions in the company, or described the great cities he had seen in his travels. He seemed as averse to the battles as Loren, for he mentioned them only in passing, and only when the story needed it.

Soon she sat by the fire as rapt as Annis and Gem whenever Albern spoke. Her heart began to burn with a lust for far-off lands. Many places and many strange things she had seen since she left the Birchwood, yet she had never seen anything half so magnificent as the places Albern spoke of.

"I would see such sights," said Loren one night when Albern had finished another tale. She said it quietly, scarcely more than a murmur, and in fact she had not meant to say it out loud. But when they all looked at her with interest, she lifted her head and went on. "I wish to see them. I have often dreamed of great cities and far-off kingdoms. You have seen them all, and more sights I never imagined. I have little to hold me in any place for any length of time. When I can, I will go to these places you speak of."

"I hope to give you that chance," said Jordel, giving her a firm look. "Our duties will carry us to many of the nine lands. Of that you need not fear."

Loren blushed, for in her excitement she had nearly forgotten about the Mystic, and how she was pledged to his service. But she did not regret it, for she sensed he was right. Jordel was not a man of Selvan, but of all the kingdoms at once, and by his side Loren knew she would see more than she ever could alone.

"Travel and see what you will," said Albern. "I will not deny I have many fond memories of the nine lands. But such memories shine a bit brighter than the places themselves. Often I could hardly see the city for my fear I would die in the next battle, or else my wits were muddled by wine and ale. Only looking back does it all seem so golden."

"I would suffer much discomfort now if it gave later years such treasured memories," said Loren. "That seems a fair trade."

"Fair enough indeed," said Albern. "But now it is time to rest."

After four days the pass dove down the mountainside again, curving back and forth upon itself as it had during their climb. The weather grew fairer, and the wide river valley sprawled before them like a tapestry all of green. It was a stunning sight. The river ran clear through wide fields of grass and small clusters of trees, like a string of sapphires laid upon a sheet of fine green satin with emeralds sewn into it. The clouds cleared at last as they reached the valley floor near the end of the day, and they reveled in the warmth of the sun. Loren threw her cloak back over her shoulders.

Jordel caught her attention with a sharp cough. When she met his gaze, he looked to her belt. Loren looked down to see her dagger out in plain sight. Quickly she yanked the left half of her cloak forwards to cover the weapon. Thankfully Albern took no notice.

That was careless, she thought. *I must never forget that I carry a great danger with me.*

Loren wondered, not for the first time, what made her keep the weapon, for it offered little help if she would not use it. But something would not let her throw it away. It had been the very first thing she stole as the Nightblade. More than that, it was a part of her now. It had saved her from certain doom more than once. She would not repay that service by casting it aside, even if she knew the dagger did not care.

They had only one day to enjoy the lush valley, for the mountain pass climbed again the day after. Albern took it, though the road on the valley floor carried on straight and out of sight.

"Why can we not keep on this way?" said Gem. "I like the wide ground far better than the narrow path in the clouds."

"Oh, this road looks fair enough," said Albern.

"But soon enough another mountain blocks it. The journey around would cost several days, while the pass runs straight."

"Then let us take it," said Jordel. "And we should hasten. I have enjoyed the sun as much as anyone, but I fear we have let it make us lazy."

They began to alternate between walking and trotting. It did not lend them very much speed, but they could not push the horses faster, for the ground was steep and rocky. The weather turned again, as if to punish them for leaving the valley floor. Once more they all had to shroud themselves in cloaks, and Gem began to complain.

The rain abated before nightfall, and Albern found them a cleft in the mountainside that would keep them dry if it started up again. Though the storm had stopped, the night was still cold.

Loren had the first watch, and she spent it damp and miserable in the mouth of the cleft, too far from the fire to dry out. Once she looked back in anger at Xain, who lay bound but warm near the flames. Then she saw his body shivering and twitching, and not from the cold. His eyes were free from blood now, but they rolled about in their sockets, and he shivered and tugged at his bonds, covered in a thin sheen of sweat. Loren turned her back, no longer envious.

She woke Albern the second both moons showed themselves above the mountains, and slept close to the fire to drive the chill from her bones.

It was lucky they had taken shelter, for rain indeed began to fall again during the night, and the next day grew wetter than the last. The third day rained even harder, and Gem began to sniff and sneeze with a cold. Worse yet, their horses began to have trouble picking their way on the path. Midnight was a fine steed and sure-footed, and Albern's bay must have been used to the mountains, but Jordel's great charger was heavy, and the children's plow horse, unsure. Every time they began to slide, Loren's heart would stop, and she pictured them pitching out over the path's edge. For safety, they rode as close to the mountain as they could.

Once, it was almost not enough. Albern had warned them of the danger of rockslides in the rain, and when at last one struck it nearly ended in disaster. A sharp crack of lightning sounded above them, and a deep rumble thundered through the ground. The plow horse grew frightened and screamed, rearing. Annis had much practice on horseback and held on, but it caught Gem unawares. He pitched backwards to the ground, straight for the edge of the road.

Loren gave a great shout and jumped from Midnight's back. She slid on the wet rocks towards the edge and snatched his arm at the last second. He rolled away from the edge and into her arms, and she pushed back with her feet as though the void beyond were reaching for them both.

For a long moment they lay there, Loren panting heavily, Gem clutching her arms as if he would never let go. When she looked down she saw that he was crying, face twisted in fear, tears spilling to mingle with the rainwater.

"There," she murmured. "It is all right."

"I am fine," he said harshly, pushing away to stand. He wiped furiously at his face with his hand, trying to look as though he were merely brushing off rainwater. "It caught me by surprise, that is all. I shall hold tighter to Annis."

Loren helped him back into the saddle despite his protests, and they kept on their way. But her panic redoubled every time the horses seemed unsure of their footing, and she held herself tensed to leap from the saddle at a moment's notice.

On the fourth day, the path ended.

They came up short against a great wall of rock. Loose earth and many boulders had slid down from the mountainside, and now completely blocked the path. All of them sat still in their saddles, staring at the debris as though they could move it with their minds.

"We shall have to turn back," said Albern.

"We would not if you had let us carry along on the valley's road," said Gem. "Now we have wasted days of travel, and I have nearly been killed. A fine guide you are."

Albern turned to the boy, and his eyes flashed. "Even the best guide cannot foresee every rock slide," he snapped. "You would have fared much worse on the road if I were not here, that I can promise you."

Gem ducked behind Annis. "I suppose we shall never know now," he muttered. "But still, I was right."

"If we turn back, how many days will it add to our journey?" said Jordel.

Albern fixed him with a look. "Does it matter? You say 'if,' but the rocks will not move themselves."

Jordel tossed his head in impatience and turned his horse back down the path.

NINE

They rode quicker on the path back down, and made the valley in three days where climbing had taken them four. But Jordel's face remained dour, and he cut every rest short. Albern seemed to pick up on the Mystic's mood, and he told no tales when they paused, only eating his food quickly and quietly.

Rain followed them all the way down, and kept pouring upon them as they rode along the valley. Soon enough they saw the truth in Albern's warning; the road ran straight to the foot of a great peak before turning west to loop around it. Since the road was clear and wide, they rode hard, and when they finally stopped after sundown Loren felt as weary as she was sore.

As Jordel lowered Xain from his charger, the wizard moaned. It was a quiet sound, and piteous, and when he lay on the grass his body twisted back and forth across the ground. Loren's stomach clenched. Albern looked at Xain with a frown.

"Is there no way to quiet him?" said Albern.

"Not without medicines I do not have," said Jordel. "Why? Do you fear discovery?"

Albern looked out into the darkness that rimmed the small circle of firelight. "I hope not. But the farther north we go, the more likely it will be that there are eyes in the darkness around us. Mayhap they will be friendly, but mayhap not." He fell silent, and no one answered him.

After she had eaten ravenously of the spare food Jordel gave them, Loren took a brief walk to ease her aching legs, as well as to escape Xain's groaning.

"Take your bow with you," said Jordel. "For protection, but also in case you spy a bird or a rabbit."

"A fair idea," said Loren. "I will not be gone long."

"Wait," said Annis. "I want to go with you." She climbed to her feet.

Jordel sat to converse with Albern about the road ahead. They had spoken every night since turning back on the pass, for now speed was more important than ever. Gem looked at the girls, and then at Jordel and Albern speaking in terse voices by the fire. He, too, gained his feet and ran to catch up. Together the three of them ventured into the darkness, away from the fire. It took Loren's eyes a moment to adjust, but the moons shone bright in the sky and painted everything with a keen silver light.

"I am sick to death of these mountains," said Annis. "Or mayhap it is the rain, or mayhap the sores my saddle has given me. I am sick of it all, I suppose."

"I do not mind it so much," said Loren. "It is good to ride without much fear of pursuit—a fine change from the last many weeks."

Annis waved a hand. "I would rather rest somewhere in peace and quiet than find it upon the road," she said. "When first I left the High King's Seat, I was excited by the journey, but now the miles have almost made me long for our manor again."

"Truly?" said Loren. "I would have thought parting ways with your mother would have made your travels seem sweeter."

Annis picked at a string on her sleeve. "I suppose. Yet I will happily retire to a bed, a chair, and a fire when the chance arises."

That brought to mind a matter Loren had long been brewing on. She stopped and turned to them both, as though she had only just been struck by the idea. "Mayhap you can have more than that. What if we found you a place to stay, once we have safely left Selvan behind us? You as well, Gem."

Both children looked at her as though she were mad, but it was he who spoke. "What sort of place? Jordel's stronghold, you mean?"

Loren shook her head. "No, not that—some noble's manor, far from any court where Yerrin or the Mystics could find you. I am certain Jordel would know of such a place. You would be safe from all prying eyes—even your mother's."

Gem's expression grew angry. "You mean to leave us behind, while you and Jordel carry on with his quest?"

The fury in his eyes confused her, but Annis' pained expression was worse. "What have I done to offend you?" she said quietly. "Why would you cast me aside?"

Loren balked. "I . . . you have done nothing. But you have seen the dangers of our road, and I think it will grow far darker before its end. You have had nowhere to go beyond my side, but I know Jordel could arrange it."

"What makes you think we *want* another place to go?" said Gem. "Did we ever ask you for one?"

"She just said so!" said Loren, pointing to Annis. "And you are always complaining of the cold and the rain and how little we have to eat. You cannot tell me you would rather have this life than one of peace and plenty. Ever since we had hoped to sell our magestones for a small fortune, I had planned to use it to send the two of you away. Mayhap to some outland kingdom like Calentin, where no one could find you."

Annis shook her head. "You spoke of such a plan—only you made it sound as though you would come with me. Did you mean to leave me there all along?"

"Of course not," said Loren, her jaw clenching. "Only I had not pledged myself to Jordel then. And you *just* told us you wished to abandon the road."

"I spoke only of wanting a rest," said Annis, her sadness slowly turning to anger. But where Gem's was like a fire, hers was like a ball of ice clenched in the fist. "I did not ask to leave you. Mayhap I thought more of our friendship than you."

"And I have pledged myself to your service!" said Gem. "You took my word and my promise, and you cannot cast them aside. It is . . . it is *dishonorable.*" He spat the word like a curse.

Loren was at a loss, and growing annoyed. "You are both acting like children," she said. "No one could wish for danger upon the road when offered a safe haven instead. Neither of you is fully grown. You should be spending your days learning, not riding from peril to peril like a matching set of fools."

"Says the fool herself," said Annis. "I have already had one woman who plotted a course for me without asking. I left her as soon as I was able, and mayhap I shall do so again."

She turned on her heel and stormed off. Gem began to follow, but stopped for his own parting words. "You may plan whatever you wish for me. But if you think to leave me behind, you will have to tie me up.

And you had better lock me in a cellar for good measure, for I can escape bonds quite easily." Then he left to follow Annis.

Loren stood there for a while in the dark, not knowing what to do and not quite sure what she had done wrong. The children were acting daft, to her mind, but she had not the first clue what to do about it.

She cast her thoughts aside and strode farther into the moonslight, seeking a target for her bow. Hunting had always cleared her mind before. But now she kept thinking of the look of hurt on Annis' face, and the anger upon Gem's. When she finally spotted a quail at roost, she shot at it, but in her distraction the arrow flew wide. The quail flew off with a startled squawk, and Loren could not recover her arrow in the moonslight. With many curses and dark mutters she stalked back to the camp, lying down to rest while trying not to look at anyone.

The journey was nearly unbearable after that. Gem and Annis rode in stony silence, and when the party stopped they sat alone to talk. They would hardly meet Loren's gaze and they ceased asking Albern for stories. Jordel was caught up in his worry for the road, but even he noticed their strange behavior. One day he took Loren from the camp and asked her what had happened. Loren told him, trying not to let her anger at the children show.

To her surprise, Jordel gave a small smile. "I wish you had spoken to me first. You should have expected no different. They are both very fond of you."

"It was only a thought, not some grand design!" said Loren.

He studied her eyes. "It does not sound like some passing fancy. Can you say in truth that you have not thought upon this for some time?"

"No plan has long survived my travels or my perils," said Loren. "Only now it seems I follow you into a war, and I only want to keep the children from it. I am fond of them as well, though just now I am nearly angry enough to forget it. I only want to keep them safe."

"Safety is rarely the greatest concern of the very young, for they have little understanding of true danger. But I do not think it is their youth that makes them act thus. Tell me, if I offered you the same chance you gave to them, would you take it?"

Loren looked at him in surprise. "I . . . I would be out of place in a noble's court."

"Gem could say the same thing. But is it your unease with nobility that holds you back, or something else? Could you sit in safety and in silence, sewing pretty dresses for dances and festivals?"

As Jordel spoke, the picture of his words found shape in Loren's mind. Yet she could not place herself inside the thought, nor see her face within it anywhere. Whenever she thought of sewing and courtly graces and curtseys, her mind shied away.

She looked at Jordel, troubled. "Anyone would wish for that kind of life. It is like a dream, and many would scheme or even kill to get it."

"Many have. But not all belong to such a life. What did Annis say when we stayed at the inn in Strapa? Mayhap such folk as us are meant for a life on the endless road, always running from place to place, never settling long enough to plant roots. Once I thought my journeys might end in a court, or at least a home, with a family. The last many years have given me cause to doubt it."

Loren turned from him. "Then you are as foolish as the children, or more so, for I think you have seen enough fighting and danger that you should have wearied of it long ago."

"What wearies one may excite another. Did Albern seem half so lively in his bowyery as he does here in the mountains? I think he convinced himself that a life of ease and comfort was his dream. But he was wrong."

"These are all very pretty words," said Loren. "But if the children stay with us upon the road, they may die."

"Yes," said Jordel, and he gave a heavy sigh. "That is my fear, too. But even children have lives, and those lives are *theirs,* Loren. We can advise them, and as their elders it is our duty to do so. We can even admonish them, or discipline them for wrongdoing. But their choices must always be their own. That is a truth not only for children, but for all people."

Loren looked at him curiously. "You have a strange mind, Jordel of the family Adair."

He bowed, brown cloak draping around him. "Ever I have sought to. Now come. It is time we were on the road again."

TEN

NEARLY A WEEK AFTER RETURNING TO THE VALLEY FLOOR, they passed the great mountain. There the path split again. One branch carried on straight, while the other rose into the range. Albern gave Jordel a pointed look.

"Which road shall it be? You have seen the risks of the faster road, but the course is yours to choose as always."

"The faster," said Jordel without hesitation. "Rock slides cannot have blocked every path north, and the weather now is milder than it was. Mayhap we can make up for lost time."

"As you say," said Albern, and he led them up.

Gem accepted this new path without grumbling, for once. Perhaps he remembered Albern's chastisement the last time, or mayhap he was still too angry at Loren to speak when she might reply. But they rode the first day in silence without trouble, and then the second, and the third.

Four days had brought them to their obstacle the last time, and as the sun wound down on the fourth now, Loren could feel relief wash through the party. It made little sense, she knew; there might well be a rock slide still ahead, just around the next twist in the path. But when they stopped to make camp, a light mood seemed to have taken hold of them all. Albern hummed a song as he removed his horse's saddlebags, while Gem and Annis spoke animatedly to each other—though still not to Loren.

But Xain did not join them in their cheer. He fared worse and worse with each passing day, and Loren had begun to worry. He seemed little more than skin and bones now. The defiance and anger in his eyes were heavily tempered with pain. More, he seemed to be senseless much of the time. Sometimes when Jordel took him from the horse, the wizard would stare at them not with fury, but with fear—a wide-eyed, frantic terror, as though he did not know who they were or why he was bound.

She drove Xain from her mind, though she thought she heard him whispering as she stood the first watch.

The night was warmer than usual, and Loren's time passed quickly. When Jordel shook her just before dawn to wake her, she found the skies clear and a rosy glow above the mountains to the east.

"A fair morning, and promise of a fair day," said Albern.

"Mayhap our luck has changed at last," said Gem.

Loren wanted to warn him against boasting again, but she held her tongue. He was angry enough with her as it was.

Mayhap she should have warned him, though, for not long after they started riding, Albern called them to a sudden halt. He waved them hastily to the side, and they all guided their horses to huddle against the mountain.

Jordel stepped up beside him, hand on his charger's reins. "What is it?" he said in a low voice.

"There are satyrs ahead," said Albern. "They have not seen us yet."

They leaned out to look. There they were: smallish creatures, a few fingers shorter than Loren, with bodies like men but legs like goats, and horns sprouting from their foreheads. At first Loren thought they were floating in the air; then she saw that they were sitting on the mountainside, though she could not see how. The cliff face looked almost sheer, yet the creatures perched upon it as though it were a flat shelf. They were perhaps ten paces above the path.

Loren quaked. "Satyrs?" she whispered. "We should run."

Albern looked back at her with a grim smile. "You have heard stories about them, then. Fear not—they are not so dangerous as many tales say, though it is true that they are nothing to trifle with, either. They are quite quick and cunning. Thankfully they do not poison their arrows."

"Will they attack us?" said Jordel, his gaze locked on the beasts.

Albern tilted his head back and forth. "That is difficult to say. Sometimes satyrs will strike at travelers, and other times let them pass with nary a word. They see the mountains as their own kingdom, and dislike others passing through. But most often their mood depends on their elder. If a satyr of honor and peace rises to power, the whole clan grows less dangerous. They will even trade with humans, if they have need to. But if a young and headstrong bull takes charge, he will encourage his followers to great violence as a way of proving himself."

"And are they ruled now by an honorable elder, or a dangerous one?" said Jordel.

"I have not been this way in many years. Last I knew, their elder was old and cautious, and bore no great ill will for men. But much can change in their clan, and quickly."

"I have heard they can rip a man's heart from his chest," said Loren, "and that they feast on children they steal from cradles in the night."

"That sounds more akin to vampires," said Annis, scoffing. "Satyrs are nowhere near so fearsome. I learned much about them in my studies. Even at their worst they are like wolves; if they are left alone or shown a sharp blade, they will leave you be. Or at least, that is what I was told."

"Then your teachers told you true," said Albern. "They are neither very numerous nor very dangerous; Loren could take one easily in a fight. Their chief strength lies in their ability to traverse the mountains, for they can strike at you from a cliff face you thought was only a wall. But now we have seen them, and can avoid them."

"How do you mean to do that?" said Jordel.

Albern's mouth twisted. "We could turn back and make for the valley floor again."

"No," said Jordel quickly. "We have lost far too much time already. At this rate I fear we shall not make Feldemar before winter, and that would be disastrous."

"I thought you might say so," said Albern. "Very well. See how the cliff face leans back, before forming a sort of wall beside the path? If we stay close to the mountainside as we ride past, and if we are quiet, I think we can pass them unawares."

"Let us do it then, and quickly," said Jordel. "Remain silent, all of you—but be ready to fight, if it should come to that. Loren, string your bow."

"I would find myself more ready if I had a blade to hand," said Gem.

"Can you wield one?" said Jordel. At Gem's bashful look, he nodded. "I thought not. Come."

They remained on foot, for on horseback their heads would be in full view of the creatures, and then led their horses forwards at a slow walk. Only Xain was not on his feet, for he remained slung across the back of Jordel's charger. The wizard did not move, and Loren thought he might be sleeping. They turned one curve, which put them in view of the satyrs for a heart-stopping moment until another curve hid them from sight again.

"They could have seen us!" hissed Loren.

"You need not worry about that," said Albern. "Their eyesight is poor, though their ears and noses are better than ours."

Step by step they went, keeping their bodies as close to the mountain as possible. Every so often Albern would duck his head out slightly, looking up to inspect the cliff.

"Still they have caught no sign of us," he whispered. "But do not speak until we are well past them."

Loren's heart thundered in her chest. Despite Annis' assurances and Albern's soothing words, still she could think only of the tales she had heard in the Birchwood. Parents would tell their children to return home at night, or else satyrs would find them in the woods and drag them away, never to be seen again. Of course her own parents had never resorted to such ruses; the threat of her father's fists had been more than enough to keep Loren from straying.

The wall of rock drew ever closer as the path narrowed. Loren felt sure the satyrs must be able to see the heads of their horses, but there was no cry of alarm. Albern had pressed himself against the rock wall now, and the rest of them followed suit. The horses seemed to catch the tension in the air, for they nickered nervously and joined their riders in hugging the cliff side.

Then without warning, Jordel's charger screamed and reared. Loren saw Xain nearly tumble from the horse's back, but his straps held. The other mounts started and shied nervously, dancing out to the far edge of the mountain path, while the plow horse dragged Gem and Annis into view.

A great keening cry erupted, a sound between a sheep's bleat and a man's battle cry, and then came the sharp *click-clack* of hooves on rock. With great leaps and bounds the satyrs came flying down the mountainside. They landed hard on the pass, both ahead of and behind the party, their hairy legs bending to absorb the shock of their fall. There were ten, by Loren's count, with three behind and the rest in front.

The moment the satyrs landed they began to shout with a terrible fury. Their words were garbled and alien to her, like listening to a warthog try its hand at speaking. She thought she caught some semblance of words she knew, but all of them were speaking at once.

Albern's bow had flown into his hand when Loren was not looking, and Jordel began to draw his blade. Loren's own hand went to her dagger, but Albern threw a hand back to stop them both. “Wait!” he said. “Do not draw your weapons. We may still be able to parley.”

“They do not look in a mood to talk,” said Jordel, whose sword remained half out of its scabbard.

“They never do,” said Albern, “and yet sometimes they will.”

He turned back to the goat-men and began to speak to them. He held both his hands out in a calming gesture, though Loren thought it less effective as he still held his bow. Meanwhile, she snatched the reins of the plow horse and drew it farther along on the path before stepping back with Midnight to put herself between the satyrs and the children.

“There now, friends,” said Albern. “Calmly now, calmly. We wish you no harm. We are only travelers. Be calm, and put up your weapons.”

His words had little effect. If anything, Loren thought she saw the goat-men grow more agitated. Most of them held long spears, though two held small bows of yew. Their arrows were little more than sharpened sticks, and slightly bent.

One great satyr stepped forth, shoving two others out of its way. He threw his head back and gave a great scream like a goat’s cry, and the other satyrs fell silent. The leader fixed his beady black eyes on Albern and crossed his arms. He gave a huge grunt, and the other satyrs echoed it more quietly.

“I take you for the leader, then,” said Albern. “Are you the elder? Do you command these brave warriors?”

So far Loren had seen nothing to show her that these creatures understood the tongue of men. But now the leader tossed his head and spoke, his voice broken and guttural. "I am no elder. I am warlord. I am Tiglak, son of the Lord, like my brothers here. And I know you, human."

Albern did not answer at first. Loren had been watching the satyrs behind them, but at the bowyer's silence she turned to glance at him. Deep concern was etched in his brows. But he quickly shook it off.

"The Lord is your elder?" he said. "I have not had the honor of meeting him. But I remember you, Tiglak. You were young when last I walked this path, but now I see you have grown tall and mighty."

Tiglak unfurled his arms and rolled his shoulders. Though larger than the others, he was still not quite so tall as Jordel, and his muscles were scarcely more impressive than Gem's. But he seemed to take the compliment well. "I am mighty—more mighty than you. Humans cannot walk the mountains anymore. The Lord has told us."

Again a shadow crossed Albern's face. "The Lord is your elder?" he asked again.

"The Lord is mightier than our elder. Our clan bows before the elder, but the elder bows before the Lord. All bow before him. Even humans, who he says cannot walk the mountains."

"We are only passing through your lands," said Albern. "We ask no boon, and we bring our own food."

"The Lord does not care," said Tiglak, growing angry. Bleats sounded in his voice now, and he gripped his spear tighter. "The Lord says no humans walk the mountains, and you are human. You will leave, or we will bring your skulls back to him."

The other satyrs gave a great shout and thrust their spears forwards, though the tips were still a few paces away. Loren realized suddenly that the creatures were not as brave as they tried to seem. She caught them looking shiftily at each other, and then back at the party, almost as if daring each other to be the one to strike first.

To her surprise the bowyer straightened where he stood, and his hands fell to his sides. "Do not threaten us, Tiglak. If you remember me, you remember that many in your clan fear my bow."

"I do not fear you!" roared Tiglak, throwing his fists into the sky. "I do not fear anyone! The Lord gives our clan strength, and weapons and much food! We do not fear you any longer, human!"

Albern did not flinch. "I have given you more than fair warning and much lenience, Tiglak. Stand aside now, or I will not be so kind."

Tiglak answered with a mighty shout, and then snatched one of the other satyrs by the neck to thrust him forwards. With the first one flung into the fray, the rest quickly followed, leaping to attack.

In a blur of motion, Albern drew and fired. He wore his quiver on his hip, not his back, a practice

Loren had always seen as strange. But now she saw its purpose; his hand could dart down to snatch an arrow and return to the bow in the blink of an eye. He drew and fired faster than a lightning strike before fetching another. Before the satyrs reached them he had unleashed three shafts, and all found their marks; three of the creatures fell to the ground, dead or dying.

But the satyrs behind the party were attacking as well, and Loren turned to face them. She nearly fell over while trying to step back, long wooden spears thrusting at her face. Then a blade caught the weapons, shattering them, and Jordel stepped forwards to protect her. His sword spun in the sunlight with a dizzying flash, and he struck one of the satyrs down where she stood. The other two backed off, still holding the broken ends of their spears forwards. Jordel held his sword at the ready, daring the creatures to come closer.

With their rear protected, Loren ran to help Albern. With the satyrs near he had drawn a short sword, and he used it with practiced ease to keep the creatures at bay while still holding the bow in his left hand. Three of them tried to surround him with their spears, while Tiglak stood in the back urging them on. But they could not breach Albern's guard, and he could not get past the long spears to reach them.

Loren snatched her new bow from Midnight's saddle and drew an arrow. After Albern's display she felt like a child, but still she reveled in the smooth feel of the fine weapon bending in her hands. She loosed her shaft, and it struck one of the satyrs in the shoulder. The goat-man fell to the ground with a cry, and the other two gaped. It gave Albern the moment he needed, and he dropped the sword in favor of another arrow. But he did not fire at the creatures before him—his arrow sailed between them, striking Tiglak in the leg.

Tiglak staggered, bleating in pain and fear. The other satyrs scampered back, leaving Albern an opening. He ran through it and tackled Tiglak, bearing him to the ground before lifting him back up, a sharp dagger pressed to the creature's throat.

"I pay the price of passage with Tiglak's life!" he shouted. "Let us go, or he dies."

"Yes!" cried Tiglak. "Yes, we let you pass! I swear it."

"By the moon goddess," said Albern.

"Do not speak of her thus, you hairless—"

Albern tightened his arm around Tiglak's throat, and the satyr fell silent. "I know the words. Swear it in the name of Skal, holy mother between the moons."

Tiglak did not look pleased, but he subsided. "I swear it in Skal's honor."

Albern waited a moment, then released his hold and shoved Tiglak away. The satyr fell to hands and knees. With a great shout he bounded back up, and Loren's heart leapt to her throat—but he jumped up the mountainside, leaping up the sheer cliff face like it was a ladder. The others followed, leaving their dead and wounded behind. Albern ran to retrieve his arrows from the bodies that lay all about. Loren ran to join him, though she had only the one shaft to reclaim.

"Will the satyrs honor those words?" said Jordel.

"They always have," said Albern. "But still it would be best not to tarry. Tiglak and his warriors are oath-bound now, but if their elder dislikes the promise they made, he will kill Tiglak and consider the burden released. Mount up and ride—and move with haste. If they do betray us, it will take them some time to muster the courage. We would do well to be quit of here before then."

ELEVEN

The children climbed on the plow horse, and Loren quickly gained her saddle atop Midnight. But Jordel waited a moment before mounting. He went to the rear of his horse first, and there he seized the back of Xain's neck. The wizard's head came up, and Jordel slapped him with a flat palm.

"Jordel!" cried Loren.

He ignored her, pulling Xain from the horse's back and casting him to the ground. Xain fought for his feet, and Jordel helped him by snatching the front of his collar to drag him up. Then he slapped him again.

"Stop it!" cried Loren, climbing down from Midnight. Albern only watched with a dark look in his eyes.

"I know you goaded the horse to rear, Xain." A dangerous undercurrent of fury in the Mystic's voice chilled Loren's heart. "We might have passed without incident but for you. You endangered all of us because of your weakness."

He seized Xain's throat in his hands, and the wizard's face began to turn red. Loren ran forwards and pulled at Jordel's arms, but she might as well have tried to move the mountain they stood on. Xain only stared daggers at the Mystic, and even through his pain she could see the hatred burning in his eyes.

"I know you suffer now," said Jordel. "I know your hunger eats away at you from the inside, until you wish you could die from the pain of it. But you brought it upon yourself. You have no one else to blame, and certainly not these children. I *will not* let you use your agony as an excuse to endanger their lives."

He pushed Xain back until they stood just fingers from the edge of the mountain path. Annis screamed in fright.

"Risk their safety again, and I will fling you to the valley floor. You are a mighty wizard, but you cannot fly. Though I need you, still I would give your life for theirs and lose no sleep over it."

He released Xain, who fell to the ground. Loren seized his coat and dragged him away from the path's edge. She looked back with worry and saw Gem and Annis watching. Annis' eyes were filled with fear, but Gem's held a curious light. He watched not with fear or even anxiousness, but with a grim sort of approval.

Jordel stalked back to his horse. From his bags he fetched a new length of rope, and a pair of leather bags. They reminded Loren of a leather hood used to shield a falcon's eyes, but larger.

Jordel wrapped the hoods around Xain's clenched hands, and then he bound them tight with straps that hung from the wrists. He undid the rope that connected Xain's hands and feet, moved his hands behind his back, and retied them. The knots were now so tight that Xain could scarcely move his hands above his lower back. Finally Jordel threw the wizard over the horse and bound him to the saddle once more.

"That will be a far harsher ride," remarked Albern.

"He has earned it," said Jordel. "Come. Lead us on, and quickly."

They rode at a gallop now, Xain bouncing terribly on Jordel's horse. At first Loren could hear him giving small yelps of pain, but they finally subsided as he slumped on the horse's flanks, senseless.

Jordel did not command them to stop at midday for a meal, or for anything else. Only once did he allow them to walk the horses, and gave them all provisions to eat as they rode. He took no food himself, but only kept glancing back angrily at Xain. Everyone seemed to have caught his dour mood; no one spoke, not even Gem to complain.

Sunset came, and soon the last sliver of sun vanished over the western mountains. Loren thought that surely they would stop then, but Albern nudged his horse over to confer with Jordel. Then the bowyer turned back to them.

"We will ride on through the night, but slower," he said. "I wish to give the satyrs no chance to track us. It might be safe here, but I shall feel more secure after a few more hours."

"Through the night?" said Annis, exhaustion plain in the slump of her shoulders. "I am ready to fall from this saddle."

"I do not recommend it," said Albern. "Keep the horses at a brisk walk. Pinch yourself if you must, but stay awake."

Silver moonslight bathed them through the night. Though it was still a bit dim, Loren found that she had grown quite accustomed to traveling by moonslight over the past many weeks, and could see almost as well as during the day. Midnight seemed at ease as well, for she followed briskly behind Jordel's charger. The plow horse, however, was unused to such stretches of travel, and began to stumble as it walked.

Soon its meandering grew too much, and Loren shouted up to Albern. "I fear for the children's horse. It looks tired enough to pitch them over the edge."

He glanced back to see. "It is only a few hours until

dawn," he said. "That horse is not well-used to such journeys, but it will not fail us. Keep on, and Annis—give him a switch of the reins every now and then."

"But who will switch me?" grumbled Annis. "I am just as tired, though I do not carry so heavy a burden." Gem's head was dug into the back of her shoulders, and Loren guessed the boy was asleep.

Dawn found them at last, exhausted but safe. The path had begun to descend again, and Loren could see by the sun's first rays that it leveled off mayhap fifteen paces above the valley floor, then ran at that height until she could no longer see it. When Albern found an alcove and ordered a halt, Loren and the children leapt from their saddles as quickly as they could. Gem flung himself on the rocky soil and fell asleep at once. Annis curled up beside him for warmth and did the same, not even bothering to secure her steed. Though Loren greatly desired to join them, she forced herself to hobble Midnight and the plow horse. Then she got her bedroll and fell asleep just as Albern began to light a cooking fire.

She woke near midday. Annis was up and sitting by the fire, while Gem still snored loudly in the same place he had been. Jordel sat against the wall of the alcove, keen blue eyes fixed unerringly upon the flames. Loren wondered if he had slept. Xain was trussed up not far away, his back to them all.

"Welcome back to wakefulness," said Albern. "We shall rest here today and through the night as well, then continue on the morrow. It would be tempting to press on now that we have slept, but it is not wise to stumble exhausted through the Greatrocks. Our limbs and bones need more time to recover."

"You need not tell me twice," said Annis. "Rarely have I ached so badly, and in so many places."

Loren smirked as she sat beside them near the fire. Though no rain fell, the day was grey and cold, and she relished the heat of the flames as they bathed her face.

Beneath her drawn hood, she studied Annis from the corner of her eyes. The girl did not shy away from Loren's nearness, nor did her eyes hold the anger they once had. Either the danger of the satyrs had made Annis forget her anger for a moment, or she had chosen to let the matter go. Loren hoped it was the latter. Annis was a dear friend, and one of her few left in the world. Without the girl, and Gem and even Jordel—and, she was slowly starting to believe, Albern—who would Loren have?

And sitting there, Loren noticed something else: Annis was no longer the plump young merchant's daughter she once had been. Though it had been scarcely a few months since they met, she seemed to have . . . changed, somehow. She was certainly a bit taller. But the change was not only in her height, nor in the fresh slimness of her waist, nor even her cheeks that were no longer as full as they once had been. Her eyes held a curious maturity, like a woman grown.

She is not a child, thought Loren. When first they met, Annis had held on to so many youthful ideas, despite the horror she had seen as a little girl. That youth seemed to be fading now. While Annis' eyes could still light up at a simple thing like a beautiful dress, she had become a different person during their time on the road.

Gem, too, was changing. He still bore the marks of a hard life in the city, with his twiggy limbs and wide, hungry eyes. But those limbs were not nearly so thin as they had once been, and Loren could see the beginnings of muscles starting to grow. He, like Annis, was taller, and growing faster than she—once he had hardly reached Loren's chest, but now she would have to stretch to put her chin on top of his head.

Loren wondered with a start if she, too, looked different. She had never had her own mirror, and rarely did she ever look at her own reflection in the waters of a still pool. When she did, she saw nothing remarkable; everyone commented on her green eyes, but beyond that she thought herself rather plain. What did she look like now, she wondered? Mayhap a bit finer in her noble's cloak, but surely more worn as well. She *felt* worn. Or rather ground down, honed—thinner, and sharper, as though the edges of her had been filed into blades, with any excess rubbed off.

With a start and a final snort, Gem finally woke. He looked around as though uncertain of where he was, and then he approached the fire to sit on Loren's other side. Together they ate a silent lunch, while Jordel stared into the fire and Albern kept watch.

Once Gem had devoured his last morsel, Jordel stood. He went to his horse and dug through the saddlebags. When his hands came out they held a short, narrow blade—hardly larger than a dirk.

"Gem, of the family Noctis," said Jordel. "Yesterday you asked me for a blade, and I scorned you for being unable to use one. I was wrong to do so, and I ask your forgiveness. I was worried at the threat to our lives."

Gem bowed his head graciously, like a king accepting a boon from a servant. But his eyes burned with an eager light as he stood and looked up at Jordel. "I took no offense."

"Then let me make you a gift," said Jordel. "Take this weapon and call it your own. And as for learning how to use it—if you wish, I will teach you."

Gem's eyes shone, and Loren thought he might weep. He reached for the sword with shaking hands. The blade rattled in its scabbard. "I thank you," he said, his voice full of emotion.

"Do you fancy a lesson now?" said Jordel. "I think we all could use a distraction after yesterday."

"Of course!" said Gem. He struggled to put the sword belt on, but could not work the buckle—he had worn only a simple belt of rope, tied at the waist, since Loren had first met him. Jordel knelt as if he were the boy's squire, and helped him secure the sword in place.

When Jordel stood, he gave Annis a curious look. "You, too, are welcome to learn."

Annis looked at both of them, both bashful and eager. "I would not presume to trouble you. I have had no experience with weapons, for it was not thought proper by my mother. She taught me to battle with words."

"I have trained many much older than you," said Jordel. "And many who had never so much as touched a sword in their life. Say the word, and my instruction is yours."

Annis lowered her eyes. "Not just now, I think. Let me watch a while first, and then we shall see if I can muster the courage."

"Come and join us, Loren!" said Gem. "Surely you would make a fine fighter!"

Loren shook her head firmly. "A sword is a weapon for killing men," she said. "I will not spend my time learning to do so, even if the knowledge is never used."

Gem rolled his eyes and shrugged. "You are a fair and beautiful flower, Loren—and one day this world will crush you under its boot for it. But have it your way."

Jordel had Gem draw, and began to teach him sword stances. Loren wandered away from them, to the mouth of the alcove where Albern stood looking out. He stood in silence and did not look at her when she approached. But when she stayed silent for a while, he glanced at her.

"You have never killed a man before?"

"Nor a woman," said Loren. "Nor will I."

"A curious rule. Not one I find often in those I meet traveling the nine lands."

"Yet it is mine. I will not break it."

"You loosed arrows at the satyrs easily enough, when they threatened us."

Loren cocked her head. Was he having a joke with her? "Those were beasts."

Albern fixed her with a hard glare. "They speak in their own tongue, and in the tongue of humans. Have you learned their language? For Tiglak took the time to learn yours. And they craft tools and weapons of war, just as we do."

"But . . . but they are not *human,*" said Loren, confused. "They are goat-men."

Albern shook his head. "Many who serve evil have left scores of dead in their wake, and roused great armies to slaughter countless more, all by saying their foes were less than human. It is a dangerous attitude to hold, no matter your foe."

"You are joking," said Loren. "Do you not kill animals for your meals? I see little difference."

"The day cattle can turn to me and plead for mercy, I will stay my blade from their throats," said Albern. "And I would not eat a satyr. But never mind. You may think on this further, or not, as you wish. But you did not come here to argue your conscience with me, I suppose."

"I . . . did not," said Loren, though in truth Albern's words troubled her greatly. She had not thought to look at the satyrs in such a way, and now that she did her heart was troubled. But she shook it off. "I saw you fighting yesterday, with your bow. I have never seen someone shoot like that."

Albern gave a little smile and looked down at his boots. "You noticed that, did you? Aye, those in Selvan often say I have some skill with a bow, though in my homeland I am accounted no great marksman."

"You do not come from Selvan, then? Whence do you hail?"

"I am a man of Calentin, as your Mystic companion could probably tell you. There we learn the bow from a very young age, for our land is hard and dangerous. And we do not use them to slay our enemies from across the battlefield, firing great shafts from on high with longbows. In Calentin you must learn to protect yourself with a bow from only a few paces away, and in the blink of an eye."

"Would you teach me?" Loren had not meant to state it so plainly, but she could not stop herself from blurting the words out. "I want to shoot like that."

Albern frowned. "A poor skill it seems, for one determined not to kill."

"More than humans may pose a danger. And I do not mean the satyrs. There are bears in the world, and lions, and tales tell of other animals far more dangerous. And besides, often I must hunt to eat. Being able to shoot so quickly would be a powerful skill when searching for food, especially if the prey spots me and bolts."

"That is why you wish to shoot, then?" said Albern, smirking. "To fetch yourself dinner?"

Loren's cheeks burned. "If you do not wish to teach me, you may simply say so."

He resumed his watch beyond the mouth of the alcove, surveying the mountains. "I am hired as a guide, not an instructor. I have concerns aplenty without spending time each day showing you my warcraft."

There came a soft *plink, plink,* upon the ground, and Loren's eyes were drawn to the sound. Albern, too, looked down to see three gold weights at his feet. They raised their gazes to find Jordel standing nearby, two fingers still buried in his purse.

"I can pay more, if you think it fair," said Jordel shortly. "Not often will she have the chance to learn from one of the famed archers of Calentin."

Loren flushed as she nodded her thanks to him. She had not thought he was listening, but she had to remind herself that Jordel often saw and heard far more than he let on.

Albern stooped to gather the coins, stuffing them into a pocket in his cloak. "It is a fair enough payment, though I cannot watch and teach at the same time."

"I will take the watch. For I would much like to see Loren learn this skill from you. And besides, I have exhausted my own student for the moment."

Loren looked past him. Gem lay on his back in the center of the alcove, sword lying loose on the ground beside him, his chest rising and falling heavily with each ragged breath. A small welt had risen on his arm, no doubt from a sharp lesson by Jordel. She snickered.

Albern gave Loren a long look and nodded. "Very well, daughter of the family Nelda. Let us teach you the true nature of a tool you have long misused."

TWELVE

ALBERN SPENT THE REST OF THAT DAY INSTRUCTING Loren in the Calentin craft of archery. First he told her to remove the quiver from her back.

"In most lands, archers wear the quiver as you do," said Albern. "They think only of the movement of their legs, and not of shooting. A quiver on the waist may be cumbersome at first, and you will often spill your arrows. But it is like a muscle. The more you travel thus, the more naturally it will come to you, until you move with the quiver at your side like another leg."

Loren tried firing with the arrows on her waist, but it was difficult. She was so used to drawing arrows from her back that this new motion came strangely. But she gritted her teeth and tried again. She did not loose the arrow, but only tried to perfect her draw. She placed the arrow to the left of the bow, the way she always had. Albern stopped her again.

"That, too, is wrong. People in the southern lands think that lends you more accuracy. But only one thing helps guide your arrows true, and that is practice. Spend enough time with the arrow on the right, and you will shoot as fine as you ever did the other way."

Loren tried, but the arrow bounced from the bow's right side. "How do I hold it steady?"

Albern raised his eyebrow. "You have answered your own question. By holding it steady."

She twisted the nock until the arrowhead came back against the bow. It put a tremendous strain on her hand, which almost cramped. She winced with the pain. Out of curiosity, she glanced over at Albern's hands, and saw for the first time how thickly muscled they were.

Something else I shall gain only with practice, she thought to herself. She ground her teeth and held the arrow steady—but she could not draw while maintaining its position, and the arrow began to drift.

"Try holding it with your left thumb," said Albern. "That is a terrible way to shoot, and your arrow will shoot wide more often than not. But it can help ease the strain on your right hand and arm while you are learning."

She tried again and again. All the rest of that day until sundown, Loren drew and drew, never loosing a shaft. Her arm burned with pain, but she kept going. The motion felt unnatural no matter how often she repeated it, but still she pressed on.

When the sun set for the day and they prepared for rest, Albern gave her a small nod of approval. "You have grit. I have tried teaching this to archers before. Most often they give up."

"It took me more than a day to learn how to shoot the wrong way," said Loren. "I will not be surprised if it takes twice as long to learn to do it right."

"It might take more than that," said Albern. "Your muscles will remember your old training for a long while yet. Do not listen to them. Your mind must rule them until at last they learn the way."

They slept well through the night. Jordel and Albern split the watch, for neither man was very tired despite the hard ride of the day before. Loren woke to a grey dawn, yet it seemed brighter and more hopeful than many of their days in the Greatrocks thus far. She ate quickly and threw on her quiver to practice. Albern watched in admiration.

"Good," he said. "Already you are quicker than yesterday."

"Yesterday I was ready to faint from weariness."

"If ever you should wish it, once you have your skill about you, I could speak to many sellsword captains across the nine lands on your behalf. They all want good fighters, but an archer who knows the Calentin craft is prized above many."

Loren tried not to turn her nose up as she replied. "I thank you, but the life of a mercenary holds little appeal to me."

Albern shook his head. "Your pardon. I had forgotten your vow. I shall put the matter from my mind."

They mounted as soon as Gem had finished his meal—which, Loren swore, was bigger than anyone else's, though she did not know how that could be when Jordel was rationing them so carefully. Once they set out upon the mountain pass, Loren's fine mood dampened. In the alcove they had had a sense of safety, even if a false one. Now, upon the road, it was easier to recall the satyr attack, the looks on their savage faces as they charged with their spears, and the terrible bleating that poured from their throats. She found herself looking up the mountainside, always fearing to see the goat-men perched above, watching, waiting for their chance to strike.

But the day passed quickly and quietly, and just after midday the sun even broke through the clouds for a while. But despite the fine day, Loren often caught Annis looking solemn, or mayhap worried. Loren had taken Midnight to the rear of the line after the satyr attack, to guard against any attack there. But that put Annis directly behind Jordel and Xain, and the girl let the plow horse drift far behind them as though she were afraid to draw too close. When Loren caught glances of her face, she could see fear in the girl's eyes, which changed to worry when she looked at Xain.

When they stopped for a midday meal, Jordel took Albern on a bit farther to scout the next turns in the pass. Gem ran after them, like a puppy following its master. They left Xain bound on the ground, and though the wizard slept, Annis still sat as far from him as she could, even leaning to the side so there was no chance of touching him.

Loren sat beside her. "What troubles you today? There is a great worry in your eyes, or mayhap a great fear."

Annis looked down at the bread in her hands. "It is nothing," she mumbled.

With a hand on the girl's shoulder, Loren leaned closer. "Annis, I want to help."

She looked over at Xain, and then back at Loren. "You know I do not like that Jordel brought Xain with us. I hate what he did to us in Wellmont, and what he did to *me*. Yet . . . yet after the satyrs attacked us, the way that Jordel . . ."

Loren thought she understood. Jordel's wrath had been terrible. Always the Mystic had been like a font of serenity, and she had been amazed how even-tempered he was even in the face of Xain's obstinate rebellion. And it was not only the wizard; when the rest of them had hated Vivien and mistrusted her, Jordel had shown her only courtesy and respect. Even when she sought to expose him for helping Xain, who had consumed magestones despite the King's law, Jordel had looked on the woman with understanding and mercy, and not with hatred.

Yet Loren did not doubt that Jordel had meant his threat to destroy Xain. And he had beaten the wizard mercilessly. It had been a terrifying display, and Loren could find no fault in Annis' fear.

But could she find fault with Jordel? His greatest concern seemed to be their safety. Loren knew how highly he valued Xain. To be driven to such rage by the wizard's actions—he must care deeply for Loren and the children, even more deeply than he often let on. Could Loren condemn his anger when she, too, was furious with Xain for all he had done?

Looking at Xain now, though, she found it hard to muster much ire against him. He had shed great patches of his hair. She could see his cheekbones pressing sharp against the skin, and his hands were like a skeleton's dressed in parchment. Jordel had to tighten his bonds every day because of how his body wasted away. It did not matter how much food they crammed around the gag that kept him from using his magic. His body was eating itself away from the inside.

She realized suddenly that Xain might die. He looked for all the world like one stricken by a terrible illness—the way Chet's mother had looked back in the

Birchwood, when her body failed her and seemed to melt into nothing. No doubt if she had tried to traverse the mountain pass through the Greatrocks, the journey would have been the death of her. Would it now be the end of Xain?

It was a troubling question, and one for which she had no answer. So she only reached out and put an arm around Annis, pulling the girl close. To her surprise, slow tears leaked from Annis' eyes.

"I . . . I wanted him to die," said Annis, her voice breaking. "I feel such shame in it, but truly I did. That hate sat with me like a festering wound, and I despised myself for it—yet I could not be rid of it. And then I thought I might get my wish, and it was awful. It seemed like something my mother would have asked for. After so long trying to escape her, I have become just like her."

"You are not," said Loren quickly. "Your mother would have had no qualms about what Jordel did. You thought you wanted him punished. Yet when you saw that punishment carried out, you knew you were wrong. You are a daughter of the family Yerrin in body, but I do not think they own your mind." She tugged Annis closer and planted a kiss on the top of her head, rubbing her shoulder gently.

"But what of Jordel? Is he, then, like my mother? Have I run from one whose violence I abhorred, only to ride with another who will behave the same when provoked?"

"That is a harder question, for I would never have suspected such a display from Jordel. Yet I do not see it in the same light. The Mystic is a good man, his patience often bordering on foolishness. Yet Xain has done great evil while we have known him. We have seen him kill. He has lied and stolen from us, and he struck you with fire. I do not understand Jordel's desire to save him. But in trying to do so, he has let Xain push him to the brink of madness, and that I *do* understand. The wizard has turned both your minds far darker than they would be otherwise."

They heard Albern's voice as he approached with the others. Annis scrubbed furiously at her eyes with the back of her sleeve, and they hastened to stand. By the time Jordel, Albern, and Gem returned, Loren stood nonchalantly over Xain while Annis made a show of checking her saddlebags.

The rest of the day passed without much event, except that near nightfall the clouds returned, and it began to rain once more. Gem groaned as the first drops fell, and Albern hastened to find them a shelter. It was not long before he spotted a cave and explored it, soon returning with news that it was shallow and empty. But in that short time the skies had already begun to pelt them. They ran inside quickly and shook the rainwater off before hobbling the horses.

"Empty it is now, but not always," said Jordel, pointing to some dried dung barely visible in the failing sunlight. "At least that will be good for a fire."

Albern started it quickly, and despite the smell they soon had gathered around the flames for warmth. After a quick meal they were all eager for bed; in dreams they did not have to suffer the cold and the grumbling of their never-quite-filled stomachs. But Loren had first watch.

It seemed an excellent chance to practice her draw, so she fetched her bow and belted on her quiver. Her muscles screamed almost immediately, the pain intense after the day's reprieve. She ignored it. Aches and sores had never kept her from learning before.

The cave was silent. The only sounds came from the crackling, noisome fire and the rain outside—and Gem's snores. So Loren never heard the footsteps behind her, nor the *whoosh* of air before something crashed into the back of her head and she fell to the ground in blackness.

THIRTEEN

LOREN'S EYES REFUSED TO FOCUS WHEN FIRST THEY opened, and her head swam in agony. Small hands shook her hard, bumping her skull against the rocky cave floor, and she cried out from the pain.

"Leave her be!" barked Jordel. "Her head is tender."

She opened her eyes just in time to see Jordel shove Gem away. The boy had been shaking her frantically, his eyes wide with terror.

"Loren," said Jordel. "Can you hear me?"

She opened her mouth and tried to answer, but only a croak came out. She nodded instead, but that nearly made her fall senseless at the pain shooting through her skull.

"Here, have some water." He raised a skin to her mouth. Loren thought it might choke her, but he poured gently, so that only a few drops came out. It touched her tongue like the sweetest honey, and she swallowed greedily. He gave her a little more.

"What has happened?" said Annis, and Loren heard a rustling out of sight. A moment later the girl's face appeared, looking at Loren in horror. "Loren! Are you all right?"

"It was Xain," said Jordel. "He loosed his bonds somehow and escaped."

Gem's face reddened with fury, and his fists clenched at his sides. "You said you knew how to bind him. And now he has nearly killed Loren!"

Jordel did not reply with the same anger. He only looked worried. "I do not understand it myself. The bonds should have held."

"Mayhap this answers the question," said Albern. Loren looked to him despite the pain and saw him holding a frayed rope. The ends had been burned. "He crawled to the fire and thrust his hands into it."

"But that would have roasted his flesh," said Annis. "It must have hurt terribly."

"It would have," said Jordel, mouth set in a grim line. "But a trapped fox will gnaw its own leg off to be free."

"What time was it when he hit you?" said Albern. "How long has he been gone?"

Loren tried to remember—then realized she did not know what time it was *now*. Outside the cave, a pale grey light shone through the clouds. No sun, at least not yet, but only the first grasping fingers of its rays, wrapping over the tops of the eastern mountain range as it pulled itself above the horizon.

"Both moons had just set," said Loren. She could hear her dry throat cracking. She reached for the waterskin again, and Jordel handed it to her.

"That means he has a few hours' lead," said Albern. "But he is not well, not by any stretch. I think we can catch him easily. And we had best do so, for if the satyrs find him first he will be easy prey in his state."

"Let them have him, then," said Gem, stamping a foot.

Jordel looked at him with a frown, but Annis spoke up as well. "Is it . . . is it wise to pursue him? After all, he still has his magic, and we have only swords."

"I do not fear him." Gem looked down at Loren, and his eyes softened. "I only think he deserves whatever he finds upon his own road, if he is so determined to take it."

Jordel frowned and looked out of the cave. To Loren's shock, she saw doubt warring with the anger in his expression. Never before had she seen him waver when asked to leave Xain behind.

Loren seized his sleeve and pulled herself up. She could not sit all the way upright, for her head spiked with terrible pain and she nearly fell. But she forced her eyes to stay open and locked them on Jordel's.

"We cannot leave him. We must find him before he gets himself killed."

Jordel's eyes widened, and he looked at her in wonder. Gem's shock was nearly comical. "After what he did to you, you still wish to risk all our lives for his?" said the boy.

"I do. We can do nothing else." Loren looked past Gem to Annis. "You told me that when you saw Xain hurt, it did not feel like you thought it would—that it nearly made you ill. Now you hope to cast him aside, out of sight, where you will not have to witness such suffering. But it is the same thing, Annis. It is not nobler to let him starve than it would be to hurl him from a cliff."

Tears welled in Annis' eyes, and she turned away. But Jordel looked only at Loren. "You, too, have hinted at leaving Xain behind," he said.

She released her hold on his sleeve to push herself farther up. But her head slumped forwards and swam, threatening to make her vomit. She raised her knees on either side of her face, taking several deep breaths until the feeling subsided.

"I wanted to leave him, it is true. And yes, he struck me. But can you not see that he stayed his hand as well? No doubt Gem thinks he meant to kill me. But if that were his intent, what stopped him? He could have taken a knife and slit all your throats as you slept. But he showed mercy in the end. Often you have spoken of giving Xain another chance, and I never understood why. But you promised there was something worth saving inside of him. Do you still think that? For if you have changed your mind, you only did so after changing my own."

Jordel softened, as though the keen blue ice of his eyes had melted into a warm pool. He bowed his head like a man in prayer. "You humble me with your mercy, Loren of the family Nelda, for I had forgotten to show any myself. You are right. We will not abandon him. As dark as his deeds have been of late, still he has done many good things with his days, and may do more still to balance the scales."

"What things?" said Gem. "I have seen no such deeds."

"You have known him only a few months, while I have known *of* him most of his life," said Jordel. "When we reclaim him, I shall tell you some of it. But now we must hasten, for even weakened he has had much time to gain a lead."

They hurried to ready their horses. Jordel finished securing his bags first and turned to Loren. "Come. I require your assistance before we venture forth."

Loren looked at Annis and Gem, but they only shrugged. So she followed Jordel to the front of the cave, where he stooped to pick up an ember from the fire with his thick leather gloves. This he carried beyond the cave mouth, with Loren hastening to keep up. The quick pace jostled her head, and she placed a hand upon the back of it. The injury there was still tender, and she winced.

Once they were out of sight and earshot of the others, Jordel turned to her. "We may be able to track Xain on the mountain pass, for you and I both know something of woodcraft, and I suspect Albern outshines us both. Yet even he might lose the trail, for still there is the rain, and much of the ground is hard and rocky. But there is something we can do to find Xain unerringly. It is a secret of the mage hunters, long lost in history, for we have had little opportunity to use it. You must never speak of this to anyone, the same as you would never whisper word of your dagger."

Loren's hand went to the weapon's hilt on instinct, and she nodded. "I swear it. What must I do?"

Jordel held out a hand. "Give it to me."

She drew the dagger and flipped it to catch the blade before placing the hilt in his hand. Jordel took it with reverence, holding it with fingertips like a fine gem. Then he knelt, placing on the ground the ember he had drawn from the fire. His hand vanished into his vest pocket, and when it came forth he held a lock of dark hair.

"Whose is that?" said Loren. But even as she spoke, she guessed the answer.

"Xain's. I have told you one gift of your dagger, that it is proof against his magics. This is another, and one of the weapon's chief purposes. Though I thought my bonds would hold him, still I collected this lock of hair just in case he should escape."

Jordel placed the dagger atop the coal to heat the blade. After it had sat there for a moment, he dropped the lock atop it. The strands began to burn, and soon had vanished in flame and a puff of smoke.

Nothing happened for a moment. Loren stared at the dagger and the coal, ready for anything. Yet no warning could have prepared her for what she saw. The black designs worked into the dagger's blade, which Jordel had told her were made of magestone, began to shift and twist. Like the branches of a tree in the wind, they twined and snaked about each other, grasping, exploring. Then all of a sudden they took on new life and stretched. North they pointed, north and slightly east, directly along the mountain pass.

"That will tell us where Xain has gone," said Jordel. "I took a good deal of hair, and the designs should not rest until he is found. They will always point in his direction. Take the dagger back now, Loren. You may sheathe it if you wish—the magic will not be affected."

Though Loren had hesitated to give it to him, now she paused equally before taking the dagger back. It seemed to her something alien and strange, a weapon of legend and not the simple if beautiful tool she had believed it to be when she stole it. With a fluttering heart she took it at last, sliding it into its sheath with a whisper.

"You have a cunning task ahead of you now," said

Jordel. "For as we ride you must look at the dagger often to see if we are going the right way. Yet above all, you must not let Albern see it. I think he is a good man, and I trust him—yet he may have masters unknown to us. It is best if not even Annis and Gem see you looking at it."

"I shall remember," said Loren with a nod. "I will not let them see."

They returned to the cave and found the others ready to set forth. Albern gave Loren and Jordel a curious look, but he did not ask where they had been. He only led them from the cave and, after inspecting the ground for a moment, he spotted the remains of footprints trailing north and east along the pass.

"He went north," said the bowyer in surprise. "I thought he might turn south, heading for tamer lands. Mayhap he thought that would be our guess."

"Then lead on, and keep a wary eye for his steps," said Jordel.

"I shall," said Albern. "Only do not be angry with me if the satyrs find him first."

They mounted, and Albern led the way north on the pass. Jordel gave Loren a look as they followed, and her hand tightened on the hilt of her dagger.

FOURTEEN

THEY RODE AS HARD AS THEY COULD—WHICH WAS NOT as fast as Jordel would have liked, for still the ground was slippery and wet. And besides, Loren could not press Midnight to go too fast, for it made her head swim and threatened to raise her gorge. Yet still they made good time, much better than Xain could have.

Loren rode at the rear as was her custom, and every so often she would draw forth the dagger to inspect its designs. Always they pointed forwards along the pass. For a long while, there was nowhere else to go. Soon, though, the path began to dip, dropping steeply down towards the valley floor.

"Here things will become more difficult," said Albern. "Though I hope the ground is soft enough after the rain to leave good marks where he has passed."

"I see no marks anywhere," said Gem, annoyed.

"I would expect no more from a boy who grew up on the cobblestones of a city," said Jordel. "Use the time to sharpen your eyes, master urchin."

The path reached the valley at last. Albern called them to a halt and dismounted to inspect the ground. Loren took advantage of his distraction to draw the dagger again, hiding it beneath her cloak. The designs twisted sharply to the left, away from the path, which ran northeast.

"That way," said Albern, pointing north. "He abandoned the path as soon as it reached the valley floor."

"How do you know?" said Annis, who seemed to share Gem's annoyance.

"Just there," said Loren, guiding Midnight up beside the plow horse. "See how all the grass stands one way, like the fibers of a rug? Then see that dip, little more than a slight darkness where the blades bend differently from those around them? They are in the shape of a footprint, and they continue off that way for some time."

"I think you are seeing things," growled Gem.

But Annis leaned forwards in her saddle with excitement. "I see them!" she cried. "I see the footprints!

Or at least, one of them. Where did you say the others were?"

"They are farther off," said Loren. "Only practiced eyes would spot them. You should take pride in seeing the one."

The girl's dark skin flushed a bit darker for the moment, while Gem rolled his eyes in a huff.

Albern led them on, and both the tracks and the dagger pointed north for a long while. The valley floor rose and fell beneath them, and on every crest Loren looked ahead eagerly, hoping to see Xain's brown coat fleeing across the wilderness. But it never appeared. They rode through midday and for two hours beyond that. Soon the ground grew rocky, and the tracks vanished.

"We should ride on anyway," said Albern. "There is nowhere to hide, and the valley is rimmed by the mountains; Xain can have gone nowhere but north."

Jordel looked to Loren, and fortunately she had just peeked at the dagger before Albern stopped them. The design still pointed north. She gave Jordel a small nod, and he looked forwards again. But Loren saw that Albern had witnessed their exchange, and he looked at her most curiously before leading them on.

Not an hour later, Albern stopped again and had them dismount. A small cluster of boulders lay just ahead, and stealthily they led their horses to it. Then Albern took Jordel and Loren forwards to peek around the edge, and they saw what he had spied from afar.

A camp waited, mayhap two spans ahead, very near to the bank of the river that ran up the center of the valley. Some figures clustered around a small fire, resting or eating. From their movements Loren knew them for satyrs, and though it was hard to count from so far away, she thought there might have been a half-dozen. She was somehow glad they were too far for her to see what they were eating—mayhap the legends about satyrs devouring children were only legends, and mayhap not.

"I suppose it is futile to try and convince you to go around?" said Albern. "I know a path that would take us west, circling them out of sight."

"And how long would that take?" said Jordel.

Albern sighed. "Longer than you would wish, I am certain. Very well. I will lead them away from the fire. Be ready to ride when I do."

He returned to his horse and seized his bow, and then rode east at a breakneck gallop. Loren waited by Midnight, stroking the horse's neck as she grazed. Jordel stayed by the edge of the boulders to watch for Albern's signal.

Then they heard it. A great whooping cry howled across the air towards them, and Loren ran to stand beside Jordel and watch. Then she saw Albern in battle, and witnessed the true power of Calentin bowcraft.

Albern rode across a narrow ford in the river straight for the satyrs, who leapt up to clutch their spears and bleat at him. But he released his reins and drew his bow, firing arrows like a man possessed. Shaft after shaft cut the air, falling upon the ground around the camp—yet Loren knew that not one of them missed on accident. He wanted their attention, not their lives. Five arrows flew wide.

But they did their job, for the satyrs bounded towards him with a roar. Some had bows and loosed their own arrows after him, but Albern was riding too fast for them to draw aim. After turning one great circle around the outskirts of their camp he rode off again, guiding his horse back across the river and into the trees on the other side.

"Go! Quickly!" cried Jordel.

They leapt atop their horses and rode past the camp. All the while Loren looked to the east, hoping the satyrs would not show their faces again among the trees. They did not, and soon the party had left the camp far behind. Jordel had them slow to a walk, and after a few minutes, Albern came riding up from behind them. He had reclaimed his arrows and held them clutched in his fist, inspecting them and returning them to the quiver one by one.

"Not too bad a job," he remarked, leading his horse to ride beside Jordel.

"That was remarkable!" said Gem. "You rode like a madman unleashed."

Albern shrugged. "It had the required effect. Come. We have lost some time."

Loren snuck a glance at her dagger. Still its markings pointed straight ahead. She sheathed it and nudged Midnight with her heels.

Xain's tracks went on and on, nearly due north, against the river's southward flow. Loren guessed he meant to walk along it as far as he could, for eventually it must lead to some sort of dwelling. There he could hide himself, and mayhap secure a horse to continue his flight. But she wondered that they had not caught him already. Xain had hardly looked fit to stand when last they saw him, and should have been slow and wandering in his escape.

A short time later, Albern called them to a halt. Again, he dismounted to inspect the ground. Loren saw what he was looking at: the prints, easy to see in the soft dirt near the river, veered sharply away from the water before disappearing to the west. Quickly she looked at the dagger. The markings still pointed north.

"He turned aside," said Albern. "For what, I do not know. Mayhap he thinks to hide himself somewhere in the mountain caves. If he does, he has a nasty surprise waiting. This deep in the Greatrocks, any caves are likely filled with satyrs. We shall ride west."

Jordel looked back over his shoulder. "Loren?"

Albern looked at her curiously, and the children did the same. Loren flushed, but she kept her eyes on Jordel's. "We should ride north," she said simply.

They all gawked at her, all but Jordel. Albern turned to him. "The tracks are clear. He went west."

"I trust Loren in this," said Jordel briskly. "We continue north."

The bowyer looked at her again, and Loren saw wonder in his eyes—along with a burning curiosity. But he tried once more. "Jordel, it is no concern of mine whether we find this wizard or not. But if you wish to, and you have hired me as your guide, then listen to me. We shall find him west of here, nowhere else."

"I do not doubt your skill in woodcraft," said Jordel. "I ask that you do not doubt my faith in Loren. If she says Xain is to the north, then north is where we shall find him."

Albern shrugged. "Very well. Only do not complain to me later when we have lost much time in this wild hunt, and have not found Xain besides. But we shall follow the daughter of the forest, if that be your wish."

Loren swallowed hard, avoiding the eyes of Gem and Annis, who looked at her without understanding. Albern gained his saddle again, and they rode north.

FIFTEEN

ALBERN GUIDED THEM FORWARDS MORE SLOWLY NOW, for he said the satyrs were thick in this part of the valley. They rarely went faster than a trot, and most of the time it was a cautious walk instead, with their eyes wandering all about, searching for any sign of danger.

In a short while, the ground west of them grew hard, though it turned back into silt where they rode. Almost as soon as the rocky ground appeared, Albern stopped them with a raised hand. He jumped from his bay and ran a short way to the west before kneeling. Curious, Loren dismounted. Her head spiked with pain at the motion, but she shook it off and went to join the bowyer.

When she reached him, Albern looked up at her with wide eyes and pointed. She saw it: a few small strands of brown cloth, and a small dark smudge that looked like blood.

"He fell here," said Albern in wonder. "You were right. Xain went this way. How did you know?"

"There is much more to this girl than meets the eye," said Jordel, surprising Loren. He had approached from behind while she studied the markings. She might have heard him coming, if not for the ache in her skull. "Now we should hasten, for that mark looks fresh."

"Indeed," said Albern as he stood, but he still looked at Loren. "Indeed. Let us move on."

They turned the horses to run across the harder terrain, for Xain had stayed on it and avoided the soft soil nearer the river. Every so often now they found a sign of him. It looked as though he was weary and stumbling, for there were many disturbed rocks and smudges of blood; he must have cut his hand, or mayhap it was from the burns he must have suffered when he frayed the rope. Midnight and the other horses began to move faster and faster without urging, feeling the excitement of their riders. Loren scanned the soil, only checking the dagger every so often, for always it pointed straight ahead.

But in their eagerness, they forgot to look up. Suddenly there was a great *snap* and a roar, and Loren raised her eyes to see a bolt of fire speeding towards them. She cried out and tugged Midnight's reins sharply to the right. But the mare had already seen the flames, and she veered even before Loren told her to. Loren snatched the plow horse's bridle and pulled it along as well, though it moved more slowly. The flame crashed down in the midst of where they had stood. When it struck the ground it splashed like a great ball of water, throwing fire in every direction. A few embers landed upon the hem of Annis' dress, making her cry out as she beat at it with her hands.

Loren vaulted from Midnight's back, ignoring the jolt of agony from the landing, and ran to the girl. Hastily she scooped up dirt and threw it at the fire. In a moment it was out, and she looked for Jordel and Albern. They had brought their horses around after avoiding the flames. Now Jordel gave a great shout as he spurred his charger forwards. Albern followed right behind him.

"Stay here, and do not move!" Loren said to Annis. She scrambled back atop Midnight and sped off after the men, gritting her teeth at the terrible jostling.

The bolt of fire had come from the northwest, just past a great mound in the earth. That is where Jordel and Albern had gone. Loren turned her horse south instead, circling the mound from the other side. In her mind's eye she saw again the day she and Xain had met. He had fled from her in the forest, and she had caught him by passing through a copse of birch trees he had avoided.

I have grown much since the Birchwood, but you have learned little, my wizard, she thought with a grim smile.

From the other side of the mound she heard Jordel yelling at Albern not to kill Xain. Then she heard another blast and eruption of flames, followed by a cry. Her heart skipped a beat. Had Xain struck Jordel with his flames? Or Albern?

It did not matter—not yet, at any rate. She could only ride on. Soon she passed the mound and steered Midnight to the right, and then she saw him. Xain ran across the open ground a few dozen paces ahead. He was making for the feet of the mountain to the west, where Loren saw a great many caves—but no satyrs.

Xain looked back and saw her then, his eyes glowing white. He did not stop, but thrust an arm behind himself and spoke a word. A bolt of lightning crackled forth, thunder threatening to burst her eardrums as it split the air. Loren flinched, her reflexes far slower than the lightning itself—but unnecessarily, for the spell split apart and struck the ground on either side of Midnight's hooves. The horse shrieked with fear, but they were unscathed. The dagger would not let Xain's magic touch them.

She reached him a moment later and tried to dive from the saddle. But the motion made white sparks of pain dance in her vision, and she lost her balance. Xain fell beneath her with a crash, but she could not wrap her arms around him. They rolled across the grass and landed paces apart.

The wizard scrambled up at once, shooting flames at her. Though Loren knew he could not harm her, her instincts did not. She hugged the dirt in fear as the flames dissipated harmlessly a few feet away, giving Xain time to find his feet and resume his run.

Thundering hooves sounded, and Albern and Jordel drew near. They looked harried but unharmed. Their horses carried them past Loren after Xain, but they could not reach him before he vanished into one of the caves that opened upon the valley floor.

Loren heard Albern shout a warning, but Jordel did not heed it. He dropped from his saddle once his charger stopped before the cave, drawing his sword and running in after Xain. Albern took a moment longer, nocking an arrow before following. Loren ran after them, one hand on her head and the other on her dagger—but she did not draw it, for Albern might turn around at any moment.

She entered the cave and found a scene of madness.

Just before her stood Jordel and Albern, weapons out as they faced Xain. The wizard stood a few paces beyond, right hand extended with flame burning in his palm. But his left hand showed flame in the other direction, deeper into the cave, where a clan of satyrs watched in fear.

There were dozens of them, many the size of small children, with some others clustered around and holding them close—their mothers, Loren guessed. Before these stood yet more of the creatures, and these were larger and thickly muscled, holding weapons of every kind. They stood between Xain and the children, braying angrily at his intrusion. They looked ready to attack at any provocation.

"Xain, if you do not leave with us, now, they will kill you," said Jordel. "Douse your flames and come."

"No, Mystic," spat Xain. "I will not go with you, not again. Not ever. I would sooner die in this cave, and let all of you burn with me!"

That was all the satyrs needed. The warriors pounced, thrusting spears and swinging axes of stone. Jordel charged, keeping one eye on Xain while fending off the goat-men with his sword. Albern fired a flurry of arrows, but he struck only in the legs and arms, felling the satyrs without slaying them.

Xain had no such compunctions. He let loose with a wave of flame that tore into the warriors. They fell to the ground bleating in fear, beating at the flames with their hands and rolling around the cave floor to douse themselves. The children screamed still louder.

"No!" cried Loren.

"Loren!" shouted Jordel. "Stop him!"

She understood at once; with the dagger, she was the only one who could attack Xain without fear. Gritting her teeth against the pain, she ran at him, boots pounding on the stony floor before she covered the last few feet in a great leap. Xain's head slammed into the rocks as he fell, and his eyes rolled back in his head, but he fought to keep his senses. Again he worked his flames on her, but they had no more effect than they had outside the cave. Seized by madness, he scrabbled for her face with his fingernails.

Loren seized his wrists and twisted them, making Xain cry out in pain. Then she flipped him over and got his arm behind his back, shoving it towards his shoulder blades until he screamed. She wrapped her elbow around his throat, dragging him upwards to stand before her, helpless. When he struggled, she only raised his hand behind his shoulder blades until she nearly broke his arm. She tightened her grip on his throat to keep him from speaking, and his flames died in his hands.

"I have him!" she cried.

"Then go!" said Jordel, backing towards her, his blade flashing in the sunlight that shone in from outside.

The satyrs drew back for a moment, giving space for a fighting retreat. Albern stilled his bowstring, though he held another arrow drawn, waiting for a threat at which to loose it. Jordel held his blade forwards. The fight had not gone from the goat-men. Their eyes glittered as they waited for an opportunity.

A moment later they were outside, and Jordel snatched Xain away from her. Then he did something Loren had never seen before. With one arm around Xain's neck, he twisted his fingers into a curious shape and pressed them to the wizard's temple. The other hand curled around Xain's wrist, pressing places between the bones and twisting his fingers into a claw. Xain screamed, but Jordel ignored him. He leaned in close and whispered into the wizard's ear—words too low and quick for Loren to catch, and when she heard snatches they were in no tongue she knew. It sounded akin to, and yet unlike, the words Xain spoke when he made his fire.

As she watched in fascination, Xain's eyes began to glow white. His face contorted as he screamed, jaw so wide she thought it might break. Bolts of fire and lightning leapt from his clawed fingers. They fell upon the mountainside above the cave, and to either side of it, and everywhere they struck they exploded in great balls of flame. The mountain shuddered, the ground quaking beneath them. With a roar and a crash, great boulders fell from above. They piled together before the cave entrance, blocking it completely in a wall of rock. Dust fountained forth, covering all of them. Loren turned away and flung up her hood to protect her mouth and nose from it.

When silence had settled at last, she looked again at the cave. It was only a wall of stones, and looked like any other part of the mountain.

"Do what you will to me, Jordel," said Xain, spittle flying from his lips, trying to reach around and claw at the Mystic's face. "I will never stop running from you. I will never stop trying to escape. One day when you are sleeping I shall break free again, and the next time I will not stop myself from—"

Jordel released the wizard's hand and wrapped an arm tighter around his neck. He squeezed briefly for a few moments, and Xain fell senseless in his arms. Jordel turned him around, then heaved him up on a shoulder without effort. The wizard had wasted away almost to nothing now, and probably weighed less than half what he had when Loren first met him.

"Will the satyrs be able to escape?" said Jordel.

"All these caves have back entrances," said Albern. "They are like a honeycomb, every cave connecting to every other. The satyrs dig them that way in case they need to run from attack. But we have time to get away before they emerge."

"I do not ask for our safety," said Jordel quietly. "I would not wish the clan to suffocate because of Xain. Beasts they may be, but they do not deserve that. If you think they can find a way out, then let us go."

SIXTEEN

The children were waiting where they had been left, staring west with wide and frightened eyes. As soon as Loren and the men returned, with Xain slung across Jordel's horse once more, Gem and Annis sighed with obvious relief. Albern guided them on quickly, riding north again along the river, for he had told them there would soon be another place where the mountain pass dipped to the valley floor. There, they could retreat into the heights.

They had not eaten all day, but Jordel did not allow them to stop. Steadily they devoured the leagues until they reached the pass, where they went up and into the clouds once more. Always they looked behind them for the satyrs, but they never saw any.

Once they were free from the valley floor, some of the thrill of excitement drained from Loren, and she felt a great weariness settle in its place—along with a redoubled pain in her head. She slumped in her saddle, the sudden motion making her hurt still worse. As they rode through the rest of the day, she felt only moments from falling to the ground in sleep. The journey thus far had been taxing enough, and the day's excitement had nearly left her undone.

Jordel finally let them halt just after sundown, and they climbed from their horses in silence. He must have seen the pain on Loren's face, for he went to her at once and gingerly inspected the back of her head.

"Does it still hurt?"

"It is not so bad," Loren said, though that was a lie. But she gritted her teeth, determined that she would not slow the party down.

"It might have been," muttered Gem.

"And we all know why," Annis agreed.

"I hear the two of you," said Jordel in a warning tone.

"Good," said Gem, louder now. "Let the wizard hear us, too. We should never have gone after him."

Jordel opened his mouth to answer, but Annis spoke first. "You know there is some wisdom in what he says. Mayhap I was wrong to say we should abandon him, alone in the mountains where he would only starve to death. But keeping him with us only puts us in greater danger. Let us give him some provisions and the plow horse and then send him on his way—which is far away from us."

"That horse is not yours to give away," said Albern. "Though I will not say I disagree with you. So far we have faced little danger in the mountains, Jordel, other than that which Xain has brought down upon us. I promised to guide you safely through the pass—yet I find that vow ever harder to keep, and I would not be made a liar by this wizard, even if his mind is swayed by want of magestone."

"We have survived so far," said Loren. "We will survive until the end of the road. No danger has yet proved our equal. If we reach settled lands and still you wish to cut Xain loose, then I might not argue against you so strongly. But here in these mountains, a horse and some spare rolls of hardtack will not suffice to save him. He is too weak to fight, and using his magic has nearly killed him. Casting him out would finish the job."

"How long, then, must we protect him?" said Annis. Though her voice had risen to a shout, it also sounded as though she might burst into tears. "I can hardly sleep at night for fear I shall wake to find him standing over me, fire burning in his fist. Every time I see him from the corner of my eye, making some sudden motion on the back of Jordel's horse, I feel as though my heart will burst from fear. How long, Loren? How long will you make me ride with the burden of this terror? You say you wish to keep Gem and me safe, hiding us away in some strange noble's manor, yet you bring our greatest danger with us and refuse to cut it loose."

Her tears spilled then, and she turned away to cast her hood over her face. She made to run from them, away from the fire and into the darkness. Loren caught her arms and pulled her in close, holding her in an embrace. Annis sobbed into her chest while Loren looked down in dismay. Over the top of Annis' head, she met Gem's gaze.

"And you? Do you think I put you willingly in danger?"

Gem did not meet her eyes, studying his dirty feet instead. "I said I would follow you," he mumbled.

"That is not what I asked you," said Loren. "If you think I am being foolish, tell me. That is one duty I will always ask of you, now and forever more."

When Gem looked up, Loren saw a fire in his eyes that heated his words. "Then yes, I do think you are being a fool. Xain is dangerous. He has nearly gotten us all killed. He nearly killed *you,* and still you wince whenever you turn your head too quickly. Yet you are forever willing to forgive him, because you will not let him die, nor anyone else. It makes me fear for you, that one day you may spare the life of one who takes yours in return. And I am afraid that day is near, and ever closer the longer we keep Xain with us."

Loren looked at Xain, curled in a ball with his hands tied behind his back, his legs held immobile by Jordel's rope. The wizard looked back in a cold fury. It was as if he did not recognize that she fought to protect him, to keep him safe from the others who wished him dead. And suddenly Loren wondered: what was she arguing for? Why did she fight so hard for him? Since the Birchwood he had abandoned her more than once, had fought against her, had told her over and again that he did not wish for her company, and had put all their lives in danger.

She turned to Jordel, seeking the reason she could not find for herself. "What do you say, Mystic? It is by your order that we have brought Xain this far."

Jordel had sat silently through all this counsel, staring into their small fire. Flames danced in his eyes, and Loren was reminded of Xain's magic, the terrible light in his face when he conjured his spells. For a moment she feared Jordel had been swayed by the others.

But when he spoke, it was not in answer to Loren. "I knew Xain upon the High King's Seat," he said in a slow voice. "Or rather, I knew of him, for everyone there had heard of his deeds, this powerful young wizard from the Academy. Often I would observe him at balls held by the nobility who live upon that island—for they have little to do with their time, other than spending it in games of intrigue and politics that would bore young Gem here to death.

"Xain was always happy and quick-witted. His

mind was as sharp with a barb as it was with his studies, and his words could sway others as easily as his magic could blast them. He did not enter into the intrigues of the Seat, which held little interest for him. But he did enjoy toying with nobles, upsetting their plans and turning their schemes awry. There was no reason to it, other than that he loved to watch their faces fall as their petty machinations were undone."

"You speak of this wizard here?" said Gem, pointing at Xain. "Hardly have I ever heard him speak so much as a word of wit. He is a sour man, not prone to laughter."

"Much has changed since those days," said Jordel. "Not the least was what happened when he had just passed his nineteenth year—the year the Lord Prince was attacked upon the King's road, kidnapped by bandits who wished to hold him for ransom."

Loren and the children gasped, and even Albern's eyes flashed as he looked at Jordel with renewed interest. Tales were told of the Lord Prince across the nine lands, of his fair hair and smile that made lovers weep, his light and easy heart, his kindness, and his compassion.

The High King Enalyn was well beloved throughout Underrealm, more so because her rule followed that of High King Trenter, who had embroiled many of the kingdoms in war. Though the throne had no heir by law, when Enalyn died, most hoped the Lord Prince would be chosen to take her place by the Council of the Seat. Even Loren, raised in a small village in the Birchwood, had grown up with that hope in her heart. But she had never heard this tale, that the Lord Prince had been in mortal danger, and from the looks on their faces, neither had Annis or Gem.

"The news was as grievous to all then as it is to you now," Jordel went on. "All upon the Seat despaired of rescuing His Highness. Yet on the morning after the bandits sent their message of ransom, Xain entered the High King's hall. I say entered—he stormed in, throwing the doors wide with a great gust of wind. The guards all leapt forth with their weapons drawn, but Enalyn bade them stay, for Xain had long had Her Majesty's favor.

"Xain went to the foot of the throne and knelt, and there he vowed to go forth and rescue the Lord Prince himself. He was a new student at the Academy, untried and untested, though as I said many had heard of his prowess. Immediately the Dean stood forth, calling Xain's boast unacceptable. The Academy could not allow such a young student to go off alone on such a mad scheme. If wizards were needed, he would select his own from the Academy's disciples and send them forth.

"I was young myself, then, and not well versed in the ways of the High King's court. Yet the Dean's words troubled me. All knew he bore no great love for Her Grace, who did not heed his counsel and often thwarted his attempts to secure more power and coin for the Academy. And there were rumors—whispers only, hidden behind hands—that mayhap the Dean himself had arranged the kidnapping, as an excuse to remove the Lord Prince from the Seat and distract the High King, leaving her with less attention to counter his efforts."

"That would be a treason most high, if it were true," said Albern. "And I would not envy the Dean his fate."

"As I said, we knew it only for a rumor," said Jordel. "But when the Dean spoke, Enalyn ignored him as she so often did. She bade Xain to rise, and then she gave him her blessing upon the quest. And she promised Xain that if he should succeed, the favor of the nine lands would be upon him for the rest of his years, and he would be wed to whichever royal daughter he found suitable, if they would have his hand. Xain shook his head and said this: 'I thank you for your blessing and your gift, but I would save the Lord Prince without them. For once he and I shared a skin of wine, and he told me a joke, and still I want to smile whenever I think of it. So I owe him a debt, you see, of years of laughter, and that is a debt not easily cast aside.'

"Then while the High King and the rest of the court sat there stunned, Xain turned on his heel and strode from the throne room. He took a horse from the stable and left the island, and no one heard from him for many days. We all thought he was lost, and many in the court wept anew, and some wore black veils of mourning. The High King wore a dark look throughout her days. But Xain did not die, as you surely have guessed. On the fourteenth day after he had left the court, someone found him collapsed by the side of the King's road in Selvan, just over a league west of Garsec. The Lord Prince was with him, covered in his blood and trying to stanch the wound, for Xain had taken a knife in his belly.

"They fetched him back to the High King's Seat in all haste, and she bade her greatest surgeons to see to his recovery. He drifted in and out of life for many days, and the Lord Prince never left his bedside.

"The Lord Prince told us that he had been brought into the woods not far from the Seat—not far from the Birchwood, either, as it turns out—and held there by bandits, including two wizards of the Academy who were under the Dean's orders. The Dean, by the way, had fled the Seat as soon as he heard the Lord Prince was recovered, though the Mystics soon found him trying to secure passage to Dulmun. We brought him back to die a traitor's death in the High King's dungeons.

"But in the bandit's camp, the Lord Prince thought himself lost. Then Xain arrived. The Lord Prince said the wizard's coming was swift and terrible, like the gathering of a winter's storm all at once. Scores of men were at that fort, but they had one great weakness: it was made all of wood. Xain burned it to the ground and all within it, bursting through the flames to rescue the Lord Prince from his cell. When he could not fend off all the bandits with his magic, he took up a sword. In the fighting he took the knife in his gut, then cut off the head of the man who wielded it. By then he had freed the Lord Prince from his bonds, and together they fought free—and not one bandit left that fort alive. The Lord Prince had to drag Xain nearly the whole way to the road, expecting at any moment that he would fall dead upon the ground.

"When Xain finally woke upon the Seat, he was not the man who had left to rescue the Lord Prince. I came to visit him then, for I was young and curious, and I got him alone when all others had left. There was a darkness in his eyes I had never seen there before, though as I said I did not know him well. When I asked him if his wounds pained him, he shook his head, and then he said, 'Well, yes. Yes, of course. But more painful is the memory of their faces.' When I asked him who he meant, he shook his head and would not answer."

Jordel's gaze turned to Xain, but the wizard still stared back at him with eyes full of hate. It was as though he had heard none of Jordel's words, or hated him even more for saying them.

"That is the man I am trying to save," said Jordel quietly. "The man who risked his own life for the life of a friend—and to whom the nine lands owe a great debt. It may not be my place to judge him thus—yet I do not think his debt is outweighed by the misdeeds that made him flee the Seat, nor any of his actions since. In fact, I think all the kingdoms will still owe him a great deal, if the Lord Prince takes the throne one day as we all hope."

"As we all hope," murmured the rest of them in unison. Loren looked at Annis, and the girl's eyes were shining.

Jordel's voice rose again as he turned to Annis, and his words rang forth with conviction. "So there is the tale you all asked for. That is the man I place my faith in. That is the man I hope to recover from the curse of the magestones. There are many powerful wizards in the nine lands. Some are more powerful than Xain. Many of them would work for me more easily than he will, if I promised them a bit of the coin that is plentiful to my order. But I do not seek their services. I shall need more than power in the times to come. I shall need good hearts, and stout minds not easily swayed by gold. Xain is one such, even if you cannot see it. And though he stands on death's door now, if I can do anything to pull him back from the threshold, I will."

He turned from the fire and stood at the edge of the darkness to take the first watch. The rest of them sat quietly, staring into the flames. Even Annis was silent, and when her eyes flicked to Xain every few moments, Loren saw that they were full of wonder, not anger or fear.

Loren hardly knew what to think. She knew only that, for whatever reason, she believed Jordel without doubt. Always Loren had seen something in the wizard, some spark of spirit, a hint of nobility that showed itself only rarely, like a gleam of red glimpsed in the cracks of coal. Though she could hardly have guessed that Xain had done such a great deed in his youth, only to break the King's law and find himself pursued across Selvan by constables.

Something had happened to twist the man. Something to turn him from the hero who rescued the Lord Prince into the bitter wizard who had abandoned Loren upon the King's road. And as she stared at Xain lying by the fire, soon asleep after his wearying day, she could only wonder what that had been.

SEVENTEEN

Loren woke when Albern gently shook her, rousing her to take watch. But when she went to the edge of their little camp and readied for her vigil, he did not go to his bedroll. Instead he came and sat beside her.

"I have had a question for you since we chased the wizard through the valley," he said. "Do you know what it is?"

Loren took his meaning at once, and her cheeks burned. "You wonder why Jordel trusted my guidance over yours when Xain's trail turned west."

"Just so. Now, granted, I am older than I was when . . . well, when I was your age. And I can see you have no small skill in woodcraft. Yet the marks on the trail seemed clear. Tell me, how did you know so assuredly that they were wrong?"

"I . . . it was a feeling." Loren stared at her feet.

"A feeling," said Albern, drawing the word out. But he looked up at the moons as though nothing were amiss. "I see. Is it, mayhap, some sort of magic in you? I would understand, then, your reluctance to speak of it."

Despite her anxiousness, she could not help but snort. "I am no wizard. Though often it seems my life would be much easier if I were. Perhaps if Jordel had a firemage in me, he would not go to such great lengths to preserve Xain."

"You heard his tale," said Albern softly. "You know it is not only Xain's powers that Jordel holds in esteem."

Loren ducked her head. "You are right," she said. "It was a poor jest. I am still tired."

To Loren's relief, he rose and made for his bedroll at last. "As are we all, O great master of woodcraft," he said over his shoulder. "But fear not. No road runs forever, and one day they all come to an end."

As the camp settled back to silence, Loren's thoughts returned to Xain and what must have befallen him. It gnawed at her, working at her mind like a dog at its bone. When Jordel woke hours later, she drew him away from the camp.

"What happened to Xain upon the High King's Seat? When I met him in the Birchwood, he was fleeing from constables, a fugitive from the King's law. He told me very little of the reason why, and I think he might have given me a false tale besides. After what you told us last night, the mystery of it burns in my mind. I can hardly believe he is the same man as the one you spoke of."

Jordel's mouth twisted, and he looked at her askance. "It is not my place to speak of the misdeeds that made Xain flee the Seat. But his heart had turned to bitterness long before that, and anger already warred with mirth in his heart. A spark ignited it, and he lashed out in his rage, much as you have seen him do since you met."

"If you cannot tell me what he did, then tell me what happened before. I want to know. I want to learn how a man can turn from a hero into . . . Xain."

Jordel chuckled. "He has done many things on the road since Cabrus that some would call heroic. Still, you are right that he is not the man he once was. I told you that the High King promised him a royal daughter. But he took no wife afterward."

"I thought not. Why?"

"Xain loved a woman well, even before he rescued the Lord Prince. Her name was Trill, and she was a daughter of a noble house."

"Trill?" said Loren with a laugh. "That is a sound, not a name."

Jordel shrugged and gave a small, secretive smile. "Her family hails from Hedgemond, an outland kingdom where customs are strange. But regardless, she was a kindly woman, and her heart belonged to Xain. But her father spurned their love, for he stood in the sway of the Dean whom Xain condemned to death by rescuing the Lord Prince. Therefore he forbade them to marry, arranging instead for her to be wed to a Yerrin, who offered a mighty dowry."

Loren thought back to her mother and father, who had sought for her a suitor they hoped would bring coin. "That is an awful fate," she said.

"Indeed. Made more so by the fact that she was with child already. The bastard boy was given to Xain when he was born, and forbidden from seeing his mother ever again. High King Enalyn gave him a wet nurse to care for the babe, but the child never had a mother."

Loren raised a hand to her mouth. "You cannot tell me the High King permitted this. Bastards were rare enough in the forest, but never were they taken from a mother who wanted them."

He frowned, his face dark and solemn. "As I said, customs are strange in Hedgemond. Trill's father is a spiteful man, and he sent her home to be wed and live in her home kingdom. Though the High King might have helped them upon the Seat, where her influence is strongest, she cannot cast aside every law in the nine lands at her whim. Still, you need not worry that the boy was unloved, for Xain treasured him above all else in this world. I think he saw the boy as a reminder of the woman he loved, and so he treated his son like a prince. The High King herself would entertain the boy on occasion. Even now with Xain a criminal, one of her guards is with his son at all times."

"But then why do Xain's eyes turn so easily to sadness and melancholy?" said Loren. "If a parent loves their child, can that not temper even the hardest heart?"

"Yet now that child has been taken away from him," said Jordel. "And they may never see each other again."

At last Loren saw it—the bitter fate that had befallen Xain and set him upon the King's road also stole the only person he held dear. She imagined herself with a son or daughter, and then suddenly having them taken away. Or worse, meeting her end in some far-off corner of the nine lands, her child ever waiting for her to come home, always looking down the road in vain hope of seeing her black cloak once more. Always disappointed. It made her want to weep.

She looked at Jordel curiously, for in his tales she had seen a thread that she felt the need to pull. "Are you kin to the High King, Jordel?"

Jordel gawked at her, seeming for once to be at a loss for words. Then his gape became a smile, and he shook his head. "You surprise me, Loren of the family Nelda, and that makes me a fool. From the start you have seen and known much more than most, for your wits are sharp. It is why I wanted you beside me in the first place."

Loren smiled. "I could tell by the way you spoke of the Lord Prince, and the High King herself. It is clear you revere them, as do all good men, yet you talk of them with familiarity. More so than could be expected even from one who frequents their courts."

"You are correct," said Jordel with a nod. "My family of Adair has close ties to many in the royal family. I am third cousin to the Lord Prince on my mother's side, and often we spent time together in our youth. Though he is my lord, and we cannot go riding or climbing as we once did, I love him dearly. My heart broke when he was captured, and it sang when Xain saved him. But there is more you have not guessed. Can you tell me what it is?"

Loren thought hard, brow furrowing. But she could think of nothing more, no clue in the Mystic's words now or the day before. "I cannot."

Jordel gave a sad little smile. "You do not think it is only the Lord Prince's rescue that endears Xain to me, do you? I did not tell you the family name of Trill, the woman he loved. Did you not wonder?"

She understood in a flash, and her eyes widened. "She is a daughter of Adair?"

"My sister," said Jordel sadly. "And his son my nephew by blood."

"But . . . but this cannot be! You told me you only

knew *of* Xain. And Xain told me much the same thing about you, when first he learned that you pursued him upon the King's road."

"And neither of us lied," said Jordel. "Already I was a Mystic when Xain courted my sister, long before their son was born. When I met Xain after he rescued the Lord Prince, he did not even know me for Trill's brother. In our order we cast off all ties to clan and kingdom. We are ruled only by the masters of our order and the High King, and it is not encouraged that we see our kin very often."

"Yet you traipse across the nine lands to rescue your sister's beloved. How do your masters feel about that, I wonder?"

Jordel shook his head. "I have told you often before: I am something strange among my order. No doubt they would look down upon my actions, if they had not already cast me from their company."

He turned then, heading for the camp, but Loren put a hand on his shoulder to stop him.

"I think your actions are honorable, Jordel of the family Adair. My thoughts might not count for much, certainly not against your former masters. Yet that is how I feel."

"I thank you," said Jordel, bowing his head. "Words of honor mean more coming from another who possesses much of it."

They made for the camp together. Loren thought of one final question just before they reached the others. "If you are third cousin to the Lord Prince, where does that put you in line of succession?"

Jordel laughed out loud, the sound ringing clear in the mountain air. "Worry not about that, for I am nearly as far removed from the throne as you are. And Mystics do not become kings."

They reached the others, who had already readied themselves for the day's journey. Loren found her mind much occupied with what Jordel had told her, and when she looked at Xain lying bound, it was as if she saw him in a new light. When Jordel moved the wizard atop his charger, she went to help him. Together they lifted Xain and laid him across the horse, somewhat more gently than Jordel had done before. Across the charger's back, he nodded in silent thanks. Loren smiled, and then she climbed atop Midnight to ready for another long day's ride.

EIGHTEEN

Though Loren's mind was much occupied after her conversation with Jordel, eventually she noticed something to distract her. Albern would stop every once in a while, letting the others pass him on the road while he stood looking behind. Then he would ride quickly to the front again, guiding them around the next bend in the pass. He did it at least twice an hour, and every time Loren passed him he looked more troubled.

Finally she stopped beside him and turned to look. She saw nothing, for the path was empty, and not a creature moved upon the valley floor. Yet Loren thought she could feel what Albern must have sensed: a curious tension on the air, something she could not identify, raising the hairs on the back of her neck.

"What is it?" Loren had not meant to speak so softly, but her voice came as scarcely more than a whisper.

"I do not know," said Albern. "Only that I do not hear any birds."

He was right. No birdsong drifted up from the valley floor. Loren chastised herself for not noticing earlier; she prided herself as a daughter of the forest, yet clearly the last few months had not been kind to her woodcraft. "Is something following us?"

"That is my guess," said Albern. "Perhaps it is the satyrs. But if so, they are skulking in the shadows and around corners."

"Perhaps that is a good thing. It means they are frightened of us."

"Satyrs do not skulk or stalk travelers," said Albern. "Either they are angry and willing to fight, all threat and bluster, or they avoid men altogether. This is something new. And that is not all."

"What else?" said Jordel, riding up behind them.

"You remember what Tiglak said when he attacked us," said Albern. "He spoke of a Lord. But satyrs do not have lords, only elders."

Loren shrugged. "It sounds like a different name for the same thing."

"Small details tell many secrets," said Albern. "And

I tell you that hearing a satyr speak of a lord—especially, as it sounded, a lord who is not a satyr himself—is like hearing a bear speak as it attacks you. The bear is no more dangerous than it was before—and yet you should be more frightened, for it should not be talking."

Loren wanted to say that she did not understand. But she saw a dark look on Jordel's face; clearly he took Albern's point, and she did not wish to look a fool. "What should we do, then?" she asked instead.

"We can only ride on," said Albern. "And be on our guard in case they decide to attack, instead of this careful stalking. It would be almost a relief if they did."

"I might not go that far," said Jordel. "Yet I, too, dislike this silence."

"Fortunately our journey will not be much longer," said Albern. "Soon our road will take us down and out of the mountains, and in two days we shall come to a small town where we may freshen our supplies, and mayhap rest."

But Jordel frowned. "We will fill our saddlebags, but we cannot afford any time off the road. Let us make for the town as quickly as possible, for already this journey has stretched overlong."

Soon after they reached a fork in the road. One way ran straight ahead, continuing their precarious path along the side of the western mountains. The other way turned east and crossed a narrow chasm, then vanished within the mountains there. There was a stone bridge built across the divide. It was old and worn, but still it looked sturdy enough.

"That way lies our path," said Albern with obvious relief. "Come, let us make haste."

They spurred their horses and rode for the bridge at a quick pace. But no sooner had their horse's hooves touched the first stones than there was a great cry from the other end of the bridge. Many satyrs leapt up from hiding places among the rocks, some bounding from the cliff faces on the other side. Arrows shrieked through the air towards them.

"Get back!" cried Jordel, turning his charger in retreat. They fell back in disarray, hiding themselves from sight behind a great boulder that stood at the fork.

"That was why they stalked us," said Jordel. "They meant to ambush us upon the bridge, where we were exposed."

"If that was their intent, they made a poor job of it," said Albern, frowning. "They should have waited until we were mostly across and their archers had a clearer shot."

"They are practically animals," said Annis. "What would they know of such strategies?"

"Satyrs may not be wise in the ways of book learning and building cities, but in mountain warfare they have no equal," said Albern sternly. "If their attack posed little danger, it is because they meant it to. They only wanted to drive us back."

"Why?" said Loren. But even as she asked the question, she guessed at the answer. "They want us to take the north road. What lies that way?"

Albern shook his head. "Nothing of any importance—certainly nothing the satyrs would care about. There is only an old fortress, abandoned for hundreds of years. But then the road turns east again, leading from the mountains to the village of Northwood. It would not stop us, but only add a few days to our journey."

"Then we must push across this bridge," said Jordel. "Come. Let us ride out and charge them. I doubt they will stand against two fighters on horseback."

Albern nodded and unslung his bow. Gem leaned forwards from behind Annis, his eyes shining. "Let me ride with you. I still have my sword."

"But you wear no mail," said Jordel. "And you have no bow with which to return fire—and if things go poorly, you will leave Annis horseless and unable to flee. No, Gem. Your time to ride will come, but not now."

So saying, he and Albern spurred their horses for the bridge. Albern gave a great ululating cry, and Jordel a shout, their voices carrying far in the crisp air.

They must have hoped to drive the satyrs back from sheer fright. But it did not work, for the creatures had nearly doubled in number while the party hid behind the boulder, and they fired a fresh hail of arrows. These all fell short, but the attack made the horses skid to a halt. Then the front line of goat-men charged with their spears. Jordel traded a few hasty blows with them, and Albern felled three with arrows, but the rest were undeterred.

Jordel cried out and wheeled his horse. Albern followed suit, and together they fled back to the others.

"That was a staunch defense," said Jordel.

"More so than it should have been," said Albern. "They are not used to facing a charge from horsemen. Something is at work here, and I do not like it."

Great jeers echoed from the other side of the bridge, along with guttural cries of *Men!* and *Trespassers!* and many words in the satyrs' tongue that Loren could not understand. Then they heard a wet *thunk* on the ground by the boulder; the satyrs had thrown something heavy. Loren poked her head out to get a better look, and then recoiled. When Albern and Jordel saw it, their faces grew stony, while Gem and Annis covered their eyes.

It was the head of a satyr. The horns had been removed—not cut off, but pulled out at the roots. It bore many welts and bruises. But still, Albern stared in grim recognition.

"It is Tiglak," he said. "He made his parley with us, and his elders disapproved. This was his punishment. Since we bargained with his life, they have rejected that gift."

"They will not let us pass in peace," said Loren. "And we cannot break them with war. It seems we must take the north road."

"That will take too long," said Jordel.

"What choice do we have?" Loren insisted. "Will we charge them all together? What if one of the children takes an arrow, or their horse is stricken with terror and bolts off the bridge? It is not a warhorse like yours."

"Yet they mean to guide us to this fortress Albern speaks of," said Gem. "They want us to go there. That means, rather immediately, that I would rather not."

"I share your sentiment," said Jordel. "I dislike the sound of this place, and I have never heard of it besides."

Albern shrugged. "Is that a great wonder? Do you know every stronghold in the nine lands, even the ones where men have never set foot in a thousand years?"

"I know enough of them that a lonely castle in the Greatrocks should have been known to me," said Jordel.

"It seems that our choices are to make for the fortress or fight the satyrs," said Loren. "And I do not think that is a fight we can win."

Jordel still looked doubtful. He turned to Albern. "You are certain the place is abandoned?"

"I am certain of nothing," said the bowyer with a shrug. "I have not seen it in ten years. Yet if it had been occupied, I would likely have heard. The movements of Selvan's armies are rarely unknown to me."

"Very well," said Jordel. "We shall take the western fork. I will ride in the rear with Loren, to ensure the satyrs do not surprise us upon the road."

They turned their horses and moved on. Behind them the jeers of the satyrs sounded long after the creatures were out of sight. And as they rounded the first bend on the mountain pass, Loren looked back a final time to see Tiglak's head in the dirt. It seemed to her that his eyes held a look of warning.

NINETEEN

NOW THEIR MOOD WAS DOUR AS THEY RODE, AND THEY neither smiled nor spoke to each other. Each of them felt that a doom hung over their heads. As the sun slowly fell behind the mountains above them, Loren heard a deep *swoosh* and looked up.

She cried out, and they all froze in fear. Albern and Jordel followed Loren's gaze skyward, and their hands went to their weapons.

Great winged beasts dove and swooped through the air. In her first flash of terror, Loren thought they were dragons, for they had great leathery wings like the beasts of legend. Yet she knew that for a foolish thought; these beasts were far too small. That was small comfort, however, for their wings still stretched far wider than Loren was tall, and their legs ended in taloned claws. Their upper bodies looked like women's, ending in women's heads with long flowing hair, though their mouths were filled with finger-long and razor-sharp teeth.

"Harpies," said Albern, and Loren knew she did not imagine the fear hidden in his voice. "Dark creatures who feast on human flesh. I have never seen their kind in the Greatrocks before."

"But you *have* seen them before elsewhere?" said Gem. His terror was much more obvious, for his voice quivered and broke. "How do you kill them?"

"The same as most things," said Albern. "An arrow in the eye or the heart is best. A blade will do. They are not Elves, impervious to spear or steel."

"What are they doing?" said Loren. "Why do they not attack?"

"We are armed. Likely they do not want to risk themselves," said Albern. But Loren thought he sounded unsure.

Gem reached for his hilt, never taking his gaze from the beasts. Jordel slapped his reins against the charger's neck. "Let us ride on. They have an evil look, and I do not like the way they circle."

The harpies followed them until sunset. Albern

searched for a cave in which to camp, for none of the party wished to rest in the open where the harpies could see them. Finally he found it, when the last of the sun's glow had nearly gone from the sky. They were so relieved that despite Albern's warning, they did not search to make sure it was empty first, but hurried inside as soon as they saw the entrance was clear. Albern shook his head and inspected the place while the rest of them laid their beds.

"We should have two on guard tonight," said Albern.

"I thought the same," said Jordel. "Gem, we shall require your help on watch tonight."

"And mine," said Annis, folding her arms. "I am older than he is, anyway."

Jordel looked at her in surprise. "Forgive me, Annis. I made a mistake, judging you both by your height. You will take the morning, and I will stand it with you myself."

Loren volunteered for the first watch, and kept Gem awake with her, for she knew the boy would never be roused early if he went to sleep with the others. They spent an anxious and nerve-racking three hours pacing the mouth of the cave, neither wishing to speak very much. But finally, as the moons neared the eastern mountaintops and their watch was almost over, Gem sat against the cave wall and leaned his head against it. His dark hair glowed blue in the moonslight.

"I had thought our jaunt through the mountains

would go a touch different than it has," he said. "This is no great adventure, but a fearful flight into the darkness."

"Most adventures are, or so I have been told," said Loren. "It is only afterwards, when they are put into story and song, that they sound anything like the tales we hear around a fire."

"Who told you that?" said Gem, looking at her with interest.

"An old man who used to travel through my village, once upon a time," said Loren. "He was a peddler by trade, but people valued him more for his stories than for his poor wares. His name was Bracken."

"That is an odd name."

"You speak bold words for a boy named Gem."

"Gem is a fine name," he said, sniffing. "It glitters."

They were silent a moment longer, and Loren thought he was done. But then he leaned forwards, folding his hands together and speaking more quietly.

"I do not want you to send me away. But I am pledged to you, and I swore to do as you told me. So I have decided that if you wish to secret me away in some noble's house, I will go there. And I will use my time to study the sword, and also to read many tomes of learning. That way I will become useful to you again. Then you will not need to hide me away, because it will be better to have me with you."

Loren looked at him in surprise, feeling her heart sink. "Gem. You cannot think that I wish to be rid of you. I have few enough friends in the world, and you are one of the finest."

Gem shook his head. "But I know that sometimes being a friend is not enough. You and Jordel have many great deeds to do. I am only in the way, as much as I like to pretend otherwise."

Her heart melted, and she sank to her knees in front of him. His hands hung limp as they rested on his legs, and gently she clasped them between her own. "Gem, nothing would give me greater joy than spending all my days with you and Annis by my side, the three of us laughing and making merry. But that coin has two sides. Nothing I can imagine frightens me more than the thought of you coming to harm. If either of you were hurt, or worse, I do not think I could bear it. I nearly went mad with worry when Xain took Annis. I only want you to be safe."

"What good is safety?" He looked up with wide, sad eyes. "I was safe enough in Cabrus. Always I could evade the constables, and even if they had caught me, they do not cut the fingers from children. I did not leave the city with you to find safety."

"And I was wrong to think that you did. You and Annis both. She was well within her rights to chastise me, for your lives do not belong to me. And if you wish to stay by my side, either of you, I will not deny you, for in truth nothing would make me happier."

He lunged forwards and wrapped his arms around her chest, holding her tight. Loren embraced him in return, and she could feel him shaking slightly against her. But he remained silent, even when she felt his tears soak through her shirt. When he had finished he let go and turned away, trying to hide his eyes so she could not see them.

"Come," he said. "I think our watch has ended, and well shall I enjoy my slumber tonight."

In the morning, Loren found Jordel awake by the cave entrance. Annis sat on the ground near him, her chin against her chest, eyes closed in slumber. Albern drew the Mystic aside to discuss the road ahead. Loren drifted closer to overhear them, making a show of fiddling with the cinch of Midnight's saddle and the straps of her saddlebags.

"I have thought much about our course," said Albern. "I share your concern, for if the satyrs and now the harpies wish to drive us towards the fortress, then I do not wish to go there any more than you do. Thus I offer another way: a track that will take us higher into the Greatrocks, riding the peaks on a more perilous path. It will add some days to our journey as well."

"Longer and more dangerous at once?" said Jordel. "That hardly seems wise."

"Yet it seems to me even less wise to carry along a course that our pursuers wish us to take," said Albern. "Though the road along the peaks may be hard, it seems better to face the dangers we know than whatever unknown peril may await us in the abandoned fortress—if indeed it is still abandoned."

"I see what you mean," said Jordel. "And I admit my heart is greatly relieved, for it has been troubled at the thought of being driven towards some unknown end. But can we change our course at all? The satyrs stopped us once. They may try to head us off again, and now they have help from the skies."

"Then at least we shall know we are being driven," said Albern with a sigh. "There is still some hope, however vain, that the satyrs are not trying to guide us, and that their display on the bridge was only some show of dominance after our attack on Tiglak. But if we make for the peaks and they stop us again, we shall know for certain that some danger awaits us in the stronghold. And as I said, better a certain danger than an uncertain one."

"A grim choice, yet it seems clear," said Jordel. "Very well. We make for the peaks. Loren, since you have been standing there eavesdropping and know our plan, you had best ready the others for the journey."

Loren gave a start and hastily turned away. "I was only tending to my saddlebags."

"Of course you were," said Jordel, a wry twist in his mouth. "Nevertheless, ready the children, and tell them to dress warmly. Our road will soon grow colder."

She did as she was asked, and it was well that she did, for the air hung cold and damp about them as they began to ride, even before they began to climb.

Soon the water formed into droplets and began to pelt them, gently at first, and then hard, like small stones falling from the sky. The road was narrow now, and rocky, and Albern bade them ride as close to the mountainside as possible.

"Walk your horses slowly, and take care not to slip," he said, raising his voice to be heard above the rain. "I hope I need not tell you what would happen if you fell from this height."

Despite the rain, the harpies still swooped in great circles overhead. The creatures seemed to give no mind to the cold, nor to the water that doused them as they flew. Birds in the Birchwood had fled for cover when rain fell, for the wet got into their feathers and turned their flight perilous. But the great leathery wings of the harpies suffered no ill effects.

Abruptly, Albern turned them from the path and climbed steeply up the side of the mountain. At first Loren was shocked, for she had not even seen a trail in the mountainside. But then her eyes began to pick it out: a stone here and there, and flat-packed dirt leading at a sharp angle up towards the peaks of the Greatrocks. None of the paths they had taken thus far had been so steep, and their mounts struggled in the mud their hooves churned up.

They had not climbed more than thirty paces when they heard a great screeching above them, and the air filled with the *whoosh* of leathery wings. Jordel drew his sword at once, and Albern nocked an arrow as the harpies descended upon them. The beasts showed their fangs as they screamed, and the sound was terrible, like pigs being slaughtered. Great taloned legs stretched forth, reaching for the travelers.

Albern loosed two arrows in the space of a second; one of the harpies plummeted from the sky and fell lifeless towards the valley floor. Its companion swerved aside at the last second, and the shaft whizzed by harmlessly. The others scattered before Loren could think to draw her own bow—but at last she did, whipping an arrow from the quiver at her hip. Drawing it as Albern did was still too unfamiliar to her, so she drew the way she had learned from Chet in the Birchwood, holding her fire until she could get a clear shot.

The harpies dove again, and this time Albern shot a pair of them down. Loren managed to loose an arrow before they retreated, but it missed its mark. She had never been good at felling birds in flight, and despite the harpies' great size, they were also more cunning, and wove a mad pattern that made it hard to aim.

They attacked again, and again, and each time Albern would fell another one or two of them. Loren even managed to bring one down, her arrow embedded firmly in the joint between wing and shoulder. But more arrived to strengthen the flock, until they looked like a great murder of crows, and Loren knew at once they did not have enough arrows to fell them all. And the harpies did not come close enough for Jordel to reach with his sword.

"We must turn back!" said Albern as the harpies regrouped again. "They will not let us reach the peaks, and if they do we shall be all the more exposed."

Jordel turned his horse without answer and led them back down, Albern and Loren keeping wary eyes skyward as they descended to the main pass. The moment Midnight's hooves touched the dirt, the harpies ceased their screaming. They swooped up and away into the sky, circling once more like vultures waiting for carrion.

"Now we know for certain," said Jordel in a voice grim with doom. "We are being herded."

"Mayhap they only attacked because they saw an opportunity," said Albern. "The fortress has been abandoned longer than anyone in the Greatrocks can remember." But even he did not sound as though he believed it.

They spent a miserable day riding in the cold and the wet, their tempers short. When Gem asked for more food at the midday meal, Jordel snapped at him, and Annis sat her saddle in stony silence the whole day. Though they could not see the sun, eventually the sky grew darker than it had been, and Albern found them another cave to rest in for the night. They were a solemn party as they laid out their bedrolls and Albern stoked a fire, until Annis crossed her arms and huffed.

"This is a journey for madmen," she said angrily. "And you are all fools for riding it."

Before Loren could answer her, Gem spoke up

in anger. "You ride it with us, and deserve the same name."

"Not by choice. Not with *him.*" She gave Xain a sharp look where he lay on the floor at the back of the cave.

To Loren's surprise, the wizard did not show anger, nor any of the madness that had plagued him of late, but only a great sadness. His mouth moved as though he wished to speak, but only a faint mumbling came out around the cloth. He cast his head down, forehead pressed into the dirt, and closed his sunken eyes as if to weep. But no tears came.

Annis turned to Jordel, her eyes flashing in anger. "The moment we leave these mountains, I am leaving. I will not walk one more league by Xain's side. I do not care what he did for the Lord Prince in his youth."

"Come now, Annis," said Loren. "We are all tired from the road. Sleep in the warmth of the fire before you say more words you will come to regret."

"I will never regret them," said Annis. "You wish to be rid of me? Fine. It cannot happen soon enough."

Loren opened her mouth, but Jordel spoke first, quietly and without rancor. "Your choice is your own, Annis of the family Yerrin. If you still wish it when we leave the mountains, I shall secure passage wherever you wish."

"I do not ask you for any more boons," said Annis, snatching up the edge of her bedroll. "I have had quite enough of them already. I am nearly dead from them."

She threw the blanket over herself and turned her back to the fire—and the others.

Gem sat there fuming in silent rage. Loren put a hand on his shoulder and murmured, "She is tired, and angry. Do not trouble yourself overmuch. Finish your food, and sleep."

But after she herself had eaten and then stood her watch, Loren lay awake long in thought, and she fell asleep grieving.

TWENTY

THE NEXT DAY DAWNED WITH LITTLE TO LIFT THEIR spirits, other than that the rain had finally ceased. But the sky was still grey with clouds, and it was hardly possible to tell that the sun had risen. They ate and made ready without speaking, and set forth upon the road in a foul mood. The harpies never ceased their swooping, and Albern stopped once at midday to look back. Half-glimpsed in the mist far back along the pass, where it snaked around the mountains and back into view, several shapes skulked among the rocks, poking their heads out every so often to peer at the travelers.

"The satyrs have followed us," said Albern. "I thought they might. At least they seem to have no interest in making a fight of it."

"Not yet, at any rate," said Jordel.

"If they planned to attack, there would not be a better time than now," said Albern. "For soon the road will descend to the valley floor again, and there a fight would not be so perilous for us."

He said it as if it were a hopeful thing, but Loren saw a darkness in Jordel's eyes that she thought she understood; the satyrs did not wish to fight them, for they were being herded.

"Is there another way to the peaks that we might take?" said Jordel. "Another path leading up?"

Albern looked at him in surprise. "One or two. But the harpies have not abandoned us."

"Perhaps we can push past them," said Jordel. "Less and less do I wish to see this mountain fortress, for my heart grows heavier the more I wonder what might lie in wait for us there."

"It would be wiser to turn aside once we reach the valley floor," said Albern. "For then the harpies will have less of an advantage, and besides we might find trees or rocks in which to take cover."

"The moment we can, then," said Jordel. "And I do not care how much longer it will take us."

That, more than anything else, filled Loren's heart with fear, and she tried to stop her hands from shaking.

The road dove soon, just as Albern had said, and before long their horses' hooves sank into soft wet dirt rather than scrabbling on rock. Albern turned them aside at once, and they spurred their horses to a gallop, making for a small wood a hundred paces from the road. The harpies screeched and dove, but the travelers only pressed their horses harder, Jordel drawing his sword in case of an attack.

They had nearly reached the wood when they heard a great braying cry before them, and satyrs swarmed from the trees. The goat-men loosed many arrows that struck the ground around the company, making the horses rear.

"An ambush!" cried Albern. "Turn back!"

"No!" cried Jordel. "They are few." And with a shout he spurred his charger. The satyrs saw death on his face and scattered, dropping their bows to flee.

But the almost-forgotten harpies swept from the sky. Their wings buffeted the riders, and Annis screamed as she was cast from the saddle. The plow horse reared, and for a terrifying moment Loren thought its hooves would come down upon Annis, crushing her. But the horse turned at the last second to come down on the grass beside her head. Somehow Gem kept his seat, until another harpy screamed by. Its great talons grazed his arm, and he cried out from the pain as he, too, toppled from the saddle. Too late, Loren nocked an arrow and fired, but the harpy flew off unharmed.

Loren rode Midnight up to the plow horse, trying to seize the reins, but the beast was terrified and bolted away from her, whinnying loudly. Albern wheeled his bay and gave chase. He snatched the horse's reins and led it back to the others. But just then more satyrs came clattering down from the mountain pass above, storming across the empty ground. From his place in the trees Jordel looked back and saw them, and returned with his charger to lend aid. He rode at the satyrs with a vengeance, but they formed a wall of spears and drawn arrows, forcing him to turn aside.

"Jordel!" cried Loren. But the beasts did not shoot at him, only forced him away. He returned to her side at the same time as Albern, and together the men studied the satyrs as Annis and Gem climbed hastily back atop the plow horse.

"How many can you fell?" said Jordel.

"Ten, if I do not miss with any of my arrows," said Albern. "Another fifteen, if I take Loren's. But there are at least twice that many, Jordel, and though I can see you are a mighty warrior I do not think even you can fight off more than a score of them."

"We must return to the road," said Loren. "Look at Gem." The boy cradled his arm against his side, and Loren could see a deep gash stretching from shoulder to elbow. He gritted his teeth in solemn courage, but his skin had gone white, and his eyes were wide and fearful.

"We do not know where the road leads," said Jordel.

"But we know what will happen if we stay." Loren's voice became pleading. "Certain death, with no chance for survival. Come, Jordel. The road may be perilous, but it cannot be worse than dying here."

"You do not know that," said Jordel. But he turned his charger and led them on a wide circle around the satyrs, bringing them back to the road. Once more the harpies retreated, and the satyrs drew back into the rocks and brush, though Loren could feel the weight of many eyes upon their backs.

The moment they were safe again, Jordel called a halt so they could tend to Gem's arm. Albern had a packet of herbs in his saddlebags, and these he fashioned into a poultice with some water from one of their skins. He pressed the poultice into the cut—which was not as deep as Loren had feared, though it was quite long. Gem winced as the pasty white-green mixture sank into his wound, but in a moment he sucked in a deep breath of air and exhaled.

"I added some mint," said Albern. "It has little curative property, but the smell of it clears the mind."

"It almost makes me forget I am hurt," said Gem, grinning. "Will the wound scar, do you think? I should greatly enjoy telling the story of how I vanquished harpies in the Greatrock Mountains."

Albern gave a short bark of laughter, and then turned his head as he tried to compose himself. Gem looked at the bowyer suspiciously.

"You have vanquished nothing more than bread

and meat since we began this journey," said Loren, her eyebrows raised.

Gem lifted his chin. "The journey is not over. Mark my words—I will take a harpy's head before we return to civilized lands."

Once Albern had finished with the wound, they rode on. The land grew more barren the farther north they went, trees and grass giving way to rocks and stones, with no signs of life anywhere—save the harpies, and sometimes the half-seen satyrs. Though the road was wide and flat, and they all had an uncomfortable sense of being hunted, Jordel did not press them to move with much haste.

"If we are being driven, I have no desire to move with speed," he said. "Mayhap if we move slowly we shall force the hand of whoever is behind this. The 'Lord' that Tiglak referred to."

"Whoever that is, I do not know that I wish to provoke them," said Albern. "Yet I, too, have little wish to run headlong into their embrace."

Had they not been harried so, Loren might have found the mountains beautiful. Though most of the green had faded away, still there were many formations that nearly took her breath. Red stone showed on some cliff faces, struck through with threads of glittering white quartz. It gave them the look of marble walls, as though they rode through a cathedral that lay open to the sky.

If only the roof were less grey and dreary, she thought.

To further slow their progress, Jordel gave them a long rest at midday to eat. The harpies seemed content to continue their endless loops in the sky, while Gem gave them many dark glances and muttered to himself. Annis seemed determined to ignore everything around her, including her companions. She did not appear to regret a word of what she had said the previous night. Loren wanted to speak with her, but she could hardly muster a scrap of attention while they were being hunted so.

The day's end came at last, and not soon enough for Loren. She longed to throw herself into slumber and forget about the dark creatures pursuing them. But first Jordel called her over.

"I wish to go with Albern and gather wood for the fire, for I think we shall all enjoy one made from proper wood rather than dung," he said. "Will you see to Xain for me?"

Loren balked. "I do not wish to go near him if I can help it."

"Do me this favor. I am well weary of this road, and I feel as though I might break if he looks at me even once more with his sullen fury."

"I feel the same. He has done as much harm to me as to you. Mayhap more," said Loren angrily. She looked down to see Xain lying nearby. Though she did not think he could hear them, still the wizard looked at her with that strange melancholy he had shown of late, as though he knew of what they were speaking.

Jordel sighed and pinched the bridge of his nose. "Very well. Mayhap you are right. I shall see to him once I return. Or perhaps I shall let him go hungry tonight. We have suffered enough trouble upon this trip on his account, and an empty belly might do him some good."

Loren pressed her lips together tightly. "Oh, all right. I shall feed him then, if only so that he does not die on us as we sleep. But are you certain he is . . . safe?"

"I think he is too weak to try anything. And besides, you have your dagger. He cannot harm you. If he should attempt to speak, replace his gag immediately. You do not have to remove it very far—only enough to shove some bread and salted meat into his mouth. He can chew through the gag. He has earned that much discomfort, at least."

So saying, he strode off with Albern into the dimming light of the day. Loren looked after them for a moment, and then she turned back down the road. The satyrs had remained out of sight, but she could feel them waiting there, watching, eyes peering into the light of the fire and at the weary travelers gathered around it.

She sighed and went to Xain. His eyes locked on to hers as she approached, and Loren thought the sadness she saw there might overwhelm her. Never had she seen the wizard look thus since the day they had met, and it unnerved her. She reached into her cloak to finger the hilt of her dagger. *I am safe,* she reminded herself. *He cannot harm me. I must only keep watching his eyes, in case they begin to glow.*

She tore a chunk of bread from the loaf in her pack and held it ready, along with some meat, and prepared to remove the gag. She held herself tense, ready to mute him again if he should speak so much as a word. But the second she removed the cloth from his lips, Xain croaked, "I am sorry."

Loren froze, bread held a few fingers from his mouth. Of all the words she had thought he might say, those had not been among them.

"What?" she said, for lack of anything better.

"I am sorry for what I did. For all I have done since we entered the mountains. For everything I did before that. I have done you much harm, and I cannot blame all of it upon the magestones."

He is playing a trick, cried a voice in her mind. *He is trying to distract you!* Yet he spoke no words of fire or thunder, and there was no glow in his eyes. In fact, Loren doubted if he could summon much magic at all in his current state. His eyes were sunken into his head, the orbs bulging out from sockets emaciated and filled with wrinkles. Only a few desiccated patches of hair still clung to his scalp, and his wrists were raw from his bindings.

"Those are pretty words," said Loren. "Yet you will pardon me for wondering if you mean them."

"I cannot blame you for that," said Xain with a sardonic little smile. "I have never given you reason to believe in me. Never. Not from the first day we met, when I abandoned you in the night. You placed your faith in me with a whole heart, something all the more remarkable from one who grew up as you did. I cast your trust aside, and that was a great evil. But I . . . much of this journey has been shrouded in darkness for me, and I hardly know my dreams from the waking world. I seem to remember that Jordel told you something of my story."

"Something of it, yes. But not all."

"Then you know I was hunted by more than just two simple constables," said Xain earnestly. "I only thought . . . I thought not to drag you into the darkness that my life had become. Yet no matter how earnestly I tried to avoid you, always you reappeared."

"To your great annoyance."

"To my salvation," said Xain. "I had only mad schemes to save my son. Had I tried to carry them out, I would surely be dead."

"I am not so sure. I have heard some say you are considered a mighty wizard, though you seem scarcely more than fair at it to me."

He stared at her for a moment before he seemed to understand that she was joking, and then he gave a croaking chuckle. "I do not know how you can laugh now, but I am glad for it. I feel as though a great weight has passed from my spirit, and my mind is free from the darkness that cloaked it." His face grew solemn again. "I wish I could undo the evil I have done. I . . .

I remember the faces of those I struck down on the road east of Wellmont. I can still see the darkfire as it consumed them. That memory will haunt me forever, I fear."

Loren's heart leapt, for she remembered what Jodel had said about the effects of the magestones passing—but then she stopped herself. This could all too easily be a trick. Xain had been dour and furious during this whole journey. He had tried to escape, and had even cast flames upon them. None of it had worked. Now, mayhap, he sought to try trickery instead. Even before the magestones, he had not sounded so hopeful as this. It was too great a change, too quickly. If he thought he could fool her, he would find himself mistaken.

"Eat your food," she said tersely. "We have a long night ahead of us."

She saw a flash of anger on his face again, the same he had worn each night as he lay by the fire. Though it dampened quickly, her heart skipped a beat. *I was right,* she thought. But Xain ate his bread and meat obediently, and did not protest when she tied the gag in his mouth again.

His words troubled her long after she had retreated to the other side of the fire to stare into the darkness, long after Jordel and Albern returned and assigned the watches for the night. As the rest readied themselves for sleep, Loren decided to speak with Jordel. When she told him what had happened, his mouth set in a grim line, and he nodded.

"He said as much to me, last night. In truth, that is why I wanted you to feed him. For one thing, I wished to see if he would say the same to another as he did to me."

"And do you believe him?" said Loren. "Do you think the magestone sickness could have passed?"

Jordel shrugged. "We cannot know for certain—not yet, at any rate. For some the process is much longer, and for others much shorter. But none ever truly shed their desire. Always it will lurk in the back of his mind, goading him, prodding him. If ever magestones are within his grasp, he will have to wage a great war against himself to resist them. If he even wants to. It is like ale and wine—some people take to them ill, and know it, and so avoid drink altogether. But some lose their wits and enjoy it, and they drink and drink until they have cast their lives down around themselves one stone at a time, and then the only way to dull the pain of it is to keep drinking. Yet the call of magestones is even sweeter."

"So you think it is a trick," Loren pressed.

"It could be," he nodded. "Or it could not. Either way, we cannot risk trusting him yet. Not now, while we are pursued on land and in the air by dark creatures eager for our blood."

Loren nodded and retired to her bedroll. But she thought much about what Xain had said—and more importantly, the deep well of sadness she had seen in his light, grey-brown eyes.

TWENTY-ONE

"We shall reach the fortress today, I think," said Albern.

It was morning, two days after the harpies had attacked them on the valley floor. Though Albern spoke with all the severity of someone commenting upon the rain, it sent a wave of unease rippling through the party.

"And what will happen then?" Gem wondered.

"Then?" said Jordel. "Then we shall see what we find, and answer it however we can. What is it you once told me? Our road is set, and what use in worrying? We can do little about it either way."

"It sounded cheerier when I said it," grumbled Gem.

Now that their destination seemed inevitable, Jordel had grown curiously calm—but Gem and Annis did not catch the same mood. Loren caught both of them looking about anxiously, as though they expected to find themselves beset by ghouls at any moment. Even Annis seemed to have forgotten some of her anger in the face of their uncertain future.

They were not much longer upon the road when it began to widen, turning from loose mud to packed dirt that hardly soaked up the rain. Then, abruptly, it turned into well-paved stone, great square blocks of granite laid out with mortar in a perfect path leading due north.

Albern stopped them at once, and from the look on his face Loren could tell he had not expected this. Jordel, too, looked solemn, for all his talk of being unworried.

"You cannot tell me this road was not here last time you came this way," said Loren.

"I can tell you that, for it is true," said Albern. "See for yourself—the stones are almost newly cut and laid. They cannot be more than a few years old. And certainly they are not older than ten years, and that is the last time I was here."

"Who would do that?" said Jordel. "Surely not the king of Selvan, for then I would certainly have heard of it."

"If I had to hazard a guess, I would lay blame at the feet of this 'Lord' the satyrs have mentioned," said Albern grimly. "And that shows the truth of what I have suspected all along: the Lord is not of the satyrs. The goat-men never lay roads like this, nor build structures of stone, or even of wood. They live in caves and in the wild, and they have no need of paving stones, since they do not ride horses or pull carts. They prefer to climb mountainsides."

"Mayhap this Lord will give us food and lodging for the night," said Gem. "Perhaps they are a benevolent ruler who will give care to five weary travelers. Six, I mean—please do not take offense." He gave a great, dramatic bow to where Xain lay on the back of Jordel's horse.

"A benevolent ruler who musters armies of satyrs and harpies to do their bidding," said Albern. "No, I do not think such a creature exists in the nine lands, little master."

"I think I prefer the title of Lord Urchin, if it please you," said Gem with a sniff.

"It does not," said Albern with a dark look. "Just now there are too many lords in the Greatrocks for my taste."

The day was dark already, but once their horses set foot upon the road their moods darkened further. Far too much was unknown, and Loren no longer held any doubt that she did not wish to see what lay at the end of this road. Whatever might be waiting in the stronghold, she could not pretend, as Gem did, to believe it was not dangerous.

Almost from the moment they reached the paved stones, the harpies swooped off and away—not out of sight, but farther back, flying in loops on either side of the road. The satyrs vanished from view. The party was headed upon the intended course; their stalkers no longer needed to watch them so closely.

The ground began to rise again, and the road with it. Wherever a hillock or mound stood in their way, a great wedge had been cut right out of the earth, as though the road had burrowed straight through it. The grey stone stretched endlessly, straight as an arrow's shaft.

When the road finally turned, they saw at last where it led.

They had been headed west of a spar in the mountains, a ridge that emerged from the eastern peaks to descend all the way to the valley floor. Once they reached it, the road turned east, rising sharply up the side of the ridge—and to the stronghold.

There it sat, perched among the Greatrocks like some ancient and terrible spider. Tall walls surrounded a large, almost bulbous stone keep, and tall towers jutted up at each of the wall's four corners like the joints of spindly legs. It sat on a great stone platform like a plinth, hacked from the ridge's side as if by a giant's axe. No fires burned in any windows. No faces could be seen above the parapets, though the party was still too far off to be certain.

"I see no signs of life," said Jordel. His voice remained calm, betraying none of the fear that clutched at Loren's heart.

"Nor I." Albern sounded almost hopeful.

"I do not like the look of the place," said Gem. "It seems as though a great evil rests within it."

"That may be, but it was not always thus," said Jordel. "For this fortress was built by my order."

"The Mystics?" said Loren, looking at him in surprise. "I thought you said you knew nothing of a mountain stronghold."

"I do not. And that is all the more strange—for I can see by the stonework and the shape of its keep that this place was built by Mystics, and for their use, though many an age ago. We must have abandoned it. I wonder why."

"Well, by all means, let us proceed directly towards it to find out," said Gem. "Nothing would please me more."

"Is there no other way to go?" said Annis, rancor forgotten in place of fear. "I am not as frightened as Gem, but nonetheless I do not enjoy the thought of drawing nearer to this place."

"You see the road," said Albern, "though it was only a small dirt path last I came here. It leads one way: forwards. And I suspect that if we try to leave it, our escorts will return and guide us back to the path. But it is as I said—no fires burn within. That, at least, is a hopeful sign."

Loren felt anything but hope.

Jordel led them on, for they no longer needed Albern's guidance. The bowyer rode in the rear, just behind Loren, and his right hand remained close to his quiver.

"Look," said Gem, his face turned backwards.

Loren looked behind them. Far below, where the road curved around the ridge, the satyrs had reappeared. But they no longer followed the party. They had drawn up in rank and file, spears held at their sides like soldiers on parade. *Or at a funeral procession,* thought Loren. It was a chilling thought, and she turned her eyes away. The only consolation was that the harpies had vanished.

They could make no attempt at stealth. The road was wide and open, with nothing behind which to take cover. Yet secrecy seemed unwarranted; no matter how close they drew, they could see no signs of life. Soon Loren could even make out the designs worked into the stone of the ramparts, yet she could see no men moving atop them.

"What do you think they—"

"Hist!" said Jordel, speaking in a low murmur. "Be silent. The place may yet be inhabited, and we would do well not to disturb anyone dwelling within."

At last they reached the walls. Still no one appeared. The eerie silence was almost worse than if they had been challenged. Loren thought she would rather be back in the battle of Wellmont, for then at least the danger had been clear and certain—she needed only keep herself alive by fleeing it. That was better than this unspoken, uncertain dread.

"Here we are at last," said Albern in a whisper. "And it looks little different from how I remember it. What do you make of it, Jordel?"

"Were the gates closed when you came here last?" said Jordel.

"Aye," said Albern. "We scaled the walls to have a look inside. But we found nothing of worth within, and saw little purpose in lowering the gates, for you can see how the road curves around the walls to lead any travelers to the other side."

"You were robbing the place, then?" said Jordel, looking at Albern with a raised eyebrow.

Albern gave an easy smile. "If no one owns a thing, is it a crime to take it for yourself? You said this place must have been abandoned. Who is to care if we found a few spare pieces of—"

His words were cut short at the deafening toll of a bell.

The clamor of it nearly pitched them all from their saddles. The bell's toll was followed by a great blast of trumpets, many of them by the sound of it, both ram's horn and brass.

"We are found!" cried Gem.

"Silence!" hissed Jordel, clapping his hand over the boy's mouth. "Be still, you fool. There is no one there to see us."

"Still, that might change," said Albern. "Come with me! Quickly!"

He turned them right, dashing headlong for the side of the ridge from which the fortress emerged. Loren had thought the walls pressed right up against the stone mountain, but as they drew near she saw that it was not so. A small lane ran between the walls and the sheer rock of the ridge, the space scarcely wider than two horses side by side. Into this passage Albern led them, and then Loren saw the mouth of a cave.

"Inside!" said Albern. They scrambled in and out of sight as quickly as they could, then turned to listen as the horns continued to blare.

"How did you know of this place?" said Gem.

"This is where we slept the last time I came," said Albern. "The cave runs far back and connects with others. Some emerge again on this side of the ridge, some on the other—you do not want to leave through those, though, for they open into empty sky."

"But what about the castle?" said Loren. "What is all the fuss about?"

"They have not seen us, or we would have heard shouts of alarm," said Jordel. "That must mean there is something else—on the other side of the fort, by the east gate."

Albern looked at him with interest. "How do you know of the east gate?"

"As I have said, this place was built by Mystics. I

could tell you how many bricks are set in the floor of the scullery."

"We must go and see," said Loren.

"We shall be killed!" hissed Annis, who still looked out of the cave fearfully, as though she expected invaders to come pouring in at any moment.

"We will not let them see us," said Loren. "I shall go alone, if no one cares to follow."

"No, you certainly will not," said Jordel firmly. "Albern, take her. Neither of you are to reveal yourselves. Only try to find out, if you can, how many are within the fortress, and what spurred them to ring the bell."

"As you say," said Albern.

Loren ran to Midnight and pulled her bow from the saddle. But Albern laid a hand on her shoulder and bade her to stop. "This is not the time for fighting. We go only to see what might be seen. Come quickly, for we might miss the show."

She nodded in reluctant agreement, and together they slipped from the cave. Loren sidled up to the wall behind Albern, walking toe-first to muffle her footsteps, and they moved east towards the other gate. Before they had gone very far, Loren heard a voice, and then another calling back in answer, ringing out from the wall above them.

"That will be the occupants," Albern whispered. "They must all be at the eastern wall to greet the new arrivals. That is why none were there to see us approach from the west. A marvelous stroke of luck, that."

"Indeed," whispered Loren, forcing herself not to wince. She did not like to rely overmuch on fortune. It seemed to her that if one was foolish enough to praise their own good luck, misfortune waited just around the next bend in the road to balance the scales.

They reached the southeast corner at last. Albern stopped abruptly, raising a hand to halt her as well, and then poked his head out. He stood there for a long time, until Loren grew impatient. She dropped to a crouch and stepped carefully up beside him, her head a few fingers below his. If Albern minded, he did not say so, only whispering, "At the first sign of trouble, turn and run."

Loren nodded, and then studied the road running east from the fort. It looked like the road they had climbed to get here, the same light grey stone set in the ground in the same fashion. Yet this road was not empty. Ten wagons traveled upon it, pulled by fine horses tall and strong. It seemed to Loren that the wagons had a familiar look.

Then the caravan drew closer, and Loren felt all the blood drain from her face. She shivered first, and then shook in earnest. She wanted to turn and run, yet she could not will her limbs to move. For leading the caravan was a carriage, much smaller than the wagons that followed it, and looking through the window of that carriage, Loren saw a face she had hoped never to see again. Grey eyes as sharp as they were cruel. Lips almost always turned in a small smile, but never a kind one. And skin dark as night, dark as Annis who waited in the cave behind them. It was the face of Damaris, scion of the merchant family Yerrin.

TWENTY-TWO

Loren could not tell Albern—she feared to make so much as a sound, especially now—so they watched in silence as the caravan proceeded. The front gate swung open with a crash, letting carriage and wagons pass inside the great stone walls. Then Albern tapped her shoulder and drew her back.

Rain began to fall as they slid back along the fortress wall, and by the time they reached the others it poured itself upon them. Albern told Jordel what they had seen—so far as he knew, a caravan like any other, proceeding into the stronghold. The Mystic listened in silence. But afterward he looked over Albern's shoulder to see Loren standing silent, arms folded around herself, staring at the floor.

"Loren?" he said. "What is it?"

She looked up at him, and then at Annis. "I . . . I know the caravan. I know whose it is."

"Who?" said Jordel, brow furrowing. But almost before the word had left his lips his eyes widened, and his lips parted slightly. He had guessed.

"Yes," said Loren. "It is a Yerrin caravan, and Damaris is with them."

There was a long moment of silence. Then Annis broke it with a scream.

"No! No, you are lying!"

Jordel pounced upon her, wrapping one arm around her shoulders and placing a hand over her mouth. She fought and kicked at him, even trying to bite his hand, though he would not let her. Albern ran to the cave mouth and looked up, peering back and forth, but he quickly turned back to them.

"No one is about, and the rain masks much of the sound in any case," he said. "But still—no more shouting."

"I cannot let you go unless you promise to be silent," said Jordel quietly. "I understand your feelings, but you will have us all captured or killed. Do you promise?"

Annis fell still, slumping in his arms. Tears leaked from the corners of her eyes. But she nodded slowly.

Jordel released her, and she fell to her knees on the cave floor. Loren went to her at once, lifting her up and finding a more comfortable place to sit against the wall.

"Is this a private matter?" said Albern. "For I do not find myself as alarmed at this news as it seems you lot think I should."

Gem stood by Jordel. His face had gone white, and his hands shook. "Damaris is a merchant, and a cruel woman. She nearly had us killed in Cabrus—well, Loren and me, at any rate."

"Did you steal from her?" said Albern, looking at them curiously. "Merchants are notoriously protective of their wares, and I should think even you two would know that."

"I took nothing from her," said Gem, raising his hands.

"I did," said Loren. "Magestones, the secret trade of their family. Their wealth has not been built only upon furs and spices and blades. They smuggle the rocks across the nine lands. That is how they came by such fortune. Also, to Damaris' mind, I took something far more valuable—her daughter."

Albern's eyes went to Annis, and for a moment he was dumbstruck. "Ah," he said at last. "Ah, I . . . oh dear."

"Indeed," said Loren. "Twice has she tried to have me killed. Third tries are charmed, they say, though I hope the charm is in my favor."

Albern shook his head. "Are all your journeys so fraught with peril and enemies, daughter of the forests? If so, and you are ever again in need of a guide through the mountains, mayhap you should warn him first."

"Never do I plan for such," said Loren, shaking her head slowly. "Yet always misfortune has a way of finding me."

"I sense more than misfortune at work here," said Jordel. "How could Damaris have come to this place? We did not even know our road would take us here."

"Nor did she, certainly," said Gem, scoffing. "She cannot be here looking for us."

Loren turned to Annis beside her. "Was this the caravan's destination? Did Damaris plan to come to the Greatrocks all along?"

Annis stared at nothing. At first Loren thought the girl had not heard. But then she shook her head. "I do not know. I was not privy to many of the discussions Mother and Gretchen had about our route. I knew only that we would be traveling all through Selvan, and mayhap to Dorsea after that."

"If they came north on the Westerly Road, the stronghold would have been only a small detour," said Albern. "A few days' ride at most. But they would have to know it was here, and occupied, or they could have had no purpose here."

"They must have known," said Jordel. "Why else would they have come? There are few places to trade at all, and no cities save for Northwood at its head. But Northwood is no place so grand as Wellmont, or even Cabrus, and I do not think Damaris would trouble herself to go there."

Annis swallowed hard and took a moment to breathe. "Then all this time, without knowing it, our steps have led us straight into my mother's arms, when all I wanted was to avoid her. We should have gone to Dorsea as I said. Or somewhere else. Anywhere but here."

"It is too late to ponder what we should have done," said Jordel. "Now we must decide what to do."

"Well, we cannot return the way we came," said Albern, "for now the guards will be back on patrol, and in any case I think we would still find the satyrs and harpies waiting for us. Nor can we leave by the road leading east, for that, too, will be watched."

"I do not mean to leave," said Jordel. "I mean to discover the business of the men within this fortress. They cannot be men of Selvan, for if the king were gathering such an army, I should have heard of it. But if not from Selvan, then who are they, and how have they mustered such strength of arms without anyone in my order knowing?"

"Are you certain no Mystics are aware of them?" said Loren.

Jordel stared at her, eyes blank.

"I do not know everything of the Mystics," said Loren. "Yet it seems to me that your order has many hands, and each does not always know what the others are holding. You say that some in your order will help you once we reach Feldemar, but not all of them. You say that Vivien reports to different masters than your own. Could not those other Mystics, placed highly and esteemed by your brothers, know of what transpires here? Could they not have withheld such information for their own schemes and purposes unknown?"

His face grew stony as she spoke. When she finished he gave a slow nod. "What you say is possible. Yet I hope it is not so. While some Mystics may play at intrigue and politics, still we are unified by the purpose of our order, to maintain a watchful peace over the nine lands. To find that some of our own had a hand in amassing an army, out of sight and without the knowledge of their brothers, would be dark tidings."

Loren thought she saw fear growing in the Mystic's eyes. "Jordel, I think you know who these men are," said Loren. "Or you may at least hazard a guess."

"I could guess many things," said Jordel. "Yet I would not, for it would be of little help, as we still would know nothing of the truth. And some things, some dark thoughts, may be given strength by voicing them aloud. No, I will not guess at who the men in this stronghold might be. I will only look, and see what may be seen with my own eyes, without fear making things greater than they are."

"Fear cannot make things seem any darker to me,"

said Annis in a small voice. "I do not think we shall escape this place. I think I shall find myself back in my mother's clutches, and once she has me, I do not think I shall ever escape again."

"I will not let her have you," said Loren. "Not while life still beats in my heart."

"If your heart is all that stands between us, I have little hope," said Annis. "Do you think she will hesitate to cut it out?"

Loren had no answer to that. Damaris had spared her life before; even when Loren had thought the merchant meant to kill her with a poisonous serpent, she had later discovered the snake's venom was not fatal. But she had little wish to rely on the merchant's mercy ever again. Annis, in Damaris' clutches, might face a terrible rebuke and a lifetime of watchful eyes. Loren would more likely have her throat slit.

She shook off such thoughts. They would not help her. And what was it Jordel had said? *Some dark thoughts may be given strength by voicing them aloud.*

"What do you mean to do then, Jordel?" said Loren. "Whatever it is, let us begin, for I wish to be quit of this place as soon as we may."

"We shall have to get inside," said Jordel. "Some of the guards and soldiers in the stronghold must know why Damaris is here. That is something I should very much like to know. I think it strange that Vivien and her masters would not know of Damaris' intention to come here, yet if she knew, she told me nothing."

"Get inside the fortress?" said Gem. "Those walls are quite tall. I am not unskilled when it comes to climbing, but I doubt I could scale them."

"But I doubt you have ever infiltrated a fortress," said Jordel. "Gaining the ramparts will be the easier part, I think. Once inside, we shall have to blend in to discover what is going on."

Gem raised a finger and opened his mouth, but Jordel silenced him with a look. "I am sorry, Gem, but you cannot come on this venture. You are only a child, however mighty your heart might be. I must do it, and I will bring Loren, for though she is young, she is very tall."

"And Albern, surely," said Loren, looking at him in surprise. "He looks like a soldier, and is well advanced in years."

"Well advanced, eh?" said Albern, giving her a wry smile. "I take it you mean that I am old." Loren floundered for an answer, but he raised a hand to stop her. "Perhaps I am, to one who so recently left childhood herself. And mayhap that age has given me more caution than I had in my youth, when I marched with sellswords. I will not come on this venture. I bear little interest in this stronghold, except that now I know it is a place to avoid if I ever guide any travelers this way again. I do not know, and do not care to know, who the men inside might be. And if they are dangerous—which I would assume for safety's sake, even if the lot of you were not so terrified at the arrival of this merchant—I have no desire to risk my life in their company. I am a guide, and nothing more, and you are my employers. If I had my way, we would be thinking of means to bypass the fortress entirely. You wish instead to break inside, and that is your choice, but I am not bound to help you."

"I guessed as much," said Jordel. "Though you do yourself a disservice by claiming to be nothing more than a guide, still I will honor your words. Only I will ask of you one favor."

He went to Albern, reaching into his coin purse and then pressing gold into the bowyer's palm.

"If anything should happen to Loren and me, I hope you will ensure that Gem, Annis, and Xain make it safely out of the Greatrocks."

Albern looked down to find eight gold weights in his hand. "This is far more than you promised me."

"Upon this journey you have found more than you bargained for. And you will face greater dangers still, if you must escape the mountains without Loren and me."

Albern took Jordel's hand and returned the coins to it. "It seems I have acquired your skill for bargaining, Jordel of the family Adair. I will not take more than you promised—nor, indeed, will I take as much as was pledged, for I would see the children and the wizard to safety whether or not you asked it of me. And I will not let you march off into death with a clear conscience. You owe me more gold when we reach

Northwood—and not before. Be sure you are there to pay me when the time comes."

"Only a guide indeed," said Jordel with a smile. "Very well, then. I return your generosity with a promise: if by any action I can ensure our safe return, I will do so. And one more thing."

He drew Albern aside, near the mouth of the caves, and they whispered for a moment. Loren strained her ears, but she could not hear the words. They spoke only a moment, and then Jordel turned to her.

"Come now, Loren. Let us set out, for the sooner we return, the sooner we may leave this place, as you wish. And do not leave your black cloak behind—for this is a time when we shall need the Nightblade."

TWENTY-THREE

While Loren fetched her black cloak, Jordel shed his brown one and placed it, folded, within his saddlebags. They slipped out of the cave and into the rain, running first to the base of the castle's wall before creeping along it as she had done with Albern before.

When they reached the southwestern corner, Jordel stopped for a moment and turned to her. "I told you this place was built by Mystics," he said. "And our strongholds have always been built with a back entrance. We know the value of information, and a messenger sent out in the night may break a siege when the army inside cannot."

"You know a way in, then?" said Loren.

"Perhaps, but only if they have not barred the door. I hope they have not, and that they do not even know of the entrance I speak of."

So saying, he took her around to the northern side of the stronghold. The great stone shelf narrowed on that side to only a few paces across, and Loren looked at the cliff's edge with some apprehension. She could see the value in such a design: even if an attacking army were to send some of its soldiers around the sides, they could be easily shoved into the abyss by defenders with stones, or perhaps long polearms. Any ladders they raised could be cast off, flinging men to the valley floor.

But she could see nothing of the door Jordel had spoken of, only the same stony surface as the rest of the walls, well-laid with mortar. Yet Jordel walked with clear purpose until he had come to the center of the northern wall. There he paused for a moment, feeling around with his fingers.

"What are you looking for?" whispered Loren.

"There will be a catch," said Jordel. "It should be . . . ah! Here."

His fingers slipped into a crack Loren had not seen, and he pulled on something. She heard a sharp *click,* and the stones began to shift. They swung in on great iron hinges, though Loren heard almost no sound—

the small scrape of stone grinding on stone was muffled by the rain that pelted them.

As soon as the gap was wide enough to enter, Jordel slipped in and waited for Loren to follow him. Once inside they pushed the door shut again and found themselves in utter blackness. Though she could feel Jordel's breath on her face, she could not see him.

"I wish I had brought a torch," he quipped. "Come. We shall have to feel our way. Place your hand upon my shoulder."

She did as he said, and slowly he led her forwards with one hand on the wall. They did not go very far before he stopped abruptly. Loren reached past him to feel a wooden surface blocking their way.

"A door?" she whispered.

"More likely a shelf. Be quiet a moment."

She felt him lean forwards, and she pushed past him to do the same. Together they pressed their ears to the wood, straining to hear any sound. But after several moments, Loren had heard nothing.

"It seems the cells are unoccupied," said Jordel. "That is good. Come, help me move this."

Together they pushed, and the shelf swung away on the same silent hinges as the stone door through which they had entered. Within, at last, there was some light—the very faint glow of a torch, but after the darkness of the passage it seemed bright as the sun. Loren saw a hallway lined with stone cells stretching away from them, each barred by an iron door. The shelf they had moved stood at the end of the passage. There was no one in sight. The door at the hallway's other end had a torch set into the wall just beside it.

"They have set a torch," she observed. "That means they must come here every so often."

"Just so. We would do well to leave before anyone sees us."

First they pushed the shelf back against the wall, sealing the passageway entrance. Then Jordel led her at a quick, crouching run to the front of the hallway. Again they pressed their ears to the wood, and again they heard only silence.

"Beyond, we shall find a passageway," said Jordel. "To the right there will be a barracks, which we should avoid at all costs. But to the left there will be a guard-room, empty except at the changing of the watch. Follow me there, as quietly as ever you can."

He swung the door open—and its hinges screamed as they turned. But there was nothing for it unless they wanted to go back, so they darted through and down the hallway, closing the door behind them with another terrible squeak from the hinges. Only a few paces down, they found the door Jordel had mentioned and slipped inside. The room was empty, and they halted on the other side, breathing hard as they listened. There was only silence.

"A stroke of luck," said Jordel. "It seems your fortune is not entirely ill."

"If my fortune were any good, I would not be in this place at all," said Loren.

"Do not be so quick to judge your fate. Look."

At the back of the room was a hearth with a low fire burning—but beside it sat many chests of drawers. Jordel opened them, and inside they found clothes of grey and dark blue, as well as shirts of chain and helmets. The helmets had slits for the eyes and another slit down the front for the mouth, but other than that they covered the face entirely. There were also swords, very plain, and belts to hold them.

"Uniforms for the guards, no doubt," said Jordel. "A great stroke of fortune. Come, dress quickly."

He threw the clothes on over his own, along with a dirty grey cloak, and traded his own broad sword for one of the blades in the chest. Loren, too, put the uniform on over her clothes. They stank of sweat and grease and ale, but she had smelled far worse. The helmets were another matter. The stench of others' breath had permeated them, and no matter how many she tried on, they all contained the reek. Most were also too small, and when she finally found one that would go down on her head, it jiggled uncomfortably.

"Put up the hood of your cloak to cover your hair," said Jordel. "Any woman among the guards would likely have cut hers short."

When they had finished, Loren hardly recognized the Mystic—or, looking down, herself. "I feel I could walk straight up to Damaris and greet her, and she would never look twice at me."

"Mayhap you are right, but let us not chance it," said Jordel. She could barely see his smile through the slit in his helmet. "Come. Let us see what may be seen. Whoever commands this stronghold will be in the main hall, the doors of which are often open. That is where we shall go first."

They returned to the hallway. There was no one about. Jordel turned right, leading her past the door to the cells where they had come in. Next they passed the barracks he had mentioned—thankfully the door was closed, though Loren could hear voices on the other side. The hallway turned left soon after, and they rounded the corner with it.

Loren almost froze. Coming down the hallway towards them were two guards dressed in the same clothes as themselves, though their helmets were off and held under their arms. They did not speak or laugh with each other, and their eyes went immediately to Jordel and Loren. She barely managed to maintain her composure and keep walking by his side. After a moment the other guards' eyes left them and grew bored, and they passed without comment. Once they had turned the corner, Loren let out a long breath.

"That went well," murmured Jordel. "And tells us something valuable. Do you know what it is?"

Loren thought hard. The guards could not have seen their faces, but surely had seen their eyes. And anyone could recognize a friend, or even a comrade, by eyes alone.

"The guards do not know each other well," said Loren. "So either there are a great many of them here, or else none have been here very long."

"Yet you see how threadbare the clothes are, and how tarnished the blades," said Jordel. "So it is the former; there are many soldiers here, enough for it to be no great surprise to see another guardsman you do not recognize at once. New guards likely arrive often, coming in caravans like the one Damaris led here. But come. Here is the main hall."

A great threshold lay ahead and to the right, with its wide wooden doors thrown open. Loren tried to walk as Jordel did, in a sort of half-march while resting her left hand upon the hilt of her sword. As they passed the doorway, she turned her head to the right as though idly curious. In the moment it took them to cross the door, she took in the room beyond.

The great hall was many paces long, with large stone pillars that rose into arches to support the ceiling. The floor was all of white stone, though it had grown dirty and Loren could see rubbish in the corners. High above, near the ceiling, many rafters of thick wood crisscrossed the space. The largest stretched all the way across the room, to small windows that let in blue moonslight to battle the orange glow of the torches set along the walls.

At the other end of the hall sat a large wooden

chair upon a dais—almost a throne, though not quite grandiose enough to earn the name. Upon that chair sat a huge brute of a man, bare arms thickly muscled and covered with designs inked into the skin, leaning one elbow on the chair's arm while his chin rested in his palm. His black hair hung thin and long, ratty and filthy, and on his chin was a thick scrub of beard. He wore a dark breastplate over a leather tunic with no sleeves. Plates covered his legs as well, which ended in great steel boots that had small spikes worked into the toes. About the room in positions of rest stood several guards, covered head to toe in metal, with great longswords hanging from their hips. Before the dais knelt a page dressed in green—*a man of the family Yerrin?* Loren thought—whose head was bowed and who spoke words she could not hear.

But more than to the man on the chair, Loren's eyes were drawn to the symbol displayed over his head: a great design worked in black metal and gold, affixed to the wall behind him at the back of the room. The black was woven into sharp, twisting shapes that wrapped about each other in an endless knot, jutting out in all directions with sharp points. She did not recognize it, but still it seemed somehow familiar. With a start, she realized it resembled the markings on her dagger, and her hand fell to its hilt beneath her grey cloak.

She could feel Jordel seize up beside her as they passed the door, though she could not be certain why. Mayhap he had recognized the man on the chair, or mayhap the symbol meant something to him. Once they were out of sight of the main hall, she whispered, "Who was that? What did you see?"

"Speak later," said Jordel. "We should not be seen muttering to each other."

The hallway stretched a long way farther on before turning left again, continuing a circuit that would lead them around the walls of the stronghold and back to where they had started. Jordel passed every door, peering in casually whenever one stood open. They saw another barracks, and once they passed a door just as a guard came through it—beyond was another room full of cells, just like the one they had entered. At last, when they had neared the southeast corner of the fortress and the end of the hallway, they saw a room with many tables laid out, and a cooking pot resting on sticks above a fire. A handful of guards sat at the tables eating, fortress men in grey and blue alongside Yerrin men in green. Here Jordel paused and turned to her.

"We shall go in here for just a moment. Do not remove your helmet for any reason, nor speak. If anyone asks, I shall answer them. We cannot risk the Yerrin men recognizing you—but they will not know my face, for I have had few dealings with them."

Loren almost answered him, but instead nodded mutely. Jordel smiled.

"Well done. Come."

He walked in, bold as daylight, going to a table very near the cooking fire and removing his helmet as he sat. Two stronghold guards sat there, a thick woman with hair so dark it was almost black, and a thin, ratty man with one of his front teeth missing. They barely looked up as Jordel sat across from them.

"Ho," said Jordel, nodding. He scooped up a half-eaten bowl of stew, abandoned by some other guard, and dug in with his fingers. The ratty man eyed him for a moment at that, but soon returned his gaze to his own food.

Loren studied them, trying to see if she could learn anything from their actions. They seemed almost determined not to notice anyone or anything around them, hardly raising their eyes from the table. She looked past them to the Yerrin guards a few tables over. Their eyes roamed more freely, but in them Loren could see distrust and annoyance. They did not want to be here, and most likely saw these guards as beneath them.

The thick woman looked at Loren after a moment and raised her chin. "Do you mean to eat, or sit sweating in that helmet all night, girl?"

"A new recruit," said Jordel. "She said she lost her appetite."

"New and green, that is plain to see," said the ratty man. "And I do not just mean her eyes."

"Speaking of green," Jordel said, tossing his head towards the Yerrin guards, "what about these ones, eh? They have a lordly bearing, that is certain."

The thick woman grunted. "That is what happens

when you work for lords and ladies—the high ones on the King's Seat, anyhow, not like the Lord."

The Lord. Loren heard in their voices the same reverence—and fear—she had heard from the satyrs. It must be the man sitting on the great chair in the main hall. But who was he?

"You mean that pretty one, eh?" said Jordel. "I have not heard what she is doing round here. What do you know?"

They both stopped eating and looked up at him. "You know no one has spoken of her purpose here, nor will they."

Jordel looked conspiratorially over his shoulder and leaned forwards, fingertips pressed to the table. "Of course—but some whispers always seep through the cracks."

The thick woman stood abruptly, the ratty man rising to join her a moment later. Both scowled down at Jordel as though he had given some great offense. "It seems you are as green as the girl you sit with," said the woman. "Still your whispering tongue, newcomer, or you might find it cut out."

They left the common room without another word. Loren moved to leave the table, but Jordel placed a hand on her arm.

"Stay for a moment while I eat," he muttered. "We must not seem nervous—now more than ever."

So she forced herself to sit still, though every part of her wanted to flee the room and the stronghold both, vanishing into the mountains as Albern had advised. But after a moment, another man came to sit with them. This one was broad as Jordel, and mayhap a bit taller. His long, sandy hair hung freely to his shoulders, and while his eyes were dark they glittered nonetheless. An easy smile rested at the corner of his mouth, and Loren thought she might find it there often.

"Do not mind those two," he said to them. "They are not half the old salts they want to appear—just experienced enough to want to make others feel less so."

"I know the sort," said Jordel. "But have no fear; it takes more than two ratty guards to put the fright in me."

"That is good to hear," said the newcomer. "Courage will matter more than petty politics if a fight comes."

"Is one coming, then?" said Jordel. "That would be more entertaining than walking a wall all day."

"You and I like different kinds of excitement, it seems," said the man, eyes twinkling as he surveyed Jordel's face. Then he leaned in closer, dropping his voice. "But mayhap we shall both have our wish. These greencloaks bring cargo for the Lord, weapons or some such. I have heard the Lord wants them badly, but you would never know it—the Yerrin woman has been waiting for his audience since she arrived. But her wait is nearly over, for she will be received soon. I brought the message to her room myself."

His talk of "weapons" held meaning for Loren. Damaris was here to bring magestones. The merchant must have retrieved more, for Loren had destroyed most of her stores before fleeing the city of Cabrus. But Yerrin's reach was long, and doubtless they had many more of the precious gems stored about the nine lands.

Loren did not want to think what this stronghold, peopled by mysterious men and ruled by an unknown Lord, would need with so many wagons full of the things. It seemed Jordel was right, and that the battle in Wellmont had been only the first step in some much greater plot.

She thought she understood, now. These soldiers must be from Dorsea. With their army invading from the south, they were amassing a secret strength in the Greatrocks to attack Selvan from the west.

They had to do something about it, though Loren did not have the faintest idea what. She supposed they could warn Selvan's king, but that road was one she could hardly imagine, even if she were not riding with an outcast Mystic and a wizard ravaged by magestones.

If Jordel guessed at her thoughts, he gave no sign. He only nodded mutely and dug the last of his stew from the bowl with his fingers. After licking them clean slowly, he stood and adjusted his belt. "It is nice to know there is at least one friendly face in these walls. Well met, friend, and may we sup again another time."

Loren realized she was still sitting and leapt quickly

to her feet. She mumbled something under her helmet, but their friend never noticed, holding his eyes on Jordel. "Well met indeed. Try not to drown in all this rain."

Jordel gave a light laugh and walked out, Loren hurrying after him.

TWENTY-FOUR

JORDEL LED HER AWAY FROM THE MESS HALL AND through the stronghold's corridors back the way they had come. At first Loren thought he must be bringing them to the exit, but he strode right past it and back to the guardroom. Thankfully it was still empty, and he threw the bolt behind them after they closed the door.

"Did I guess right from his words?" said Loren. "Did Damaris come all this way to bring her magestones to this stronghold?"

"That would be my guess," said Jordel. "And it explains why she should come on such a roundabout path. If she were to ride straight for Northwood, she would surely have caught the attention of the King's law."

"We must warn Selvan, I suppose," said Loren, her mind turning to how they could possibly cross the whole kingdom with the Mystics and constables both at their heels.

"Hm? No, we can send no word of this yet," said Jordel, as if distracted. "Not until we have tended to more pressing matters."

"What could be more urgent? These are Dorsean men, intent on invading Selvan."

Jordel shook his head. "I wish that were so, but it is not. These are no men of Dorsea, nor any of the nine lands, I fear. They are something far darker, far more terrible. When first I saw this stronghold I thought I might find them within, though I held to a faint hope that it would not be so."

"Who are they, then?"

Jordel shook his head and paced the room. From within his helmet, his keen blue eyes pierced hers of green. "You remember that in Wellmont I spoke with Xain? I told him much that I have told few other souls, much more than it seems I should have. I am not eager to repeat that mistake again, yet I must trust you with some of it."

"I have shown you time and again that I am worthy of such trust," said Loren.

"So you have." He hesitated a moment before nodding. "So you have. Then know this: the men in this stronghold are Shades, a name that for centuries was nothing more than a frightened whisper in the dark. Yet some among the Mystics remember them, and I recognized the symbol they have hung above the throne in the main hall."

"And yet I have never heard of them," said Loren. "Are they a type of wizard, then?"

"No, nothing so simple," said Jordel. "In truth they are like the Mystics. Some of their number are among the Mighty of the nine lands, while some are simple soldiers like me."

"You have never been a simple soldier," said Loren. "But if these Shades are like the Mystics, why are they so feared? I thought the Mystics obeyed the will of the High King."

"So we do. But they are like us only in formation. Where we are light, they are the darkness. Where we are red, they are the ghostly grey of death. They serve a master far more terrible than any Wizard King you have heard of in tales—or they served her, I should say, for they have not been seen in many hundreds of years."

"Do you mean the man in the main hall?" said Loren. "Is he the Lord the satyrs spoke of?"

"No, I very much doubt that. Their master would not be seated so clearly in view, and yet in such a mean place as this. The master's place is atop the gilded throne of a kingdom torn to rubble, or else in the shadows of a land about to fall."

Despite the darkness of his words, Loren thought she could see a sense of excitement growing within him, an itching impatience that made his fingers twitch and his feet stamp. He resumed his pacing, a growing light in his eyes.

"But if she is back—or he, I might say, for it could be—then that means the other, too, has returned. I have not been misled. After all this time, I can tell my masters with certainty. And yet no, not yet. Some other purpose may have brought the Shades here. We must learn more."

He was talking to himself now, and though Loren understood the words, their deeper meaning eluded her. She gripped his arms and turned him towards her. "Jordel. What master do they serve, and if no one has seen her in centuries, how can she still live? You speak of her as if she were Elven-kind."

Jordel shook his head. "No, nothing like that. Then we would certainly be doomed. Now there is still hope. But we must learn what Damaris is doing here. And more than that, we must learn how much she knows of the Shades. They must be powerful, more powerful than I could have dreaded, if they have kept her waiting so long since her arrival. Seeing how the man in the main hall comports himself around Damaris will be as valuable as hearing the words they speak."

"I still do not understand. You have explained nothing."

"I have told you all I know for certain," said Jordel.

"They are Shades, and they once served a dark master who means to do no good to any within the nine lands. I do not know if they serve her still, or how great her might may have grown. This could be some forgotten remnant of their number, hiding in the caves of the Greatrocks for centuries, who have only recently emerged to take this stronghold. Yet I do not think so. It is far more important to learn what Yerrin is doing here, and what Damaris hopes to gain from associating with such dark partners in trade."

"And just how do you mean to do that?"

Jordel smiled. "The answer is simple, though you will not like it. I mean to attend her meeting with the master of this stronghold."

Loren felt her stomach clench. The thought of being in that long hall at the same time as Damaris made her ill. But she steeled herself—this, after all, was the sort of life the Nightblade should expect. "You mean to be one of the guards in attendance, then? At least we are dressed for the part."

"I do not think so," said Jordel. "Who knows if the master of the stronghold will even allow guards to attend? And if he does, we should not test our guises so stringently as that, for no quartermaster would be as easily fooled as the soldiers on patrol have been."

"How, then?" said Loren. "I can keep from being seen in my black cloak, most of the time, but I cannot become invisible—nor can you, unless you have some magic you have not shown me before."

"No. I think we require a more ordinary sort of trickery here. Did you see the roof of the great hall when we passed by?"

Loren cast her mind back. She remembered great wooden rafters stretching above, and set high in either wall, large windows that stood open to the rainy sky, giving the whole place a gloomy chill. "You mean to sneak in through the windows? But how can we get there?"

Jordel went to one of the room's cabinets and searched through its drawers. From the bottom one he pulled a length of rope. "With this. The rear of the hall is joined to the keep, which rises to the pinnacle of the stronghold—a final refuge against any invading force, from which the commander and his chosen guard can hold off an army. The top of the tower reaches some ten paces above the roof of the hall. You should be able to climb down to it easily enough."

She balked at his words. "*I* should? You speak as if you will not come with me."

"Who will lower you down? And if some other guard should happen by, who will turn their eyes from the rope tied to the battlements? It must be you, Loren—but I have great faith in you, and I know you shall not fail me."

Loren wished she had his faith. But she had little choice other than to obey; and indeed, she much preferred the idea of perching in the rafters above the hall to the thought of standing in attendance while Damaris was there.

"Very well. What must I do?"

"Only listen," said Jordel. "Keep yourself from being seen—that should be easy, for it is a dark day and the rafters are shadowed. Remember everything that is said, even if you do not understand it, and then return to me when they are done. You must recall every detail, no matter how slight. The manner in which a word is said can be just as important as the word itself."

"I understand," said Loren. "Let us go, then, before I lose my nerve."

Jordel placed a hand on her shoulder and gave her a smile. "I admit to knowing little of you, Loren of the family Nelda—less than I should, at any rate. But I know, at least, that you have no shortage of courage. Come."

First Loren ran to the drawer where she had hidden her black cloak. She folded it tightly and held it beneath her arm. Then Jordel tucked the rope beneath the folds of his cloak, and he led her from the guardroom into the torchlit halls of the stronghold.

TWENTY-FIVE

THE STRONGHOLD HAD SEEMED DARK ENOUGH BEFORE. Now it appeared even more gloomy, and Loren thought she could imagine a cloaked figure hiding in every shadow. Her heart thundered at her within her chest, like a great war drum beating hard in alarm. *Fire! Foes! To battle!* But there was no battle, and the guards they passed in the halls gave them no more scrutiny than before.

Jordel took a different way this time, left and around the corner, and soon to a staircase leading up. This took them to a small room with a fire set in one wall and two guards in chairs, huddled near the warmth of the flames. The guards barely looked up as Jordel proceeded swiftly to the door.

"Close that behind you," said one of the guards. "The latch sticks."

The sudden sound of his voice almost made Loren jump in fright, but she maintained enough control to nod hastily instead. When Jordel opened the door, she understood the words better: they found themselves outside, within the courtyard of the stronghold, and the wind had turned bitter.

She glanced around to get her bearings, trying to be inconspicuous. They had emerged from one of the gate towers in the stronghold's northern wall. Beside them was a great corral, and many horses stood inside it, pressing close to each other for warmth against the rain. The weather seemed even harsher than it had when they first arrived; Loren could not see more than five paces in any direction. But she could see that the eastern gate was now closed, and dim shapes in the gloom seemed to be the Yerrin caravan, arranged in rows in the courtyard. The drivers were smaller lumps atop the wagons, pulling their cloaks tight and shivering in the downpour. Loren knew those wagons contained magestones—those drivers would not be allowed to leave their posts for any reason, even if fire should rain from the sky.

Though more Yerrin men stood in rings around their wagons, they were not the only ones present. Loren saw many stronghold guards there as well, forming another ring around the caravan. But these guards were not present to keep anyone from straying too close to the wagons, she realized; they were there to keep the Yerrin guards from wandering too far away. The two groups faced each other in the downpour, both sides glaring, both trying not to show their discomfort in the cold and the wet.

Jordel pressed on quickly, turning left and leading her to the stronghold's other wall. From the gloom appeared the great hall, and above it, the keep. Tall and imposing, the walls of the keep were like a mountain all on their own, and though the real mountain stretched high above the structure, still Loren thought the keep was the more impressive sight. It was round, not square like most of the other towers, and it stretched into the sky for what seemed like twenty paces.

But they did not make for the keep—and drawing closer, Loren could see there was no door to enter it from the courtyard. Instead they made for a building built into the southeastern end of the courtyard, to a door just like the one in the gate tower. Inside was a room filled with arms, swords and spears and bows all lining the walls.

"The armory," said Jordel.

"I would never have guessed," said Loren. If Jordel knew it was a jest, he did not smile.

Another sharp turn and another door placed them in a corridor again, much like the one they had found when they first entered the stronghold, and Loren realized that they stood now within the southern wall. At the end of the hallway stood a great door that took up nearly the whole wall. It was made of iron, and looked to be very thick. Jordel went to it and knocked, and after a moment, a hatch slid open. On the other side, two beady eyes squinted at them.

"What is it?" said the woman.

"Orders from above," said Jordel, sounding weary. "It seems there is a leak in the roof. We have been sent to look at it."

The eyes squinted more tightly, and the eyes turned to Loren before sliding back to Jordel. "I have seen no leak."

Loren blanched, but Jordel barely reacted at all. He only shrugged and tossed his head behind him. "Nor have I, but then I have yet to enter the keep. I only know what I was told. I was a mason once, and so they have sent me to see if there is aught I can do."

"Who sent you?" said the guard. "If there was a leak, I should have heard of it."

"We are newly arrived," said Jordel. "I do not know his name—only that his rank was higher than mine, and most likely yours. A captain, I think."

Through the viewing hatch, her squinted eyes finally widened. "The . . . a captain? Ah . . . well, you had best come in, then."

The view hatch slid shut with a rusty shriek, and then Loren heard a thump as a bar was moved on the other side. The door slid inward, grating on the stone floor and filling the corridor with its scream. Jordel stepped in as soon as the gap widened enough, and Loren was quick to follow.

She found herself in a room that seemed small, but when she took a second look she saw that it stretched quite far in every direction. But the ceiling was low enough to touch, if she jumped, making it feel cramped. Fine weaponry lined the walls, finer than that in the armory. Above a fireplace hung two swords crossed over a shield. Well-made spears stood in rows, and there were bows on display that put even Albern's fine crafts to shame. A great tapestry hung on the back wall, bordered in red and worked through with threads of gold and silver. In it Loren saw a tall figure in black armor holding a silver sword high, though she was not close enough to see any more details. To their right was another iron door, much like the one through which they had entered. If she had her bearings right, that door led into the stronghold's hall, behind the dais they had seen.

"Take the stairs all the way up," said the guard who had let them in. She was alone. Loren saw a small table and a single chair nearby. Though they were modestly carved, there was obvious skill in their making.

"Thank you," said Jordel. "Though I certainly will not enjoy going out into that rain again."

"Welcome to the Greatrocks," said the guard with an ugly look. "I wish we had never left the forest."

Loren's ears perked up sharply at that, but Jordel seemed not to hear. "I would know little of that," he said. "Stay warm."

Against the opposite wall there was a narrow stone staircase with no banister, and it vanished into the ceiling above them. They climbed it and found themselves on another floor just like the first—except this one had no weapons or tapestries on the walls, only a great table in the middle surrounded by many fine and cushioned chairs. A council room, then, from which the stronghold's commander could coordinate their defenses. The staircase ended, and Loren saw another one on the opposite side of the room, again vanishing into the ceiling.

"Why did they build it that way?" she said quietly. "Why not have only one staircase going all the way up?"

"Anyone who breaks into the keep must cross each floor before they can keep climbing," said Jordel. "It gives the defenders many places to retreat. Attackers cannot push all the way up a single staircase in one great surge. They must fight to take each floor, and conquer each staircase anew."

Loren nodded, imagining it. Soldiers fighting and dying for every pace of stone floor, blood pouring down the steps of each storey. She shuddered and hoped she would never know a battle like that, men killing each other just to own a few stone walls.

The next floor up held provisions and rations.

Great barrels lined one wall, likely filled with wine or ale, while everywhere there were great sacks holding flour and wheat and even some vegetables. A few had spilled out upon the floor, and Loren wondered how often the place was inspected. The next floor held beds, and one side of the room was blocked by a curtain—the quarters of the lord of the stronghold, no doubt, in times of siege.

A final staircase led to a wooden hatch. Jordel pushed against it, but it did not budge. He thudded on it hard with his fist, and when no answer came, with the hilt of his sword. Finally they heard footsteps above, and a sharp sliding sound as a latch was thrown. The hatch rose, and immediately they were pelted by raindrops.

Hastily they emerged into the rain atop the keep. Two guards stood there already, both huddling beneath their cloaks and cowls, trying to stay dry in the lee of the ramparts. It was a fruitless attempt; there was no place to hide from the downpour.

"We have only just started our watch," said one of the guards, shouting to be heard in the rain.

"I am not here to replace you," said Jordel. "I have been sent to look for a leak."

"There is no leak," said the guard.

"Well then, my search will be fruitless, but I have orders, same as you."

"Waste your time then, if you wish. It is no trouble to me." The guard turned from them with a shrug and went back to huddle away from the wind, crouching against the wall at the edge of the roof.

Jordel made a great show of his inspection. He went to the eastern side of the roof and crouched there, running his fingers along the seam between wall and floor. In a stooped walk he moved along, leaning down to look carefully at the joins between stone and mortar. He was so busy, in fact, that even Loren began to wonder if he actually had some skill in masonry. If not, he was certainly convincing enough. He was so animated in his inspection that soon the guards began to watch him curiously.

When he had come all the way around to the northern side, Jordel straightened and shook his head. Loren stepped closer, and the other guards craned their necks forwards to see.

"See here," said Jordel, looking to the guards and pointing down. "A chink in the mortar. Very small, hardly more than a hair's breadth. But water needs less than that to find a way in. This crack lets it run all the way through the walls and into the Lord's chambers."

Loren certainly did not expect the guards' reactions. Both of them recoiled, straightening where they stood and going white as sheets. "The Lord has arrived?" said one of them. "I had heard nothing of this. When?"

Jordel raised his hands quickly, shaking his head to calm them. "Apologies. I am newly arrived, and it is an affectation from my prior service. I was footman to a minor scion in the royal family once. I meant the commander of the stronghold."

The men sagged, like sealed sheep's bladders with the air suddenly let out. "The brute, he means," said one of them, sounding greatly annoyed. "Never call him by that name again, if you know what is good for you. If any of the higher-ups heard it . . ."

Jordel ducked his head, as though chagrined. "I will not do it again," he said. "My apologies. Please, let me do you a service to make up for frightening you. Leave this sopping roof and go get yourselves warm by a fire. Eat something, and let the chill seep from your bones."

The guards traded glances. Loren could read the eagerness in their eyes, but also their fear. "I have traveled with him for many a league," she said, jerking a thumb at Jordel. "Once he sets to his stonework, he will be at it for hours. Tell the woman downstairs we shall be here till sundown at least. Or, that is, what passes for sundown in this weather." She looked up at the sky, where the sun was not so much a glow as a part of the sky that was slightly less dark than the rest.

Still the guards hesitated. "No one has told us we are relieved."

"The captain sent him," said Loren. "When we told her that below, she snapped right into line. Mention it if you must. Besides, what kind of watch can you be keeping? I can scarcely see my hand in front of my eyes."

The guard who had opened the hatch for them gave a rueful laugh. "She speaks true enough. That is fair. We shall thank you for your kindness, then, and once more advise you: never call another the Lord, not unless you mean who you say."

"I will not," said Jordel. "And thank you in return."

The guards hurried through the hatch in the roof. Loren closed it behind them, and then slid into place the wooden bar that held it shut.

Quickly she threw off her guardsman's cloak, shivering for a moment in the chill, and donned her black one instead. Immediately the rain seemed to lessen—the thick, velvety cloth kept the water from soaking through, while also lessening the chill of the wind that pelted her. Compared to before, she felt almost warm. Meanwhile, Jordel unfurled the rope and tied it quickly around one of the ramparts on the northern side. He let the rest of the length drop down into the grey.

"The hatch is sealed. You could still come with me."

"When stealth is required, fewer bodies are harder to see," said Jordel. "Besides, what if someone came and wanted to open the hatch? How would it look if neither of us answered?"

"How will it look if you answer, and I am nowhere to be found?"

"I shall think up some excuse. Or throw them into slumber a bit quicker than they might wish."

"But not kill them," Loren said, looking into his eyes.

He met her gaze a long moment, blue eyes almost glowing in the faint light that managed to seep through the clouds. "Not unless I have no other choice."

"They are only soldiers, following orders."

"I have told you, they are Shades," said Jordel. "You cannot know the evil that drives them."

"They have eaten with us. You have made jokes with them. They seem to represent no more evil than any other we have met by chance upon the road. No doubt some are here only for the coin. You know the Shades' dark history. Do these men?"

"Enough, Loren," said Jordel firmly. "I promised when I took you into my service that I would not force you to fight, nor to harm another. I made no pledge for myself, but you know I will not do so if there is another way. If you thought so little of me, you would not be in my company now. But you are, and now we have work to do."

Loren's jaw clenched. But the Mystic was right. Even now, Damaris might be in the hall below, meeting the stronghold's commander—"the brute," as the guard had called him.

She went to the wall and pushed herself up, sitting on the edge of it. It was a great height, but she had spent half of her life at the tops of trees, looking down at the ground far below. Gripping the rope, she slid from the rampart's edge.

The rope swayed beneath her, and for a moment Loren spun out of control, her left shoulder slamming into the stone wall. She gritted her teeth and forced herself to hold still, letting the sway of the rope bring her around. Once she stilled, she planted her feet on the stone and began to lower herself hand over hand. She whispered a quiet prayer of thanks for her years spent climbing and the strength it had given her arms.

But a tree with branches was quite different from a rope made slick with rain. As she went farther and farther down, the rope grew ever wetter, soaking up the rain that had been unable to reach it beneath Jordel's cloak. Her hands slipped once, but she swiftly recovered, wrapping her whole body around the rope. But moving her feet from the wall made her swing again, and she thudded painfully into the stone. It was a moment before she could steady herself with her feet, and by the time she did, her hands had gripped the rope so tightly they were almost frozen.

She leaned forwards and breathed on them a few times, trying to imbue them with warmth, but it was fruitless against the biting chill. Her best hope was to descend as quickly as she could, while her fingers still felt anything at all. Faster now she began to slide down, but each time it was harder to grip the slick line.

Finally, disaster struck. Loren's boots slid out from under her, and she swung towards the wall. She struck it with a crash, and her fingers loosened against her will. Air screamed in her ears as she plummeted, and without thinking she seized the rope again. It sliced through the skin of her palms like a knife, and she cried out with the pain of it.

The roof flew up to meet her, and she slammed into it on her back. The impact knocked the breath from her and left her gasping, but she had no time to recover—the slope was slick with rainwater, and she began to slide towards the roof's edge. She scrabbled to catch a hold, but the shingles slid beneath her bloodied palms. Sharp stabbings told her of splinters sinking into her flesh.

Loren rolled, flipping onto her back, and the thick cloak slowed her descent—but not nearly fast enough, for the edge still sped towards her. She planted the soles of her boots, but that was a mistake. Her boots caught, but her speed made her flip up, so that for one brief second she stood before pitching forwards again towards the edge, now headfirst.

She tried desperately to twist around again, but only managed to turn sideways before reaching the roof's edge. That saved her life. There was a tiny lip, no more than a few fingers high, and she struck it with her whole body. Still she nearly went over, but she managed to hang on with one arm and one leg wrapped around the stone lip. Her cloak dangled into the empty air, weighing her down. She groaned hard as she managed to pull herself back up, flopping onto her back at the very edge, tucked against the lip.

For a long moment she lay there, trying to still her hammering heart. Images flashed in her mind, of her body spinning out into empty space to slam into the ground of the courtyard. Even if she survived the fall, she would be doomed; surely the guards would see her, and then all would be lost.

Through the dim haze, Loren thought she could just glimpse the figure of Jordel peering at her over the edge of the keep's roof. She raised a limp hand and gave him a small wave. His face disappeared.

That is enough rest, she decided. She still had work to do. She forced herself to get up, though in truth she wanted to lie there forever and never rise again. Kneeling at the roof's edge, she peeked cautiously over the side. In the wall beneath her was a window, easily large enough to slip through. But it was more than a pace down, and its sill was not wide.

She would have to risk it. Much time had passed already, and who knew but that Damaris was already within the great hall, speaking with the stronghold's commander? Loren tried to still her shaking and bloodied hands, wrapping them around the stone lip at the edge with a grimace. Then she kicked off. Her body swung around and towards the window, her body slamming into the wall just above it. Now her feet were only a pace from the sill. But to reach it, she would have to drop.

A terrifying thought came to her mind. *Once I get down, how shall I get back up?* At that her nerves failed her, and she hung there for a long moment. She was too terrified to drop down, and too exhausted to pull herself back up. And her arms had begun to ache.

The choice was removed from her. The slick rainwater on the stone finally made her lose her grip, and she fell with a lurch in her stomach. Her feet found the sill, but she was still leaning too far backwards. She teetered, and for the second time pictured herself falling lifeless into the courtyard. But her hands acted when her mind could not, snatching the edge of the window, scrabbling at the stone. One of her nails ripped off in a chink between stone and mortar, but she found her grip. She pulled herself inside and out of the pouring rain.

She was in the hall—well, almost. A rafter sat only a pace ahead, at the perfect height for her to step forwards onto it. Almost she did so, but then she remembered her cloak. It was soaking wet. The last thing she wanted was for it to drip onto the floor as she hid in the rafters, for then they would surely find her. She reached up and untied the cloak from her throat, folded it quickly, and left it on the sill. Then she stepped onto the rafter, holding herself steady with one hand while sucking on her mangled finger to ease the pain. The ache in her palms had become a fire in the freezing air.

At once Loren saw her: Damaris, standing alone in the center of the hall, some five paces from the throne at the end. From so far up near the ceiling, Damaris looked very small indeed, and certainly not the imposing figure that Loren often imagined her to be.

Just behind Damaris stood a large man, broad and muscled, though not quite so imposing as the stronghold's commander that Loren had seen earlier. The guard wore a breastplate and had a helmet under one arm, while his other hand rested on the hilt of a sword nearly as long as Loren was tall. She knew him at once: Gregor, Damaris' personal bodyguard. Where Damaris was a serpent with two faces, Gregor was a battering ram. He had disliked Loren from the first, and nearly killed her even before she stoked the merchant's ire. Many of her most fearful dreams were of finally falling into his clutches. The other guards were unknown to Loren, but they stood close by their master and watched the room with wary eyes.

As she studied Damaris, her mind drifted back to the road where they had met. To Loren, the merchant had looked then as she did now: calm, serene, even kind—a worldly woman with a sharp eye and a quick tongue. It had not been hard for Loren to imagine the two of them working together, and even becoming friends in time.

She shook the thought away. She and Damaris would never be friends now. Not after Loren had seen her order the deaths of so many. Not after Cabrus, where she had ordered Loren thrown into a cell with a viper. For all that Damaris seemed to be, Loren had seen the merchant's true colors far too clearly to ever be fooled again.

But then all such thoughts vanished, for there was

a great groan at the head of the hall. Iron hinges wailed as a door opened, and from behind the dais emerged the commander, walking languidly to sit upon his chair.

TWENTY-SIX

Now Loren had more time to study the man than she had had before. Her first glance had told her much: he was as thickly wrapped with muscle as anyone she had ever seen; his face was covered with a great shag of beard; and his hair hung limp and greasy to his shoulders. But now she could better see the designs etched in tattoos across all his skin, for they were plainly visible under his leather vest lined with black fur. He wore no weapon, but one leaned against the arm of his chair: a great hammer, as long as Loren was tall, and its head was as large as hers. Two guards filed in behind him, taking positions on either side of his dais. Both were musclebound warriors in their own right, but neither came close to the immense bulk of their master.

The commander regarded Damaris coolly for a long, silent moment, and the merchant met his gaze unflinching. Loren wondered what they were waiting for, until finally Damaris collected her fine silk skirts and knelt in a deep curtsey that landed one of her knees on the floor.

"Hail, Commander Trisken, honored of the Lord, master of their forces here in Selvan," she said. "I, Damaris of the family Yerrin, come before you, as was promised to your master."

"My master and yours," said the man—Trisken, she had said his name was. His voice was deep and rumbling, and yet Loren had thought he would sound somewhat . . . stupider than he did. Though his deep bass reverberated within Loren's chest, his tone and inflection reminded her of Xain or Jordel, whose tongues flowed easily with the graces one expected at court.

"Of course," said Damaris, rising from her curtsey.

Her deference was so complete, so absolute. Loren had never heard her sound thus. Who was this man Trisken, and who was his master, that they could cow such a proud woman so easily?

"I greet you, Damaris of the family Yerrin," said Trisken, "and bid you welcome to my keep. You have no need of your guards here, and our further council will be conducted in their absence."

Gregor stiffened behind Damaris, but she turned her head at once and nodded. He hesitated only a moment before turning away and striding towards the great hall's door, motioning the other guards to follow him with a flick of his wrist. Once they had gone, guards in the hall swung the doors shut behind them. Now it was only Damaris, Trisken, and the guards on either side of his dais. *And me, of course,* thought Loren.

Trisken drummed his fingers on the arm of his throne. His nails were long, longer than Loren's at any rate, and they made a soft *tap, tap* upon the wood. "Your road here has been fraught with many dramatics, or so the Lord has told me."

"Nothing more than I could deal with," said Damaris, annoyance slightly tinging her voice. "Often the more foolish dogs of the King's law have snapped at my family's heels. Always we have dealt with them swiftly, for after all we have much practice."

"And yet, if the King's law were to learn of your journey's ultimate end, what then? The Lord would have greatly preferred it that no one took any more notice of your passing than a mouse creeping by in the night. And thus he bade you, very clearly."

A thin sheen of sweat broke out on Damaris' forehead. Loren felt her own stomach turn a flip, as though she stood in the merchant's place. She had never seen Damaris show so much as a moment's fear or hesitation, much less this long pause that seemed to stretch on for eternity. To her great surprise, Loren found herself wishing desperately that Damaris would turn and flee the great hall, for the air seemed suddenly fraught with danger.

"We took every precaution on our journey, and I am well-practiced in such plans," said Damaris. "But even I cannot predict every end. And ultimately, I was only betrayed by my own desire to help the Lord, for I found someone upon the road who I thought might one day serve him. But she betrayed us, as I could not have foreseen, and stole away that which is most precious to me."

With a start, Loren realized that Damaris was talking about her. Had that been the merchant's plan all along? To recruit her into the service of this Lord, whoever he might be? But then why had she tried to turn Loren over to the constables? Why had she had Loren pursued, and thrown into a cell?

But then again, Loren realized that even at their worst, Damaris' motives were never entirely clear. She had thrown a viper into that cell with Loren, where it had poisoned her with its bite, and yet later the apothecary had told her the venom was not lethal. And the merchant had spoken highly of her even in opposition, hinting at things Loren did not understand and lamenting that the two of them had not become friends.

At the time, Loren had taken her words for lies through a forked tongue, the subtle manipulations of a woman who excelled at controlling the fates of everyone she met. Now she was not so sure.

"I have heard all of this," said Trisken. "It does not concern me. All I care about is that you have done what the Lord commands—and for which he has paid your family most handsomely."

Damaris lifted her head slightly, seeming to find familiar ground again. "I have, Commander. And more than that. I bring you a bounty of magestones even greater than was promised—and for the excess, I have a boon to ask of you. Will you treat with me in the name of the Lord?"

The great hall fell to silence, marked only by the pounding rain on the roof and a gentle *tap, tap,* as Trisken drummed his long fingernails on the throne.

When finally he spoke, it was not in answer to Damaris' question. Instead he asked, "How is it that so simple a girl as has been described to me could thwart you so utterly? The Lord was not aware that the family Yerrin could be so helpless against one young child of the forest."

Loren's cheeks burned. Though she knew it for foolishness, a part of her mind felt as though he were speaking directly to her, as though he knew she lurked in the rafters and could hear him.

"You say a young child of the forest," said Damaris, and her tone had grown bitter now. "I thought the same. But since then, I have learned much that turns my mind in another direction. No doubt the Lord knows much of the doings surrounding the battle of Wellmont. But what he may not have heard is that this girl was in the company of Mystics all throughout that engagement, and afterwards as well, and was last seen still in their company. I know now what I could not before: she is their agent, a redcloak herself, but in disguise, and has had their help from the beginning."

At that, Trisken shot forwards in his chair. "Do you think the Lord has not guessed at this already? And do you think it pleases him? That you, Damaris of the family Yerrin, might very nearly have brought one of them straight here, to our stronghold in the Greatrocks?"

Damaris had made a mistake, and she knew it. Once more she fell into a curtsey, and this time she bowed her head.

"I would never have brought her here, Commander. I would have sent word to the Lord directly and had her vetted by one of his agents. The family Yerrin will never reveal the Lord or any of his places of power, this one least of all."

Loren took note of that to tell Jordel later. This was not the only stronghold of the Lord—whoever he was, for Loren still had no idea. Even more of interest to her was Damaris' mad theory, that Loren had been a Mystic all along. If she was not so fearful of being discovered, Loren might have found it funny.

"See that you do not," said Trisken in a voice of steel. "For if that were ever to come to pass, the Lord would end you. He would wipe the family Yerrin from the very face of history. No bard would remember any songs of you, and no tome would contain the record of your name. All the land you own would be burned and salted, a blight upon the face of the nine lands that all would know only as a nameless fear."

Damaris' head ducked still lower. "I know it, and my family knows it. We wish nothing more than to serve him."

"Then serve him by being more cautious with your dealings." Trisken sank back into his throne, going from angry to almost bored in an instant. "Now. You spoke of a boon you wish to beg of the Lord—in return for more magestones. What would you ask of him?"

Damaris waited a long moment, as though ensuring it was safe, before she finally rose from her curtsey. But still she stood cowed, with shoulders drooping and head bowed. "Commander, my boon and the Lord's concern are one and the same. Along our route I had planned to sell much of our cargo—for as the Lord well knows, Yerrin is valuable to him only so long as we continue to be profitable, and ensure that we can provide him with whatever he desires. But after Cabrus, I proceeded straight here as quickly as my caravan could travel. I sold no magestones to anyone else. As a consequence, I have half again the amount that the Lord purchased—and they are his, if he wants them."

Trisken shifted in his seat at that. Loren well knew that magestones were beyond value—and in fact were the true source of the family Yerrin's immeasurable wealth. Honest goods could only accumulate so much coin. Smuggling magestones for generations had filled the Yerrin coffers beyond accounting.

"That is a hefty cargo indeed," said Trisken. "And must accompany a hefty request."

"A request not so great for the Lord to carry out as it has been for me, I think. That is why I ask. I think that for your master—and mine—the task will be but a trifle. I ask that he finds my daughter Annis and returns her to me."

A small smile appeared at the corner of Trisken's mouth. Loren wondered if he had been expecting the question, for it did not seem to surprise him.

"I see. You have failed to track her down yourself, have you?"

"Many agents within our family have tried. And we have pressed many of our contacts within the Mystics to aid us. Yet therein lies the problem. If, as we both suspect, the girl Loren is allied with the redcloaks, then they will make every attempt to thwart our efforts to find her. And if we cannot find Loren, then we cannot find Annis, for I believe they still travel in company."

Trisken rapped his nails. *Tap, tap.* "Prudent thinking. But so much magestone seems a price too great, and I find myself suspicious."

"The Lord has considerable resources at his disposal," said Damaris. "Yet to mobilize them for such a task may cause him some minor annoyance. The magestones are a token, a gift to thank him for his kindness, in this smallest of matters."

"Smallest of matters indeed. I will beseech the Lord upon your behalf. You will leave your . . . token with me regardless."

Damaris did not answer that at first, and Loren caught a sharp jerk of her head. Trisken's eyes narrowed. Loren realized it was a test. He meant to make Damaris prove her loyalty by accepting her payment, but on different terms than those she had strictly offered.

Finally Damaris nodded. "Of course. As I said, they are a gift."

"Good. Then—"

Trisken's words were cut off as the front door of the great hall slammed open. The commander's guards leapt to the fore and drew their blades, and Damaris whirled—but it was only a stronghold guard, running in with her grey cloak fluttering behind her. She flew past Damaris to the foot of the dais and knelt.

"Commander," said the messenger. "We have found a small party of spies in the caves south of the stronghold."

Trisken shot to his feet. "How many? Have we taken them?"

"Not yet, but a force has been dispatched to bring them into the cells—or kill them."

TWENTY-SEVEN

Gem. Annis. Albern. No.

Trisken's guards sheathed their blades, but the commander went to the hammer that leaned against his throne. He seized its handle and, though it looked heavier than a boulder, lifted it easily to slide it into a sheath on his back. "Take me to the caves. Lady Damaris, your request has been heard. Wait for me within your quarters while I deal with this nuisance."

"Of course," said Damaris, curtseying a final time. Trisken swept past her and out of the room.

As if he had held her in a spell, once Trisken was

gone Loren found herself able to move again. She stood from her crouch in the rafters, wincing as her knees screamed with pain from holding position so long in the chilled air. Swiftly she slunk back to the rafter beside the window and stepped out to the sill.

As she clasped her black cloak around her once more, her gaze drifted upward. There was the lip of the roof, a pace above her outstretched hand. It seemed impossibly out of reach, but she had to try. Gem and Annis were in mortal danger, and Jordel did not even know it.

She let herself wait one long moment, then crouched and jumped as high as she could. The angle was wrong, and she nearly missed the grip. Her right hand slipped away, her left hand clinging desperately to the roof's edge. A spike of pain shot through her torn finger, and she gritted her teeth to keep from crying out. She swung out and away from the wall, thinking for a moment she would lose what little hold she had, before finally swinging back in and seizing the lip with her other hand. Every muscle in her arms and chest burned with the pain of her earlier fall and the biting air, but still she heaved with all her might. Her right elbow came up over the edge, and after a little more pulling and wriggling, she collapsed upon the rooftop in a heap.

But she could not take even a moment to rest. Leaping to her feet, she darted for the rope and seized it, wincing at the pain in her mangled hands. She tried to pull herself up, but that was far too slow.

The rope jerked, and suddenly she found herself flying upwards through the air. Looking up, she saw Jordel's strong gloved hands leaping over each other as he pulled her up one arm's length at a time. Loren wanted to keep climbing, to help him lift her, but the pain left her unable to do anything more than hold on as he tugged her to the top.

The Mystic seized her arm as soon as she was within reach and nearly flung her onto the rooftop. She lay on her back, gasping and clutching her hands between her knees, trying to stop the fire in her palms.

"Come, Loren. You must rise." Jordel seized her arm and pulled her up. "I heard shouting in the courtyard. If you have been discovered, we must flee, quickly."

"Not me," said Loren miserably. "It was not me they found. The others."

Jordel's keen blue eyes went wide as he froze. He looked at the hatch leading down, and then to the edge of the roof.

"We cannot go all the way back through the stronghold," he said. "It will take far too long. We will lower the rope over the outer wall and climb down that way."

Loren felt fear spread across her expression, and Jordel's eyes grew troubled. He seized her wrists and flipped her palms upward. His brows drew close at the blood and the sight of her finger where the nail had been torn free.

"We have to help them," he said softly. "Here. Take my gloves. They will help, at least."

He ripped them from his hands and gave them to her. Loren pulled them on gratefully. They were wet straight through from the rain, and she felt her blood begin to soak into the leather, mingling with the rainwater. Meanwhile Jordel untied the rope from the north end of the roof and retied it to one of the ramparts on the south side. He looked over the edge and turned back with a frown.

"It ends four paces from the ground," he said. "We shall have to take care with the final drop. Are you ready?"

"I must be," said Loren. Though her body did not wish to obey her, still she forced herself forwards.

"A moment," said Jordel, holding up a hand to stop her. In a few seconds he pulled the rope back up to the roof, then handed her the end of it. Loren took it in her gloved hands and looked up at him in question.

"I will lower you down," said Jordel. "It will be easier on you, and make you less likely to fall, I think."

Loren felt her heart flutter. "But . . . what if your grip should slip? What if guards arrive while you are lowering me?"

"It is not my grip I worry about, and if we are quick, no one will have a chance to come. Quickly! We have no time for argument."

He lifted Loren up as if she were a child and perched her on the edge of the rampart, then took the rope in his thick hands. At his nod, Loren pushed herself from the edge.

She felt the rope give slightly in Jordel's grip, and in a panic she thought he was losing her already. But it was only his arms stretching to full length, and she jolted to a stop just a pace down. She planted her boots on the wall the way she had before, an attempt to control her descent and lessen Jordel's burden however she could.

Loren need not have worried. Jordel's hands moved swiftly, end over end as he lowered her quickly down the stronghold's outer wall. She felt for one mad moment that she was walking backwards down the stones, as if they were a floor and she were playing some children's game.

Just as Jordel had said, the rope ended four paces from the ground. Loren stopped with a jolt and looked up to see Jordel's face peering over the rampart. Now she must drop the rest of the way. She let her feet fall free of the castle wall, dangling at a height nearly double her own.

I must let go, she thought. *Annis and Gem need me.*

Her frozen fingers finally obeyed her, and she plummeted through the air.

Loren had spent long years dropping from trees in the Birchwood, and knew how to absorb the shock of a landing in her legs. But the ground of the Birchwood had been soft loam, and now she landed on rock. Her ankle twisted beneath her, and she fell backwards, landing hard and slamming her head on the stone. After the blow Xain had given her in the cave days ago, this felt like a spike had lodged itself in her brain. For a moment she lay senseless, mouth open in a wordless scream, unable to move. When she lifted her head, it hurt—but not quite so badly as she had feared. And when she tried to move her ankle, it responded with only a small twinge of pain.

"Not so bad as it could have been," she muttered to herself, climbing to her feet—and then leaping quickly out of the way, for Jordel had scurried down the rope like a squirrel down a tree. Already he had reached the bottom. He hit the ground a pace from her and tumbled into a somersault before landing on his back, then leapt to his feet.

"Are you hurt?" he said.

"Not badly," said Loren. "Let us go."

Jordel led the way along the stronghold wall back to the cave where the others lay hidden. *Not hidden any longer,* thought Loren.

The stronghold guards came into view first. Several lurked outside the cave mouth, hidden around the edge of the stronghold. Loren soon saw why: three bodies lay just outside the mouth of the cave, arrows sticking from their chests like flagpoles.

Loren ducked for the stronghold wall on instinct so that the soldiers would not see them—but Jordel pushed onwards, and then she remembered that they still wore guard uniforms. So she followed closely behind him, throwing back her cowl and casting her cloak back over her shoulders, so that hopefully the other guards would not notice it was black, not grey. But she made sure the edge of the cloak still concealed her dagger, which hung near the back of her belt.

One of the guards spotted them. "Take cover, friends, or you'll end up like our comrades there." He gave a significant nod to the bodies sprawled outside the cave.

Jordel and Loren darted around the corner, but Loren stood in full view of the cave, holding her head high, hoping Albern would look out and recognize her. Jordel, meanwhile, ducked in company with the man who had spoken to them. Three other guards stood behind, each afraid to press forwards.

"How many are in there?" said Jordel.

"I cannot count for certain, but I have seen at least two," said the guard. "But one of them was a child."

"A child?" said Loren, feigning surprise. Had they seen Annis? Everything might be lost if Damaris learned that Annis was here.

"Aye, a thin boy, dressed all in rags. Looks like he belongs begging on some city street, not up in these mountains," said the man.

Loren breathed a quiet sigh of relief. Jordel turned and gave her an urgent look. He tossed his head in the direction of the other guards. She sized them up. There were four of them against Jordel and Loren, and who knew when more would arrive? Trisken might come at any moment, and Loren did not enjoy the thought of testing herself against that warhammer. The guard at the back was smallest, a thin woman with short red hair who did not look much older than Loren herself, though her eyes were filled with a grim determination. To Loren's other side, she was shocked to recognize the thin, reedy man who had spoken so rudely to Jordel and her in the mess hall. He did not seem to recognize either of them, for his eyes were fixed on the cave.

With surprise on her side, she thought she could take the two of them. She nodded to Jordel and drew her dagger.

In a burst of motion, Jordel drove his elbow into the face of the thick man beside him. Loren crashed her pommel on the back of the thin man's head, and he slumped to the ground. The woman's eyes flashed with surprise, but she quickly brought her sword around in a swing at Loren's head. Loren barely ducked it, and then kicked the woman's shin to fell her. But the Shade kept her grip on her sword and swung it again. Loren had to dart back to avoid the strike, but then she seized the woman's tunic, striking her three times in the face with her fist while still holding the dagger's hilt. It lent extra weight to her blows, and the woman fell, senseless.

Loren looked up to find Jordel with his arms wrapped around the neck of the final soldier, choking the breath out of him. The man struggled to strike back, but he could not loosen the Mystic's grip. His eyes fluttered up and rolled back in his head, and he fell unconscious. Jordel dropped him unceremoniously to the ground.

"Now let us find our friends, and hope they do not shoot us," he said.

They ran for the cave mouth, their weapons sheathed and their hands held high. Loren stepped distastefully around the bodies on the ground, averting her eyes from them. There was so much death, no matter how she tried to avoid it. Albern must have recognized them, for no arrows came flying out of the darkness. No sooner had they entered the cave than Gem and Annis seized Loren in a hug. Xain lay behind them all, near the horses, his eyes filled with concern.

"Well, you certainly took your time getting here," said Albern, stepping forwards. He still held an arrow nocked, but he had relaxed his draw. Despite the jovial tone of his words, Loren saw the relief in his eyes.

"When we heard the shouts of alarm inside the fort, we thought you had been found," said Annis. "It was not long before we realized they had spotted us, not you."

"We held them off admirably though, I think," said Gem, stepping back from his hug as though embarrassed. "Certainly they were no match for our determination and prowess."

"Yes, the little master here cowered so fearfully that the enemy took pity on him and fled," said Albern.

Gem opened his mouth to answer, but Jordel interrupted him. "We have no time for words, only flight. Fetch the horses and Xain, for—"

THOOM

The heavy crash of a gate striking the ground drowned out his words. All of them stopped in their tracks and turned to the mouth of the cave—just as from around the corner of the stronghold, Trisken stepped forwards, his great warhammer clutched in both hands.

TWENTY-EIGHT

To either side of Trisken walked the bodyguards Loren had seen at his dais, and before him marched a half-dozen stronghold soldiers. They made no attempt to hide behind cover as they advanced, though the soldiers in front glanced uneasily at each other. Trisken paid them no mind.

"Well, he is an ugly one," said Albern, raising his bow and drawing.

His shaft struck one soldier in the chest. The others flinched and made to stop, but Trisken's guards shoved them forwards. The soldiers raised shields, but against

Albern they might as well have had no protection at all. Twice again his arrows struck, and twice again killed. That made them duck at last behind the edges of the cave mouth.

"Back!" said Loren. She seized Gem and Annis and tried to pull them farther into the caves.

"No," said Jordel. "We cannot flee without leaving Xain and the horses behind. It will be a fight." He drew his sword and stepped forwards.

"Aye, and we could use more than two blades," said Albern, looking at Loren sidelong.

"I will help," said Gem, though his voice quivered as he said it. He reached for the small sword Jordel had given him, buckled to his waist.

"Do not be a fool," said Loren, grabbing his wrist as he drew and shoving the blade back in. "You will be slaughtered."

"He will likely be slaughtered in any case, if they get through Jordel and me," said Albern. "Let the boy die with a sword in his hand if he wants."

"I told you I would not ask you to kill," said Jordel. "And I will not do so now. But if we do not fight, then likely we will all die here."

Loren looked at the cave mouth where the soldiers' heads could be seen poking into view, no doubt goaded by Trisken and his men. Even Gem meant to take up a blade in their defense. And Annis had stooped to pick up a rock from the ground, holding it ready to throw.

There was a shout from the mouth of the cave, and the soldiers rushed them, with Trisken coming close behind. There was no more time for thought; Loren ran to Midnight and seized her bow from the saddle, and then turned with a shaft already drawn.

She planted one arrow in a man's leg. Albern, without any such compunction, slew one of the bodyguards with a shaft through the eye. Two soldiers remained, as well as Trisken and one bodyguard.

Albern drew his sword, and he and Jordel met the Shades in battle. Beside them came Gem, thin voice raised in a battle cry—but one of the Shades struck out with a mighty fist, and Gem was dashed aside into the cave wall where he slumped to the ground.

Jordel and Albern traded blows with their opponents, backing up a step at a time. Loren drew her dagger, but the cave walls pressed too tight, and she could not find a place to step in. She was not even sure her blade would help against the longer weapons of their foes. But the narrow space also forced Trisken to hold back.

The bodyguard nearly broke Albern's defense, and Loren was about to go to his aid. Then from nowhere a rock flew into the bodyguard's temple. Loren saw Annis' empty hand. The moment's distraction gave Albern an opening. His sword found its mark at last, plunging through chain mail and into the guard's gut. As the woman died, Albern stepped past her and cut down one of Jordel's opponents as well.

Jordel pounced as the last Shade tried to flee. His stolen sword plunged into the man's back. Before he could withdraw it, Trisken stepped around his henchman and struck with the hilt of his hammer, driving the pommel hard into Jordel's chest. The Mystic fell to his back with a great *whoosh* of air and curled up, clutching his chest where he had been struck. Albern leapt to his defense, trying to keep Trisken at bay, but the stronghold commander forced him back as easily as if he were Gem before turning back to Jordel.

"No!" Loren could restrain herself no longer. She scooped up Gem's sword and leapt at Trisken, swinging wildly. She wished suddenly that she had taken the chance to learn sword fighting. Even to her, the strikes seemed clumsy. But they gave Trisken just enough pause for Jordel to find his feet again, and he pressed forwards beside her while Albern circled around from behind.

They had Trisken surrounded in the center of the cave, his head turning back and forth to keep them all in sight. Loren held her sword awkwardly before her. Albern moved to strike, but Trisken turned the blade aside with his hammer. He used the advantage to step back and around the bowyer, putting his back to the cave wall.

The air grew quiet in a sudden lull. Only the rain outside and the heavy breathing of the fighters could be heard. Trisken's eyes sought out their faces one by one, studying them. Then he looked past them, to where Gem lay crumpled on the floor, and where Annis knelt beside him.

A cruel look of recognition slid over his face.

"No," he chuckled. "No, this cannot be. This is too wonderful." He threw back his head and laughed loud and long, the deep, terrible sound echoing off the walls of the cave until it became a choir of dark voices all joining in his mirth.

"If you call dying in a cave wonderful, then you are a madman," said Albern.

Trisken acted as if he had not heard. His eyes were still only for Annis, his lips split in a wide grin. "The Yerrin girl. I thought finding you for your mother would be difficult. How could I have imagined you would walk into my arms? The Lord will be most pleased."

Annis' eyes filled with fright, and she clutched Gem's unconscious form a little tighter.

"Yes, I will bring you to your mother shortly. After I have dealt with these." Trisken's gaze went to Loren. "You must be the other one—the Mystic spy who stole her away. The one some call Nightblade. Your corpse will make the Lord a fine gift, I think."

Thinking him distracted, Jordel lunged. But Trisken sidestepped the blow, moving far more quickly than such a large man should, batting the sword aside with his hilt. He turned the movement into a swing that came speeding towards Loren's head, and she barely ducked in time.

Trisken fell back into a fighting pose, and kept speaking as if nothing had happened. "And you. I can smell the stench of a Mystic upon you. The outcast. Where is your fallen wizard, Jordel? Ah, there he is upon the floor." He laughed again, shaking his great head slowly. "What marvelous fortune for me. And for the Lord, whom fortune shall always favor. But how tragic for you, to come so far only to find death in the Greatrocks."

Loren had an idea. If she could distract the man, it might give Albern and Jordel a chance to bring him down. Certainly she could do no more good than that, for she was no fighter. As Trisken began to speak again, Loren leapt forwards with a cry, bringing her sword down in a heavy overhand swing.

Trisken's warhammer swung to meet it, and Loren's sword rang painfully in her hand. Then one leg came up, his plated knee smashing into her ribs. Loren cried out and fell, but before she could reach the ground Trisken brought the hilt around again, sending the pommel crashing down between her shoulder blades.

Jordel attacked with a wordless roar of fury, smashing the warhammer aside and driving forwards with another strike, pressing in close where Trisken could not bring his weapon to bear. That barely gave the commander pause; he seized the front of Jordel's tunic in one meaty fist and drew him forwards, slamming his forehead into Jordel's nose.

But that gave Albern the chance he needed. His

blade found its home deep in the back of Trisken's knee, the bloodied tip of it exploding through the front of the man's leg and shoving away the plate. Trisken sank down with a grunt, but in a desperate final attempt he raised his hammer above Jordel's chest.

Albern's sword swung around and nearly clove his arm in two, hacking through skin and muscle and into the bone. Trisken's hammer fell useless, his arm limp and wasted. Jordel rose, dagger in hand, and plunged it to the hilt into Trisken's neck. The giant fell at last, facedown on the cave floor, his blood pooling around him to mix with the rainwater.

Loren rolled onto her back, gasping for air, and winced as she landed on a rock just where the pommel of Trisken's warhammer had struck her. Slowly she was able to gain her hands and knees. Her fingers prodded at her ribs. The bones were certainly bruised, but they did not feel broken. At least she hoped not, for then she had no idea how she could make it out of the Greatrocks alive.

She could do nothing more than crawl, so she made her way to Gem on the other side of the cave. Annis was already there, holding his head in her lap and looking down into his face. Silent tears rolled down her cheeks.

"He lives," she said. "I can feel his breath. He is only hurt."

"Good," said Loren. "But he needs to wake. We must flee, now."

"He knew me, Loren," said Annis, her voice breaking. "He knew who I was. He knew my mother."

"She wanted his assistance searching for you," said Loren. "I will tell you all of it, everything we have learned, but later. For now, rest easily. He is dead, and it no longer matters what he knows."

Loren shook Gem by the shoulders. Still his eyes remained closed. She slapped his face, gently at first, and then harder. Finally she went to a dip in the cave floor, where water had pooled as if in a bowl. She scooped it up in both hands, then dropped it onto Gem's face. He came up sputtering.

"What happened?" he said weakly. His words were slurred by thick lips, for a large bruise was already covering most of the left side of his face.

"You were struck down in the fight," said Loren. "But you fought bravely."

"Of course I did," Gem grunted. "I—"

He froze, his eyes widening in terror as he looked beyond Loren and Annis.

Loren whirled just in time to see Trisken rise to his knees. His mangled right arm still hung limp by his side, but with his left he seized Jordel's cloak and dragged him down. His arm wrapped around the Mystic's throat, squeezing tight as he throttled the life out of him.

"Stinking Mystic," hissed Trisken, voice bubbling with blood through his torn throat. "All your kind are doomed—but I am content to start with you."

Albern flung himself forwards, sinking his knife into Trisken's neck again. The commander only laughed. Albern withdrew the knife and plunged it into the man's spine. Trisken only laughed harder, while Jordel's face grew purple and Loren heard a weak rattle escape from his throat. She ran to seize Trisken's wrist and pull his arm away from the Mystic, but she may as well have tried to move a mountain.

The bowyer stuck the knife into Trisken's eye, the blade sinking six fingers deep into the man's brain. His whole body went slack at once, his arm finally falling away, and he sank to the ground once more.

Loren pulled Jordel away from the body, where he fell to his face on the ground. He took great, wheezing gasps of air, sucking it down like sweet wine.

"What manner of witchery was that?" cried Annis. "He was dead. Jordel killed him."

Albern shrugged, stooping to wipe his dagger clean on Trisken's cloak. "Do not think too much of it. In war, I have seen men fight on through worse. But not a dagger in the eye. It is over now."

Jordel forced himself up. "We must leave." His voice was a horrible rasp. "More will come when their commander fails to return."

"Indeed," said Albern. "Strange that he would even risk himself out here, when he has a whole garrison at his back. But no matter. Where will we go? The west road and the east will both be watched. Farther into the caves?"

"No," said Jordel. "Once they find his body, they will send their whole strength to scour this place. We have but one choice. We must go into the fort itself."

"You are mad," said Gem, voice shaking.

"He is not," said Loren. "There is a place we can hide. But Jordel, what then? It hardly seems a better hiding spot than this, and still we have no means of escape."

"I do not yet know," said Jordel. "Only we cannot remain here."

"But the horses," said Loren. "They will not fit into the secret entrance. What will we do with them?"

"We must abandon them," said Jordel. "Bring everything from the saddles that you can, and leave the rest."

Loren felt her heart seize up. She looked far back into the cave, where Midnight still stood hobbled with the other horses. The plow horse and Albern's bay nickered and danced at all the bloodshed—but Midnight stood stock still, her gaze fixed on Loren. The thought of leaving the mare made Loren want to weep. More than a month they had spent on the road together, until Midnight seemed as much a friend as Annis or Gem did.

"Do not despair," said Jordel, seeing the look on her face. "We may yet have a chance to recover them. The soldiers within the stronghold will no doubt bring the horses in for themselves, and from there we might rescue them."

The odds against that seemed strong, but Loren did not say so. She only nodded, for she knew he was right. With heavy hearts, they all went to their saddlebags and fetched their provisions, waterskins, and bedrolls. Albern stroked his horse's mane for a moment. Then he removed its hobbles and gave it a pat on the neck. Loren spent a little while holding her forehead against Midnight's muzzle. The mare turned and nudged her, as though she could sense Loren's distress.

Meanwhile, Jordel went to Xain, bound hand and foot on the cave floor. The wizard had watched the whole fight in silence, for a gag still bound his mouth. Now Jordel hauled him up to his feet and looked solemnly into his eyes.

"I am going to unbind your feet, and you will come with us," said Jordel. "If you should try to flee, you will die. Even if you should escape my grasp, the soldiers within the stronghold will find you and kill you. Do you understand?"

Xain nodded, neither eager nor fearful. Loren remembered the brief words he had had with her, his apology that had seemed so sincere. She found herself wanting to believe those words now, to have some assurance that his time of madness had passed. But still, she was not eager to break the bonds that held his hands, nor to remove the gag from his mouth.

They stood at the cave mouth, ready to emerge into the rain. But then, just before Jordel took his first step beyond the opening, Loren heard the scrape of metal on stone.

She looked back and froze. There on the cave floor, Trisken moved. His boot slid slowly on the floor as he tried to bring it up beneath him. His arms sought for purchase on the stone—both of them, the right and the left. Even as she watched, the torn flesh and skin of his right arm stitched together, as though under the hands of a seamstress. The hole where his eye had been was sealed over with skin, and it bubbled and rippled like a boiling kettle.

"Jordel," she said, her voice barely above a whisper.

"Run," said Jordel. "Run, *now!*"

They fled out into the rainy night as quickly as their legs could carry them.

TWENTY-NINE

JORDEL LED THEM AT A CROUCHING RUN ALONG THE stronghold's wall, around the corner towards the gate that led in from the east. All of them kept a wary eye above, watchful for any guard who might poke their head over to see them. But they went unnoticed, for they clung closely to the wall.

Loren led the way after that, for she knew where the hidden entrance was, while Jordel pushed Xain on ahead of him. But the wizard caused no trouble at all, running along behind her obediently, halting whenever the rest of them did without complaint.

They found the eastern gate closed, and so they crept by it without incident. Before long they stood in front of the secret entrance that Jordel had shown Loren before. While Albern kept a hand on Xain's arm, Jordel pressed his finger into the chink in the wall, and the stone gave way before them.

Quietly they crept inside, and Jordel pushed the door closed behind them. Then they were trapped in silence and darkness, within the very bowels of their enemy's stronghold, from where Loren had no faintest idea how they might escape.

Jordel bound Xain's feet again, which the wizard suffered without struggle. Then for a while they simply rested, nearly all of them nursing injuries from the fight. Loren tried to feel on her back where Trisken had struck her, but her arms could not quite reach it, and trying to do so made her ribs flare with pain. She could hardly see the others, who were visible only by a hair-thick sliver of light that came in beneath the secret door to the outside world.

"We shall need a light," said Jordel. "There should be a torch fixture on the wall—here it is. They had a torch in the cells beyond, if you will recall, Loren. Fetch it for us, will you?"

"What if they notice its absence?" said Loren.

"I do not think they would guess that we took it into the walls," he said. "But be quick about it, so that you are not seen."

Loren went to the other end of the passageway,

where she found the wooden wall that was, in fact, the back of the shelves in the dungeon room. She pushed it open on its silent hinges and ran to the torch. When she lit it and fixed it to the wall in the hidden passage, it seemed bright as the sun.

"Much better," said Albern. He had unstrung his bow to lay it across his knees, and was now polishing his knife, which still bore some stains of blood from the fight.

With the room lit, Loren could see the children sitting against the opposite wall. Gem was poking with interest at the bruise that covered his face. But Annis sat huddled, arms wrapped around her knees, her eyes staring at nothing.

Loren sidled over to sit between them and placed an arm around the younger girl's shoulders. "Do not be so fearful, Annis. You look like a woman awaiting her execution."

"Am I not?" said Annis. "Are not we all? We sit trapped in the fortress of our enemy, and their leader cannot be killed."

Loren had no good answer to that, for she too had been badly shaken by the sight of Trisken rising to life again after Albern killed him twice. "It must be some kind of magic," she said.

"It is," said Jordel. "A dark magic that Underrealm has not seen in centuries. Not since a much, much darker time than ours. It is an evil portent indeed." He turned to where Xain sat against the wall. The wizard glanced at him with troubled eyes. Jordel gave him the slightest of nods.

Loren shot them both a dirty look. The last thing they needed was to rob Annis of what little hope she had left. "And yet, we escaped from him."

"That hardly helps," said Annis. "For still we are trapped."

"And we shall escape from here, too," said Loren. "Just as we escaped from Cabrus, and Wellmont, and Vivien upon the river. Only after here, there will be no more dangers, no more foes trying to harm us. In no time we shall be in Feldemar, well on our way to . . ." She turned to Jordel. "Where are we going, exactly?"

He must finally have understood that Loren wished to cheer the girl, for he nodded slowly. "To my stronghold of Ammon, in the southeast of that kingdom," he said. "It was once a castle of my family's, set to guard against invasion from Dulmun. But it has long been abandoned, for it was built in a time of war that has long since ended. Feldemar and Dulmun have been at peace for many hundreds of years. When I joined the order and learned of Ammon, I took it for my own, and from there I have long planned my efforts throughout the nine lands. It is no place of luxury, or even of much comfort, but it has two great strengths: it is secret, and it is safe."

"But will the other Mystics not know that you have gone there?" said Annis, her voice still filled with worry. "Will they not find us?"

"Mayhap," said Jordel. "The High King herself knows of the stronghold, and may send her agents there to find me. But I have allies there, and loyal soldiers, who will spare no effort to help us and conceal us from any search. It has always seemed prudent to me to keep one place where I could retreat, where not even my masters could reach me if I did not wish it."

"Do you see?" said Loren. "Once we leave the Greatrocks we shall lose ourselves in the Birchwood, my home. No one will find us there. And beyond the Birchwood, it is but a short journey to Feldemar."

"A short journey, you say," grumbled Annis. "I feel as though we move from one short journey to another, except they are always longer than we think, and more fraught with peril."

"You may be right, and yet I promise you this, Annis of the family Yerrin," said Jordel. "I vow that I will see you safely to Ammon. While life remains in my body, I will not abandon you or turn aside. I will see you—and all of us—to safety."

Annis peered at him in the torchlight. She did not say anything, but she nodded, and Loren could feel her relax.

"All very good words, and I do not doubt them," said Albern. "But it seems that before they can be carried out, the lot of us have much to do."

"He is right," said Gem. "We cannot very well reach Ammon while we lurk in these castle walls."

"No, we cannot," said Jordel with a sigh. "But we

have learned much about the foes who wish to prevent our escape: one of them—the Yerrins—known, and the other largely a mystery. It is the unknown that worries me, of course—and yet with each encounter, I learn more and more of them. But at the same time, the family Yerrin becomes more of a question."

"How do you mean?" said Loren.

"Think: why should Yerrin seek the help of this Lord, whoever he may be?" said Jordel. "If they desire his help, he must be more powerful than they—or at least, capable of things they are not. But if that is true, how could he have hidden himself so well that I have never heard even whispers of his arrival?"

"You would know better than us," said Gem.

"And yet I know nothing—but I have guesses. And if I guess correctly, then we have already fought the first battle of a war I have tried to stave off for many years."

He looked at Xain as he said that. The wizard sat with his hands bound behind him, very near the secret doorway through which they had come. His eyes were clear now, as they were most days, and in them Loren saw a great worry. She remembered how, in Wellmont, Jordel had spoken to Xain for most of a day. He had desired the wizard's services ever since Loren first met him in Cabrus, and on that day Jordel had finally revealed why. But not to her.

Gem stirred where he sat, reaching for the saddlebag he had brought. "I wish you would speak more plainly. All this double-talk makes me quite hungry, yet I am certain you will insist I do not eat as much as I wish."

"In that you are correct, for if you ate as much as you wish, no doubt your stomach would rupture," said Jordel, snatching the saddlebag away from him. "And it is wise to fear speaking plainly about that which you do not know plainly. Those who speak with both authority and ignorance may plant ideas that cannot be shaken off, even after seeing the truth."

"More double-talk," grumbled Gem. "Give me what food you will, and that will sate my curiosity."

Jordel chuckled and divided their food, handing Gem some small morsels of bread and the last of an old cheese that was nearly spoiled. The rest received their rations in silence, all of them lost deep in thought. Loren wondered if their minds were turned to the same thing as hers: the sight of Trisken struggling up from the floor, as his ruined eye stitched itself together.

"Loren, will you feed Xain for me?" said Jordel.

She nodded and took the food Jordel held forth, then went to where Xain lay. Loren noted with interest that the wizard looked better than he had in a while. His limbs were still thin and wasted and his cheeks gaunt, but his eyes were clear and bright, and they no longer sank so deeply into his skull. He had lost much of his hair to the magestone sickness, but what remained had thickened and grown lustrous again. He looked at her eagerly as she removed the gag.

Carefully she untied it and pulled the cloth from his mouth. The moment his lips were free, Xain said loudly, "Jordel, let me help."

His voice, so strong in the cramped space, made Loren jump in surprise. Jordel and Albern reached for their knives on instinct. But Xain did not move at all, and spoke no further word. Jordel had warned her that a firemage's words of power were dangerous, and that is why Xain had been kept gagged. The wizard must have recognized their fear, for he did not utter so much as a murmur as Jordel studied him silently.

Annis, however, did not remain silent. "Indeed, let him help us," she muttered, looking down at her hands. "That has turned out so well in the past."

Xain looked at her sadly, but then he returned his gaze to Jordel. His eyes were so eager, so earnest . . . Loren wanted him to speak, to explain himself. But he waited.

"Go on," said Jordel, his voice entirely passive. Loren could read nothing in the words.

"We must escape this stronghold," said Xain. "Yet there are only six of us, and an army of our foes. But you know my strength. You know I can tip the scales in our favor. Let me do it, Jordel, and prove my remorse."

"You ask us to trust you, Xain?" said Annis, trembling as she beheld him. "You would have done better if your first words were an apology. For your actions in the valley—and for this." She drew down the collar of her dress, pressing a finger to her neck. There was the terrible scar Xain had left in her skin, the twisted, melted flesh where he had burned her with his fire.

"I shall never be able to apologize enough for what I did to you, Annis, and to the rest of you as well," said Xain quickly. "No words will ever make it right. Only action. Let me stand beside you, and atone for my wrongdoing by aiding our escape—or give my life to enable it, if need be."

"Then the debt of honor would certainly be paid," said Annis, turning away.

"Annis," said Jordel in a warning tone.

"Still your tongue," she said. "I am done. Trust him if you wish, or not. I cannot sway you either way, and I will not presume to try."

Jordel looked solemnly at her for a moment before turning back to Xain. The wizard sat still, looking up expectantly.

"Though she is overzealous in her condemnation, Annis is not entirely wrong," said Jordel. "With such peril surrounding us, it seems an ill-advised time to test the limits of your honesty. Even so, I might do it—yet if you are recovered, it is only recently, and still you are weak from the magestones' hunger. We would gain precious little advantage by freeing you, and yet we would risk a great deal."

"I feel strong," Xain insisted, voice rising. "I know I can help you, and I do not speak idly—if it comes to it, I shall stay behind to ensure your escape. It is the least that honor demands of me."

Jordel frowned, and his hand stole beneath his cloak, where Loren knew it gripped the hilt of his blade. "I have given you my answer, Xain."

Xain's brow wrinkled, and Loren grew afraid—afraid he would lash out with words of power, afraid of what his magic could do in such a small space. But as her gaze rested upon his face, she saw it relax. His eyes grew calm again. He shook his head sadly and turned away from them.

"As you say," he muttered quietly. "I suppose I deserve no better."

Loren fed him and replaced the gag. She took no pleasure in it.

As they sated their hunger, they sat around Jordel in a small semicircle. First Loren told them all that had happened within the stronghold, and all she had heard between Damaris and Trisken. But she did not say how much they had spoken of her, because that seemed somewhat akin to boasting. Jordel sat quiet, cross-legged with his hands across his knees, like some village elder telling children a story, as she told her story and the others asked their questions. When they had finished, he spoke his thoughts at last.

"Whatever their ultimate purpose here, I know one thing: this fortress must not be allowed to stand," said Jordel. "We must cast out both the Shades and the family Yerrin, for no scheme of theirs will bring anything but evil to the nine lands."

"I thought our intent was to escape," said Albern. "It seems you speak of a fight instead."

"Tell me how you think we can escape without a fight, and I shall call it good counsel," said Jordel. "But they have guards with torches on the wall by night, and can see the road for mayhap a league in either direction by day. By vanquishing them—or, at least, by wreaking great havoc upon the stronghold, and thus distracting them—we stand our best chance at slipping away undetected."

"But Jordel . . . understand I am not afraid," said Gem carefully. "But we are only six—five, without the wizard, who we cannot rely upon. You have said there are scores of soldiers here. One does not need cowardice, only prudence, to see that the odds in such a battle are more than a little stacked in the favor of our enemies."

"Yet where so few may be weak in open battle, they may have great strength in silence and secrecy," said Jordel. "And I think I have a way to use our small number—and the fact that the Shades do not yet know where we are hiding—to attack the fortress."

"Say on, then," said Gem. "I should love to hear how five fighters can conquer more than fifty. Mayhap they will sing a song about it."

"If they do, it may be because we failed in our secrecy," said Jordel. "But no matter. The family Yerrin has placed their caravan in the stronghold's courtyard. They hold many goods, but we all know their true cargo is magestones."

Loren glanced at Xain. His eyes had lit up with interest, and she felt a shiver climb her spine.

"Magestones empower wizards, but they have other properties," said Jordel. "If a magestone is set ablaze, it burns with darkfire."

"Darkfire," whispered Loren. "Like Xain used upon the Dorsean ships outside of Wellmont?"

Jordel nodded. "And upon the road when he struck down Vivien. Darkfire cannot be doused without magic, and I would be surprised if they have any wizards here within the castle walls. Water only spreads it, and it will burn through wood, cloth, flesh, and even steel."

"You mean to set the caravan ablaze," said Albern. "A fine distraction, to be sure—so long as we do not let ourselves be caught in the fire, here within our hiding place."

"That would be ill-advised, to be sure," said Jordel with a small smile. "My thought is that Annis and Xain will hide here, within the walls. As soon as the flames are set, the rest of us will return to join them, and escape as our enemies are occupied by the destruction of their stores."

"It would be a grievous blow to the family Yerrin, to be sure, to lose so valuable a cargo," said Loren.

"And if the Shades are already angry at them for their dealings with you, believing you to be a Mystic spy, think of their wrath after this," said Jordel. "Such a blow could forever sunder this dark alliance, and that could do nothing but help us in the future."

And best of all, in Loren's mind, they would take no lives in the process. When Jordel had first begun to speak of attacking the fortress, she thought he meant to break his vow by asking her to slay the Shades. This plan, however, would do their enemies great harm without spilling a drop of blood.

"You mean to leave me alone with the wizard again," said Annis. "The last time that happened, I did not enjoy the experience."

"Yet then he was unbound," said Jordel. "And if you wish to leave this stronghold as badly as you claim, I think this gives us our greatest chance."

"Very well, then," said Albern. "Tell us what you mean for us to do."

THIRTY

LOREN AND JORDEL STILL HAD THEIR SHADE UNIFORMS, but Jordel planned for Albern to go in disguise as well. Loren remembered the guardroom where they had found the clothing the first time, so she slipped quickly from the hidden passageway to fetch clothes for him. Her heart thundered the whole time, for though she was still unknown to most in the fortress, she was well aware that Trisken had seen her. If he had returned, and happened to chance upon her in the hallway, he would recognize her at once. But she saw no one at all; in fact, the stronghold seemed curiously quiet and empty.

She returned with clothing that she thought was of a size with Albern, and was pleased to see that it fit. But Albern lifted his arm and sniffed at the blue and grey cloth, wrinkling his nose.

"You could not have found anything cleaner?" he groused.

"That might be your own stench," said Loren haughtily. "Tell me, bowyer, when was the last time you bathed?"

He smirked at her. "Your sharp tongue wounds me. The clothes will do, I suppose."

"We shall wait for nightfall," said Jordel, "and hope the rain holds. If it does, the courtyard will be a dark place, where Loren and Gem can slip in among the shadows with ease. You will come with Albern and me, and while we distract the Yerrin guards, the two of you will sneak in among the wagons. Flee the caravan as soon as you set your fires, for the alarm will be raised, and swiftly."

"Mayhap I should go alone," said Loren. "The danger seems great."

"And when has great danger ever swayed me?" said Gem. "I am not some frightened child. I fought in the cave when even you wished to stay your hand."

Loren was about to cuff him, but Jordel spoke quickly. "Boasting aside, I am afraid we need Gem," he said. "One fire might be put out before the magestones catch, or perhaps they could separate the wagon from the rest of the caravan to cut their losses.

By setting two flames at once, I hope to double our chances."

As they waited for the sun to set, Jordel showed Annis the catch to open the secret passage, in case the rest of them were lost and she had to flee with Xain. Annis' eyes were filled with fear as he explained it to her, and she looked often at the wizard. Loren found it hard to meet the girl's gaze. She would have done much to avoid leaving the two of them alone, especially after what Xain had done to Annis the last time. But she had little choice. And within her heart, she secretly believed the words Xain had spoken the day before. She only hoped that that trust was not a mistake.

The sliver of daylight faded beneath the door of the secret entrance, and they set forth from their hiding place.

First they listened carefully with ears pressed to the back of the shelf, but they heard no sound. They slipped out into the jail cells and listened again at the door leading into the hallway. Still all was quiet. Gem stood beside Loren with his eyes wide and face pale. But his hands were steady and his mouth set firm with determination. Loren reminded herself that Gem had long been a thief—no doubt he had experience sneaking about and avoiding guards.

They took leave of the jail and turned left, heading towards the guardroom. That way lay the closest exit to the courtyard. It also took them farther from the great hall, where Trisken was likely to be. None of them had any wish to see the commander again.

But just as they neared the guardroom, they heard a door creak open around the corner. Footsteps entered the hall. Loren froze, and Gem beside her. But Jordel moved quickly, throwing open the door of the guardroom and shoving them both inside. He and Albern, still clad in their uniforms, closed the door and stood in the hallway.

Loren pressed herself to the door to listen. The footsteps stopped not far away. "Well met," came a voice that sounded familiar. After a moment she placed it—the man who had spoken kindly to them when they ate the day before.

"Well met," said Jordel easily. "You look as though you lost a fight with a raincloud."

"This blasted storm will not cease. Even in the caves, there are many holes in the ceiling through which the rainwater leaks."

"You have come from the caves?" said Jordel.

"Have you not?" said the man. "More than half the stronghold has been sent in, to scour them for the spies."

"I have not yet had the honor," said Jordel. "But I would guess, from the stoop of your shoulders, that nothing yet has been found."

"Nothing more than the horses, which are in the courtyard now," said the man. "Yet the commander will not let us give up the search. Those caves are dangerous, but he pushes us on. His rage is like a whip at our backs. Some men have fallen into pits, and at least one is lost—mayhap more, but we will not know until the next time comes to report in."

Loren gave Gem a look, and he returned it with a smile. Their horses were safe, at least.

"Still, the spies must be there," said Jordel. "Given enough time, we shall find them."

"Mayhap," said the man. "And yet . . . you know of the rope."

"I do," said Jordel solemnly. But Loren did not know, at first—and then she remembered. They had climbed down from the top of the keep and left their rope hanging there. Her stomach did a somersault.

"Some of the men think they are within the walls of the stronghold now," said the guard, now in a muted tone. "Though it seems unlikely, for where could they be hiding? Yet you know how rumors persist. And I must admit I have looked cautiously over my shoulder more often than normal on my watch tonight."

"A silly fear," said Jordel. "The rope might well have been their means of escape, not entry, for they say it ended four paces or more above the ground."

"I had not heard that," said the man. "But still, if once they entered the fortress and escaped, who is to say but that they could return?"

"I think they are well away from here," said Jordel. "Probably in some passage in the caves we have not yet found, one that leads out of the mountains."

"Let us hope you are right," said the man with

a sigh. "But here I have stood too long in soaking clothes. I shall leave you be now, and get out of them."

"As you say," said Jordel. "The guardroom awaits you."

Loren saw it for a signal at once—the man meant to enter the very room where she and Gem were hidden. She seized the boy's arm and pulled him after her. At the back of the room was a large chest of drawers set away from the wall. The two of them ducked behind it just in time, Loren's bruised ribs flaring at the motion and making her wince. The door swung open, and Loren heard footsteps enter the room.

Slowly the steps drew closer, and Loren heard the soft *squish* of wet leather. The man stopped a few paces away, at one of the other chests of drawers. Gem's eyes were wide with fright. His hand crept to the hilt of a knife at his belt.

Loren seized his arm and shook her head. Gem glared back at her, his fingers tightening on the handle. Loren stared him down. He subsided, but only for a moment. They heard the man remove his cloak and toss it atop the dresser with a wet *slap*. Then he approached the drawers behind which they were hiding.

Gem jumped from his hiding place with a cry and the *hiss* of his dagger leaving its sheath. "Gem, no!" said Loren, coming up behind him. The guardsman fell back, his hand flying to the hilt of his sword at his belt, staring at the two of them in shock.

"Who in the nine lands are you?" But then his eyes

narrowed, and his blade flew from the scabbard. "The spies," he growled.

Behind him the door flew open. Albern and Jordel stormed into the room. The guard looked back at the two of them with obvious relief.

"Brothers!" he said. "I have found our hidden foes—or two of them, at least. Quickly, take—"

His words cut off in a gurgle as Albern drew a knife across his neck. The guard slumped to the ground, staring helplessly up into Jordel's keen blue eyes.

"I am sorry," said Jordel quietly. "Would that we had met in other circumstances."

The guard's body slackened as he died.

Loren wanted to be sick. "He helped us, Jordel," she said. "In the stronghold's mess. You spoke with him and called him friend."

"Then this is not the first time I have befriended a man, only to face him later on the other side of a battlefield," said Jordel. "Were he wearing a cloak of red and not blue, gladly would I have fought beside him."

"Remind me to choose my clothing carefully then," said Loren, turning her eyes from him.

Jordel did not answer—but at least Loren was glad to see him look sick, rather than satisfied at the man's death.

"None of us are blameless," said Albern. He wiped his blade off on the fallen guard's cloak, but Loren saw no trace of triumph in his eyes.

"If you are weary of this talk by now, I am ten times

more so," said Gem. He had sheathed his knife, more irritated than disgusted. "Let us be rid of this mess and on with our mission, before someone else comes."

At first Loren wanted to refuse to touch the body, but she soon realized that was foolish. Someone had to keep watch at the door, and better it be Jordel or Albern in full uniform than she with her cloak of black.

So while Gem scrubbed at the blood on the floor with the man's cloak, she and Albern lifted the guard and stuffed him into one of the tall standing closets. It was not much of a hiding place, but it would have to do, for they all felt the need for haste.

When the room was clear, with no signs of struggle, Jordel scouted the hallway ahead. He turned to wave them on, and Albern walked before Loren and Gem. They slunk along behind him, trying to make themselves as small as they could. Soon they stood before the door that would take them into the courtyard. Jordel paused to give them one last instruction.

"It will be dark outside, but they will still have torches," he said. "Keep yourselves to the shadows until you see an opening in the guards' lines, and then make for the wagons quickly. Your escape will be easier, for the whole stronghold will likely be distracted by the burning. When you strike your flames, take great care not to get any darkfire on you. It will burn you as easily as the magestones and the wagons, for it knows no difference."

Loren and Gem nodded silently. Jordel opened the

door a crack and put his head through. Once satisfied that no one was about, he stepped out with Albern. Loren slipped into the night behind them, Gem at her side.

The door came out in the middle of the northern wall. To their left was the horse corral, where one guard stood watch, while to their right were three small buildings—guardrooms, most likely. Great pools of shadow lay where those buildings met the castle wall. She and Gem lost themselves in the inky dark, waiting for an opening.

Between the black of night and the rain that poured ceaselessly down, they could not make out the bodies of the Yerrin guards surrounding the caravan. They were visible only by the light of their torches, which seemed to float back and forth in the downpour. But the line of guards was too thick, and Loren did not see a gap where they might slip through.

Jordel and Albern soon saw to that. Loren saw them step up to one of the guards, obscuring the light of his torch. They began to speak in voices she could not hope to hear. And as they continued their conversation, other torches drifted towards them in the darkness. Soon one whole side of the caravan lay nearly empty of Yerrin men. Loren and Gem ran forwards. She ducked her head to hide any flash of her pale skin, and walked before Gem so that her black cloak shielded him. Then they were in and among the wagons, hidden from all eyes, and they paused to catch their bearings.

Loren pressed her mouth to Gem's ear to be heard over the rain. "We should set our blazes in the middle of the group," she whispered.

He nodded, and they crept forwards in the darkness. As they reached the corner of the wagon, Loren risked a look out. Jordel and Albern still stood speaking with the Yerrin guards, and now she could clearly see their faces in the torches' light. But also she recognized the massive shape of one Yerrin soldier: it was Gregor, Damaris' bodyguard. Loren could hear his angry voice booming through the storm, though she could not make out the words. He gestured sharply with his hands, pointing away. Evidently Albern and Jordel were not welcome.

"We must hurry," she said. "Come."

They ran on. Soon she judged that they were somewhere near the middle of the wagons. Loren pointed to one, and Gem ran for it, reaching for the flint he had tucked in his belt. Loren swung herself into the back of another wagon. She sighed as the rain stopped pounding on her head. The wagon held bolts of cloth, much the same as the one she had hidden in the first time she had come upon the caravan. *It might be the very one,* she mused.

She knew just where to go; in the floorboards at the center of the wagon, she found a small hole through which her finger could slip. When she pulled on it, a panel came up. It was almost too dark to see, but she would have known the shapes beneath even in pitch blackness: small packets, wrapped in brown cloth, each holding several magestones, each worth a fortune.

Loren paused, flint and steel in hand. She had had a sudden thought. Quickly she looked back over her shoulder. There was no one about, and the torches of the guards danced a good distance away. They looked like Elven-light or imp fire. She was alone.

She seized one of the magestone packets and slipped it into her cloak. Then she placed another into a pocket on the other side. Jordel would have been furious if he saw. He thought of the magestones as evil, and after what they had done to Xain, Loren could not argue. Yet they were also beyond value—and she was the Nightblade, after all. If the Mystic could murder guardsmen against her wishes, it seemed only fair that she could steal and sell magestones against his.

But now she had wasted precious time. Gem had likely already set his flames and would be coming for her soon. She struck the flint against her hunting knife. Sparks leapt forth, casting the inside of the wagon in a ruddy glow. Jordel had assured her that the magestones would burn easily, and he was right. The sparks lit upon the brown cloth, which began to smolder. Soon a small black flame sprang forth.

Loren suppressed a shudder. She had seen darkfire used twice before. Xain had used it to burn ships upon the Dragon's Tail, and even the river's waters could not douse the flames. Then upon the road east of Wellmont, he had cast down Vivien and six other Mystics.

She still remembered the way their bodies had bubbled. Then, as now, the terrible darkness of the fire hurt her eyes, twisting her nerves until she wanted to crawl out from within her own skin.

She fled the wagon, eager to put some distance between herself and the fires. But as her boots struck the courtyard, the air exploded with the clamor of a bell—the same bell they had heard when they reached the stronghold.

Loren froze, listening. She heard no voices shouting, no clash of steel on steel. It was not Jordel and Albern, then, who had raised the alarm. That could mean only one thing: someone in the stronghold had found the body they had left in the guardroom.

Gem darted into view, his eyes wide. "Loren, what is it? Have we been spotted?"

"They found the body," said Loren. "We must flee, and in haste."

They made their way back to where they had last seen Jordel and Albern. The two of them still stood with the Yerrin guards. All faces were turned up towards the keep, where the bell had only just ceased its clamor. Just as Loren ducked behind the closest wagon, Gregor and his guards sprang into action.

"Spread out!" said Gregor. "Keep watch over the wagons. Let no one approach. And as for you—" he thrust a finger at Jordel and Albern "—withdraw, or I will slay you myself."

"As you say, friend." Jordel raised his hands. But

he did not back away. Loren knew he did not want to leave while she and Gem were still among the wagons.

"Come on," said Loren, snatching Gem's sleeve. They withdrew to the other side of the caravan, but the guards had pressed close together again. Swiftly they ran to the eastern end, but there was no opening there, either. They were surrounded, unable to escape.

Then she heard a voice that sent chills sliding down her spine.

"Gregor," said Damaris. "A body has been found. The spies are inside the walls." She stepped into view, and though Loren knew the merchant could not see her, still she ducked a little farther behind the wagon's edge.

"We are vigilant, my lady," said Gregor, giving Jordel and Albern a foul look. "They will not approach the wagons."

"You must take every precaution," said Damaris. "Have some men patrol the—"

Her voice was interrupted by a sudden roar of flames blasting into the sky. The wagon Loren had set afire had finally caught in earnest, and now darkfire blazed, a deeper black against the night sky.

"They are here!" cried Damaris, her voice a clarion call of rage. "You fools, they are here already! Find them! And save the caravan!"

Yerrin guards rushed in among the wagons. Just in time, Loren dove between the wooden wheels and pulled Gem down with her. She gave a sharp grunt as her bruised ribs struck the ground, and then covered her own mouth with her hand. Gregor led his men in, Damaris beside him.

"Find them!" cried Damaris. "Do not let them escape!"

At first Loren thought Damaris would pass them by. But the merchant's fine boots paused by their wagon, just a pace away. Then in a flash, Damaris knelt and thrust her head beneath the wagon. Her eyes found Loren's, and in her gaze Loren saw a bitter, bone-deep fury, hotter than darkfire itself.

"You," hissed Damaris.

Loren tried to scramble away, but in an instant Gregor dove down and seized her ankle, dragging her out from under the wagon. She swung upside-down in the air, her cloak billowing to the ground beneath her head.

Though clearly it threw Damaris off guard to see Loren there, she tried to maintain her composure. "Loren of the family Nelda. How is it that you are here? What have you done with . . ." Her eyes widened. "Annis is here. She is within the stronghold. Gregor, kill this one at once, and then send your men to search for my daughter. Tear the walls down stone by stone if you must!"

Gregor's sword was already in hand. He drew it back and swung—but then Jordel was there, his blade flashing in to halt Gregor's. Damaris cried out and backed away, producing a knife from her belt. But Jordel had no interest in her. His other hand struck Gregor beneath his armpit. The bodyguard grunted and dropped Loren, who fell to the cobblestones in a heap. A meaty hand reached for her again, but Jordel swung with his sword, and Gregor had to withdraw.

From the other direction, strong hands seized Loren and hauled her up. She drew her dagger without thinking, thrusting it in front of her—but then she recognized Albern and stayed her hand. The bowyer's eyes fell upon the dagger for a moment, and then he was dragging her away from Gregor, while Jordel held his ground to give them a chance to escape.

"Gem!" cried Loren. "Gem, run! Jordel, *run!*"

"Ignore him," said Damaris. "Get the girl!"

Gregor tried to press past Jordel, but he was blocked on either side by the caravans. The Mystic's sword leapt about like a serpent. Loren could not see Gem anywhere. She had lost him when Gregor snatched her from beneath the wagon.

More Yerrin guards erupted from amid the wagons, and swiftly they moved around to encircle Jordel. He glanced over his shoulder to find his retreat blocked, and turned so that his back was to the wagon. Gregor pressed forwards, mouth set in a grim line.

"Jordel!" cried Loren. "Albern, help him!" She tried to go to his aid, but Albern's grip on her cloak was firm, and he pulled her back.

"We cannot, Loren. They would only catch us, too."

He pulled her farther away. Loren fought him, but he was too strong. And then her heart broke, for Gem emerged from nowhere and leapt into the fray, trying to free Jordel. He screamed thinly, thrusting his knife at one of the men standing between Jordel and escape. The blade sank into the man's arm, and he cried out. But the knife became stuck and was ripped from Gem's grasp. The Yerrin guard's mailed fist struck the boy in his face, and he fell to the ground.

Jordel lunged for him, but Gregor forced the Mystic back. Another blade came from nowhere, striking him in the side. His mail held, but he twisted with the pain of the blow, and then Gregor struck him with his fist. Jordel fell, and Loren could not see him behind the bodies of his foes.

More guards were coming. Albern pulled Loren through the door and into the stronghold, their footsteps echoing hollowly as they ran down the hallway.

THIRTY-ONE

LOREN KEPT FIGHTING TO FREE HERSELF, DESPERATE TO go back, but Albern forced her on. Once they were in the hallways, he did not make for the jail where their escape lay, but pulled her in the other direction.

"Where are you going?" said Loren.

"Our foes are too close on our heels. We must draw them away, or risk leading them right to Annis and Xain. If we must die, let us not be their doom as well."

As if to lend strength to his words, guards erupted from the hallway ahead. Albern pushed her ahead of him as they fled, running until they reached the thick wooden door of the northeast watchtower.

Two guards waited within, swords drawn and eyes wide with alarm. They paused in confusion when they saw Albern in his guardsman's uniform.

That gave him the moment he needed, and one guard fell, his chest laid open by a heavy strike. The other guard traded blows, but only for a moment, for Albern was strengthened by wrath. He plunged the blade deep into the guard's belly, then withdrew it before the man could hit the ground.

Loren winced as each body fell. So many dead, and whatever Jordel had told her, still she only saw men and women following orders. But she held her tongue, for she could hardly think of a worse time to chastise Albern. He had saved her life countless times by now, and did so anew with every stroke of the blade.

"Thank the sky," said Albern. Loren followed his gaze to a bow standing in the corner, a quiver of arrows just beside it. Quickly he sheathed his sword and snatched up the bow. She could almost see his body relax at the familiar feel of the weapon.

They heard boots pounding down the hallway through which they had come. Up the stairs they ran, Loren in the lead once more, until they reached the middle door that led to the battlements.

Once again they emerged into the rain, but this time the night was bright with the flames of many torches set into stands along the wall. Another guard stood just beyond the doorway. Albern did not pause in his run, but merely planted his shoulder in the woman's chest. She pitched backwards, slipping across the wet stones to fall with a cry into the courtyard below.

Looking down, Loren saw that most of the caravans were now black with darkfire. Yerrin guards ran among them, trying to separate the wagons that might still be saved, but none would venture too close to the black flames, which made their work more difficult. She could not see Jordel or Gem—they must have been taken away already. A hopeful thought struck her; mayhap they would be taken to the cells next to the secret passage, where Annis and Xain lay hidden. They might still be rescued.

But first they had to make good their escape. As they ran forwards, Loren heard a shout. An arrow hissed as it flew by. She ducked on instinct before glancing down. They had been spotted. Yerrin guards and stronghold soldiers stood together, some half-dozen of them, bows out and aiming. Albern fired three shots in quick succession, felling two and making the rest scatter for cover. Hidden among the wagons that had not yet caught flame, they kept up their barrage.

"They are only trying to slow us until their friends arrive," said Albern. "Come!"

The door behind them flew open and two guards came out into the rain. Ahead, at the other end of the wall, another pair emerged. Loren and Albern skidded to a halt. He dropped his bow—only two arrows remained in the quiver—and drew his blade as the Shades charged.

Loren drew her hunting knife, and then ducked as a blade swept towards her face. She leapt forwards with a feint, not to draw blood but to drive the soldier back. Her fist swung hard into the man's nose. It crunched beneath her knuckles, and he seized his face, cursing. But she heard another moving up behind her, and had to turn before she could strike again. Her new foe swung overhead, which let her sidestep easily, but her back was now against the ramparts. She leapt and rolled across the stones, a sidelong swipe passing so close she felt the wind of it.

She found her feet and held the knife out again—but then a stray arrow from the courtyard struck the soldier in her face. Her eyes went dead in an instant. The arrow's impact pitched her body over the wall onto the rocks far below. Loren watched in horror; the woman's limbs flopped about like a doll's, and when she struck the ground she bounced, then pitched out over the cliff to plunge into the darkness of the valley.

A hand seized Loren's elbow, snapping her back to the moment. Albern pulled her onwards, stepping over the bodies of the other three guards—all slain. They ran on, Loren feeling more and more nauseated with each passing moment.

Then a figure appeared in the outer doorway leading to the great hall, all the way across the courtyard. Even from the corner of her eye, the massive form caught her attention, and she turned to look. Her heart quailed. It was Trisken.

The stronghold commander stood illuminated in torchlight, shorn of his armor but still wearing his thick leather vest. He looked at the two of them through the rain, his face an impassive mask. No fury marked his expression, nor any confusion. Only a heightened interest, and a dark intent, like a wolf with its eyes on a wounded elk. He stepped into the courtyard, walking around the edge of the caravan towards them, his gaze never leaving Loren's face.

"Albern!" she cried in warning.

Albern turned and saw Trisken, and his look grew dark. He had recovered his bow, and now he drew. The shaft sped true, planting itself in the commander's heart. The brute fell back with a grunt, then sank to one knee. A second shaft sped forwards, striking him in his neck. It almost toppled him backwards, but he put out a hand to steady himself, and Albern's quiver was empty.

Slowly Trisken found his feet again. First he seized the arrow in his neck, tugging it out as though pulling a knife through a hunk of roast meat. He took the arrow in his chest, and to Loren's horror, pushed it deeper until the head erupted out his back. Then he snapped the shaft in two, and threw the fletching away before reaching back with his other hand and pulling forth the arrowhead. With blood pouring down his chest, he continued his advance.

"What manner of creature is he?" cried Loren, voice thick with fear.

"The kind you cannot fight," said Albern, and they ran on.

They made the northwest tower only a few moments before Trisken reached the bottom of it. Before they could run to the next part of the wall, a door crashed open below them. There came the sound of iron-shod boots slamming into stone.

"Come, children." Trisken's voice floated up the stairs towards them. His voice echoed loud as thunder off the stone walls, like the clamor from some dark creature of myth. "We have two of you already, but I want the rest. Come to me, and end your useless flight."

Albern made to pull her on, but Loren stopped him. She had spotted a rope in the corner, and it gave her an idea. After picking it up, she ran on beside Albern—but up the stairs, and not back out to the wall.

"What are you—" Albern hissed, but then understanding flashed in his eyes, and he came without question.

He followed her up, until they found a hatch and burst out onto the top of the tower. Loren's fingers already struggled to tie the rope in a knot, but her mangled palms made every motion difficult.

"Here, let me," said Albern, taking the rope and finishing the knot.

He threw it around the battlement and let the

end trail off into the darkness below. Loren waved her hand. "You first," she said. "My hands are still injured, and it will make me slow."

"All the more reason I should go behind, to protect you in case we are discovered." Loren tried to argue, but he very nearly threw her from the top of the tower. "I will brook no argument. Go! Now!"

Though she thought his stubbornness might get them both killed, she had little choice. Loren seized the rope and swung out into emptiness, lowering herself an arm's length at a time as quickly as she could, boots planted on the wall. The torn skin on her hands, only recently healed, pulled itself open again almost immediately. Loren gritted her teeth and tried not to scream. The rain and blood mingled to make her grip slippery, and she barely made it to the bottom without falling. Once her feet struck the mountain, she kept her hands on the line and tried to steady it, for Albern was coming much faster than she had.

He let himself fall the last few paces and landed already running. Together they fled along the north wall to where Loren knew the secret entrance lay. Her bloody fingers scrabbled along the lines between stone and mortar. At first she could not find the catch, and in a panic she thought she had forgotten where it was. But then her fingers vanished into the wall, and she pulled at the latch. The door swung open, and together they rushed inside.

Annis stood as the door opened, her face a mask

of fear. When she recognized the two of them, she relaxed—but only for a moment. Loren began to swing the door shut, and Annis saw that Jordel and Gem were missing. The door closed with a soft click, and Annis leapt forwards with a cry.

"Where are the others?" she said. "What happened to Gem? What—"

Loren snatched her and pressed a bloody hand over the girl's mouth, drawing her down to the floor. Albern picked up a waterskin and doused the torch on the wall. Pitch darkness enveloped them.

Loren whispered in Annis' ear. "They are gone. I lost them. They were taken. They are gone." The thrill of their flight seeped from her veins, and she felt tears spilling down her cheeks, mingling with the rain water and some stray drops of blood. "They are gone. I lost them."

Then she could say nothing more as her chest heaved in wracking sobs that she tried desperately to silence. They heard footsteps running by outside and the shouts of soldiers. The dim glow of torches shone in the tiny crack between the door and the ground, and then vanished, and then reappeared. But Loren hardly cared. She did not even notice when at last the footsteps and the shouts receded, the thin line of light disappearing from the bottom of the passageway.

"Gone," she sobbed, as Annis took her in an embrace. She pressed her face deep into the girl's shoulder, letting her tears spill forth anew.

Albern managed to light the torch again, and she could see the pain in his eyes as he looked at her. Across the passageway, Xain looked at his feet, his head bowed in grief.

"Gone. I lost them. Forgive me."

THIRTY-TWO

"We have little time," said Albern. "There is no other choice. We must flee the fortress."

It was some time later, and the thin grey light of dawn seeped in under the door. Loren hardly noticed. She sat against the wall, head bowed so far forwards that it hung between her knees. Her hair fell thin and scraggly, reminding her of Xain's when he had suffered from the magestone sickness. Wordless, she nodded.

"What about Jordel and Gem?" said Annis. "You cannot mean to leave them."

"We do not know if they live," said Albern. Though

he spoke sternly and without hesitation, Loren could hear a thickness in his voice that she had never heard there before. "And I made Jordel a vow. I mean to fulfill it, as atonement for leading you upon this road."

"You have nothing to atone for," said Loren. "We have had little choice since the moment we set out from Strapa. I curse the moment we laid eyes upon this fortress. I would rather have walked back into the spears of the satyrs than this place."

Albern's eyes filled with fresh pain, and he turned away from her. "Curse not the fortress, but Strapa itself and the day you met me there. I am to blame, and no other, for the fortune that has befallen you."

Loren raised her head to look at him, not understanding. "You saved us in Strapa, Albern. Without you, the Mystics would have taken us."

"Without me, they would never have known you were there," said Albern, eyes cast downwards. "I was the one who told the Mystics I had seen you. They had reached the town already, and put out word that they sought a party matching your description. After you came into my shop, I followed you back to your inn, and then sought out the Mystics to tell them where you were."

Loren felt as if the ground had vanished beneath her. "But . . . but you saved us. When the Mystics ambushed us, you arrived to lead us to safety."

"That was my plan. I never meant to let them have you, not for long. I would either save you from their clutches in the village itself, as I did, or ambush the Mystics once they left Strapa with you in tow. I thought it was the only way you would choose to take the mountain pass, which I thought safer than the Westerly Road."

Her confusion vanished, but only to be replaced by a rising fury. "And because you thought it would place more coin in your pockets," said Loren. Her voice grew dangerously loud. "All along the road you pretended to befriend us, when in truth you thought only of Jordel's gold."

Albern shook his head. "That is not so. I swear it. How often did he offer me more coin, only to have me refuse him?"

"A fine show," hissed Loren. "Mayhap you thought to steal the rest once we were safely out of the mountains."

"I vow to you, on any oath you could ask, that I thought the mountain pass would be safer," said Albern. "How could I know this stronghold had been occupied in my absence? I thought we would face no danger greater than satyrs. I knew nothing of these Shades, or the Lord who rules them. I promise you."

"The promises of a liar mean nothing," said Loren. She went to the secret door and leaned her arm against it, shaking as she tried to calm herself. It would be fitting, she thought, to open the door and cast him out, to let him be caught by the Shades as Jordel had. He had brought this fate upon them. Let him reap what he had sown.

But slowly, as her blood cooled and her fist stopped twitching before her eyes, she realized that that would do none of them any good. Gem and Jordel were gone, and would not be helped if she lost Albern in the bargain. Despite what he had done, he was the only one of them who knew the mountains. If they managed to escape the stronghold, only Albern could lead them the rest of the way to Northwood. But how could she trust him, now that she knew the truth of him?

Loren turned from the wall and looked at the bowyer, whose face was still cast down and shadowed from the torch's glow. Both Annis and Xain were looking at him as well, the girl and the wizard joined in a rare moment of unity by their anger.

"If, as you say, you feel any remorse for leading us astray, then prove it," said Loren. "We must escape this fortress, and I cannot do it alone. Help me save those of us who remain."

"I will," said Albern, looking up at her with pain in his eyes. "I swear it. Even at the cost of my own life, for that would be a small payment."

"Very well," said Loren. "How shall we do it?"

"I have thought on that," said Albern. "To escape, we shall need two things: horses, and an open gate. If you can take care of the gate, I shall fetch our horses from the corral."

"How?" said Loren. "Guards are posted, and they will not let you simply walk in and take them."

"Let me tend to that," said Albern grimly. "I promise you, they will not stand against me."

"Even if I trust you, how shall I open the gate?" said Loren. "Rarely in my life have I seen a gate at all, much less a guarded one, and I know nothing of their working."

"There is a winch that opens it," said Albern. "It will be in the guard tower, likely on the first floor. You will see a great wheel, with a catch to hold it once it is raised."

Loren remembered when she and Jordel had visited the gate tower together in disguise. She had seen the wheel then—large, almost as tall as she was, and made with many spokes. "I saw it. But I do not know if I can open it myself. It was very large."

"Fortress gates are cleverly made," said Albern. "A single person may turn the wheel. Still, it may take you some time, and the guards will know something is amiss the moment you begin. So we must work in concert, you and I. The moment you hear commotion in the courtyard, which there surely will be once I make off with the horses, you must open the gate as quickly as you can. My distraction should give you time."

"Fine," said Loren. She looked from Albern to Xain. "Then there is only one matter left to tend to."

She went to the wizard and knelt before him. His eyes were clear as he looked back at her, clear and bright and free from madness. Loren quailed at what she was about to do. But then she reminded herself that Jordel had believed Xain's remorse. If she could not trust Xain for herself, she could at least trust in Jordel.

"I mean to free you from your bonds, Xain," said Loren. "Tell me, can I trust you not to betray us when I do?"

Xain nodded slowly, but Annis' head jerked up. "You mean to free him? Now? This plan seems dangerous enough already."

Loren did not take her eyes from Xain. "Jordel said he would not leave Xain behind. In his absence I am bound to carry out his orders. And we cannot make good our escape if we must drag a man with us. I cannot lift him atop a horse as Jordel did."

She reached out and seized Xain's ankles before drawing her hunting knife. The ropes parted easily before her blade, as did the ones at his wrists. She waited. He made no move to pull the gag away. After another moment's pause, she reached up and removed it herself.

"If you mean to speak words of power, say them now," said Loren. "I would rather your betrayal come before our escape than in the middle of it, where it would put us in the hands of the Shades."

"I told you I would do you no harm, Loren of the family Nelda." His voice croaked, but he cleared his throat and went on, stronger. "I meant it. My magic is weak within me, and I doubt I shall be able to make more than sparks for a long time to come. But if I reach for those sparks, it will be only in your defense. And I will echo Albern's vow: if by my life, or death, I can see the two of you to safety, I will."

"I shall hold you to that," said Loren. Her mind drifted to the pockets of her cloak, where she still held the two packets of magestones. She suppressed a shiver. "You know I will not take your life. But if you should betray us again, with my last breath I will ensure you spend the rest of your days in the Greatrocks, under the knives of Shades."

She stood and turned back to Albern. "As soon as the sun rises, we move."

THIRTY-THREE

LOREN THOUGHT LONG ABOUT KEEPING HER BLACK cloak. But daylight was almost upon them, and so it would be useless outside, and the black cloth would give her little help within the castle. So she cast it off and donned instead the blue cloak of her Shade uniform. She had stowed the helmet in their hiding place, and now she put it on as well. The guise would not withstand close scrutiny—surely by now the guards would be on the lookout for strangers in disguise. But it might give her the half-second advantage she would need in a fight, or in an escape.

Xain had wanted to come with Loren, but she refused. He was still too weak to help, and she did not want him unleashing magic that might draw the guards' attention. Instead, Xain and Annis would wait until they heard the stronghold's alarms, and then leave the secret hallway to meet Albern and Loren in front of the fortress gate.

After looking to be sure the way was clear, she and Albern slipped from the secret chamber and into the fortress. Loren had hoped Jordel and Gem might be brought to the jail cells just outside their hiding place, but they had no such luck. As much as it pained her, she knew it was her duty to get Annis, at least, out of the stronghold and to safety. But once they left, she meant to convince Xain, and mayhap Albern, to return and rescue the others. She would have tried it before escaping, but if they failed, Annis would sit wasting away within the stronghold's walls, and either die there, or fall into her mother's clutches.

They hoped to find the hallways empty, but the moment they entered the stronghold, they heard heavy footsteps coming down the hall towards them. They had prepared for this, however, and with hands on their hilts they marched quickly down the hall in the other direction. The guards rounded the corner and saw them coming, but Loren and Albern marched with such conviction that the Shades gave them no second glance. Both pairs passed each other in the hallway, and soon Loren and Albern rounded the corner out of sight.

"Carry on this way to the guardhouse while I make for the courtyard," said Albern. "But hurry. It shall not take me long, I think, to free our horses, and then we must ride with all haste."

Loren nodded, and he stepped outside. She half ran to the end of the hall where the gatehouse door waited, but she paused before opening it. She and Jordel had seen two guards when they came this way before. If they were still here, she planned to try again the ruse Jordel had played; Loren would say she was there to replace one of them, and when one left, subdue the other. She drew a deep breath and stepped through the door.

To her surprise, she found only one guard on duty. He sat near the wheel to open the gate, leaning back in a wooden chair. He shot to his feet when the door opened, but relaxed once he saw her.

"I thought you might be the commander," said the man. "He has been making rounds ever since the spies escaped again."

"In that case I am surprised to see only one on guard here," said Loren, looking around the room to make sure there was no one else about. It was empty.

"Of course there are two of us," he scoffed. "My partner had to take a piss. She shall return in a moment. I told her it was a mistake, leaving post with command breathing down our necks. But I guess some things cannot wait." He snickered.

"Then it is your good fortune, I suppose," said Loren. "I am here to replace one of you. The commander has issued new orders. We are to stagger shifts to keep everyone more alert. And if the spies have learned our movements, they will be misled. Since your partner is missing, I suppose your shift has ended early."

At once his eyes narrowed suspiciously, and Loren knew she had made a mistake. "I have heard no such orders. What is the password, then, if you are to replace me?"

Loren cursed herself for a fool. Of course they would have set up a password. She rolled her eyes and stepped closer, letting her hand drift idly to the back of the chair opposite his, just a pace away. "Are you truly surprised they have not told everyone yet? Things are a mess since—"

She seized the chair with both hands and swung it for his head. The man barely got an arm up in time, and he cried out as the wood cracked against his forearm. Loren leapt forwards, swinging again from above. This time she struck his helmet with a rattling clang, sending it flying to the floor. Still he did not fall. In desperation she dropped the chair, seized his cloak, and struck him. He fell back, slamming his head into one of the spokes of the wheel. His eyes rolled back, and he collapsed.

"There is your password," she said, breathing heavily.

She seized the spokes of the wheel, but then she

stopped. Albern had told her to wait for the clamor of his escape before she turned it. What was taking him so long? A window looked out into the courtyard, giving her a clear view of the gate itself. The spikes at the bottom of the portcullis were sunk deep into the ground. Two guards with spears sat near it, heads hanging down, sheltered from the falling rain by the wall.

Perhaps she should test the gate before Albern stole the horses. Surely no one would notice if she moved the gate only a finger or two. They might think it was just the chains settling. With both hands on the wheel and one eye firmly on the portcullis, Loren tried giving the wheel a spin.

It did not move.

Her pulse thundered. She heaved and heaved, but the spokes would not budge. She looked desperately for the catch Albern had mentioned, which held the gate open but could be knocked out to close it again quickly. She found the mechanism and the catch, just as he had described, but it was not in place. The gate should have opened easily.

No matter how hard she pulled at the wheel, it would not turn. Her nerves turned to panic. Albern would escape with the horses at any moment.

In frustration she struck the wheel with her fist. It shuddered and spun—in the opposite direction. Loren bit her tongue hard enough to bleed, and then seized the wheel and tried again. It turned easily, from right to left instead of left to right.

But through the window she saw the gate fly up—not just a few fingers as she had intended, but almost a pace. The guards stood and seized their spears, shouting in alarm. After looking at the portcullis in confusion, they turned as one to look at the gatehouse.

She froze in fear—but then she heard the shouts of more guards in the courtyard. Horses began to scream, and she heard the ring of blades clashing. Albern had made his move. Loren hauled again at the wheel, pulling as hard and quickly as she could. It moved easily now, and the iron mechanism caught with each turn to keep the gate from falling down. The guards outside wavered, unsure of whether to help in the courtyard or stop Loren from raising the gate farther.

The wheel stopped turning. The gate had reached its full height. Loren turned to make for the door—which crashed open, and two men rushed in with drawn swords. Outside, the keep's bell sounded the alarm. Loren took one look at the doorway, now blocked by two burly soldiers with bared steel, and turned to run up the stairs instead.

They gave chase, shouting, but without armor Loren moved much faster. She passed the middle landing, which was empty, and emerged atop the gate tower into open air. Rain soaked her at once. She threw the wooden hatch closed behind her, and then turned the wooden lever to hold it fast. In a moment she heard pounding from below.

Looking down into the courtyard, Loren saw Albern atop his bay, with Midnight's reins in one hand and the other horses tied to the mare's saddle. They had run in circles to avoid the grasping hands of the guards, but now that the gate was open they made for it at a hard gallop. One whole side of the corral had been cast down, and the other horses were near stampeding at the sudden noise of the bell and the shouting guards. Beyond, the burned husks of the Yerrin caravans still stood, little more than piles of ash and the broken remains of wheel housings. Loren smiled grimly at that.

The pounding at the hatch redoubled, and she heard the splinter of wood as the catch began to give. A narrow walkway, thankfully abandoned, connected the top of her gate tower to the other. Loren ran along it, looking for some means of escape. But the hatch atop the next tower burst open, and guards surged forth. They saw her and charged with a battle cry.

Loren skidded to a halt on the wet stone. She could not go forwards, nor could she go back. In desperation she looked over the back of the walkway, but the courtyard lay some eight paces below her. The front was the same—but then she saw the portcullis. Raised as it was, its iron grid was only two paces below the top of the wall.

Just before the guards reached out to grasp her, Loren vaulted over the front of the wall and caught the gate. She wore the leather gloves of a guards' uniform, but still the impact shot agony through her mangled hands.

She had no time to think of that now. Swiftly she climbed down, one arm's length at a time, using the iron bars like a ladder. She reached the bottom just as Albern shot out from the gate atop the horses.

"Albern!"

He wheeled around to look up at her. "Jump!" he cried.

The distance still seemed too great, but she had no choice. Loren let herself fall. She came down hard on the paving stones of the entranceway, but thankfully her ankle did not twist beneath her. She rolled with the impact, crying out as pain lanced her ribs. She came up scrabbling and ran for the horses.

Behind her, Yerrin men and Shades had gathered. They came pouring out after her, scarcely a few paces behind. Xain and Annis burst into view and ran for Albern. Loren wanted to faint from relief.

She and the others reached the horses almost at the same time. They vaulted into their saddles. With a cry and the kick of his heels, Albern spurred his bay out and across the bridge. The other horses followed, and together they rode away from the Shade stronghold as the curses and cries of their pursuers faded away on the air.

THIRTY-FOUR

"WE WILL NOT HAVE LONG!" CRIED ALBERN, SHOUTING over the thundering hooves. "They will not let us escape so easily, and soon they will recover their steeds. Ride as hard as you can, and do not stop for anything!"

They hardly needed his urging. The stronghold had already vanished in the rain behind them, but still Loren could feel its presence, like a great malevolent being with all its thought bent upon them. Mayhap it was only her imagination, or mayhap some dark magic of Trisken's, but either way she urged Midnight on to greater and greater speed.

She caught a glimpse of Annis' face as they rode, wide-eyed and filled with fright as Loren knew her own must be. Xain rode silently, his eyes filled with quiet intensity as he gripped the reins. He must be in great pain, she realized, for likely he was still weak from the magestone sickness.

Despite Loren's sense of a watchful presence behind them, they saw no sign of pursuit. The road from the stronghold delved straight into a crevasse in the mountains, where a peak looked like it had been cloven in two by a giant's axe. The cleft made a passageway that had been flattened by craftsmen long ago, and was wide enough for all of them to ride abreast with room on either side. The passageway ended after a time, and Loren was surprised to see another gate looming ahead. But this one had long fallen into disrepair, and the Shades had not yet occupied it. The stone bridge between the towers had fallen to rubble, and the towers themselves looked ready to collapse with a strong gust of wind. Not a soul observed them as they passed through, slowing to a brisk walk so the horses would not lose their footing upon the stones.

"I am glad to see this place empty," said Albern.

"You knew it was here?" said Loren.

He tossed his head. "It was here when last I came this way. I guessed that the Shades had not yet taken it, for as you can see it is in far worse repair than the stronghold."

"And what if you had been wrong, and we found soldiers waiting to stop us?" said Annis angrily.

Albern shrugged. "Then we would have devised another plan. It hardly seemed likely that we would get this far."

Beyond the gate lay another narrow pass snaking through the mountains. They seemed to be heading gently downwards now, and Loren thought this must be the descent out of the mountains that Albern had spoken of. The horses stepped with more vigor, almost as if they could sense freedom ahead. But still Loren felt darkness haunting their steps, and she could not shake the feeling.

Then, as they crested a rise and prepared to climb down the other side, they heard a screeching on the air. Instinct made them duck even as their horses reared beneath them. Harpies swept down out of the air to attack.

"Now we know they are minions of Trisken—or mayhap of his master," cried Albern. "I thought our escape seemed too easy."

He had his bow in his hand, and had stolen many arrows from within the stronghold. Shafts flew up to strike the creatures as they dove, and several fell before him. The rest swooped up and away, screaming at the party in fury. They dove again, and Loren brought her own bow up to shoot them. But they dodged and wove in tight curves as they descended, and she could not find her mark; only Albern's arrows sped true.

Beside her, she saw a familiar glow. She glanced over and saw light blooming from Xain's eyes. His hand twisted into a claw as he whispered words in a strange tongue. He raised the hand skyward, his flames streaking for the harpies. It was a weak, sputtering fire, far more meager than she had seen from him before, but it curved in the air and struck one of the beasts, singeing its wings. Once more the harpies broke off their attack.

Xain slumped forwards over his saddle, holding the horn tightly to keep himself from falling. With a nudge of her heels, Loren brought Midnight alongside him and gripped his shoulder.

"Are you all right?" she said.

"I have not the strength," he gasped. "Not yet. I am sorry."

"Do not blame yourself," said Albern. "We are too exposed. Come! Let us ride."

Their horses flew down the mountainside now, needing no urging from their riders as they caught the harpies' scent. The harpies swooped low, emboldened by the party's flight. But Albern took them off the path and into the thin, scrubby trees to the right, where the harpies could no longer see them.

"This will not last," said Albern. "But mayhap we can remain under cover until we think of a plan, or until those creatures give up."

"They will not give up," said Loren. "And if we wait too long, no doubt the Shades will find us."

"What is your counsel, then? Ride back out into the open?" said Albern gruffly. Then he ducked his head. "I am sorry. I have no right to speak thus."

Before Loren could answer, braying erupted from the mountains all around. They wheeled their horses about, Albern nocking an arrow quicker than blinking. Loren's eyes went wide. From the crags all around them came satyrs, clutching weapons and vaulting down on their hairy hind legs. There were far more than they had seen before reaching the Shade stronghold, and the goat-men's faces twisted in rage.

"More minions of the Shades!" said Albern. "Ride on!"

They had no choice except to return to the open path, and their horses raced down it in panic. But the road twisted and turned, and the satyrs could leap straight over any rise the road had to avoid. They gained ground swiftly. The harpies drew ever closer, until Loren could feel the wind of their wings.

"They will be upon us in moments!" said Loren. "Albern, we must find some hiding place."

His face was grim as he brought his horse to a halt, looking at her from across the road. "There are none. No places where they will not find us. Yet mayhap there is somewhere to make our stand."

Loren's throat went dry. She understood his words: a *last* stand, some place where they could fight until they were overwhelmed. It seemed a cruel way to die, here on the road so far from home. Would anyone find her bones, or would they be mere fodder for the satyrs?

Albern took them off the road again, to a small hollow that lay close by. The mountainside curved up and over it, forming a sort of cave that blocked the harpies. There were many boulders laid across the opening to offer cover from the satyrs' arrows. Albern led them in at a gallop, and when they came to a halt they all dismounted.

At once Albern went to the mouth of the hollow, bow half-drawn in his hand. The satyrs pulled up short, out of bowshot, beating their spears against each other and bleating. The harpies circled, screaming with their eyes fixed on the travelers. The hollow ended some ten paces in. There was no way out, except through their enemies.

"The satyrs will strike first," said Albern. His voice was matter-of-fact, as though he were giving them directions to the nearest inn. "Likely they are waiting for some champion to come forth and drive them onwards."

"What do we do?" said Annis, gripping Loren's arm. "How do we escape?"

Albern turned to her and spoke flatly. "We do not escape. We fight until we are killed. If you wish to die with a weapon in your hand, I shall give you one. If you wish to use it upon me before our enemy strikes, I will not blame you, or stop you."

But Loren ignored him and Annis both. She pulled

her arm from the girl's clutching hand and went instead to Xain. The wizard leaned on a boulder near the entrance. His eyes were closed, and he drew deep, hasty breaths, as though he had just run a league without stopping.

"Xain, how deeply can we trust you?"

He opened his eyes to stare at her in confusion. "With your lives, though I do not blame you for doubting me. Yet I can be of little help now. You saw my flames upon the road. I could not defeat Gem with my magic, much less this army of evil beasts."

"If you had such power, would you use it to help us?"

"Of course, I—" Xain froze. His eyes found hers, and in his face she saw a curious light. But it dampened in an instant, and he turned away.

Loren went to Midnight's saddle, where she had thrown the bag Annis had brought during their escape. She withdrew her black cloak, and from its pocket she produced a brown cloth packet. Annis gasped. Loren returned to Xain and held the packet out to him.

"Here is all the strength you need," she said. "Prove that your words are not an empty boast. Use your power to help us."

"You are mad," said Xain and Annis at the same time. They looked at each other for a moment, and then Xain went on. "You saw what they did to me—when I used them, and after. I would not wish that pain on my most hated enemy."

"He is right, Loren," said Albern. "This course seems unwise. I have seen magestone sickness; it is not something I would witness again."

"Yet with the stones' power, you vanquished Vivien upon the Dragon's Tail," said Loren. "You were starved half to death, yet you defeated her. You staved off the Dorsean invasion of Wellmont. You sank their fleet upon the river west of the city."

"And I nearly killed all of you," snapped Xain. "Loren, I *tried* to kill you. I wanted to, desperately. You do not know the whispers that magestones plant in the mind. You cannot imagine how hard I had to struggle just to keep you all—"

"Enough!" roared Loren. Xain fell silent and took a step back. "You claim you are sorry for what you did. You say you wish to atone for your wrongs. Prove it. Prove it now, or we all die here. You say the magestones whisper to you, and that it is a struggle to resist them. Then struggle, and win. Was it torturous to suffer the magestone sickness? Then suffer that torture again. Do it to save us, and to save our friends, and prove you are worthy of the trust that Jordel placed in you."

Xain stared at the ground and did not answer her at first. Outside the hollow, the satyrs brayed louder. Albern had not fired at them yet, and they were growing bolder. Xain looked over his shoulder, out into the open air where the beasts waited.

Then, in one sudden motion, he snatched the brown cloth packet from her hand and ripped it open.

With thin and wasted fingers, he plucked one of the magestones from the packet and shoved it between his lips. His teeth crunched down, and he swallowed.

Xain bent his head, his shoulders shuddering. Though he was the same height as always, Loren would have sworn that she *felt* him grow, somehow. As she watched in fascination, the skin of his hands and hollow cheeks filled out, and where his hair had been patchy and thin before, it grew thick and lustrous, glinting in the grey sunlight that filtered down through the clouds. From behind his closed eyelids, Loren saw white light spill forth, like fire hidden behind a doorframe. Slowly the white light turned black. He opened his eyes, and they were bottomless pools of ebony, looking at her without emotion. Loren had to restrain herself from stepping back.

"Xain?" she said tentatively.

"I am here," he said. "I am myself."

He turned on his heel, so suddenly that Loren jumped. He strode out between the boulders and into the open air. Albern reached to grab the wizard's arm, but Loren stopped him.

The satyrs had edged slowly forwards. When they saw Xain emerge, they fell back bleating. But when they realized he was alone and unarmed, they cried out in rage and swept forwards to attack.

Xain called out a word and swept his arm in a wide arc.

A wall of fire erupted from the ground, casting

earth high into the air with a tumultuous explosion. The fire swept forth, and though the satyrs turned to flee, they could not run fast enough. The flames covered and consumed them, and they fell wailing to the ground, their bodies burning away.

The harpies, seeing the satyrs' fate, wheeled in the air to flee. But Xain put forth his power, and a gale of wind swept down from the sky. The rainclouds above turned into a storm, black and terrible, and lightning crashed from on high. It struck with terrible fury, turning great circles of earth into molten rock. The bolts struck the harpies down, and in moments the skies were clear.

Xain's magic subsided, and all was silent.

Loren stood beside Albern, both of them frozen in awe. Annis hid behind them, clutching Loren's sleeve as if for protection.

As if I could save her from Xain, if he chose to harm us.

Xain turned back, and the black glow faded from his eyes. His eyes were grim, but curling the corner of his mouth was the same smirk he had worn the day Loren first met him. She swallowed hard, hoping she had not made a terrible mistake.

He tossed his head. "Come. Fetch the horses. We ride for the fort."

THIRTY-FIVE

LOREN SWUNG ONTO MIDNIGHT WHILE ALBERN mounted his bay. She snatched the reins of Jordel's charger, which Xain had ridden from the Shade stronghold. But then she saw Annis climbing atop the plow horse.

"Annis, you should remain here," said Loren. "We are in for a fight, and even if Xain can defeat our enemies, still it will not be safe."

"I am coming," said Annis. "My mother awaits, and I have spent too long running from her. She will never give up her hunt until I make her."

"She will not give up even then," said Loren. "She knows you do not wish to return. Telling her again will not change her mind."

"I did not say I would *tell* her to leave me alone, I said I will *make* her," said Annis, shaking with rage. "She meant to bargain with those Shades in order to find me—killers, serving a dark and secret Lord. I shall never be free unless I stop her."

"What will you do?" said Loren. "Kill her yourself? How, then, will you be better than her?"

"I . . ." Annis stopped, her fists shaking as they held her reins. "I do not know. But let her see me riding at your side. Let her see that I myself have chosen where I stand, and it is with you. Still she thinks of me only as her daughter. Let her see me across a battle line, as her enemy. Then mayhap she will think twice before trying to bring me back."

Loren looked at Albern helplessly, but the bowyer only shrugged. "I would be unwise to give you counsel. You know far more of this tale than I do."

"The longer we wait, the greater the danger to Jordel and Gem," said Xain harshly. "Let her come, if she wishes it. Unless you want to tie her up and leave her helpless here, where she might be found by some passing wolf, or more satyrs lying in wait."

"Very well," said Loren, kicking her heels into Midnight's flanks in frustration. "But if you get yourself killed, I will find you in another life and box your ears for your stupidity."

They led the horses back to the road, and then spurred them to a gallop up it. Hoofbeats warred with the howl of wind and rain. Often Loren looked over at Xain, still not entirely sure her choice had been wise. But at least he rode alongside them now. If he could save Jordel and Gem, even if he used his magic to escape afterwards, then it would be worth it.

They soon passed the crumbled outer gate, but a moment later they pulled their horses to a halt. Darklight blazed in Xain's eyes, and Albern nocked an arrow.

On the road before them was an army. Yerrin men, all bedecked in green, every man wearing a helmet and a shirt of chain. They bore spears and swords and marched in formation, and as soon as they saw the party they drew up behind their shields. At the rear of the column were some on horseback—and Loren saw Damaris there, with Gregor on a great steed beside her. The merchant saw Annis, and her eyes widened in relief before she turned on Loren with white-hot fury.

"So, thief," said Damaris. "You return to my open arms. Have you come to fling yourself at my feet and beg for mercy? You have a convincing tongue. Mayhap you will even earn it."

"I have never needed your mercy before, and I will not ask it now," said Loren. "Order your men to stand aside. Our quarrel is not with you."

"You and I shall always have quarrel," said Damaris. "So many times I could have ended your life, but always I stayed my hand. I thought I saw the seed of something useful in you. I thought to shape you into wisdom and skill. I was a fool for it. I should have slit your throat in that jail cell, you puppet of Mystics."

"I am no one's puppet," said Loren. "I stand for myself, and for my friends. Mayhap you could have killed me, once upon a time, but that chance is long gone. Stand aside. I will not ask you again."

Damaris ignored her, turning to Annis. "Daughter. Come back to me. You ride with fools. They stand against foes they cannot hope to comprehend. They will be ground to dust under the boots of their enemy. Save yourself from that fate."

"And resign myself to a worse one?" said Annis. "No, Mother. I will not come back to you now. I have longed to escape you since I was only a little girl."

"You are a little girl still." The merchant's eyes darkened. "You prove it over and over again, like a bard who knows only one song. Tell me, Annis, how rich has been your life since joining Loren's company? How flea-ridden the beds, how meager your meals? I see scars upon you that were not there before, and you dress in the rags of a pauper. Oh, but you are wise to choose such a path, surely. Any child in the nine lands would kill their own siblings for the wealth and plenty I gave you."

"Because they would not know the cost," said Annis, shaking. Though tears leaked from her eyes to mingle with the raindrops on her cheeks, still she sat tall and proud in her saddle, looking at Damaris with barely contained anger. "When I was barely old enough to walk, you made me give a man a goblet of poisoned wine, and then forced me to watch as it choked the life from him. You sat me down to watch as your dungeon keepers flayed their victims to death, all for a morsel of information that would let you earn another hundred gold weights."

"How terrible for you," said Damaris, face twisting in mock pity. "To see so many terrible things—and then turn around and enjoy all the coin my actions provided us."

"We never lacked for coin in the first place," cried Annis. "And one day I came to see the truth. Of all the evils you have committed, none were for wealth. You enjoy it. You love to cause pain, and grief, and misery. You drink it in and cannot stop, like a woman who is always searching for another wineskin. And you hoped to make me like you, because then you would not be so alone in your misery. For you *are* miserable, Mother, a miserable woman whose only pale shade of joy is found in the hurting of others. But you are also alone, for I shall never be like you."

Damaris' hands tightened on her reins, the dark skin of her knuckles paler for a moment. "Take her, and the girl," she said. "Kill the others."

Gregor bellowed the advance, and the Yerrin soldiers pressed forwards. Albern raised his bow and drew—but then the black light in Xain's eyes blazed, and he put forth his hand. A gale sprang from nowhere to blast the soldiers, casting them off to either side of the road. Then great wells of fire bloomed around them, encircling them in fences of flame. The soldiers cried out in terror and fell back, pressing into each other in tight knots, trying to keep their limbs from burning.

The ten horsemen at the rear had not advanced, and were as yet unharmed. With a battle cry, Gregor drew his sword, and he and five soldiers spurred their mounts.

"Stop!" cried Damaris.

Gregor yanked on his reins at once, and his riders did the same. Their horses slid to a stop in the mud, and Gregor looked back at his lady.

"Magestones," said Damaris, looking at Xain with seething fury. "You use my own strength against me. Very well, Loren of the family Nelda. It seems I cannot contest you—not today, at least."

"My lady—" said Gregor.

"No," she snapped. "It is done. I will not lose you in a fight you cannot hope to win. Get off the road and let them pass."

Gregor fixed Loren with a long, ugly look, as his men led their horses off the road and towards the others, who were still surrounded by Xain's fires. Only when they had removed themselves did he turn his steed and ride back to Damaris. Then they left the road together, clearing the way for Loren and the others.

Slowly, half expecting a trick, Loren led Midnight forwards. The other horses fell in behind. She felt prickles on the back of her neck under the eyes of the Yerrin soldiers, but no one moved so much as a muscle—until they had nearly passed the soldiers by.

One footman, probably hoping to earn the favor of his lady, drew and loosed an arrow that sped through the air towards Xain. But the wizard caught the shaft in a fist of air, flinging it aside where it buried itself in the dirt. With a flick of Xain's wrist, the archer flew screaming into the air. Then the dark glow of Xain's eyes increased, and with a clench of his fist the Yerrin soldier erupted in darkfire.

"No!" cried Loren. But it was too late. The man was past saving. His screams were hideous, and Loren shuddered. Xain glanced at her, and the anger fell from his face. His fist opened, and the darkfire guttered out. The soldier fell limp to the ground.

Gregor and his horsemen reached for their blades, but Damaris cried out again, "Stop!" She looked in disgust at the fallen archer, whose body lay smoking near his comrades. "I told you it is pointless. The fool deserved his fate. Stay your hand unless you wish the same."

Loren and the rest now stood on the other side of the Yerrin guards. She turned Midnight one last time, fixing Damaris with a steely look.

"Do not come after us. You know Xain's might. He will not hesitate to unleash it upon you."

Damaris snorted. "Save me your threats. They are for fools who do not know their enemy's strength. I know yours all too well, for it came from me. Everything you have came from me—*Nightblade.*" She spat the word like a curse. Then she looked to her daughter one last time, her eyes softening. "Annis. I know you have been led astray. I know you think this girl is your friend. She is not. Ones such as you and I, we have no friends. There is only family. One day you will remember it, and when you do, come home. We can never forget, but I will forgive. Always remember, Annis: I need you."

With that, she turned her horse and led it down the mountain road. Xain let his flames subside, and the Yerrin guards, though cautious at first, soon fell in to march behind their lady. Gregor stayed the longest, his ugly look fixed on Loren, but then he, too, turned to follow. Soon they had all vanished into the rainclouds.

THIRTY-SIX

THEY FOUND THE STRONGHOLD DRAWN UP AND READY to defend itself against them.

The party halted just out of bowshot. The bridge before them was empty, as was the rock shelf all around—but the walls were well occupied, with many Shades in blue and grey standing with spears and bows in hand.

Albern looked to Xain. "I imagine you have some way to get us in?"

"That gate cannot stop me. Nor will the soldiers on the walls. We need not fear their spears and arrows."

"And what of Trisken?" said Albern. "You saw him when we fought in the caves. Some dark magic protects him. He cannot be slain by blade or bolt."

Xain's smirk widened, becoming a smile that was almost cruel. "I have neither blade nor bolt at my disposal. But let him test himself against my flames, and we shall see if ashes can come back to life."

He dismounted and walked for the bridge. Loren and the others made to follow, but he turned sharply.

"Stay," he said. "I would rather not worry about protecting you. Let me clear the path first."

Loren hesitated, but Albern spoke in her place. "As you wish." He nodded to Loren, and they stilled their horses while Xain walked on.

As he reached the bridge, someone on the wall gave a shout. The archers lifted their bows and drew. Arrows sailed through the air towards him. Though she knew his powers well, still Loren straightened in her saddle, and she almost cried out for him to flee.

But Xain reached out, and even from behind him she could see the dark glow emanating from his eyes. The arrows halted in midflight, trapped inside a wall of air. As Xain cast his arm forwards, the arrows flew back towards their enemies, showering them with death. The Shades ducked behind the battlements, but several were too slow and pitched into the courtyard, screaming as they died.

Loren turned away, refusing to look. But she could not block out the sound, even when she covered her ears. *It is Xain's doing,* she told herself. *I could not stop him even if I tried.*

Xain came to the far end of the bridge, just a few paces away from the stronghold gate. The archers dared to loose another volley, but he cast it back just as easily. This time they were ready and ducked behind the battlements. They must have thought to keep shooting until they broke his defenses, thinking they were safe behind their gate.

They were wrong. Xain sent forth a roaring ball of flame that crashed into the gate with a thunderous explosion. It blew inwards, shattering into a thousand shards of molten metal. The shrapnel tore at the bodies of the men gathered on the other side. Their screams turned Loren's stomach.

Albern caught her eye. "What now of your promise not to take a life?"

"It is not my choice," said Loren, shaking. "Xain casts the flames. I would not have killed them."

The words sounded hollow, even in her own ears. She had given him the magestones, without which Xain would have no such power. Not for this, and not to kill the Yerrin guard who had shot at them upon the road. But then, if she had not given him the stones, they would all be dead. That was what she had to remind herself.

And after Jordel and Gem were rescued? Then, Loren could only hope he would remember his vow to remain true.

Shades ran down from the battlements to assemble in the courtyard, standing before Xain in rank and file. Loren could barely glimpse them through the gate. Xain sent forth another wall of flame, just as he had against the satyrs in the hollow. This time, though, he showed mercy, and did not send it rushing towards them. The heat of it put terror enough into their hearts, and they turned to flee. She heard a crash as the stronghold's west gate was thrown open. The Shades ran for their lives down the road and into the valley far below. Then Xain let his flames die, and he turned to look at her across the bridge.

His eyes were lit with battle-wrath, and a fierce smile twisted his lips. But then he saw Loren's face, and the anger and smile died as one. The flame guttered to sparks, and then to nothing, and his hands fell to his sides.

"Come forth now," he called. "But keep a wary eye still. There may be more of them skulking about."

Albern put himself at their head, riding forwards with an arrow nocked but undrawn. Loren and Annis followed close behind, their eyes searching for threats in the deathly silence. There was no sound but the hollow wind whistling through the peaks. Even the rain had finally stopped, though the air still hung thick and wet, threatening to resume the downpour at any moment.

One thought nagged at Loren: they had yet to see Trisken. She knew she would have spotted him upon the castle wall, and she could not picture him fleeing into the valley with the rest of his men.

"Beware of Trisken," she said sharply—though part of her wanted to remain silent, as though by speaking his name she would invite him to appear.

"Aye," said Albern. "And if we see him, you run. Let Xain and me deal with him."

"Easily promised, and still more easily done," said Loren.

The courtyard was quiet, and empty but for the mangled bodies of the Shades. Loren was relieved to see fewer than she had thought, but still she felt sick at the loss of their lives. Whatever promises had led these men to join the Shades, she doubted they had agreed to face a wizard wroth with magestones.

"We know they are not keeping Jordel and Gem in the jail beside the secret entrance," she said. "But there is another in the south wall. Let us search there."

No one wanted to be the first to open the door leading inside, but after a moment Xain threw it open and strode in. For him, mayhap the fear was not so great. The hallway was empty, bare even of torches. Xain threw forth a ball of blue magefire that floated in front of them. Loren led them to the jail, but the cells were empty.

"Where else would he keep them?" said Annis. Loren could see the worry on the girl's face, and knew that nearly all of it was for Gem. "Are there dungeons below the castle, perhaps?"

"Not likely," said Albern. "Few masons would burrow into the land beneath a fortress and thus weaken its foundation—especially so high in the Greatrocks, where faults in the stone are common."

"They might be in the great hall," said Loren. Her heart was heavy; she had feared it might be so since they first entered, for some whisper in her mind said they would not find their friends in the jail. The great hall was where they had seen Trisken for the first time. If the foreboding in her heart held any truth, it was where they would find him again.

Albern must have sensed her mind, for his face grew as grim as she felt. But he led them back to the courtyard without comment, and together he and Xain approached the wide wooden doors that opened into the hall.

"Quiet as we enter," said Albern. "We cannot know what—"

Xain gave a snort and sent forth wind, blasting the doors open with a gust. They slammed into the walls and sent a great thundering *boom* to echo throughout the stronghold.

"Or we could cast prudence to the winds," said Albern amiably. He motioned Loren and Annis back as he sidled up to the edge of the doorway.

Loren ignored him and crept forwards, hand on her dagger, though she knew better than to draw it except at utmost need. But Xain strode in without hesitation, straight through the center of the hall. As

Loren and Albern followed him more cautiously, they saw their worry had been baseless. Trisken did not lie within, nor did any other Shade—but there were Jordel and Gem. They sat in simple wooden chairs, facing away from the door towards the dais. Their hands and feet were bound, and they did not move.

Their heads hung limp upon their chests. From behind, Loren could see the knots of gags. Even at the great din from Xain's entrance, neither of them stirred. She saw blood soaking their clothing.

Loren's heart quailed, and she felt rooted to the floor.

Annis had no such restraint. *"Gem!"* she screamed, running forwards as tears ran down her face. "Gem, no!"

She came around his front and seized his face, lifting it up. Tears spilled anew as she shook him, his head flopping limply in her hands.

Then he yanked his head back and out of her grasp, shaking it with a muffled groan.

"Gem!" cried Loren. Her limbs answered the command of her mind at last, and she ran to him.

Annis hurried to remove his gag, and once free of it, Gem looked up at the two of them. "Why would you do that?" he groused. "I think my head hurts enough without your help, thank you."

When Loren saw his face, she gasped and covered her mouth. He was purple with bruises, and a gash in his forehead stretched from temple to hairline. His arms, too, were covered in welts, and beneath his collar she could see great purple splotches where he had been struck again and again.

"Gem," cried Annis, holding his head in her arms. "Gem, Gem. We thought we lost you."

"You did not, though you will if you keep strangling me," croaked the boy. "I would kill half the kingdom for even a drop of water."

Annis hastened to fetch some from the horses in the courtyard, while Loren turned to Jordel. His head lolled like Gem's, but she could see the rise of his chest as he breathed. He looked, if anything, worse than the boy. But as she shook him gently, his eyes snapped open, and he looked up at her with a gaze as sharp as ever.

Loren quickly untied the gag, and then held his gaze as Albern knelt behind him to cut his bonds. "Greetings, Mystic," she said lightly. "Your rescue has arrived—though late, for which I hope you can find forgiveness."

"Loren," said Jordel, his voice quiet but still strong. "How . . . where is Trisken?"

Loren felt a shiver down her spine, but she shook it off and smiled at him. "Hidden in some hole, no doubt. We have not seen him, though we managed to frighten off his army."

Albern finished with the bonds, and Jordel rubbed at his wrists, which were chafed raw. "What . . . how did you manage it?" But then he turned, and his eyes fell upon Xain. He saw the strength in the wizard's limbs, and the harsh look upon his face. The Mystic's face grew grim.

Before he could say or do something rash, Loren laid a restraining hand on his shoulder. "It is all right, Jordel. He saved us, and you as well. Without him we would already be dead."

"You gave him more stones," said Jordel. He looked at her in smoldering anger. "Loren, did you learn nothing from Wellmont?"

"We would already be dead," Loren said again, more harshly this time. "I had a choice: trust him, or become a feast for satyrs and harpies. You yourself said you believed his remorse. I put my faith in him—and you as well, rather than let us all be killed."

"A long enough time it took the two of you," said Xain with a bitter laugh. "But fear not, mighty Mystic. The sickness has not claimed me yet, nor will I let it again. It seems I am your puppet once more, as I think I was fated to be."

Jordel met his eyes and frowned. "That is something I have never asked of you. I want you by my side of your own choice, or not at all. If you think I hold you upon some leash, then you are worse off than when the magestone sickness ate away at your limbs, and would do well to be quit of us as soon as you can."

Xain's anger faltered, and he cast his eyes away. "I . . . I am sorry. I did not mean you insult. The . . . the power, it . . ." He trailed off and shook his head. "No matter. We should leave here."

His arm over Albern's shoulder, Jordel shuffled outside. Gem tried to walk with Annis' help, but his steps came too slow. Loren scooped him up in her arms like a babe, at which he squawked—but then he settled down in her grasp, as though she bore him on a litter.

"I would travel all the nine lands if I could find transport like this," he said.

Loren made as if to drop him, catching him at the last second. Gem whimpered at the pain of his bruises. "My pardon," she said, smiling brightly. "I am not so steady a steed as a good horse, you can clearly see."

Gem only glared at her and muttered darkly.

They mounted their horses. Jordel took back his charger, while Xain fetched another from the corral, which the Shades had abandoned. Gem sat behind Annis, clutching her tightly and wincing at every step the plow horse took. To ease their injuries, they walked slowly to the stronghold's east gate, stepping out before the bridge and to freedom.

But just beyond the gate, they reined to a halt.

Loren's blood turned to ice, and she felt the children quail on their horse beside her.

Trisken stood on the bridge to block their escape, and an evil smile split his face from ear to ear.

THIRTY-SEVEN

THE COMMANDER STOOD UNCARING IN THE MIDDLE of the bridge, his warhammer standing on its head beside him, the handle leaning against his thigh. But he did not wear the sleeveless shirt and vest they had seen him in before. Now he wore a suit of full plate, gleaming dark grey metal that covered his arms and legs and breast. Upon his head was a helmet with two small black horns jutting forth from the forehead. Loren remembered how he had slammed his face into Jordel's, and was nearly sick at the thought of those horns punching through flesh and bone. Even his hands and feet were shod in metal, with interlocking plates that looked thick as a finger. Loren wondered how he could even move in such armor.

Trisken's smile widened as they watched him. "Why do you wish to leave my company so early? Have I proved such a terrible host? I know that Jordel, at least, enjoyed his stay with me. Why, you cried my praises all throughout the night."

Jordel glared from a face that was a mass of bruises. But before he could speak, Xain spurred forwards, and when he reached the bridge he dismounted.

"You might think to frighten the others—but not me," said the wizard, his voice rumbling with hidden power. "I was bound and helpless when last I saw you. I am not so now. Do you wish to test yourself against my strength?"

"I hear the magestones that lie behind your words, wizard," said Trisken. "I am not impressed. Scuttle back to your master before I teach you the meaning of courtesy."

Xain's eyes glowed, and he formed balls of flame in each fist. "I have been freed by one who holds life sacred," he said. "At her wish, I will give you one chance, since you have not yet raised a hand against us. Turn and fly. Vanish into the mountains, and never show your face in the nine lands again. Fail to obey me, and I will end your tale here."

"I raised my hand against the Mystic and the boy, while you hid somewhere in these mountains," said

Trisken. "They still bear the marks. But of course, you were not there to see it. Here. I shall show you."

He seized the handle of his warhammer and swung it in a wide arc. It slammed into his left hand with a loud *clang* of metal. Then he took one step forwards—only one, his plate boots grinding on the stone.

Jordel and Albern nudged their horses, but Xain turned to them and raised a hand. "Stay back, for my fires may fly wild, and I would spare you from their heat."

They halted. Albern wore a look of relief, but Jordel's frown only deepened.

Xain put forth his power, and the sky darkened above them all. The clouds swirled down into a great spiral, channeling towards Trisken where he stood on the bridge. Then a great lightning bolt arced forth. Its thunder was deafening, leaving a ringing noise at the edge of hearing. The ground where Trisken stood erupted in a burst of light, throwing up a plume of stone dust.

But through the dust, Trisken stepped through, rolling his shoulders as though an ache in his neck pained him.

Xain paused. Loren saw it, and could almost feel his hesitation. But then he loosed his power again, this time with flame. It rolled towards Trisken in a great wave. But when it reached the commander it rippled and roiled, splitting before him as though upon an invisible wedge, and passed him without harm. The man did not even seem to sweat inside his armor.

"Stop toying with him, Xain!" cried Annis.

Terrible knowledge dawned upon Loren. "Xain is not sparing him," she murmured. "He is . . ."

Her words cut off as a deep and terrible laugh issued forth from Trisken's helmet. "What is wrong, little firemage?" he said. "Come, throw more sparks my way. I shall use them to roast you all on a great spit."

He was getting closer now, and Loren wanted to cry out for Xain to flee. But the wizard held his ground. He let loose with a gale to blast Trisken back, but the winds guttered and died almost before they had fled his fingertips. In desperation he shot white-hot flames at the stones of the bridge. Rock and mortar melted, turning it from a solid roadway into a pit of red liquid. But as Trisken continued his relentless advance, the stone cooled beneath his feet. Each place he stepped turned solid again, giving him a narrow walkway across the guttering flames.

Cursing, Xain finally stepped back, but even in his retreat he struck again. Darkfire sprouted from his fingers, twisting with a fury blacker than a night without moons. In grasping tendrils it stretched forth, like the fingers of the dead, twisting around Trisken and wreathing him in ebony flames.

And then Loren saw, or thought she saw, a dark glow—not from Xain's eyes, but from Trisken. Its darklight emanated from the commander's head, or somewhere about his neck, and its malevolence matched the cold fury in Xain's glare.

It lasted only a moment, and then it vanished. But the darkfire fell back as though a wind had blown it away, and vanished to nothing on the air.

Jordel and Albern leapt forwards, but too late. Trisken reached Xain and struck, swinging his warhammer around for the wizard's chest. Xain twisted, but not far enough—he took the force of the blow on his shoulder instead of his chest. It spun him around and tossed him to the ground. He cried out with pain.

Then Jordel was there. His sword struck twice on Trisken's armor before the larger man backed away. With more space between the combatants, Albern let loose two shafts. Both found joints in Trisken's armor, in the shoulder and the groin, and pierced the chain mail there. But now that she was looking for it, Loren saw the glow of darklight again—just a flash of it, and this time she was sure it was the neck. Trisken stumbled, but then he ripped the arrows free and attacked Jordel with a vengeance.

Albern ceased his volley to stoop and grip Xain's boot, pulling the wizard across the stones and out of the fight. Loren leapt from her horse and seized her bow, running to stand beside the bowyer. Behind her she saw Gem struggle to climb down from his saddle, but Annis seized his bruised arm in her hands and squeezed. "Do not be an idiot, Gem! You will only get yourself killed."

Loren drew an arrow as Albern had taught her, the motion coming easier now. But she did not have his aim, and she knew it. Jordel and Trisken were locked in a frantic dance, and she could not find a clear shot. Albern planted one more arrow in Trisken's knee. A second ricocheted from his helmet, and then Jordel was in the way again.

Trisken swung in wide, swooping arcs. He moved much faster than his armor should have allowed. Loren could hardly follow the motion of the weapon. But Jordel was faster still with his sword, and he was a seasoned fighter besides, never reaching too far nor withdrawing too quickly.

The brute swung too wide at last, leaving an opening. A dagger appeared in Jordel's hand. It punched through the chain mail at the side of the breast plate, and Trisken grunted. Loren leaned forwards, mouth open, hoping he would fall.

But it was a ruse. Trisken grinned with bloody teeth and seized Jordel's tunic. He gripped his hammer just below the handle and slammed the head into Jordel's chest. The Mystic nearly fell, choking. Somehow he managed to bring his sword around and hack at Trisken's neck. But the swing was weak, and the mail held.

Trisken's metal knee found its place in Jordel's stomach, and the Mystic dropped. The hammer came up to finish him, but Loren and Albern shouted and charged. Albern reached for his sword, but without a weapon of her own Loren wasted no time. She seized Trisken's neck, trying to bowl him over backwards. He lost his balance and stumbled, but somehow managed to catch his feet. Leaning back as he was, his gut was an easy target, and Albern drove his sword up and under the breast plate, deep into the giant's belly.

The helmet came off under Loren's arm. Trisken's hair swung wildly, streaked with the blood coughed up from his lungs. Loren glimpsed a tattoo worked into his neck—a twisting, intricate design of black that looked very like the designs on her dagger. It flashed with darklight for a moment, and she recognized the glow she had seen before.

Then Trisken reached back and seized her by the hair. He flung her bodily over his shoulder to crash into the side of the bridge. Only its low wall kept her from sliding off into the chasm and falling to the valley floor impossibly far below. He ignored the sword in his stomach and grabbed Albern. The horned helmet was gone, but his head was plenty hard enough. He smashed it into Albern's nose with a *crack,* and the bowyer's head snapped back with a fountain of blood.

Jordel lay only a few paces from Loren. His eyes were glazed and wild, searching around for something. He was nearly senseless, but still he fought for his feet. His breath came in wheezing gasps, and Loren heard a gurgle in it. Though his chain mail was whole, there was a dent in his chest that should not have been there.

"Jordel," she said. "Jordel, look at me."

The Mystic's eyes tried to focus on her face. Their keen blue seemed clouded as if by some spell, but at last she saw him recognize her.

Loren scrambled to hands and knees and went to him. "The back of his neck. A tattoo, like the signs upon my dagger. It glows whenever we strike him. It is what keeps him alive."

Jordel's head swung around, far slower than it should have. Albern had broken the giant's grasp and was fending him off with a sword, but Trisken was pushing him ever farther towards the edge.

"A tattoo," mumbled Jordel. He coughed, and a bloody lump spattered upon the stones. "Dark magic. I was right."

He fought to his feet, using his sword like a crutch. Loren stood and helped him. At first he could gain no more than one knee, but in another moment he got his feet under him.

"I must help Albern." Loren let go of Jordel to run at Trisken. But Jordel seized her sleeve and pulled her back. He dragged her around to look into his eyes.

"Hear me, Loren. The Shades' dark master has returned, and Trisken is one of his favored champions. Ask Xain of it. I told him everything."

Loren looked over the Mystic's shoulder at Xain. He stirred while Annis and Gem knelt by his head, trying to rouse him.

"No magic," said Jordel. "It is no proof against them. I never told him that. Tell him."

Then he broke away from Loren's grip and charged at Trisken's back.

Loren reached for him, tried to grasp his arm. She

missed her grip. The chains of his shirt slid away under her skin.

In his hand he still held his sword. But he cast the blade aside and reached for a hunting knife in his boot. Stooping for it almost made him fall. But he kept going.

Trisken's metal fist struck Albern in the jaw, knocking him to the ground. Then Jordel hit Trisken from behind, wrapping his arms around the commander in death's embrace. His knife plunged into the back of Trisken's neck, and together they pitched over the edge of the bridge and into the chasm below.

THIRTY-EIGHT

THEY FOUND THE BODIES SHATTERED ON THE FLOOR of the valley.

Albern thought it was too dangerous to take the long road down, but Loren would not hear it. She would not leave Jordel's body to rot where the crows and the wolves—and the harpies—could peck at it.

So they went through the stronghold, to the long stone road on the other side that descended to the valley floor. Then they traversed all the way around the foot of the mountain.

The land beneath the bridge was mostly soft loam,

punctuated by rocks that jutted from the soil like rotten teeth. A fine mist clung to the ground, swirling around their boots and cloaks as they picked their way along, searching.

Jordel lay on his back. Mercifully, his eyes were closed. Loren did not think she could have borne to see them open, their keen blue robbed of life. Those eyes had mesmerized her the very first time she had seen them, and had given even the mightiest warriors pause. That they would no longer be beside her, to watch over her and all the nine kingdoms, seemed a crime beyond punishment or any hope of justice.

Trisken's body lay not far away. Jordel's knife was buried to the hilt in the tattoo on his neck. The commander had struck one of the rocks when he landed, and it had shattered his back so that his body was almost in two. His neck was twisted, and every part of his armor was dented and tarnished. Not a muscle of his body stirred.

They dug a grave for Jordel. They had no shovels, and so had to make do with their fingers and sharp stones. It took an eternity, and they could not make it deep enough, so when they had laid him in it they covered him with stones. Before, though, Loren wrapped him in his red cloak, fetched from the saddlebags of his charger. His clasp she kept, stowing it in one of the pockets of her cloak. If she could no longer walk by his side, she would keep that to remember him by. And some urge of her heart told her to bring it to his brothers in the Mystics. Disgraced though he might be, still she guessed that there were some of his brothers and sisters who would want to see him honored for the services he had rendered to the nine lands—for she would have hazarded a guess that he had performed many.

They stood beside the stones a while. Loren's eyes leaked steady tears, slowly, for she tried to still them. Annis did not weep, but that might have been because she was trying to comfort Gem.

The boy was inconsolable. He buried his face in his cloak and threw himself down upon the stones, refusing to leave them. Albern had to carry him away from the grave, but he did it gently, with soft murmurs as though to a wounded animal.

Xain stood there with Loren the longest. His eyes were wet with tears, but he did not let them fall. Albern had helped him bind his arm in a bandage, holding it against his chest, for his shoulder would be long in healing. His other arm fidgeted with the hem of his coat, as though itching to take some action, if only he could determine what it was.

"I was not strong enough to save him," said Xain.

"No one would have been," said Loren. "He said Trisken's mark made him proof against all magic. No wizard could have stood against him, no matter their power."

"Mighty they have called me, all my life. I wish I were mightier still."

Loren said nothing, for those words sounded dangerous.

"Did he say nothing else?" said Xain, looking up at her.

Their dark master has returned, Loren thought. *Ask Xain.*

"Nothing that needs saying now," she murmured. "We shall talk upon the road."

They finally left the grave near midday. As they walked from the hollow where he lay, Loren turned back one final time. The sun had come out at last. She thought shafts of light should have come piercing down, down through the overcast, to light upon Jordel's grave. But it was not one of Bracken's stories. Still, the day was warmer and gentler than any they had seen in weeks. Gentler than it had any right to be, for one of the great men of the nine lands lay dead.

Trisken's body they left for the harpies.

The road back up was harder, for every step away from the valley felt like they were leaving him behind. Loren knew they were not, not really. But it was hard to still the pain in her heart, and more than once Gem asked if he could go back one last time. Annis shushed him each time, and by the time they reached the stronghold he had fallen silent.

They returned to the bridge. Its stones were stained by blood—Loren's, and Albern's, and Jordel's, and even Trisken's. Her eyes shied away from it. She could look only at the spot on the edge where Jordel and Trisken had gone over for the last time.

Xain stopped his horse and dismounted, and then went to the edge of the bridge. Loren climbed off Midnight and stood beside him. They looked down over the edge. The valley was too far below for them to see the grave, but Loren could imagine it. *It would be just there,* she decided. *There, in between those rocks.*

Xain reached out his hand, and his eyes glowed—still black, for the magestone still ran in his veins. Fire spilled forth from one finger, small but white-hot. It ran over the stones of the bridge like a pen, painting words there in liquid rock. When he had finished, he sent forth a gust of air to cool it.

"I never learned to read," said Loren quietly. "What does it say?"

Xain looked at her in surprise. But only for a moment before he turned back to what he had written and intoned,

Here fell a great man
A clarion trumpet against danger
In darkness where none could see
His name was Jordel

"It is beautiful," said Loren.

"I am no poet."

"It fits him. He was never one to bandy words.

And in those few lines are hidden a great many secrets, which was very like him."

"You speak the truth there."

"And what will you do now, Xain?" said Loren, turning to look at him. "Your powers are at their peak. Even with one of your hands injured, we could not stop you if you wished to leave. Not even if we were at our full strength, and we are battered and broken."

Xain looked sharply at her. "You still have the rest of those magestones?"

Loren swallowed. But she nodded. He knew she did.

"Give them to me."

She did not move.

"You know I could take them if I wanted to," said Xain. "I do not want to. I want you to put them in my hand."

He held forth his good hand, palm outstretched. Loren marveled again at how smooth his skin was. He looked as though he had never worked a day in his life—and, now that she knew from whence he came, she supposed he never really had.

Loren reached into her cloak and withdrew the magestones. She had barely tied the packet together, and it sat lumpy in his fist.

With one sweep of his hands—like the casting of a spell—Xain hurled the magestones into the void. They spun as they fell, flashing in the sun's renewed light, and vanished into the chasm where Jordel would lie forever.

Silently Xain mounted and rode on. Loren watched him for a moment. Then a hand stole beneath her cloak. She fingered the inside pocket—the one on the other side, that hung just by her right hand. She brushed against the fine brown cloth of the second packet of magestones. It was cool and rough against her skin.

Loren gained Midnight's saddle and followed Xain.

THIRTY-NINE

THEIR ROAD FROM THE GREATROCKS AND INTO THE village of Northwood was pleasant, more pleasant than any days since they had set out from Strapa. The sun emerged brighter on the second day than it had when they left the fortress, and brighter still the day after that. The path wound down out of the mountains, sharply at first, and then more and more gently as it reached the foothills that sloped away into the wide land of Selvan.

To the north of their course, Loren could see the

Birchwood laid out wide and verdant, like a carpet of brilliant green fibers. It made her heart swell in her breast, and to her great surprise she found herself aching to walk among the trees again. It had been long since she had been in a forest—a good and proper one—and the Birchwood was her home. Soon, she knew, their road would take them north and into its reaches. They still meant to make for Feldemar, and for Jordel's stronghold of Ammon. What they would do then, Loren did not know, but it was the only course they had.

They rode mostly silent through the days, and at night they sat quiet about the campfire. The only talk was of gathering wood, and hobbling the horses, and setting a watch. Only one of them stood awake at a time, for they were tired, and no satyrs came from the mountains to bother them. It seemed that with the defeat of the Shade stronghold, the evil creatures of the mountain wanted no more trouble with the travelers, and had retreated into their caves to lick their wounds.

On the fourth day, Albern began to sing. He sang as loud and as clear as he had in the early days of their journey. But his voice now was tinged with grief, and he sang songs of heroes that had fallen in battle long before, and lovers who lost each other in storms of war that swept the nine lands, and ships lost in the three seas. The songs brought fresh tears to all of their eyes, but also a quiet calm to their hearts. Loren imagined bards writing songs of Jordel and his battle against

Trisken on the bridge, and she wondered if the others were thinking the same thing.

At last she gave voice to the thought. "You should write a song about him," she told Albern.

"I am no songwright," said Albern. "Only a bowyer with a voice that doesn't quite send sheep running. My words could do him no justice."

"Nor could any of ours," said Loren. "But you know the most songs, and you knew him. His tale should not be told by someone he never met."

"I doubt that friends of Jordel are in short supply across the nine lands," said Albern. "But if you insist, I will think upon it. Come and visit me the next time you go to Strapa, and I will sing for you what I have."

"You do not mean to come with us after Northwood?" said Gem, who looked like he might cry again.

"No, little master. I will see you safely there, as I vowed. And then I will go home—upon the Westerly Road, and not the mountain pass." He gave a harsh chuckle. "I think it will be a long time before I travel that way again, if ever I do. When I was in Strapa, I thought the wind tugged at my branches and made me yearn for the freedom of the road. But now that I have walked it again, I find the roots I planted have grown too deep. I long for nothing more than my little shop, and the meager custom that comes my way, and a good tankard of ale in the evenings."

"We should all be so lucky," said Xain. The wizard had grown pale, and his skin broke out in sweat though they had not yet descended all the way into the lowlands' heat. The magestone sickness was coming upon him once again—but milder this time, and though his hands often trembled, Loren saw no trace of madness in his eyes.

"Still, I hope you will come my way if ever you have a chance," said Albern. "For though I lament this trip and my role in you taking it, mayhap one day we might look back on it with fonder memories." He fell silent and bent his head towards the saddle, as though he were afraid to say more.

Loren thought she knew his mind. "Do not blame yourself for the journey's end. Jordel learned much that he would not have known otherwise, and he passed that knowledge on to the rest of us. We will give his order the warning they need to deal with these Shades. He would have wished for nothing more."

Albern nodded swiftly and turned so that she could not see his face. Gem hid his eyes behind the edge of his cloak and wept again.

On the sixth day after they left the fortress, they at last saw the town of Northwood before them. A low wall surrounded it, not even two paces high, something to stand behind rather than atop. The town spilled out beyond the wall like wine from an overfilled waterskin, running among dikes and troughs that brought water from the Melnar River to the farms. Smoke floated gently upwards from every chimney, soft and white, as from the fires in the simple wood cottages of Loren's village.

"It is bigger than I thought it would be," said Annis. "Almost a city."

"Aye, for it is the northernmost town on the Westerly Road," said Albern. "In one sense, it is Selvan's northwestern border, though law says the borders lie in the Greatrocks to the west, and in the Birchwood to the north. And border towns are often large."

"Should we be wary of a Yerrin ambush upon those streets, do you think?" said Xain, eyes sharp as he surveyed the place.

"I do not think we need worry," said Annis. "We destroyed my mother's caravan. Without it she has nothing to trade, and therefore nothing to do. And she has many men with her who must be fed, but probably scant coin with which to feed them, if she brought all her cargo into the mountains for the Shades. She will scuttle home as fast as her horse's legs can carry her, there to gather her strength once more."

"And to plan revenge," said Loren.

"Aye, and that, too," said Annis quietly.

"I know an inn here, where the ale is sweet and the beds are soft," said Albern. "The matron will give you your custom as a gift."

"We have coin," said Loren. It was true, for Jordel had always carried much with him, and it sat still in his saddlebags.

"Do not deny this gift," said Albern, fixing her with a solemn look. "It is the very least I can do. Let me do it."

Soon they reached the first houses, little more than shacks set out upon the wide fields of farms. Little children ran up to them and scuttled about the legs of the horses, tugging at Loren's fine cloak and waving to Gem. He waved back at some of the boys with a smile, though Annis only wrinkled her nose.

"They do not often see riders coming down out of the mountains," said Xain.

"I should say not," said Albern. "I know very few who take that road, and none who have done so in the last many years."

"Where is this inn?" said Annis.

"A good ways off from these farms," said Albern. "What is wrong, my lady? Not fond of the smell of pigs' dung?"

"Are you?" she asked pointedly.

Albern tossed his head. "Fair enough."

Soon the streets turned from dirt to cobbles, and then from cobbles to well-paved stone. The town rose atop a hill, where sat a cluster of many low buildings. Loren saw a great hall there, probably where the mayor lived—for any town so large as this had to have a mayor. But the other buildings were much like those she had seen in Cabrus and Wellmont, low stone structures with signs out front advertising the owner's trade: smiths and clothiers, cobblers and bowyers. Albern peeked in through the door at some of these last, giving their wares a passing glance. He lifted his nose and sniffed, as haughty as Annis ever was on her worst day.

Finally they found the inn he had spoken of. Its sign was the largest Loren had ever seen on an inn, showing a great rock thrusting out of the land, with a wave and a howling gust of wind crashing against it.

"The Lee Shore," said Albern. "And does it not feel like one after those mountains?"

"Let me lie on one of their beds and I will tell you how it feels," said Gem. "It is all well and good to look pretty, but it is what you can feel under your back that counts."

The stable boy took their horses and gawked at the two silver pennies Loren threw him. Albern led them inside and to the back of the common room, where stood the matron behind the bar. Her eyes fell upon Albern, and her face beamed in a warm smile.

"Now there is a face this place has missed for far too long. Come here, you great lummox!"

She came out from behind the bar, leaving two patrons waiting for their drinks, and wrapped Albern in a warm embrace. Though she was a head shorter than him and very slim, still she managed to lift his feet up off the ground, and just below her long sleeves Loren caught a glimpse of sinewy muscles.

"Xain, Annis, Gem, and especially Loren," said Albern. "Take great pleasure in the company you now keep. This is Mag, and we have known each other since we were nothing more than children."

"A little more than children, you mean. Children do not get up to the things we did at that age," said Mag, laughing. Then, catching Annis' scandalized expression, she laughed still harder. "Oh, do not mistake me, my lady. We got into all sorts of trouble, but more the sort you make with a blade than the sort you make with . . . well, *his* blade."

Albern's face turned a deep red, and he bowed to the rest of them. "Forgive Mag. She has a tongue like the saltiest dock girl, and she has always had the gumption to back up her talk. Also, she has belonged to another man for years now, and so she means nothing by it."

"Belonged to him as much as he belongs to me, you mean," said Mag, punching Albern's shoulder before returning to the bar.

"Of course, Mag," said Albern. He leaned close to Loren. "She is also the best fighter you have ever seen. Every army in the world poured a glass of wine into the dirt the day she gave up soldiering."

"What are you whispering there, Albern?" said Mag sharply.

"Nothing, Mag," he said quickly, "only my friends need rest and food, mayhap for a while. Let me pay for them, eh?"

Mag caught his eye, and her smile dampened. When she looked at Loren and the rest of them, her eyes looked sad. "Aye, I can do that," she said. "Stay as long as you need, loves. You are most welcome here."

"We shall find ourselves a table," said Albern. "But you must come and have an ale with us, Mag, as soon as you have a moment."

"As soon as that man of mine finishes his piss and comes back," grumbled Mag. "I shall be there in a minute, loves."

Albern led them away, picking his route between the tables, careful not to jostle anyone. Annis stepped close behind him. "Albern, what was that business with you two? I felt like you spoke words none of us could hear."

"Just a minute," said Albern. At last he found an empty table, and they all fell into chairs around it. Xain tucked himself against the wall, leaning back and picking at his sleeves. Loren studied the wizard with worry, but when he caught her staring he gave a weak smile to reassure her.

"Mags and I have seen some things best left forgotten," said Albern softly. "Friends dying. Battles lost. Cities sacked, and kings hung. The kinds of things that keep you up at night. When we both hung up our swords, I chose Strapa, and she chose Northwood. But we have stayed close since, and each knows the other's mind. I have never paid for another's custom before, and she caught the meaning in the words. She will not trouble you for coin while you are here, and she will let you have your privacy, if you want it."

"She must let us pay," Loren insisted, leaning forwards. "I wish to be no burden on anyone else's purse."

"Look around you," said Albern, giving a wry smile. "Do you think Mag lacks for custom?"

It was true, Loren realized as she scanned the room. There was hardly a seat empty. And everyone at every table had their hands wrapped around a mug of ale, most with empty cups sitting before them. Business was booming, though it was barely afternoon.

"Half of them come here just for her," said Albern. "It was no jest when I said Mag is the best fighter you have ever seen. Men come from across Selvan to see her. And then they stay for the ale."

But Loren went stone still in her seat. As she scanned the room, her eyes lit upon a face across it. Albern's voice became an indistinct buzz.

"Loren?" said Gem, seeing her look. He followed her gaze with concern. "What is it? Danger?"

"No . . ." said Loren. Her voice was weak, like a dream. Slowly she rose from her chair. She walked, and then ran as she became sure of it. She knew that face. She knew it as well as her own.

"Chet!"

He looked up at her from a tankard of ale, his face filled with confusion. Loren reached up and cast back her hood. Then his eyes bulged, and a smile crashed upon him like a wave on the sea, and he shot to his feet.

"Loren?" he cried. "Loren, is it really you?"

Then they were laughing, arms wrapped around each other tight, and he picked her up off the ground. She buried her face in his shoulder, still laughing, laughing until the laughter turned to tears, the first tears of joy she had shed in time beyond memory.

She turned to find Xain and the others standing behind her, looking confused but no longer alarmed. Then there were introductions to be made, and somewhere in the middle of it all Mag came over with a platter full of mugs.

"Now you know them, and they know you," said Loren. "But Chet, what on earth are you doing here? You are leagues from home—weeks of travel, unless you took a boat."

"That I certainly did not," said Chet with a chuckle. "Nasty things. But I . . . Loren, I am here looking for you."

She blinked at that. "Looking for *me?* Why would you be . . . and of all places, why would you be looking for me here?"

The joy that had lit his eyes since first he saw her dampened, and his smile fell. He looked at the others quickly, and then back to her. "Because . . . because of how you left. Because of what happened."

Loren froze. Her stomach lurched. "No. Your father. Tell me he is all right, tell me—"

"Da's fine," said Chet quickly. "It was a knock on the head, it was nothing. I am speaking of . . ."

Again he looked at the others. Loren's brow furrowed. "Speak. They are my friends. More than that, by now."

He looked at her askance. "Friends enough to speak of . . ." Chet froze, his mouth hanging open. "Sky above. You do not know."

"Know *what,* Chet?" Loren could feel a panic at the back of her mind, climbing to the forefront, clawing its way there and threatening to overwhelm her.

"Not here," he said quickly. He turned and spoke to the rest of them, placing his hands on the table. "I beg your pardon, all of you. But these words are not mine to tell. I must speak with Loren, alone, and if she tells you afterwards, so be it. But I cannot."

"Loren?" said Albern, looking at her with a question in his eyes.

"It is all right," she said, nodding. Chet rose and held out his hand to her. She did not need it, but she took it with a small smile nonetheless, relishing the feeling of her hand in his. Then he took her outside the inn and into the streets.

"I have been here a few days," he said, mumbling, as though uncomfortable. "There is a nice waterway not far from here. Come, let me show it to you."

"Chet, tell me what you must," said Loren. "It will be no easier to hear beside a dike than here on the street."

"Just come," he said, taking her hand again.

So Loren let herself be led off, and soon they had reached the place he spoke of. It really was beautiful, though Loren would have appreciated it more if she were not so afraid. The grass was green, and the water lapped at the edges of the waterway with a quiet murmur. He sat down on the edge of it, eyes fixed on his lap, and she sat across from him.

Chet reached out to hold her hands between his own. "It really is so wonderful to see you, Loren," he said quietly. "I set out to find you, but it was only ever half a fool's hope. I was nearly starved by the time I got here, and I never knew when I would be able to leave the town again, for I had little coin. But now it matters not. I have found you, like I meant to."

"I am glad to see you, too, Chet," she said. "But tell me. Why have you come looking for me?"

He glanced over his shoulder, and then back at the ground. He picked at his nails, and then nibbled on them with his teeth.

"Stop that," said Loren, snatching his hand away. "If you cannot tell me, then start by telling me of home. You said your father is well? And your mother?"

His face filled with sadness, and Loren swallowed hard. "She . . . she died, finally," he said. "It is why I finally left. I would have come sooner, I swear it, but—"

"You have nothing to explain. You were with her, as you should have been."

"I was," he said. "Though I have often thought of coming to find you. After . . . after what happened with your father."

Loren's heart chilled. "Oh?" she said. "Did he

make some kind of trouble after I left? He and Mother were furious, no doubt. I cannot imagine they made it pleasant for anybody else."

Chet studied the ground again. And then, with a cold clarity, Loren knew what he had to tell her. But still she waited for him to say it. And finally, after a long while, he met her eyes.

"He never came back, Loren," he said softly. "He is dead. They found him in the woods, not far south of the village. He bled to death from an arrow in his leg. They . . . they do not know who did it."

He looked away. Loren thought she heard the question in his voice. And she, of course, knew the answer. Chet would know that Loren had stolen a bow from his home, as well as many arrows. And he knew she had fled with that bow, on the same day her father had been shot. Chet knew. He knew Loren had killed her father.

But Loren could think of only one thing. *He is dead. He is dead, and I killed him. I killed him.*

She tried to stand up, but her arms gave way trying to lift herself. Chet took her arm and helped her to her feet. Loren looked out over Northwood, seeing none of it.

I killed him. I killed my father.

All her talk since then. Every time she had withheld her hand. The times she had despised Damaris for killing so easily, and had looked down on Jordel for killing at all. All of that, and she had killed her first man before she ever left the Birchwood.

I killed my father. I did it.

My father is dead.

And at that thought, something broke inside her. As if in the distance, at the back of her mind, she heard Jordel's voice. He had spoken the words to her on the Westerly Road, weeks and weeks ago.

I have met boys whose fathers were taken with drink or horrid memories of war, or simply with black hearts. Yet when these boys told me of the day their fathers died, they wept hot and bitter tears. Few hold only hatred for home and family, no matter how justified.

Loren fell against Chet, seizing the front of his tunic. She had no more tears—she had spent them all when Jordel died. But now grief made her blind, so that she could not take a step without help, and she leaned her head hard into Chet's shoulder as he helped her back to the inn.

My father is dead.

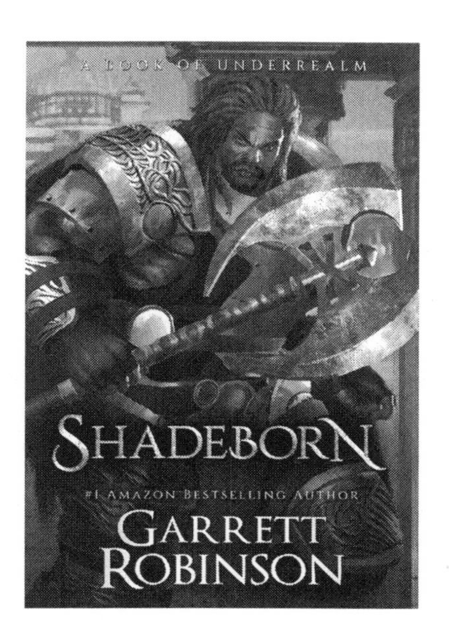

GET THE NEXT BOOK

You've finished *Darkfire*, the third book in the Nightblade Epic.

Your next book is *Shadeborn*. Get it here:

Underrealm.net/Shadeborn

CONNECT ONLINE

FACEBOOK

Want to hang out with other fans of the Underrealm books? There's a Facebook group where you can do just that. Join the Nine Lands group on Facebook and share your favorite moments and fan theories from the books. I also post regular behind-the-scenes content, including information about the world you can't find anywhere else. Visit the link to be taken to the Facebook group:

Underrealm.net/nine-lands

YOUTUBE

Catch up with me daily (when I'm not directing a film or having a baby). You can watch my daily YouTube channel where I talk about art, science, life, my books, and the world.

But not cats.

Never cats.

GarrettBRobinson.com/yt

THE BOOKS OF UNDERREALM

THE NIGHTBLADE EPIC

NIGHTBLADE

MYSTIC

DARKFIRE

SHADEBORN

WEREMAGE

YERRIN

THE ACADEMY JOURNALS

THE ALCHEMIST'S TOUCH

THE MINDMAGE'S WRATH

THE FIREMAGE'S VENGEANCE

CHRONOLOGICAL ORDER

NIGHTBLADE

MYSTIC

DARKFIRE

SHADEBORN

THE ALCHEMIST'S TOUCH

WEREMAGE

THE MINDMAGE'S WRATH

THE FIREMAGE'S VENGEANCE

YERRIN

ABOUT THE AUTHOR

Garrett Robinson was born and raised in Los Angeles. The son of an author/painter father and a violinist/singer mother, no one was surprised when he grew up to be an artist.

After blooding himself in the independent film industry, he self-published his first book in 2012 and swiftly followed it with a stream of others, publishing more than two million words by 2014. Within months he topped numerous Amazon bestseller lists. Now he spends his time writing books and directing films.

A passionate fantasy author, his most popular books are the novels of Underrealm, including The Nightblade Epic and The Academy Journals series.

However, he has delved into many other genres. Some works are for adult audiences only, such as *Non Zombie* and *Hit Girls,* but he has also published popular books for younger readers, including The Realm Keepers series and *The Ninjabread Man*, co-authored with Z.C. Bolger.

Garrett lives in Oregon with his wife Meghan, his children Dawn, Luke, and Desmond, and his dog Chewbacca.

Garrett can be found on:

BLOG: garrettbrobinson.com/blog
EMAIL: garrett@garrettbrobinson.com
TWITTER: twitter.com/garrettauthor
FACEBOOK: facebook.com/garrettbrobinson

Made in the USA
Middletown, DE
11 April 2018